"Someone To Come Back To"

By

Róisín Black

Dedication

Heroes come in all shapes, sizes and guises. Some wear a uniform, some sling a stethoscope around their necks, some do a job they get very little thanks for but they do it to make a difference.

Other heroes get quietly on with their lives, whispering words of encouragement, offering guidance and support.

This story wouldn't be before you today without the presence of such a hero in my life.

His encouragement never wavered, his words always pushed me on and his belief in me gave me the wings I needed to fly towards my dream.

This book is dedicated to my husband.

My hero.

Someone To Come Back To

Book One In The Omega Security Series

Copyright © 2016 Roisin Black

All rights reserved.

Editor – Sheryl Lee

http://sherylleee.wix.com/editor

Cover Design – Hang Le

http://www.byhangle.com/

Cover Art – David M Portraits

https://www.facebook.com/davidmportraits/

CONTENTS

"An Alpha Male MUST absolutely be perceived by his peers as the toughest, most popular, and smartest. An **Omega Male** cares little for this recognition...but knows that he is all those things and more." – Urban Dictionary.

ONE

"Satellite connection lost," announced the plummy-voiced satellite navigation device in her best queen's English.

"Oh shut the hell up, Lizzie," growled Maggie O'Brien as she looked in desperation at the landscape around her for some sign that she wasn't, as she suspected, driving around in circles. As soon as she spotted the big tree with the broken branch, for the third time now, her suspicions were confirmed - she had spent the last hour doing laps around the forest.

"Execute a u-turn," came the plummy-voiced advice.

"Oh for God's sake, shut the hell up," shouted Maggie as she ripped her phone out of its holder and smacked her finger down on the off button.

"Just turn off the main road, follow Old Creek Road for a few miles, then take the first left turn and then the second right and follow that road for two miles and take the first left and follow that road to the end and the cottage is there on the shores of the lake," Maggie mockingly repeated the directions Dr. Matt had given her as to how to get to his family's vacation cottage in the Adirondacks.

It had taken her five hours to get as far as the turn-off onto Old Creek Road and she was tired, hungry and losing light. She pulled over and dug a crumpled old map out of her handbag. Something had told her to bring it with her just as she'd been running out the door to beat the Brooklyn traffic.

She smoothed it out as best she could on the passenger seat and located Old Creek Road and the myriad of roads that led off it. She looked for "Little Lake" and punched a "yes" into the air when she found it but then realized none of this was much good to her as she had no idea where she was. She could hardly navigate herself to a point on the map when she didn't know where to start from.

"Damn," she cursed into the confines of the empty car. She looked around again in the hope that something, anything, might inspire her to figure out her location.

Nothing.

"Okay," she informed herself, "there's nothing for it but to try and find a road with a name on it or some other kind of identifying feature and take it from there."

She whipped the car out onto the road and took off with renewed vigor at a speed that, somewhere in the back her mind, she realized was probably not a good idea on a dirt road but imminent exhaustion, growing frustration and an increasing pressure in her bladder spurred her on.

Springsteen was belting out "Born To Run" at top volume, which is why, she later reasoned, she remained blissfully unaware of anything having happened until a warning light started flashing at her from the dashboard, accompanied by a very worried beeping sound.

"Oh shit!" she exclaimed as she pulled over and examined the light more closely.

The icon, which was practically on fire at this point, seemed to indicate there was a problem with the brakes or suspension, she wasn't sure which but she decided the best thing to do at this stage was to get out and have a closer look.

The crunching of her boots on the gravel only served to emphasize the silence surrounding her and she realized soon it would be dark. The trees loomed threateningly in the twilight and as she squeezed herself under her car she hoped there was nothing seriously wrong with it.

She had only just contorted herself into a position where she could see behind the wheels when something wet connected with the exposed part of her leg where her pants had ridden up her calves. To be more precise, something licked her leg. She froze. What the hell would be wandering around the forest at this time of the evening and licking people?

Do bears lick? she thought as a voice broke the silence and gave her such a shock she jerked and banged her head.

"What the hell?" she exclaimed. "Who the hell are you and why are you licking my leg?

A soft chuckle was all she got in reply and another lick accompanied by what seemed like a sniff.

Oh just my luck, Maggie thought to herself, *I'm stuck in the middle of nowhere with car trouble and a lick-freak.*

"Okay mister," she announced, "you lick my leg one more time and I'll come out from underneath this car and split your head open with this tire iron."

Her bravado was rewarded with a laugh this time and annoyance flashed through her. The fact she didn't have a tire iron or that the guy could be standing there with a gun, hence his laughter, didn't occur to her as she wriggled furiously out from underneath the car. A trickle of fear did, however, wind its way down her spine as her eyes fell on one of the biggest men she had ever seen. Beside him sat what she now guessed was the source of the licks.

"It'd be a pity if you hit him with your invisible tire iron after he took such a shine to you" laughed the big guy before her, his eyes brimming with mirth.

"Oh very funny," snarled Maggie but within seconds a smile bloomed across her face and she was laughing too at the ridiculousness of the situation. Had she really just accused this guy of licking her leg in the middle of the forest!

She walked over to her new four-legged friend who sat by his owner looking the picture of innocence.

"What's his name?" she asked.

"Rock," replied the big guy.

"Pleased to meet you Rock," laughed Maggie as she ruffled the fur on the top of his head and tickled him behind the ear. He leaned in to her approvingly and licked her hand.

"Hmmm, he sure seems to like you," the big guy informed her, a look of curiosity in his eyes now.

"So what's the problem with the car?" he asked in a voice so deep and rich it seemed to fill the space around them.

"Oh, I'm not sure," Maggie replied, "seems to be a problem with either the brakes or suspension."

"Can you drive it?" he asked.

"Well yes," Maggie replied, "if I ignore the flashing red light, manic beeping and the shudder in the steering wheel."

"Hmmm, doesn't sound like driving it too far is such a good idea," mused her new companion. "Mind if I take a look?"

Maggie had no idea how a guy his size was going to fit underneath the car but she shrugged her shoulders and said, "Be my guest."

The forest seemed eerily still and there wasn't even the sound of a solitary bird chirping to disturb the silence. An icy shiver washed over Maggie as she watched Big Guy remove his back-pack and place his fishing rod carefully on the ground beside Rock. He took a flashlight out of the back-pack and slid under her car with the ease and grace of a cat, a very big cat.

"Ah, I see what the problem is," he announced, a note of amusement in his voice. "Hmmm….I don't think you'll be going far tonight."

Irritation flashed through Maggie.

"What?" she exclaimed. "It can't be that bad."

Big Guy came out from underneath the vehicle.

"Oh you don't think so, eh?" he asked her, a look of bemusement on his face. "Well, you can drive it if you like but I'd say you'll get a few miles at best before you're in trouble with the steering and the brakes and you'll only be doing more damage along the way."

"Huh?" snorted Maggie, not quite believing her ears. "What the hell is wrong with it?"

"You've done some damage to your suspension and got what looks like gravel stuck in your brakes. I'm guessing you were driving at a speed considerably more than is recommended on these roads," he finished, his face saying what his words didn't, that is, *dumb-ass city slicker.*

Maggie ignored his expression, she had far too much on her mind than to worry about what some huge mountain man thought of her.

Damn, she thought to herself, *what the hell am I going to do?*

Lieutenant John Sullivan of the U.S. Navy SEALs stood back and considered the situation before him, especially the flame haired female currently chewing her lip in consternation. A damsel in distress scenario wasn't exactly what he had been expecting on his return hike back to the cabin but here she was in front of him and he didn't like the look of his options to deal with the situation.

Ordinarily he'd fix the car and drive her to wherever she was going and, if it wasn't too far, hike back or he'd send her on her way with clear directions to her destination. The only problem was a mega-storm was on its way and he didn't fancy sending her off into the wilderness by herself and he also didn't fancy hiking back to the cabin in the wind, rain and dark with the possibility of trees coming down. An ominous sense of inevitability crept over him.

They were too far from anywhere to hike to the nearest town and there was no cell phone signal for miles. Not that it would be fair to expect a taxi or tow-truck to come out in the storm. The answer to his dilemma was staring him in his face but he didn't want to look at it just yet.

He had come out to his grandfather's old cabin to straighten his head out. The last thing he wanted was contact with another human being, especially a cantankerous female because in his experience cantankerous females always meant trouble. He supposed the first thing he'd better determine was where she was headed.

"Where are you headed?" he asked.

Maggie's head whipped up and the look in her eyes suggested she'd been dreading him asking that question.

"Little Lake," she answered, "Dr. Matt Fraser's place."

John's eyes widened, if it was Old Doc Fraser's place she was talking about, it was a good six miles from where they stood. Hiking her over there was out of the question at this time of the evening. A gust of wind tugged at his jacket. The storm would be on them soon, it was time to make a decision.

"Then I guess you'd best come with me," he suggested.

Maggie's eyebrows shot up and her mouth dropped open at the same time. She looked around as if looking for something.

"Well where are you headed?" she asked. "Do you have a place nearby? Can I get a cab from there?"

John tried to suppress his smile but he only succeeded in looking like he was smirking.

"Er, no," he replied, "you can't get a cab from there. I live a short walk down the trail here," he said, pointing down the track, which seemed to Maggie to go on for miles.

"Oh, that's okay then," she announced. "No need to worry, I'll simply call a cab and I can organize a tow-truck to come and get the car in the morning."

This time John couldn't suppress his smile. This lady was a classic and she believed she had all the answers, proposing city appropriate solutions to the most un-city like situation. Somehow he guessed telling her there was no cell phone coverage wouldn't make a difference to her trying to call a cab anyway.

Maggie considered the giant before her and the fact she seemed to cause him great amusement. Yet again he was smiling as if her suggestion to call a cab was some kind of hilarious concept. She was quite sure the local "tires for hire" would be more than delighted at the prospect of being handsomely rewarded for coming to get her and bringing her to the nearest hotel. She'd stay there for the night and simply get the car towed and fixed tomorrow and be ensconced in blissful solitude in Matt's place tomorrow evening.

The last thing she wanted was to spend any more time than was necessary with another human being. She had come out to the wilderness in search of peace and a place to think things through without any distractions. She'd had just about enough of people at the moment and the thoughts of spending any more time than was necessary with anybody brought on a slight ache in her head. However, she had to admit that the guy, even though easily amused, seemed kind and had been helpful.

The thought then occurred to her if she couldn't get a cab from his place then where did he mean for her to go? The wind blew her hair off her face and the realization hit her like a bolt of lightning.

Good God, she thought to herself, *he means for me to stay at his place. Oh, no. Oh no, no, no, no…* she told herself and turned towards her car.

"Ahem," John cleared his throat, "I don't mean to put you under any pressure or anything but there's the tiny matter of a storm coming, so whatever it is you are thinking of doing could you maybe hurry up and do it. If you're coming with me then we need to start moving."

Maggie ignored him, opened the car door and grabbed her phone out of her bag. She looked at Mr. Impatience and asked him if he happened to know the number of the local cab company.

He rattled off a series of numbers.

Maggie punched them into her phone and brought it to her ear.

John smiled, this wouldn't take long.

Seconds later a very annoyed red-haired female shook her phone like it simply needed clearing of some sort of blockage and pressed re-dial.

John waited.

"What the…" Maggie started to say as realization dawned on her. She looked at the man opposite her who, yet again, was smiling! He really was starting to get on her already frayed nerves.

"You knew that didn't you?" she accused him.

"Yep," he admitted, nodding his head slowly.

"Where is the nearest cell phone signal?" she clipped at him.

"A few miles that way," he said, his thumb pointing in the opposite direction to where he said he was going.

"Fuck," Maggie swore under her breath.

What to do, she thought to herself, *walk a few miles in the opposite direction to where the only other human being for miles around is going, in the hopes of getting a cell phone signal and convincing a cab driver to come and get me in the middle of nowhere or head off into the wilderness with the aforementioned human being and spend the night at his place?*

John smiled at the expletive and turned in the direction of the car. The solution, as unpalatable as it was to him, was obvious and it was just like a woman to try and deny it. Watching the flame-haired vixen before him mentally scrambling for another alternative was highly amusing but the wind was really starting to pick up and he knew they needed to make tracks so he intended to see just what she had in the way of luggage.

"What are you doing?" the vixen demanded.

"Just checking to see what sort of luggage you have," John replied.

"No, no, no, there's no need for that," she announced, a tremor of panic in her voice. "I'm not going with you, I mean I can't go with you. I'll just sleep in the car tonight and first thing in the morning hike down to where I can get a cell phone signal and call a cab. Please, you've been kind enough, I don't want to impose on you any more than I already have."

John considered the vision of obstinacy before him. There was no way he was going to hike off into the night and leave her out here in the storm by herself but how was he going to make her see that?

"Really?" he asked. "You want to stay out here for the night, by yourself, in the middle of nowhere, in a broke down car with a massive storm about to hit? Really? What kinda crazy are you?"

Maggie visibly smarted at the suggestion she was in any way mentally unhinged. The wind whipped around her head and her hair started to lift from her shoulders. She fixed her green eyes, as hard as emeralds now, on Mr. Unreasonable.

"Oh, because heading off to God knows where with a guy I've never met before is such a saner option?" She threw at him.

John was about to throw a retort back at her when he was momentarily floored by the flashes of green from her eyes, they were unlike anything he had ever seen. That and the way her hair was starting to float in red waves around her head gave her an almost unearthly aspect. He shook his head, was this really happening or was this some sort of post-traumatic stress incident? He closed his eyes for a moment, hoping when he opened them it would be just him and Rock on the darkening trail. He opened his eyes and to his dismay the red-haired witch was still there, only now she looked even more pissed off than before.

He decided to appeal to her sense of logic, if she had any.

"Do you at least have a blanket?" he asked.

The glimmer of understanding in her eyes and subsequent doubt about her intention to stay in the car, gave him hope.

"Toilet paper?" he pressed.

A look of panic and embarrassment mixed in with the green and he knew he had her.

"Okay," he announced, "let's get moving."

To his delight, he discovered a lightly packed rucksack in the trunk, most women he knew took the equivalent of an overnight suitcase just to go shopping. He was about to throw it over his shoulder when she grabbed it and threw it over her own. He saw she had put on her jacket and slung her handbag over her head and across her chest. Amusingly, she beeped the alarm on the car and with a flourish of her arm announced, "After you."

John picked up his rod and rucksack and struck off down the trail. Rock bounded ahead, overjoyed to finally be heading home and then he did something totally unexpected. He ran back to their guest and jumped at her, landing a lick across her face, as if to say he was delighted she was coming with them. John was glad at least one of them was happy to have company.

***

Maggie estimated they had trekked at least a mile and still there was no sign of any sort of habitation. She kept having to tell herself the guy marching beside her had a kind face and heading off with him to God knows where wasn't a totally crazy idea. As if to further convince herself, she stole a glance up at him. The forest was shrouded in shadows now and they cast a dark aspect over his face. His features were set in firm determination as he stared straight ahead and strode unquestioningly into the encroaching night.

In contrast, Maggie was squinting to see a few feet in front of her and she supposed the last few weeks spent working nights and the subsequent fatigue didn't help. Seconds later an uneven part of the trail caused her to turn over on her ankle but before she even had a chance to call out in pain a strong arm shot out and grabbed her.

"Hey, you okay?" He asked, genuine concern in his voice.

"Yes, I, erm… I'm fine thanks," Maggie replied, "nothing serious, just twisted my ankle a bit."

Her knight, in rather dull armor, looked down at her foot.

"Sorry," he said, a strange look on his face, as if somehow her injury had been his fault, "I've been setting a bit of a pace but I'm only trying to get back before this storm really hits."

He looked to the sky and then over at the trees. The sky looked furious, with clouds of black, grey, purple and even green pushing at each other for dominance. The trees danced in wild abandonment as if trying to gain the attention of the heavens to plead for mercy.

He stuck out his arm. "Here," he said, "grab on."

Maggie looked at him as if he had completely lost his mind.

"Pardon?" she asked.

"Grab on to my arm," he replied, a note of impatience in his voice, "I'll help steady you the rest of the way. It's about another two miles."

Another two miles! Maggie screamed silently to herself. *What the hell happened to, 'just down the road'? And this damsel in distress thing has gone on for long enough, I might not be able to do anything about fixing my car but I can damn well walk unaided.*

John could see from the vixen's expression that his offer of physical assistance was about to be blown out of the water. He had noted, however, her dismay on hearing there were another two miles ahead of them, he figured he'd better not mention the other half a mile after that. The upturn of her chin told him she wasn't about to disappoint.

"I may not be able to fix cars but I am perfectly capable of walking entirely unaided, thank you," she announced and with that stomped off into the shadows.

John thought he heard, "See if you can keep up," fly past him on the wind but he couldn't be sure so instead he fell into step beside crazy chick and wondered what the hell he was doing bringing her back to the cabin.

It was nearly dark now and the wind howled all around them. Maggie was glad she wasn't spending the night in the car, although just where she would be spending the night she didn't know. She reasoned to herself that the man walking beside her had to be a decent sort, after all he didn't have to stop and offer his assistance, he could have just pointed down the trail and told her to walk until she got a cell phone signal. There was a kindness in his eyes but there was something else there as well, something that disconcerted her, something she seemed to recognize but at the same time couldn't place. If he turned on her she wouldn't have a hope against him. He was huge and bristled with physical fitness. She could almost feel the testosterone coming off him.

She figured they had walked at least another mile and wondered how much further they had to go as the wind ripped angrily at their jackets and all around them was pitch black.

The trees continued their panicked dance and John was sure he could smell rain, lots of it. He reached into his backpack and pulled out the flashlight.

Maggie was glad of the illumination. The darkness had combined with her overall fatigue to bring about a wave of exhaustion which she was finding difficult to control.

Come on Maggie, she berated herself, *push through. It's not the first time you've faced a wall of exhaustion. Get over it!*

She thought of many nights in the E.R. surrounded by chaos, exhaustion washing over her and having to dig deep to keep going. Of course she knew this time it was a little different as she hadn't slept properly since her last fateful shift which in itself had been twelve hours long.

Has it really only been fourteen hours since it all happened? she asked herself.

It felt like a lifetime ago.

She concentrated on putting one foot in front of the other and then help came in the unexpected form of Rock, who sidled up beside her and placed his head under her hand as if to let her know he was there to offer extra support. The dog's simple act lifted her spirits and she smiled at him in the darkness. She wasn't so sure about his owner but she decided Rock was one special kind of dog.

His timing couldn't have been better as seconds later the heavens opened and enormous drops of rain splatted onto their jackets. Maggie quickly tied her hood tight around her head and pushed on, her eyes and all her energy focused on following the crescent of light ahead of her.

A flash of lightning crackled across the sky and seconds later was followed by an ominous rumble of thunder. The wind howled all around them now as if enraged by their presence. John turned to Maggie, "It's not much further," he shouted over the wind, his voice seeking to reassure her in the dark. Maggie nodded her head, she was grateful he cared enough to tell her but she was too tired to talk. It seemed like the wind wanted to blow her back down the trail to her car. Somewhere close there sounded an almighty crack and they heard a tree crashing to the forest floor. She thought how much worse it would have been facing a night like this on her own in her broken down car in the middle of nowhere and she was very grateful for the stranger in front of her.

Seconds later he grabbed her arm, "This way," he commanded as he led her down a smaller track to the left. Immediately it was as if they had entered a wind tunnel and the wild mountain air sliced at their jackets and the rain chipped at the exposed parts of their skin. Maggie could feel herself being pushed back and instinctively she reached out and this time was relieved to find a strong arm extended in an offer of support. She gladly took it as she figured it was better than having to be dragged out of a ditch. Big guy tucked her hand in under his arm and then powered into the storm. Maggie thought her legs would give way on more than one occasion but somehow she managed to stay upright and put one foot in front of the other. Another flash of lightning illuminated the landscape and to her great relief revealed a small cabin about one hundred meters ahead.

Five minutes later she was standing just inside the door of what was obviously an ancient cabin as big guy lit a paraffin lamp. Somehow the rain had managed to find a way through the waterproofing in her jacket and she started to shiver from the cold. Her host noticed immediately and advised her to get out of her wet clothes before turning his attention to lighting a fire in the enormous fireplace.

Exhausted and slightly disorientated Maggie started to strip off on the spot, as she couldn't see what other option was open to her. The place was tiny and consisted mainly of a seating area in front of the fire, a double bed to the left of the fire as you came in the front door and a kitchen just off the seating area. A desk and chair, surrounded by bookshelves, was just off to her right where she stood with her back to the door.

She removed her jacket and hung it over the back of the chair. She leaned down and undid her boots and placed them beside the door. She took off the light baseball style top, which then left her standing there in her saturated jeans and a tiny tank top and bra.

She was just about to undo her jeans when John turned around. Embarrassment shot through him as he realized he hadn't shown her the bathroom and a stab of panic hit him at the thought of him about to see her standing in front of him in only her knickers and top.

"Whoa there," he said in a louder than intended voice, "let me get you a towel and show you to the bathroom."

Maggie quickly did her button back up as it slowly dawned on her he hadn't meant for her to take her clothes off where she stood. Embarrassed, she grabbed her dry clothes and followed him over to the other side of the fireplace where she now noticed there was a door. With her eyes trained on the floor she gladly accepted a towel and the lamp and slipped into the bathroom, which she was relieved to see as she had been wondering just how she was going to deal with her pressing need to pee.

She sat on the toilet for longer than was necessary, glad of the rest and the opportunity to think and breathe. The events of the last few hours were slightly overwhelming, especially following on as they did from the tumultuous events which had seen her flee New York and head for the seclusion of the Adirondacks. Ending up in a cabin in the absolute back end of nowhere with a giant of a man who she had never met before had most certainly not been part of her plan. It hadn't even been on her outermost radar. Yet, here she was.

She reasoned with herself the guy showed no signs of being a crazed psychopath but then again, she argued, wasn't that how most serial killers first appeared to their victims, as some sort of helpful, charming stranger? She sat with her head in her hands and as her head swooned with fatigue, she decided she didn't care. All she wanted to do was lie down and sleep but she figured that wasn't an option just yet. She splashed her face with cold water, hung the towel on a peg on the back of the door and quietly opened it.

The cabin was illuminated by a number of lamps and the fire was crackling to life in the hearth. Maggie came around by the side of the fireplace when she stopped dead in her tracks. Over beside the bed, his back thankfully to her, stood her rescuer, totally naked. Maggie clamped her hand over her mouth to stifle the gasp that was rapidly making its way up her throat. She had seen thousands of bodies in her time but never one quite like the one before her now.

Christ, thought Maggie, *even this guy's muscles have muscles.*

She knew she should retreat in to the bathroom to give him enough time to get dressed but she stood transfixed. The breadth of his shoulders and the way his muscles flexed as he reached down to the bed for his shirt held her spellbound. The perfect form of his back as it tapered flawlessly down to his hips and the tightness of his ass, followed by the incredibly toned muscles in his legs all combined to immobilize Maggie into a state of almost euphoric appreciation.

She had never seen a man quite like this before and she couldn't help but gape. However, as she looked closer, she began to notice scars and the more she looked the more she realized the embodiment of male perfection before her was covered in them. Some seemed a few years old but her medical knowledge told her some were quite recent. Worryingly, she noticed a few were gunshot wounds.

Oh God, she groaned to herself, *who is this guy?*

He threw the shirt over his head and she started to back up towards the bathroom when he turned around.

"No need to leave because of me," he grinned at her.

Maggie blushed the color of her hair.

"I...., I...., I'm sorry," she stuttered as she tried to look anywhere except between his legs.

"It's ok, I'm not the shy type," he chuckled as he pulled on a pair of boxer shorts and slung a pair of jeans across his hips. He left the shirt hanging loose and it was then Maggie realized, as she looked into his laughing brown eyes, just how incredibly handsome he was, like Henry Cavill and Eric Bana all rolled into one. She didn't think it was possible but she blushed even more.

Rock looked at her from his position in front of the fire and she was certain the dog shot her a look of understanding.

"By the way," Mr. Ruggedly Handsome grinned, "my name is John."

Maggie continued to stare at him, not realizing he was waiting for her to tell him her name, she really had never come across a man quite as manly as this guy and she was finding it quite disconcerting.

Where do guys like this come from? she thought to herself.

"And you," John prompted her, "do you have a name?"

"Oh, er me, yes my name is Maggie," she replied.

"Well Maggie I hope you like fish, because that's all that's on the menu tonight," he informed her.

Maggie rustled into her bag and produced a chicken curry ready meal.

"Oh please don't worry about me," she said, "I've been enough trouble. I'll just pop this in the microwave and that's me happy."

A look of disdain crossed over John's attractive features.

"Do you like fish?" he asked in a no-nonsense tone.

"Erm, yes," replied Maggie, "but really there's no need..."

"Then fish it is," John calmly informed her as he loomed over her and relieved her of the chicken curry.

"Well is there at least something I can do?" insisted Maggie.

John noticed the shadows around her eyes and the way she stood with her knees slightly bent as if she was carrying some unseen load and was about to keel over.

"Why don't you take a seat over by the fire," he suggested in a voice Maggie found surprisingly tender.

Something within her shifted a little and gave way and she decided if for once in her life a gorgeous man wanted to cook her dinner then she was going to let him. It seemed she was having a day like no other so why not just go with the flow and let things be. So, against everything in her nature, she sat on the floor beside Rock with her back to the sofa and rubbed the dog behind his ear as she stared into the flames.

John observed his guest from his vantage point in the kitchen. If he wasn't mistaken she was exhibiting some of the classic signs of post-traumatic stress and serious fatigue, God knows he'd seen them often enough. He watched as she stared into the fire as if lost in another world. Her hand was still now and Rock was looking up at her but it was obvious she didn't see him.

Hmmm, wondered John, *just what do I have on my hands?*

He shook his head as he reasoned with himself that at least it was a one night only deal. He could cope with that and then get back to some serious solitude and straight thinking. He opened the fridge and poured a glass of perfectly chilled Chablis. He walked over to the fire and offered it to Maggie.

"I think you've earned this," he smiled.

She looked at him with a faraway look in her eyes.

She couldn't quite believe this mountain man, whose man-cave she had seriously invaded, was cooking her dinner and was now standing before her with a glass of wine. She was definitely going with this flow. She accepted the glass.

"Thank you," she said as she bent her head to take a sip. "Wow," she exclaimed, "that's wonderful. What is it?"

John smiled.

"Un Petit Chablis," he informed her in a perfect French accent, "I find it goes particularly well with fresh trout."

"I'd say it goes particularly well with anything," remarked Maggie as this time she took more than a sip.

John smiled as he returned to the kitchen, her appreciation of one of his favorite wines pleased him in a way he found strange. He wondered if she was Dr. Matt's current girlfriend. If so, he had certainly deviated from his usual blonde, cosmetically enhanced, scrawny-assed, run-of-the-mill type.

There was nothing cosmetic about the woman sitting in front of his fire and he was willing to bet every curvy part of her was real. She was tall and striking rather than pretty and those eyes of hers could cut a man in half. She turned to look at him and embarrassment burned through him at being caught watching her. She looked equally embarrassed and quickly glanced away.

Awkward moment alert! John thought to himself.

"So what do you do when you aren't rescuing damsels in distress?" Maggie asked from across the room.

Shit, he thought, *the last thing I want to do is talk in any way about my job.*

"Oh I'm a fixer," he blurted out. "I fix things."

"Oh, like what?" Maggie asked.

Like bad guys, he thought to himself but he didn't say that.

"Like cars," he replied.

Hmmm…. Thought Maggie to herself, *I was thinking more along the lines of a cop.*

"You, er, obviously work out," she observed, a slightly embarrassed tremor to her voice.

"Yeah, I like to stay in shape," he grinned at her.

Rock rolled over onto his back and Maggie leaned across to tickle his tummy, much to his appreciation, judging by his subsequent contented groans. Maggie laughed and John was caught unawares at the unusual sound filling his cabin. Her laugh was almost musical and a peculiar sensation washed over him as he looked over at the flame-haired woman sitting in front of his fire, tickling his dog, her face alight with joy and her green eyes sparkling in delight.

It was a sensation he wasn't quite familiar with and it pissed him off that a woman he had rescued from the side of the road and never met before could so easily disturb the equilibrium of his carefully controlled emotions. He scowled as he turned his attention to the fish, now this situation he wasn't comfortable with at all.

"How old is he?" came Maggie's voice and he presumed she was enquiring about Rock's age.

"Four years," replied John.

"Ah, that's a great age for a lab," stated Maggie, "they've pretty much calmed down by then."

"You've had dogs?" asked John.

"Oh, yes, some," Maggie replied, "I miss having a dog in my life."

"Well, get this fish into you before he nabs it," John advised, "It's one of his favorites."

Maggie didn't need to be told twice. It was simply the best trout she had ever tasted and the bread and salad he served with it were perfect. The bread especially, tasted homemade and she made a mental note to find out from him where he'd bought it. The whole thing beat her chicken curry ready meal by a very long shot. And the Petit Chablis went so well with it that she happily accepted a second glass.

God, she thought to herself, *I'm almost feeling happy…*

"So what do you do when you're not being a damsel in distress?" John asked from across the small wooden table.

Oh shit, Maggie thought to herself, *the last thing I want to talk about is my damn job.*

"Oh I'm a hairdresser," she quipped and surprised even herself with her choice of fictional occupation, she barely even went to the hairdressers!

Hmmmm, John thought to himself, *I was thinking more nurse or paramedic, because you sure look like one strung out hairdresser to me.*

He grinned.

"Maybe you could fix me up a little before you leave?" he teased, running his hands through his hair.

It occurred to Maggie he could quite easily be a L'Oreal model such was the thickness and glossiness of his dark locks. The last thing he needed was her anywhere near him with a scissors but she had to admit she wouldn't mind running her hands through his hair and possibly down those muscular shoulders…

Shit, she thought to herself, *this wine is going straight to my head. Get a hold of yourself Maggie.*

"It would be my pleasure," she smiled at him.

Something in the way she looked at him, some emotion buried deep in her eyes set off a peculiar tingling sensation in John's abdomen. It was as if he'd been exposed to a low voltage electric current. He was so disturbed by this development he jumped up from the table and started to clear away the plates.

"Oh no," Maggie protested, "please let me do the clearing up, it's the least I can do after you cooked me such a beautiful meal."

She reached out and put her hand on his arm to stop him from picking up her plate. He was about to tell her it was okay when he was aware of an intense tingling in his arm where her hand was and the voltage was significantly higher than a few seconds ago.

Maybe she really is a witch, he thought to himself as he released his fingers from her plate.

He knew it was a while since he'd been with a woman and maybe that was the reason for his physical over-reaction to the one before him now but he didn't remember ever having such a response before. He figured at thirty-four years of age that was probably a bit weird.

"Actually, I need to go to the bathroom," he informed her, anxious to be out of her touch-zone, "just leave the dishes on the draining board and I'll dry them when I come out."

"Sure," Maggie replied as he made his way across the room.

"Fuck," he exhaled into the mirror as the toilet flushed behind him.

"Fuck, fuck, fuck," he continued as he reasoned with his reflection that the last thing he needed right now was the distraction of a physical attraction to a female and a stubborn, single-minded female at that, who he suspected was recovering from some sort of traumatic event.

He had come here to straighten his head out, to try and sort out the storm of emotions which had been building in him since his last assignment. It had been a success but not in the normal SEAL way. They'd had poor intelligence and had sustained casualties.

The whole thing had felt wrong from the beginning but he'd had to follow orders and that's what didn't sit right with him. He'd never questioned orders before, they'd always made sense to him and he could follow their logic. They'd always meticulously planned their missions on the best and most available intelligence possible but not this time and it had cost them. Or was that it? Was that what bothered him or was he simply in this game too long? Had the intelligence been sufficient, as the top brass seemed to think? Was the problem with him?

It seemed to him politicians and the media had an increasing influence on their actions and he'd felt a gnawing cynicism growing inside him for some time now. These were the things he needed to be focused on, to be able to think through, not a green-eyed, flame-haired temptress.

He went back into the cabin. The kitchen was clean, with the pan and dishes dried and stacked neatly in the corner but there was no sign of Maggie. He looked over to the bed but she wasn't there. Then he walked around to the other side of the couch and not for the first time tonight was taken completely by surprise. There, on the floor, cuddled up to his dog in front of the fire, was his guest, her hair a fan of crimson silk as it spread out over one of the cushions she had taken off the couch and her eyes closed in what seemed to be a deep sleep.

Something told him not to disturb her and he grabbed a blanket out of the cupboard beside the fireplace. He gently covered her with it and stepped back to take in the view. His stomach did a strange sort of flip and he immediately determined he would fix her car as best he could the next day and get her the hell out of his life.

***

He went over to the kitchen and took a twelve year old bottle of Jameson whiskey out of the cupboard, poured a generous amount into a mug and sat on the bed.

Outside, the storm clawed mercilessly at the cabin but John remained unperturbed, his great grandfather had built the place over a hundred years ago, it wasn't the first storm it had seen and he presumed it wouldn't be the last.

No, John Sullivan was more perturbed by the presence of the storm, calling herself Maggie, lying in front of his fire. He had never brought a woman here. It was his sanctuary, a sacred place where he came to deal with the things he had to do as part of his job, where he came to heal and contemplate, to internalize and compartmentalize. Some of the team had accompanied him on occasion and some had used the place for their own downtime but these were his blood brothers, men he stood back to back with in the most challenging of situations, men who would die for him without question. He knew these men, knew the respect and loyalty pumping through their blood and knew none of them would ever disrespect his place. Each of them knew the value of having a place to go to deal with the things they did, the decisions they made and to have the chance to re-calibrate in order to function as a "normal" member of the general population before they had to go and do it all over again.

Now, a member of that population, who he didn't know from Eve, was cuddled up to his dog on the floor, quietly snoring. Already he could feel a difference in the internal atmosphere of the place, his place, and he didn't like it, even though he had to grudgingly admit there were some things he didn't mind, such as the fire in those green eyes and her pig-headedness which had given him a much needed laugh.

But women weren't his thing. It's not that he didn't enjoy their company from time to time, he was even quite fond of some of the guys' wives but a full-time female partner wasn't his scene. All his relationships had faltered at the few months mark.

He thought of Sandy, the last girlfriend he'd had, gorgeous, long-legged Sandy, sweet as honey and crazy for him. But they had come to that point in all relationships where she expected more and he hadn't been prepared to give it. She hadn't wanted a ring or anything, just to know they were going somewhere, to know he was worth waiting for when he was gone on deployment, to know there was a chance of a future with him.

A part of him had even wanted to give her all those assurances, to take the next step with her but a bigger part of him couldn't do it.

He thought of the guys happily hooked up with wives and girlfriends and he honestly didn't know how they did it, how they reconciled the job and its merciless, unrelenting demands with the needs and expectations of a permanent, long-term relationship.

He couldn't imagine walking away from someone who you loved to the depths of your soul, not knowing if you would ever see them again and trying to park that, put it aside and focus on the mission, where the chances of you coming back to that person were not stacked in your favor.

As for the women left behind, he didn't even want to think about them, how they got on with their lives, some of them raising children, not knowing if the sight of the man they loved walking away was the last they were ever going to see of him. Of course that wasn't something he had to exert any effort in imagining as he had watched his mother wave his father off on too many occasions and he had watched it take its toll on her, watched the love of a man in uniform exact its price. He had vowed he would never want or expect any woman to pay that price for him and he knew his decision came with a price of its own.

Anxious not to get caught up in painful memories from his past, he turned his thoughts to his team-mates, Wolf and Freezer, and his visits to them in the hospital before he had headed to the cabin.

He had just been about to walk in on Freezer when something had stopped him before he'd had the door fully open. Thankfully, he had stopped himself just in time from disturbing a moment between Freezer and his wife Karen.

Freezer's left leg was "shot to shit" as he had so eloquently put it himself and only time would tell if he would heal enough to return to active duty. The realization maybe his SEAL career was over had obviously hit Freezer as he lay in the hospital bed and seeing Karen had brought a number of other realities home.

Through the crack in the open door John had observed Freezer, so named because he was built like a side by side fridge freezer and as cool as ice under fire. He had watched as one of the toughest guys he knew had broken down and sobbed like a small boy in Karen's arms. She was his safe place, his sanctuary, where he was stripped of all emotional pretense and could find release. She would be there to help him pick up his pieces and put them back together.

Wolf, a man so wild only the SEALs had managed to tame him had been lying in his bed looking at some distant point out the window when

John had entered the room. His injuries were more serious and it was practically a certainty his career as an active member of SEALs was over.

They hadn't exchanged much in the way of conversation when the door opened and Maria, the only woman brave or stupid enough to take on Wolf had stepped shyly into the room. It was obvious from the change in her shape and the bump she carried proudly in front of her that she had been waiting for Wolf's return to tell him their special news.

"A baby wolf?" Wolf had managed to ask, not believing his eyes.

"Wolves," Maria had laughed in reply.

As long as he lived John would never forget the transformation that came over his friend in that moment and how he had gone from quiet despair to a place of hope and was suddenly looking at a life full of prospects rather than dead ends.

John knew his decision to stay on his own meant if he was ever injured he would cry his tears alone, there would be no-one to shelter his pain. The prospect of another type of life, should his SEALs career be over prematurely, simply didn't exist.

He had felt an emptiness in him on leaving the hospital that had stayed with him throughout the drive to the Adirondacks and troubled him for the past two days. It came at him in waves and he knew he needed to get it and a number of other emotions under control. He needed to strip things back, compartmentalize and move on.

But the first thing he had to do was get rid of the distracting red-haired creature snoring on his floor.

**

Somewhere behind her eyes Maggie was back in the emergency department at Hillview, New York's oldest public hospital. It was Thursday night, chaos prevailed as usual and it seemed everyone wanted a piece of her. She had just stabilized a young gunshot victim in trauma bay one when Nurse Luisa Gonzalez came running at her and dragged her into trauma bay four.

Three year old Kayla Smith's broken little body had just arrived and Dr. Maggie O'Brien knew immediately she would need to draw on all her years of experience and expertise to save this little girl and she would need to draw on it fast.

The paramedics had been told Kayla had fallen down the stairs, which meant a high chance of brain and / or neck injury. However, as soon as Maggie removed Kayla's clothes another story started to emerge and she knew they didn't have all the facts and the situation was potentially much worse than reported.

The child's body was a litany of abuse with new bruises forming where old ones were in the process of healing. What looked like cigarette burns, old and new, littered the child's arms but the most worrying of all were the marks made by a shoe or boot, the largest of which covered most of the child's upper right thoracic area. Maggie also suspected malnutrition and dehydration as the child looked more like a two year old than a three year old.

Maggie's stomach churned in anger and disgust at what something calling itself a human being had inflicted on this child. She was only grateful for the fact Kayla was unconscious but then, with horrible inevitability, she woke up and started screaming.

Maggie could see from the terror in the child's eyes she didn't know where she was or what was happening to her. Maggie tried to comfort her, to tell her where she was, that it was okay, the doctors and nurses would look after her. Kayla fixed her ice blue eyes on Maggie and whimpered, "hurts," and Maggie drew on all her reserves not to let the tears behind her own eyes become a reality. She knew the child was in severe pain and she needed to park her emotions and get on with the job of alleviating that pain and saving her life. She shouted for one of the nurses to get an IV going, when there was a commotion outside the trauma bay.

"My baby, my baby," a woman screamed at the top of her voice, "I need to see my baby."

Somehow, Kayla's mother had managed to get past security and was trying to gain access to Kayla. Two security guards were trying their best to restrain her whilst at the same time trying to have some compassion for her situation. Maggie decided a quick introduction from her with an explanation as to the team's need for no distractions in order to be able to focus on Kayla's treatment, might be the quickest way to diffuse the situation.

She was wrong.

It was obvious the mother was either inebriated or high or even both and logic wasn't something she was capable of right now. She looked at Maggie like she was speaking in a foreign language and then looked past her and proceeded to scream, "My baby, my baby, let me see my fucking baby."

Maggie told the security guards to get her out of there and returned back to caring for Kayla. The child was in and out of consciousness and Maggie hoped the pain meds were starting to take effect. Her breathing was labored and she needed a CT scan as quickly as possible. The x-ray team were just moving the equipment in place when all hell broke loose outside the trauma bay.

Kayla's mother had bitten one of the security guard's cheeks and with his blood running down her chin, was now making a renewed attempt to gain access to Kayla. The injured security guard was trying to ignore the pain from the bite and was attempting to help his colleague subdue her. All the time the mother was screaming, "Get off me, get the fuck off me, I'm a good mom, I need to be with my baby."

Then, a man appeared, just under six-foot with his hair shorn to a dark shadow on his head, he was wild-eyed and crazed looking.

"Get the fuck off her," he shouted at the guards and proceeded to launch an attack on the uninjured guard, whilst Kayla's mother raked her nails down the side of the injured guard's face, scratching at the bite-mark as she did so.

At the sound of the man's voice Kayla's condition took a turn for the worse. She gasped for breath and the monitors beeped in a concerto of panic. Kayla's eyes flew open and Maggie could see the terror in them.

"We're losing her," one of the nurses shouted.

Maggie looked into Kayla's eyes, "Stay with me Kayla, please stay with me," she pleaded.

Then she was shouting orders but the beeping of the machines told her nothing she was doing was working.

The scuffle outside the trauma bay continued and the crazed looking guy was shouting all sorts of threats at the staff as he proceeded to kick and punch the security guards. The sound of his voice was having an obvious traumatic effect on Kayla and Maggie shouted at the security guards to get him the hell out of there. As she did so the heart monitor beeped that long, slow ominous beep.

"No!" screamed Maggie. "No! Stay with me Kayla, stay with me, stay with me..."

Holy shit! thought John as he woke to the sound of screams filling the cabin, *What the fuck is going on?*

He was out of the bed before he even had his eyes open and was primed for a fight as his feet touched the floor. He looked around the cabin but saw no-one there. He looked for the source of the screams and realized Maggie was screaming in her sleep. Tears were running down her face and her arms were outstretched as if someone was running away from her. The deep distress on her face was only matched by the agony in her voice.

"Please don't go honey, please, I promise they won't hurt you anymore, pleeeease," she begged.

So I was right, John thought to himself, *this woman's been through something and from the sounds of it, something bad.*

John walked over to where she still lay on the floor and spoke to her in a soothing voice.

"Maggie, hey Maggie, it's okay," he told her, "you're dreaming."

He put his hand lightly on her shoulder and shook her gently.

Maggie heard a voice off somewhere in the distance, a voice deep and strong that seemed to fill the space in her head. Then she felt a hand on her shoulder, crazed guy, it must be crazed guy she thought to herself and screamed, "Get off me you bastard!" as she lashed out.

John recoiled from her attack until he realized she was still asleep. Again, he shook her gently.

"Maggie, hey Maggie," he said, a little louder this time, "you're asleep, having a bad dream, wake-up."

Maggie's eyes flashed open but John could see she wasn't actually awake. He let her be. She closed them again.

There had been a momentary brightness and then darkness. The trauma bay was dark now but a tiny voice whimpered, "No more hurts." She turned around and Kayla was disappearing into the darkness. Maggie reached out but in an instant she was gone.

"No!" Maggie sobbed, "No!" and then she gave in to the sobs that erupted from deep within her and shook her body until she thought she would get sick.

And then somehow there was a warmth around her and a voice, that deep, soothing voice telling her it was okay, it was just a dream. Slowly she returned to semi-consciousness and realized she was being supported by a pair of arms, a pair of incredibly strong arms and her cheek was up against a chest, a very hard, muscular chest.

Hmmmm……. This feels good, she thought, *very good,* as she burrowed into the chest, the chest she now realized was naked and smelled faintly of sandalwood and amber, a very male chest. Then the realization hit her and she bolted straight back into one hundred percent reality.

Mountain man, the guy, John, *yes that's his name,* she thought to herself, was holding her and soothing her and it felt amazingly good. In fact, it felt so good she didn't want to move, didn't want to leave the security of those strong arms holding her like they could protect her from the ills of this world, from such horrors as a little child being so beaten and abused she died from a combination of her injuries and sheer terror at the sound of her abuser's voice.

"You okay?" John asked, his voice so gentle and tender she nearly didn't catch what he said.

She nodded her head and reluctantly started to pull away from his chest. Embarrassment was setting in now and she couldn't look at him.

"I, er, I'm sorry," she stuttered, "I obviously woke you, I'm really sorry."

"Hey, it's okay," John replied as he let one arm fall away. Maggie was surprised at how much she wanted him to put it back where it was.

"I think you might have upset Rock a bit more than me," chuckled John, "he is rather fond of his beauty sleep."

Maggie looked round to see Rock sitting like a sentry on the other side of the fireplace, watching her intently but not making any approach.

"Oh I'm sorry puppy," she smiled and patted the cushion beside her, "come on over here to me."

Rock was beside her in an instant, looking searchingly into her face and licking what was left of her tears off her cheeks. Maggie laughed and shivered at the same time. John jumped up and grabbed the blanket which she had discarded in her distress and draped it around her. He then went to the kitchen and poured a generous measure of whiskey into two mugs.

"Here," he said, as he proffered one of the mugs to Maggie, "take this, it'll make you feel better."

Maggie took the mug and sipped at the twelve year old liquid. Whiskey wasn't her drink of choice but as its heat spread out from her tummy, dispelling the death-like shivers, she had to admit she felt a little better. John threw some logs on the fire, then sat on the couch and cradled his own mug in his hands, Rock plopped his two front paws in her lap and continued to snuggle into her.

"Want to talk about it?" John asked.

Maggie shook her head, the last thing she wanted to do was talk about it, the dream had rattled her to her core.

"Okay," he said in a tone that told her he respected her decision and wouldn't pry, "but you should know Rock is a pretty good listener," he smiled at her.

She smiled back and then down at Rock.

A strange, unfamiliar sensation shot through John as she smiled at him, her eyes still harboring some of the distress from whatever it was she had dreamt about and a part of him wanted to know what had caused her to be so upset, and to make it go away.

A silence fell over the cabin and all that could be heard were the last vestiges of the storm, reduced now to a mournful howl throughout the forest.

They sat like that for some minutes, the silence growing between them like an unwanted present neither of them wanted to unwrap. In the end it was Maggie who broke it, she had never been good at silence.

"So do you fix things from here?" she asked.

John looked puzzled for a second but only for a split second until he obviously remembered their conversation from earlier.

"No," he replied, "I mostly come here to fix myself, I fix things out of Virginia Beach."

"Oh," Maggie replied, "so this is like a holiday place?"

"That's right," John grinned at her, "I try to get up here as much as I can to recharge my batteries."

And reset myself, he thought.

What about you?" He asked, "if I'm not mistaken that's a New York accent, I'm guessing Brooklyn?"

Maggie was impressed, to place her as a native New Yorker was one thing but to pinpoint her correctly as having been born and raised in Brooklyn was another thing altogether.

"You'll be telling me the color of my childhood bedroom next," she smiled.

John smiled back, "Well I'm betting it wasn't pink."

Hmmmm… now things are getting uncanny, she thought.

She laughed, "No it wasn't but how you'd know that, I have no idea."

"Oh," John grinned at her, "you'd be surprised at the things I know."

Maggie looked at him, at the warm light in his eyes as they reflected the glow of the fire and thought how she wouldn't mind finding out more about the things he knew. Then her eyes slid shyly down to his impressive chest and the strong muscularity of his legs. A heat started to spread from her abdomen and she blushed as she realized its significance.

No, I wouldn't mind getting to know you better at all, she ruefully acknowledged to herself.

In the half-light of the cabin John noticed some of the color returning to his guest's cheeks.

"Feeling better?" he asked.

"Yes, lots," Maggie nodded, "I think we probably need to quit talking and let Rock get back to his beauty sleep."

John chuckled.

"Yeah, I suppose you're right, otherwise he's going to be barking on about it all day tomorrow."

He stood up and this time a flash of heat leapt across Maggie's abdomen. The man was simply in perfect physical shape and he was starting to have a most disconcerting effect on her. He leaned down to take the mug and it was all Maggie could do to wrench her eyes away from his torso, smile up at him and hand it to him. But she wasn't quick enough to hide the flicker of desire that lit up her eyes.

Shit, she thought, *I don't need this right now, I need to be on my own, to think. I need to straighten my head out and make decisions about what I want out of my life. I most certainly don't need to be lusting after some guy I met in the middle of the woods. The type of guy who would never be interested in me.*

Embarrassed, she quickly looked into the fire and in a hoarse voice, she barely recognized, said, "Thanks."

John took the mugs and made his way to the kitchen sink. He'd caught the look in her eyes and recognized the unadulterated desire. He'd had looks like that before, he was well aware his body had a certain effect on some women but there was something else involved with the look from Maggie, a hunger and an intelligence he found mesmerizing. He wondered what sex with a woman who could look at you like that would be like and he took longer than necessary to rinse the mugs as the realization dawned on him he was more turned on by that look than he had been by anything else in a long time.

Fuck, he swore to himself, *I've really got to get rid of her first thing in the morning.*

He walked back over to the couch and, with his eyes fixed on Rock, informed his guest she could take the bed. With her eyes also fixed firmly on the dog, she gently refuted his kind offer and informed him she was just fine on the floor.

"Really, I'd like you to take the bed," John repeated stiffly, this time looking at her.

"Seriously, I'm fine here," she insisted, her face focused on the fire now and her chin raised in that defiant manner he was quickly learning she had when she didn't want to do something.

John released an exasperated sigh and wondered who the hell slept on the floor when they had the option to sleep in a bed? Only a crazy, green-eyed, flame-haired, pig-headed woman that's who, he reasoned to himself. Then the thought occurred to him maybe she was some kind of clean-freak and was afraid of catching something off his sheets.

He shrugged, "Okay have it your way but at least sleep on the couch."

Maggie was relieved he had dropped the bed idea. She was seriously trying to avoid looking at him as she didn't want to fan the flames of desire any further and the thoughts of lying in his bed with the intoxicating smell of him surrounding her was proving somewhat overwhelming.

"Yeah, okay," she agreed with an edge of huskiness to her voice that hinted at her inner battle.

She gently prised Rock off her and crawled up on to the couch with the cushion and blanket. She knew she should face into the back of the couch with her back to the bed but she couldn't resist the opportunity for one more peek at the embodiment of male perfection as he walked past her. After all, when would she ever see the likes of him again.

Liquid heat rippled through her groin as she watched him move with the grace of a panther across the room. She tried to tell herself her appreciation of his perfectly proportioned body was from a purely medical point of view, an appreciation of what a combination of positive lifestyle choices and exercise could achieve. However, she knew on a purely visceral level she was bullshitting herself, she appreciated his perfect chest, abs and ass as a red-blooded female and it was as simple as that. She squeezed her eyes and legs shut.

"Good night," she husked to the object of her lust across the room.

John caught the husky undercurrent in his guest's voice and instantly wished he hadn't. He remembered the feel of her against his chest, how she had pressed into him, the softness of her curves, the whisper of coconut and jasmine from her hair and the tremulous, embarrassed smile as she had woken up and realized where she was. It was one thing admitting he had an attraction to *her* but the look in her eyes and the huskiness in her voice told him she just might have an attraction to him and with that thought in his head it was all he could do to stay in the bed.

"Good night," he replied as formally as he could.

It was some time before either of them fell asleep.

TWO

Maggie knew she was alone even before she opened her eyes. The internal atmosphere of the cabin was different, as if missing a huge presence, and a cursory glance around its interior confirmed it was. The bed over in the corner was perfectly made and the giant of a man who had been in it last night was gone and so, it would seem, was Rock. Maggie felt a sliver of disappointment that her new four-legged friend had abandoned her. Then she realized she was both disappointed and relieved his owner wasn't around either.

She padded sleepily to the bathroom and after a quick look in the mirror was suddenly relieved no-one was around to witness the wild-looking wreck known as Maggie O'Brien. Her hair stood out at all angles to her head and the paleness of her complexion accentuated the dark circles under her eyes. She looked like something out of The Exorcist.

She padded back into the main part of the cabin and it was then she noticed the silence, the beautiful sweet silence. No traffic, no police sirens, no constant hum of human beings and no howling storm. She smiled to herself and opened the cabin door, gasping at the stunning vista before her. She hadn't realized it last night but the cabin was at the top of a rise and commanded incredible views of the forest and the valley below. The air was so fresh and crisp she could almost bite it like an apple and the sun shone in a flawless blue sky. Maggie smiled, what a perfect start to the day.

She went into the kitchen and found some ground coffee and what was left of the bread from the night before. Under the coffee tin was a note; "Gone to fix your car, back in a while – John." She was touched by the fact he had been considerate enough to leave a note. Apart from a seriously bossy streak, he seemed to be a decent enough guy, actually if she was honest, he seemed more considerate than your average guy, at least any she had gotten mixed up with anyway.

Hmmmm… she thought to herself, *my failed love life, is that what I am going to start thinking about now? Really? When I have other, more serious things to consider? I don't think so.* With that she took her coffee and pan-fried toast and settled into one of the Adirondack chairs on the cabin's veranda.

The issue refused to leave her alone though and niggled at her constantly as she tried to sort through the jumble of emotions in her head. Finally she had to admit if she was honest with herself, her love-life, or lack of it, was one of the areas she needed to look at.

She'd had her fair share of boyfriends in the past, despite being taller than a lot of men, with a shock of red-hair that refused to be tamed and a temper to match. The latter had mellowed over the years and some industrial strength products had worked wonders on her hair but she hadn't had a proper relationship in over two years. All of them had faltered at the altar of her career.

She remembered her last boyfriend Tim, and his pleas to her to leave the E.R. and get engaged, to become Mrs. Taylor and follow him to a life in the burbs, from where he intended to commute to work every day and leave her rearing their children. His vision of domestic bliss had only revealed itself under the influence of a lot of alcohol at the staff Christmas party and Maggie had realized there and then their relationship was over. It had spluttered on for a few more months, mainly due to their hectic work schedules but Maggie had finally ended it.

The idea of her as some sort of housewife, trying to juggle domestic commitments with raising children was the stuff of her own personal horror movie. She could barely manage her life as a single woman, never mind trying to keep small people alive and cared for. And there was the rub, the thing she didn't understand, the thing she wanted to put under a microscope and examine forensically and the thing she was simultaneously terrified to look at.

She was a successful trauma surgeon, a key member of the E.R. team at Hillview. She was an intelligent, accomplished woman, excellent at her job and committed to her work. But that's where her success stopped.

Her apartment was a disaster zone. It was constantly a mess. She struggled to keep on top of the basics such as washing, ironing and cleaning. Her bills were consistently overdue and she'd had her phone and power disconnected on more than one occasion. She barely had time to shop, never mind cook and her diet consisted basically of take-outs and frozen dinners. And this for a trauma surgeon! She knew if she kept going in this vein she'd be bringing a major trauma on herself.

Then there was her social life. Apart from the occasional drinks with colleagues and the few times a year she met up with former friends from university, she didn't have a social life. She didn't *do* anything. She seemed to remember a time when she used to go for a run or a bike ride but there just didn't seem to be any time in her schedule anymore to do those things. And then there was her sex life.

Hmmmm… she thought to herself, *I'm back to that old bogey.* She simply didn't have a sex life. Other than a fumble with an intern about a year ago, she had zip, nada, zilch.

No wonder I'm swooning over some guy I met in the woods, she thought baldly to herself.

How was it her life differed so greatly from her father's? He had worked the E.R. all his life and had always been impeccably turned out, not slinking into work in yet another crumpled shirt and the same pants for three days in a row. He had eaten like a king and found time for a walk every day, his "constitutional" he had called it. His bills were always paid promptly and she never remembered a time when their phone or power had been disconnected. He had always had time to spend with each of his kids every day. She barely had time to herself. He had been her hero and she had grown-up wanting to be just like him.

Hillview had welcomed her with open arms, delighted to have the daughter of E.R. legend Dr. Dan O'Brien on staff. And she was doing her best to live up to that legend. She'd always thought that was what she wanted and in the beginning it had felt great. She'd been totally buzzed up following in her eminent father's footsteps but after a few years and the sheer grind of the E.R. the buzz had started to fade.

She loved her job but lately it didn't feel the same. Was it the changing nature of many of the cases they dealt with such as the increase in stabbings, gun-shot wounds, and worst of all battered and abused children or was she burnt out? Did she need to go into a saner part of medicine, to specialize, and work scheduled hours, maybe even just during the day?

Her father had worked E.R. all his life until the day he retired, he could never have imagined doing anything else. Why then should she not be able for it? Why was she struggling to balance her work life with some semblance of a personal life? Why, for God's sake, was she lucky if she had a clean pair of panties to put on in the morning!

The answer, of course was back in Bay Ridge in the perfectly maintained brownstone she had grown up in. But it wasn't the answer she wanted. It was the answer, the truth of which, she refused to acknowledge. However, here she was in the middle of nowhere, a place she had driven over five hours to get to so she could have some peace and solitude to finally figure out exactly what it was that had been bothering her for months now. She had promised herself it was a time for brutal honesty, so there was no point hiding behind half-truths and fairytales.

The answer took the form of Kitty O'Brien her indomitable mother and a woman with whom she had a less than straightforward relationship. She'd always laid the blame for the type of relationship she had with her mother squarely at her mother's feet but the thought had been slowly formulating over the past few months if that was strictly fair. And now, sitting here on this glorious morning, looking at the incredible scenery before her and actually spending time alone, sitting and thinking, she had to finally face the unpalatable fact she hadn't been fair to her mother at all, not one little bit.

Kitty O'Brien had been a doctor in her own right and if any of the comments from some of her father's colleagues were to be believed, had been a brilliant and gifted physician. However, her career had been sacrificed upon the altar of motherhood and domestic servitude. Maggie was aware her mother had kept working for a few years after she was born and even after the birth of her brother Patrick but had never gone back to work after the birth of Lucy. Maggie always assumed that had been her mother's choice but now she wondered how much of a choice she'd actually had.

Even nowadays it was difficult to successfully juggle a career with a home-life, she was single with no kids and couldn't pull it off. She could only imagine how impossible it would have been for a woman of her mother's generation, who, after dealing with the general criticism for choosing to be a working mother, would have been expected to handle all of the child-rearing and housework as well. As much of a hero as her father was to her, she never recalled him once cooking a meal or vacuuming the floor, much less cleaning a bathroom.

She cringed as she recalled her unadulterated adoration of her father whilst at the same time all her mother had got from her was grudging acknowledgement at best and snooty disdain most of the time. No wonder, her mother's response was a guarded prickliness. She had kept the cogs of all their lives running so smoothly for so long, none of them had even been aware of it.

The house had always been immaculate, a perfectly cooked meal was on the table every evening, impeccably ironed clothes were ready to wear every morning, homework was supervised every night, football games, swimming, drama recitals and school plays were never missed, bills were paid on time and holidays were planned with military precision and no special occasion went unmissed.

In later years her mother had even volunteered at a local women's health clinic. Maggie had been vaguely aware of her mother being highly regarded by local women, obvious in the affection they demonstrated to "Dr. Kitty" whenever they'd met any of these women on public occasions. However, she had been too focused on her father as the hero to consider her mother might actually be just as equally regarded.

"Damn," Maggie swore to herself as she shifted uncomfortably in her seat, no wonder her father had been able to pull off a thirty year career in the Emergency Room, he'd had the unequivocal, total and absolute support of his wife who had managed every aspect of his life.

All he'd had to do every day was get up, put his perfectly ironed clothes on, eat the breakfast his wife had prepared for him and go to work. He hadn't needed to worry about where the food was coming from or who was going to cook it, how his dirty clothes were going to get cleaned and ironed and put in the wardrobe or who was going to pay the bills.

Of course he could just have fun with his children because the homework was already done and he'd never had to take time out of his busy day to carefully plan something as mundane as a family holiday, much less do all the packing for it. It was easy to go and be super-doctor every day when you had a whole other human being managing every aspect of your life.

And there was the problem, Maggie didn't have the equivalent of her mother, or anyone remotely close, to manage *her* life. Disgruntled, she got up from the chair and went back inside the cabin. She had finally faced up to what had been niggling at her for so long but how to solve it? She was hardly going to find herself a wife any time soon.......

She decided to have a shower.

***

It had only taken John twenty minutes to run the few miles to where Maggie's car lay abandoned in the middle of the forest but it had taken him considerably longer to fix it and if he wasn't mistaken she had done some damage to the front tie rods. She'd probably have to get them checked before considering a drive back to New York.

He finished tightening the wheel nuts and threw his backpack onto the passenger seat. He stretched and surveyed the scenery before him. It was a beautiful morning with the sort of crackling freshness in the air that only comes after a storm. He'd love to be running the few miles back to the cabin but that would only delay his plans to deposit his guest at Dr. Matt's place as soon as possible. So he beckoned Rock into the car and jumped in behind the wheel.

Five minutes later he crunched up in front of the cabin. The door was open but his guest was nowhere to be seen and the reason why became apparent as he walked inside. "Stayin Alive" was, ironically, being murdered in the shower. John chuckled to himself as he thought of how embarrassed she was going to be when she realized he'd heard her singing efforts. America's next Idol she wasn't.

He went into the kitchen and put the kettle on to boil, he figured a decent mug of coffee was just what he needed. The singing stopped and John realized a second too late that the bathroom door opened far too quickly for its inhabitant to be dressed. He looked up to find Maggie desperately attempting to cover her curves with the hand towel. His reaction to her ivory skin, endless legs and partially revealed breasts that spilled out either side of the towel, was immediate, and now *his* eyes sparked with desire, not to mention the other part of him, hardening by the second.

"Oh my God!" she exclaimed. "Where did you come from?"

John tried to drag his eyes away from her but failed miserably as he answered, "I live here, remember?"

His voice sounded throaty and his tone a lot more sarcastic than he intended but he had been completely unprepared for the sight of a near naked woman in his cabin, and what a woman.

He knew he should look away but his mind had shut down. His eyes, however, remained very much alive as they continued to drink in every incredible curve of Maggie's body. The towel came to just above the top of her legs and rose tantalizingly with each breath. Her hands tried to hold the top part in place over her breasts and the lower part over her hips but the outer edge didn't quite reach, revealing the delicious arc of her hips as they nipped in towards her waist. John was spellbound.

"Right, yeah, ok," Maggie stuttered as she started to back her way into the bathroom, "erm would you mind bringing my bag over and leaving it just outside the door?"

Apart from her obvious embarrassment there was something else in her tone and a spark of something in her eyes that took John a few seconds to place but when he did, he was the one who was embarrassed. She had tried her best to hide it amongst the shock and indignation but John was an expert in this particular emotion and knew even the tiniest trickle of fear when he saw it.

God, he thought to himself, *did I look that bloody desperate?*

He was mortified to think she would consider him incapable of controlling his desire and capable of hurting her. He was also a little annoyed considering all he had done since meeting her was help her out and look after her. But he hadn't been able to take his eyes off her when she'd stood before him, exposed and naked and he supposed it *was* just the two of them in the middle of the wilderness, so maybe she was justified in her thinking but still the idea rankled with him.

He deposited her bag and a larger towel in front of the bathroom door, grabbed his mug of coffee and headed out to the veranda. This woman brought out behavior in him he didn't recognize and he was glad her car was fixed and he would be rid of her within the hour.

Maggie sat on the edge of the bathtub trying to steady her breathing and calm the hell down.

Jesus, she thought to herself, *how does this guy always sneak up on me? He's like a ghost.*

As her heart rate returned to normal and she toweled herself off, her ire increased.

And staring at me like that, Christ, I'm sure I'm not the first naked woman he has ever set eyes on, he could have had the decency to look away.

On the surface she was angry but on a deeper level she knew her anger was fueled by the fact no other man had ever looked at her like that before, with raw animal lust, and she found it a little scary and yet another side of her found it incredibly exciting.

Maggie O'Brien quickly consigned both emotions to the, "things Maggie doesn't think about" box and, fully dressed, with her head held high, marched into the cabin. She was slightly deflated to discover John wasn't there, after all she had quite a speech prepared for him. She continued out to the veranda where she found him languishing in one of the chairs.

He looked up at her, his eyes neutral orbs of brown now as if the raging desire of minutes ago had never happened.

"I'm sorry," he said in a quiet voice. "I didn't mean to frighten you."

His apology took Maggie completely by surprise and she was lost for words. Ostensibly, he was referring to the fact he came back to the cabin unannounced but she knew he was really referring to the way he had looked at her like a wolf about to devour its prey. She was touched by his sincerity and appreciated his attempt at trying to put her back at ease. It worked. She flashed him a huge smile and told him not to worry, it was just one of those things.

"All forgotten," she blithely reassured him, knowing she would never forget how he had looked at her and even the slightest thought of it sent butterflies scattering across her tummy. She really needed to get away from this guy before she did something stupid.

"Oh wow, you drove my car back," she observed, anxious to move the conversation along and forget about being practically naked in front of him only ten minutes ago.

"Yeah," answered John, also glad to talk about something else, "it's driveable for the moment but I'd say you best get the guys at "Autoworks" in Little Creek to check it out before heading back to New York, I think you might have some damage to the front tie rods."

"Oh right, yeah ok, I'll do that, probably tomorrow as I just want to settle in to Matt's place tonight," she agreed.

John found her agreeability disconcerting, after all it wasn't something that seemed to come naturally to her.

"I'm ready when you are," she announced.

John practically jumped out of the chair and started to climb into the driver's seat until he was interrupted by a very caustic, "Er, where do you think you're going?"

"Driving," he replied, somewhat confused, "to Dr. Matt's."

"Erm, it's *my* car," Maggie pointed out.

John looked at her, all hands on hips and flashing green eyes, she really was a piece of work.

"Yes, it is," he drawled, "but I think we determined within the first five minutes of meeting that you don't have a clue where you're going, so it's easier if I drive you there rather than trying to direct you. Plus there is probably less chance of further damage to the car if *I* drive."

Maggie considered the bossy control-freak in front of her and thought about objecting, especially to his insult about her driving style but then somewhere in the back of her mind her psych training kicked in and she thought to herself, *okay he's obviously an alpha male who is used to being in control, so in the interests of expediency I'll just let him think he is in control and we can get the hell out of here.*

John could see her objections formulating and her chin beginning to rise, so was flabbergasted when she announced, "All right then, you drive."

With that she threw her backpack in the trunk and climbed into the passenger seat.

John shook his head and sat in behind the wheel, this was one female he had no handle on at all and thank God he was getting rid of her. Just as he turned on the ignition a bark sounded from behind the car. Rock, it seemed, wanted to come along too.

John looked at Maggie.

"I'm planning on hiking back so is it ok if Rock comes along, you don't mind him in your car?" he asked.

With all that had happened in the last half hour and in her eagerness to leave, Maggie hadn't considered how he was intending to get back to the cabin and was now slightly embarrassed she hadn't even asked, especially in light of everything he had done for her.

"Of course," she exclaimed, as she reached back and opened the door behind her.

Rock made no attempt to get into the car.

"Er, I'm not sure he wants to come with us though," Maggie observed.

John couldn't suppress his grin.

"He's kinda used to the front seat," he explained.

Maggie shot him a "what the fuck" look and he couldn't suppress the chuckle that rose up from his chest.

"Usually it's just me and him," John laughed, by way of explanation, "I think he's waiting for you to get out of his seat."

Maggie was incredulous and the thought occurred to her that the old adage about dogs being like their owners was obviously true. Domineering owner, domineering dog. Again, in the interests of just getting to Matt's place, she climbed out of the passenger seat and held the door open. Rock duly climbed up onto the seat but at least the dog had the good grace to look somewhat sheepish about his actions which is more than could be said for his owner. Maggie sat in the back and with an exasperated edge to her voice announced, "Can we just go now."

The muscles in John's stomach were clenched tight from trying to keep his laughter in and he didn't dare look at what he suspected was Rock's smug face or he would explode and he didn't think his female passenger would appreciate it. He had to hand it to her though, most other females wouldn't have budged.

He eased the car down the track and sneaked a peek at his back-seat passenger. She was looking at the scenery on either side of the car and smirking to herself. He couldn't help wondering what she found so funny.

Men, Maggie thought ruefully to herself, *they were simple creatures really, even the non-human ones*.

She ruffled the top of Rock's head, "Happy there buddy?" Rock turned and licked her hand as if to say, "Yes, thank you."

"So does your girlfriend have to sit in the back seat all the time?" she asked.

John thought of Sandy, and how, as sweet as she was, she had never conceded to letting Rock sit in the front passenger seat.

"Erm, no," he replied.

An unexpected stab of disappointment shot through Maggie. *So he has a girlfriend*, she thought to herself.

"I actually don't have a girlfriend," John continued and for some reason she couldn't quite define, this information made her happy. Why the absence of a girlfriend in this guy's life, who she only knew for about twenty hours, should make her happy, she had no idea. It wasn't as if she was looking for a boyfriend, she had enough to do to figure out how to have clean clothes on a regular basis. Still, she couldn't deny the tingle of possibility sitting low in her tummy.

They had already driven a few miles and Maggie began to realize it was going to be a hell of a hike back to the cabin.

"You know, I can drive you back," she offered.

"Oh that's ok," John replied, "I'm actually looking forward to the hike, it's a perfect day for it."

"Well okay," Maggie conceded, "but there's no problem if you change your mind."

"Thanks," smiled John and her tummy did a strange kind of wobble as she caught his reflection in the rear view mirror. He really was disturbingly handsome and when he smiled she felt his dark eyes revealed a tiny part of the bigger picture that made up the man she simply knew as John.

He turned onto what was obviously a main road, "This is Old Creek Road," he explained to her.

"Oh, okay," she replied.

He drove for what seemed a few miles and then turned left, he took the second right, drove for about two miles then took another left turn. He followed this tiny track for about a mile and then Maggie spotted the sunlight twinkling on the waters of a small lake, like thousands of magical diamonds.

She was entranced and knew instinctively the decision to come here was the right one, so she was somewhat dismayed at the, "Oh fuck," that filled the interior of the car but then she noticed John wasn't looking at the lake. No, he was looking at the picture perfect old lakeshore cottage that had been in Matt Fraser's family for generations. Picture perfect, that was, except for the tree now dividing it neatly in two.

"Oh no!" Maggie exclaimed as her plans for a few days of lazy solitude came crashing down as surely as the tree had. "Oh you've got to be kidding me."

John was speechless, what the hell was he supposed to do with her now? His plans for a leisurely hike back to the cabin were well and truly over as he realized he at least had to drive her into the nearest town with a hotel.

"Do you have a number for Dr. Matt?" He asked her.

"Of course I do," she snapped at him, "I work with the guy."

It seemed to John he wasn't the only one disappointed with the unfortunate turn of events. It hadn't occurred to him she might have wanted to get away from him as much as he wanted to be rid of her. And then he realized maybe she was here for the same reasons he was, to try and figure things out. Maybe she was at a turning point in her life too. Whatever she had been dreaming about certainly seemed traumatic enough. Then it hit him – she'd said she worked with Dr. Matt, so he had been right, she *was* a nurse.

"I thought you said you were a hairdresser," he observed dryly.

"What?" Maggie narked back at him, she really wasn't in the mood for small talk about her job right now and then she remembered she'd told him she was a hairdresser, oh shit.

"Yes I am," she lied and John noted how she raised her chin just like when she didn't want to do something, "I do some of the patients' hair in the hospital."

It was an outrageous lie and she couldn't believe she had just come out with it but her brain was consumed with other things right now, like what the hell was she going to do? She actually felt like crying and Maggie O'Brien never cried, ever.

She needed to get out of the car. The last thing she wanted was for him to see her upset. She opened the door and marched towards the cottage. She wasn't exactly sure what she was doing but she desperately needed some space. She was vaguely aware of a car door banging shut behind her but she marched on.

"Maggie," John shouted after her, "what are you doing?"

She ignored him and continued moving forward. Somewhere in the forest behind the cottage she heard a loud cracking sound. Maggie ignored it and kept going.

"Maggie!" John shouted after her again and if she wasn't mistaken there was a note of concern in his voice.

The cracking sound got louder. She stopped. She'd heard that sound before.

Oh shit, she thought to herself as she realized it was the sound she'd heard in the forest last night during the storm before a tree had come crashing down. Only this time the sound was much closer. She looked up just in time to see a huge fir tumbling in her direction. She was about to turn and run when she felt a pair of strong arms encircling her and then she was on the ground rolling. A few seconds later she stopped and realized she was entangled in the gigantic form that was John. She would never understand how he always managed to sneak up on her but as the tree connected violently with the spot she had just been standing on, she was very glad, on this occasion, he had.

Adrenaline rushed through John's veins. What the hell had she been thinking? He was starting to wonder if her mind had been affected by whatever it was she was here to try to deal with. He knew she was upset at not being able to settle in to some serious alone time at Dr. Matt's place but that was no reason to try and get herself killed. He loosened his arms and she raised herself up off his chest. Her face was a mixture of shock, confusion, relief and total vulnerability.

"Thank you," she mumbled and John was just about to lecture her on the dangers of approaching a damaged building when he noticed the tears threatening to escape out the sides of her eyes.

Oh no, he thought, *don't do that to me, don't cry.*

A sense of mild panic started to make its way up from his stomach and he scrambled to try and get up. As he did so his hand brushed against her breast and something akin to an electric current crackled across the palm of his hand and sent shockwaves of desire rippling through to his groin. Maggie froze and so did he, then slowly, with a growing sense of anticipation she turned her head to look at him.

Her eyes were wide with, "what the hell was that?" and her mouth parted slightly as if the question was on the tip of her tongue. Her breasts were pushed against his chest and her endless legs were tangled either side of his. John had never wanted to kiss a woman so badly in all his life but he knew to do so would be madness. However, when the green of her eyes darkened with understanding, he could hold back no longer.

Something about her as she lay on top of him was like a deer caught in the headlights and he didn't want to spook her, so with almost superhuman restraint, he kissed her gentle and slow. It came as a surprise to him then when she not only returned his kiss but crushed her lips against his, demanding more.

John parted his lips in invitation and she gladly accepted, darting her tongue into his mouth as if laying claim to him like a hungry tigress. Molten desire ripped through him, as the fingers of his left hand entangled themselves in the hair at the back of her head and held it firmly in place as he pressed his lips tighter against hers. Meanwhile, his right hand moved to the exquisite curve of her buttocks and he pulled her closer to him.

Somewhere in the long-forgotten recesses of Maggie's mind a voice screamed, *oh God, what am I doing?* Her head was spinning and an intense heat was spreading from her abdomen to the space between her legs. She was kissing this annoying giant of a man and loving it! In fact she couldn't get enough.

His tongue invaded her mouth and he pressed her head closer as if he wanted to completely devour her and then he pulled back and teased her with little nips along her lips before invading her again. His hand moved to her buttocks and he pulled her against him in unspoken need. But there was no mistaking the full extent of his need when she felt the hardness of him against her pelvis. Her response was visceral and she clawed at his shoulders in an effort to bring him even closer to her.

A fire was burning in John's loins and he wasn't quite sure how he was going to put it out. He'd never had such a lightning fast, full-on reaction to a woman before but then again he'd never met a woman quite like Maggie.

Maggie was rapidly losing herself in this guy's kisses. *Mmmmm,* she thought to herself, *where does a guy learn to kiss like that?*

The lines between reality and desire were blurring beautifully in her mind and a feral hunger started to build deep within her. She wanted this guy and she wanted him now. She returned his kisses with a ferocity she'd always suspected she had but had never let loose till now and her body moved in ways that could only be described as totally wanton.

John could feel his grip start to slip. He wasn't sure what he had expected to happen after he kissed her, he hadn't actually stopped to think about it, but he hadn't expected the tornado of desire as she met his kisses with a furious passion he had never experienced before.

He was already past the point of simply being turned on, his whole body was inflamed with a need for this woman he couldn't comprehend. Rational thought was starting to desert him and all he could see was him fully satisfying his need for her, here on the shores of the lake, in broad daylight, without so much as a condom, and the realization of how much he wanted that scared him. And John Sullivan of the U.S. Navy SEALs didn't do scared, ever. He needed to get this situation under control.

With his lips still locked on hers he rolled the two of them over until he was the one on top. He tried to pull his head away but she was having none of it and grasped hungrily at his head, keeping him firmly in place. Then she thrust her body against him and he groaned as an almost uncontrollable urge to rip at her jeans came over him.

Maggie surrendered her mind to the bliss that had taken over the rest of her body. All conscious thought had deserted her and she didn't care about anything except getting more of the gorgeous man who was kissing her like she was the last woman on earth. He groaned, a groan so visceral and full of need she craved the feeling of his skin. She wanted to run her hands over his bare flesh and explore the hidden contours of his muscles. She clawed at his shirt and pulled it out from the top of his jeans, her fingers connected with his skin and slowly, deliciously savoring the feel of him, she ran them all the way to the top of his impressive shoulders.

John was at the tipping point, his breathing was ragged now and all he could think of was satisfying the overwhelming need he had for the woman beneath him. Her hands travelled up his back and it was as if her fingertips had lasers embedded in them such was the trail of heat they left in their wake. His manhood throbbed painfully and it wouldn't take much to push him over the edge.

Her hands came back down to his waist, their touch an excruciating delight as she raked the tips of her fingers over the muscles of his abdomen which were clenched in a desperate bid for self-control. She groaned, a low animalistic groan which told him she wanted him as much as he desperately wanted her. Then her hands moved to his belt and he knew this was it, if she released what was in his pants, if she so much as touched him below the hips, there would be no stopping him.

He had never felt this way before with a woman, so completely out of control and it scared him in a way he didn't understand. Control was what he knew, what he understood and he knew right now he had to try and scrabble some back or he would be lost. This was a crazy, beautiful insanity but insanity nonetheless. His hand flew to hers and he wrenched his lips away from her mouth.

"No," he croaked.

Maggie stilled and looked up into John's handsome face. His pupils were fully dilated, his eyes two black pools of feverish desire. His breathing was coming in disjointed breaths and she could feel the strain of restraint in every muscle of his body.

She let her hands fall away and he visibly relaxed with relief. Bitter disappointment washed over her and she looked away. The cogs of her mind started to click back into place and slowly she started to return to reality and the wonderful, mindless bliss of only moments ago disintegrated into dreamlike wisps.   Rejection, confusion and embarrassment bit into her consciousness.

Had I really been about to have sex with a guy I've only just met, in the middle of nowhere, in broad daylight? she thought incredulously to herself. *And did the same guy, just refuse me?*

Shame and mortification consumed her and she couldn't look at him. She needed to get as far away from this guy as possible. She pushed against his chest but he held her in place.

John was starting to regret his decision. The throbbing between his legs had abated into a deep ache which he suspected might take some time to deal with. He looked down at the wildcat beneath him, at her lips swollen from the pressure of his kisses, her flushed cheeks and unabridged hunger in her eyes. He'd never seen anything as incredible in all his life.

He watched as the hunger, the hunger that burned for him, changed to embarrassment and she turned away. His need for control had come at the cost of her pride and he felt bad. He put his fingers to her cheek and turned her face gently so that she was looking up at him. Rejection and anger flashed at him and his regret deepened.

"Hey," he whispered, "I want to…. I want you…. It's just…." Words failed him. What was he supposed to say?

It's just that I've never felt this way with a woman before? I've never been so completely out of control? You seem to be able to sidestep all my defenses and reduce me to a mindless neanderthal? Your effect on me terrifies the crap out of me?

Oh yes, all that would be just dandy, he thought to himself, *confess her complete and utter power over you and just surrender.*

Confusion clouded her eyes and a part of him wanted to kiss all her doubts away, forget he had said no and obliterate the ache in his loins that was refusing to go away but a greater part of him shouted, *no, get up and walk away. Now!*

She raised her head slightly and for a moment he thought she was going to kiss him. Panic flashed through him, if her lips connected with his again then he knew instinctively the tiny semblance of control he was hanging onto would disintegrate and it would be all over.

The cogs of Maggie's mind were whirring furiously now and she had returned to full consciousness and one hundred percent rational thinking.

Of course a guy like this was never going to fall for you, the rational part of her brain lectured her, *guys like this are the absolute preserve of the cheerleader and the prom queen, which you definitely ain't honey.* A cynical cackle echoed in the recesses of her mind, *huh, you think you would have learned that by now*, it laughed and her sense of foolishness and shame deepened even further. And yet there was something in his eyes, something sincere as he told her he wanted her…

The irrational urge to kiss him again came over her and then she saw the panic in his eyes and the unspoken plea, *please don't*. She shrank back into the ground and he rolled off her at a speed which left her breathless. She lay on the ground and looked up at the perfect sky.

Now would be a good time to beam me up Scotty, she thought ruefully to herself.

John walked as best he could to the shores of the lake. Even the mere prospect of her kissing him had him hard all over again and his cock strained painfully against his jeans.

"Fuck," he swore to himself under his breath, "fuck, fuck, fuck."

Now what? he wondered, *what the hell do I do now?*

He couldn't even look in her direction, much less talk to her. He considered drawing a map for her to get to Little Creek and letting her drive there herself. He could hike back to the cabin and never see her again. However, there was the problem of the possible damage to the tie rods of her car and she could run into difficulties.

No, he thought to himself, *I've got to see her safely delivered to Little Creek and then I'm done with her.*

As much as the prospect cheered him, a sliver of something else licked at his gut, something akin to fear, a shard of nervousness. He had never experienced such a potent reaction with any other woman in his entire life. Whereas he grudgingly had to admit this fact, it also scared the shit out of him. He was used to calling the shots and controlling the pace when it came to sex and he always had himself under total control. He prided himself on it.

He was powerfully built and most of the women he had been with were much smaller than him and he had always been conscious of how easy it would have been to unintentionally hurt one of them if he had tipped over the edge. So he kept himself in check, controlled the pace and everyone walked away happy. But today a mere kiss had him heading in a direction from which he had felt it nearly impossible to come back from.

True, Maggie was a strong woman but he wondered if she was strong enough to withstand what she had the power to unleash? Did he really want to walk away from such a tempting prospect? A trickle of doubt licked at his gut. He promptly ignored it. He would do what was best for both of them. He had started this and then decided to call a halt when things hadn't turned out quite as he expected, so he should be man enough to apologize to her. He turned around.

She was sitting facing the lake now, her hands around her knees and her hair blowing around her face like flames from a fire and her eyes were a blue-green as they reflected the color of the lake. Her lips were still slightly swollen from his kisses and the unmistakable flush of desire remained on her cheeks. She wasn't conventionally pretty but the more he looked at her the more she took his breath away. He was just about to walk over to her when she got up and started to walk in the direction of the car. He adjusted his direction accordingly. She scowled at him and started to walk faster.

"Maggie," he started, but she scowled even more ferociously at him this time and picked up speed.

"Maggie, please," he pleaded in a low voice. She stopped and looked at him.

"What?" she spat and the look in her eyes was like a wire in his gut.

"I'm sorry," he faltered, he wasn't sure what else to say, "I'm really sorry. I shouldn't have…" he couldn't say the words.

"What?" she interrupted him. "Kissed me?"

It would seem she wasn't afraid to dissect what had happened between them.

"It's okay John, I understand," she announced in a hard voice laced with bitterness, "guys like you don't bother with girls like me. I get it. It's ok."

John was shocked at her vehemence and confused. *Guys like him? What did that mean?*

"What do you mean, guys like me?" he demanded.

She smirked at him, a most unpleasant addition to her striking features.

"Oh come on, John, don't be disingenuous, a guy like you, a jock, a work-out warrior, a guy who doesn't want all his hard work at the gym ruined by escorting the wrong kind of girl on his arm. I get it, it's okay," she stressed, "I'm not your type."

She said the word "type" as if it was some sort of unpleasant disease.

John was incredulous.

"What the hell are you talking about?" he demanded, "I'm not some sort of 'work-out warrior' and my decision to halt things between us has nothing to do with you, it's about me."

He was so angry he could hardly go on. God but this woman got under his skin.

Her eyes raked mercilessly over him, "Not a work-out warrior eh? Come on," she snorted, "look at you."

John took a deep breath, yes he worked out to some extent but he could hardly tell her his physique had been honed over the years through open ocean swimming, mixed terrain runs with a full pack on and trekking some of the most remote and high altitude mountain ranges in the world.

He looked her square in the eye, he needed her to believe him. "It's not about you Maggie, it's about me."

Again, she smirked, and he decided he really didn't like it when she did that.

"Oh come on John," she snarled, "I was serving it up to you on a plate, what kinda guy turns down no holds barred, no strings attached sex?"

The self-recrimination in her voice and pouring unchecked from her eyes pulled the wire along his gut like a knife. He stepped towards her and knew instantly it was a mistake. She put her hands out and backed away from him. "Don't come near me," she hissed.

John couldn't believe a woman as sexy as her could think any man wouldn't consider himself lucky to get a chance to be with her. The thought of her believing he stopped things between them because she wasn't some sort of arm candy to complement his looks infuriated him. He was starting to think it would have been easier to just have had sex with her.

She stood in front of him, glaring at him, accusing and defiant. He decided to take one last stab at convincing her and opt for a portion of the truth.

"Look, I've been through a bit of a rough time lately and I came out here to sort myself out. I'm a bit messed up at the minute and the last thing I expected was to run into a woman like you. I feel it wouldn't be entirely fair to drag you into what's going on with me right now. You're a beautiful woman and I'm sorry."

Maggie looked at the gorgeous man standing a few feet away from her, a man she wanted to kiss and slap across the face at the same time. She was so embarrassed she could barely look at him and the last thing she was interested in was some trite apology. However, his admission to being a bit messed up struck a chord with her, after all wasn't that the same reason she was here? And the note of sincerity in his voice was unmistakable, along with the plea for understanding shining out from his eyes.

Is it possible? she thought to herself, *is it possible he genuinely finds me attractive but is finding all this a little too hard to handle at the minute?*

The thought intrigued her and her anger and embarrassment started to fade and were fast replaced with something akin to hope. She had never met a guy quite like him and whereas he annoyed her with his bossy ways, at the same time she had never been kissed the way he had kissed her and she had never responded to any other man the way she responded to him.

He made her feel safe, not in a helpless female kind of way but a way in which she could be herself and let her wilder instincts run free. She had a feeling he could handle anything she threw at him and she blushed as she remembered the way her body had instinctively moved against him, God, how she would like the chance to do that again.

She doubted there was any chance of a relationship with him, after all where would she find the time for that. However, she was happy with the possibility of seeing him again at some point in the future and taking things up where she was willing to let them drop, for now.

She smiled at him, a shy smile and nodded, "Okay, apology accepted."

John's shoulders slumped in relief and he grinned at her, "I think we'd better let Dr. Matt know he has some D.I.Y. ahead of him."

Maggie fished her cell phone out of her bag and called Matt. It was something of a hotch-potch conversation as the cell phone coverage was patchy. She walked in random directions trying to find the best coverage.

John watched her and it was with some relief he realized the ache in his groin was starting to ease, despite the smile she had bestowed on him a few moments ago. His head, however, was still spinning from all that had happened in the last twenty minutes. How could one woman have such an effect on him? And how was it she was the only person in the entire world to whom he admitted having had a tough time recently and how come he felt slightly better for it?

John Sullivan never spoke to anybody about how he was feeling, not even the navy counselors who he had to interact with after each combat mission. The way he felt about things was the way he felt about things and, to him, talking about the way he felt wasn't going to change anything. It wasn't going to bring anyone back from the dead or replace blown-up arms or "shot-to-shit" legs.

A shaft of something he recognized as sorrow moved through him as he thought of Wolf and Freezer back in their hospital beds. Talking wasn't going to do anything for them but he knew he still needed to deal with the shame and helplessness he felt in relation to their injuries. His rational brain told him there was nothing he could have done to change the outcome of the mission but his emotional brain, the one that loved these men like brothers, tormented him with what ifs. What if he had moved faster, what if he'd shot with more accuracy, what if he'd listened to his gut telling him something was wrong? What if, what if, what if......

He shook his head and the weight of regret lay heavy on his shoulders. He was lusting after a crazy woman he had only just met, when Wolf and Freezer lay shattered and broken, wondering what they were going to do with the rest of their lives. Shame and guilt ripped through him and all he wanted to do was run through the Adirondack wilderness until he reached the sanctuary of the cabin, his legs burning and his body purged, with only the dark shadows of his mind to deal with. But he had a package to deliver to Little Creek and the sooner he did that, the sooner his life could return to some semblance of normality.

THREE

The drive to Little Creek was a quiet affair with nothing more than a cursory conversation about Dr. Matt and his plans to get someone up to the cottage and assess the damage.

On finishing her call Maggie had returned to the car, where John waited for her but he seemed distant and inscrutable as if he was wrestling with a situation somewhere off in the distance, a situation which, if she wasn't mistaken, was causing him considerable pain. Further attempts to engage him in conversation resulted in monosyllabic answers and she finally took the hint and shut up.

She sank back into the seat and couldn't help grinning at the incongruous sight of John's enormous shoulders spilling out either side of the driver's seat and Rock's head focused totally on the road ahead.

They're quite a pair, she thought to herself.

Soon they were in the picture perfect riverside town of Little Creek.

"I think the best thing to do is take the car to the guys at Autoworks first and then we'll see about getting you a place to stay," John suggested from the driver's seat.

Maggie nodded, "Sounds good to me," she agreed.

John drove on through the town and Maggie wondered what it would be like to live in a place like this, with a constant supply of fresh air, where everyone knew everyone else and greeted each other on the street, where life moved at a much slower pace.

Would she like living in a place like this she wondered or would she eventually crave the rush and mania of the city? Did people hurt each other here as much as they did in the city? She thought about the endless stabbings, shootings and beatings which had formed the bulk of her caseload in recent months and the increasing incidence of battered and bruised children. She thought of Kayla, of her ice blue eyes full of terror and pain. Would she ever be likely to treat a child like Kayla if she lived in a place like Little Creek? One thing she knew for sure, if she stayed at Hillview, there were going to be plenty more Kaylas.

If? She thought to herself, *if? Would I really consider leaving Hillview?* The thought hit her like a thunderbolt and she straightened involuntarily in the seat. She had never even considered it before, at least not consciously. She had always planned on the same career as her father, if he could do it then why couldn't she? But as she now realized, she didn't have the incredible support system her father had enjoyed and also she doubted if he ever had to deal with the constant traumatic caseload she and her colleagues dealt with day in and day out. But if she left Hillview where would she go and what would she do?

John had been stealing surreptitious glances at his backseat passenger. She was gone off into a world of her own again, thinking about something and he was willing to bet, from the distressed look in her eyes, it was the same thing she had dreamed about in the cabin.

He wondered what it was that haunted her? The thought occurred to him he was likely to never find out and a pang of regret scratched at his gut. Was he really prepared to let the chance of having something with a woman like Maggie slip through his fingers?

Yes, a voice inside his mind insisted, *you can barely control yourself when you are around her, how do you think having a woman like that in your head will affect you when you have to deploy? Play with this particular fire John and you will definitely get burned.*

However, before the voice had even finished, a wave of intense emptiness washed over him and he couldn't help wondering if it wasn't more dangerous, in the long run, than the woman in the rear-view mirror.

***

Samuel Taber couldn't quite believe his eyes. Lieutenant John Sullivan of the U.S. Navy SEALs was driving into his auto-repair shop in a ten year old Toyota Prius. His usual companion, Rock, was sitting by his side but if he wasn't mistaken there was a woman sitting in the back seat.

"Well wonders will never cease," he exclaimed under his breath. A broad grin broke out over his face as he extended his hand, "A slight change of transport for you John," he laughed as he took the big man's hand.

"Don't worry Sam, I haven't joined the socks and sandals brigade just yet, this here is the vehicle of my friend, Maggie," he informed Sam.

Sam swept his eyes appreciatively over Maggie.

Friend? he thought. *She wouldn't be my friend for long.*

"Pleased to meet you," he announced as he offered her his hand.

Maggie shook his hand and smiled at the mischief twinkling in his sky-blue eyes. It seemed she had been looking for a hot guy in all the wrong places over the years.

Who knew they were all hiding in the Adirondacks? she thought wryly to herself.

"So what's the problem with your wheels then?" he asked.

"It's more to do with her tie rods," John replied. "I think they're damaged and I was wondering if you could check 'em."

"No problem," Sam announced. "Why don't you come back to me in an hour or so and I'll let you know."

"Sounds good," John smiled, "see you in about an hour."

"An hour it is," announced Maggie emphatically, in a bid to remind them both she was still there and able to speak for herself.

The two of them looked at her as if she was slightly unhinged and then a look passed between them which she couldn't quite fathom. It was a look of mutual understanding and, if she wasn't mistaken, respect, as if there was something else in the mix between these two, other than just two guys who knew each other.

John turned to her, "Come on let's find you a place to stay," he said as he started to walk down the road in the direction of the town.

Interestingly, Rock, at least, waited for her. She smiled at the dog and ruffled his head, "Thanks buddy," she whispered as the two of them set off in pursuit of his owner.

Maggie watched the powerful frame of the man striding purposefully in front of her. It was as if he literally couldn't wait to put some distance between them and she wondered what "tough time" he had gone through recently that seemed to be eating him up from the inside out.

Fifteen minutes later they were standing outside The Little Creek Lodge and Maggie's cheeks were flushed from the brisk nature of the walk. Hardly a word had passed between them, except for John to inform her that the Lodge was probably her best bet for accommodation.

The two of them entered, leaving Rock outside on the veranda that ran the length of the main building. Maggie was worried about him but John assured her Rock wouldn't move from his spot once he was given the command to stay.

He held the door open for her and she went inside. The main reception area was classic Adirondack rustic with a large open stone fireplace and leather couches to the left and the main reception area directly ahead, with a small bar to the right leading to the main dining room. Behind the reception desk was a twinkly-eyed, grey-haired man who looked like he had been there since the place first opened in 1896.

He smiled at them, a full-faced smile of genuine warmth and friendliness, "What can I do for you two lovebirds?" he grinned.

John stopped dead in his tracks and Maggie couldn't help chuckling at the look of shock on his face.

"We, er… we," she started to explain but John cut her short.

"My *friend* here would like a room," he declared and his emphatic emphasis on the word friend was unmistakable.

The old man couldn't hide his disappointment.

"Ah, I'm afraid I can't help you there," he announced, "we're completely booked out."

Maggie could swear she spotted a twinkle of mischief in his eyes. Was he serious or was he trying to play cupid?

"Oh I'm only a wee slip of a thing," she joked, "surely you must have a cupboard or something you can squeeze me into for a few nights."

The old man's eyes sparkled with mirth and he laughed, "Oh I wouldn't mind squeezing *you* into a cupboard for a night or two but they're all full too."

Maggie couldn't quite believe the place was full on a Saturday night in the middle of October but she decided to play along.

"Ok," she announced, "perhaps you could recommend somewhere else?"

The old-timer's eyes positively glistened with laughter at this stage. "Well I could," he replied, "but they'd all be full too."

Whatever this guy's game was, Maggie was starting to lose patience. Still, she reckoned a show of impatience wouldn't help her case much at this point so she pasted on her sweetest smile and exclaimed, "What? It's not possible everywhere is booked out, that just doesn't make any sense!"

"It does when there's an international fishing competition on," chuckled old blue eyes.

A low groan escaped from John and she turned to see him running his hand down his face. A look of resignation sat upon his handsome features. "Shit, I forgot about that," he sighed.

Maggie couldn't believe her ears. Her head swiveled around to look at the old man. It swiveled back again to look at John. Old twinkly eyes was smiling. John most certainly wasn't. Old Twinkly eyes was giving her a "here's your chance" look. John couldn't bear to look at her at all. A crushing sense of inevitability crept over her.

"Just how far do you think I'd have to go before I'd find a place to stay?" she asked the last of the great matchmakers.

"Oh I reckon you'd have to go as far as Saratoga Springs or maybe even Albany," he replied and gave her a look that suggested she was crazy to even be thinking about it when she had her "friend" to stay with.

It was Maggie's turn to groan.

So much for a few days of blessed solitude, she thought dejectedly to herself, *I'll be half way back to New York at that rate.*

Then a thought occurred to her as she recalled seeing a camping supplies shop down the street. She could still get the solitude she craved - all she had to do was get her car and buy herself a tent, or at least a sleeping bag and a Bunsen Burner or whatever it was they called those things you cooked on in the great outdoors. Throw in a few supplies at the local grocery store and she was set.

Buoyed by her new plan she smiled at old twinkly eyes, "No problem," she winked at him, "thank you so much for your time." She grabbed the pen on the desk in front of him and wrote down her cell number. "I'd appreciate it if you could give me a call if a cancellation comes up."

The old man gave her a puzzled look and then looked at John to see if he could make any sense out of her actions but John looked just as confused.

"Well I suppose we'd best go and get my car," Maggie announced as she turned and headed for the door. John said goodbye to old twinkly eyes as he chased after her.

Old twinkly eyes stared after them in bemusement. He'd seen a lot of things in his time as the owner of Little Creek Lodge but nothing quite like the chemistry that sizzled between the two people who'd just left. He wondered how much longer they would be able to deny it.

FOUR

John was starting to think there was some sort of cosmic conspiracy at work.

What the fuck am I going to do now? He wondered.

He sent up a silent prayer everything would be okay with her car and she would decide to find accommodation in Albany or Saratoga Springs - a good two hours drive away. In the interests of expediency he decided to make his way back to Autoworks on his own. The day was moving on and he could make it out to Sam's place in half the time it would take than if he had Maggie with him, even though she suddenly seemed to be in a big hurry.

"Hey, hold up," he cried after her as she marched ahead.

She stopped abruptly and turned to face him. He was surprised to see something akin to zeal sparking out from her eyes and she definitely looked like she had a plan. Then again, this woman always had a plan and John couldn't help wondering what it was this time.

"I was thinking," he started, "there's no need for the two of us to go and get your car, why don't you let me go and get it and I'll meet you back in town."

Maggie cocked her head to one side and looked at him like she needed to give his offer some serious consideration.

"That'd be great," she told him, "if you don't mind."

John didn't mind at all, he was craving some alone time, some time to think straight. However, he was a little suspicious of how quickly she had agreed to his offer, after all, agreeability didn't seem to be in her nature.

"Where will I meet you?" she asked.

"How about Bridget's Home Bakery and Tea Shop?" he suggested. "I can show you where it is on the way."

Maggie smiled, "Sounds great," she agreed as she stepped aside to allow him to take the lead. She had to fight the urge to link her arm through his as she walked beside him through the picture perfect town of Little Creek. She patted Rock gently on the head instead as he happily trotted along beside her.

The town basically consisted of a main street which followed the path of the river that flowed parallel to it. The street consisted of restaurants, antique stores, craft shops, fishing and hunting supply shops and boutique bed and breakfasts which Maggie now noticed all had "Full" signs in their windows. In between buildings there were beautifully manicured green areas that ran seamlessly down to the river. Some of the restaurants had back decks overlooking the river and so it was with Bridget's Home Bakery and Tea Shop, possibly the quaintest little tea shop Maggie had ever set eyes upon. It looked like it belonged in a bygone era, all polished timber and chintzy decor.

Maggie grinned as John ducked his head to get in the door. The interior was rustic comfort personified and antique tea-sets lined the shelves on the walls. An old pot-bellied stove dominated the main wall and a large arch-way led out onto the sun-drenched deck. There were only a few patrons dotted about here and there in quiet conversation and John led her to a small table in the corner with a perfect view of the river. Maggie smiled, "I hadn't figured you for frequenting a tea shop," she told him.

He looked at her and was about to say something when a squeal of obvious delight came from inside.

"Oh my good God, would you look at who finally turned up," exclaimed the squealer in an accent that suggested she had never left the Emerald Isle. Maggie turned and saw a slightly plump, grey-haired, blue-eyed woman in her sixties barreling towards John, her arms outstretched and a smile as wide as the state of New York on her face.

"Come here and give your Aunt Bridget a hug," she demanded.

John looked slightly embarrassed but smiled and took the woman into his arms nonetheless, whereupon there could be no doubt as to who was the one doing most of the hugging. After what seemed an eternity she finally loosened her hold and stepped back to look at him.

"It's great to see you John," she said, a slight tremble in her voice, "it's great to see you in one piece and safe."

At the word "safe" John shifted slightly and looked in Maggie's direction. Aunt Bridget's head swiveled around and Maggie found herself pinned by a pair of laser-like, sapphire-blue eyes.

"Oh, and who is this?' she inquired, not once relinquishing Maggie from her gaze.

"This is a friend of mine," John answered, "Maggie."

"Maggie? A friend you say?" she exhaled, as she extended her hand towards Maggie, all the while firmly holding her in her sights. "Well, I'm pleased to meet you, Maggie," she announced as she shook Maggie's hand.

Maggie felt like she had been turned inside out and forensically examined. She didn't know who Aunt Bridget was but she was willing to bet her jolly exterior masked a shrewd character.

"Likewise," Maggie replied, smiling.

Peeling her eyes away from Maggie, Bridget demanded to know what she could get them.

"I'm actually going to run out to Sam Taber's place," John informed her, "he's fixing Maggie's car but I think Maggie would at least like a coffee while she waits for me."

"A coffee it is," Bridget reiterated softly as she smiled at the two of them and Maggie was willing to bet it would come with a slice of interrogation.

As Aunt Bridget headed back in the direction of the kitchen, John smiled at Maggie, "I'll be as quick as I can," he assured her. "I'm sure you're anxious to get on the road."

Maggie's tummy went into freefall at his smile but she managed to return one of her own, "Oh don't put yourself under any pressure on my behalf," she informed him, thinking silently to herself, *after all I'm not going far*.

"Oh no pressure at all," John announced with something of a false note in his voice as he proceeded to make his way out of the restaurant.

As soon as Maggie was sure he and Rock were out of sight she got up and went to the counter where Bridget was looking after a customer.

"Can you hold that coffee for me?" she asked the older woman, "I'll be back in ten minutes."

She skipped out the door as Bridget nodded, "Of course."

Maggie had waited until she was rid of John to put her plan to acquire some new camping equipment into action. From what she already knew of him, she suspected he wouldn't approve of her plans and she wasn't in the mood for his bossy objections. What she did, once she got her car back, was none of his business anyway she reasoned to herself as she dashed down the street to the camping supplies shop.

Exactly twenty-five minutes and a few hundred dollars later she was back on the deck overlooking the river with the autumn sunshine warming her face and happily sipping her coffee, feeling very satisfied with herself. She'd come to the Adirondacks for some much needed solitude and that was what she was going to get, even if she was a little nervous at spending the night alone, in a flimsy tent, in the middle of the forest. Okay, a lot nervous.

The restaurant was busy and Aunt Bridget was run off her feet, thereby preventing the interrogation from taking place that Maggie was sure she had planned as soon as she got a few spare minutes. She had just started to make her way over to Maggie's table when John's huge frame appeared in the archway. A scattering of butterflies skipped across Maggie's tummy at the sight of him and she groaned inwardly to herself, *oh God, this guy makes me feel like a sappy teenager.*

Bridget turned to see what had made her newest customer suddenly go all doe-eyed and immediately understood when she spotted John. She wasn't sure what was going on between them, the curvy red-head was the first woman Bridget knew of that John had ever brought with him to the Adirondacks, but she hoped it meant he had finally opened his heart to someone. She looked heavenwards and sent up a silent prayer, *please let her be the one,* before she turned and having smiled at John, made her way back to the kitchen.

John made his way over to the table and from the look on his face Maggie wondered who had died.

"Is everything all right?" she asked.

"Not exactly," John huffed as he sat on the opposite side of the table, "your tie rods are fu.... finished, we were lucky we got as far as Little Creek without anything happening."

Maggie looked at him, at his beautiful face and couldn't believe her ears. What sort of evil bitch-fairy had put a spell on her?

"What?" she spluttered. "What did you just say?"

John, who had studiously avoided making eye contact, now looked her straight in the eyes.

"I said...."

"No, No, don't say it again, I actually heard you but what does it mean? Why is it a problem? Can't Sam just replace them?"

"Er, no. There aren't too many Toyota Prius models in these here parts so he doesn't carry spares for them. He can order them in but they'll take a few days to get here."

Maggie stared at him like he was speaking outer most alien and he had to admit he felt sorry for her, all her plans kept going to shit. The problem he now faced, was what he was going to do with her. He dropped his gaze and fiddled with the keys in his hands, he hadn't thought about anything else since Sam had dropped the bomb about the tie rods. Of course his old navy buddy had seen it as a perfect excuse for John to get Maggie back to the cabin for some "one on one" as he had so succinctly put it. And therein lay the problem, if he offered her the chance to stay at the cabin with him for the next few days, John knew keeping his hands and tongue and other parts of him away from her would be tougher than hell-week.

"Are those car keys?"

Maggie's voice broke through his thoughts.

"Yes," he replied, "as a favor to me Sam offered you the use of....erm.... one of his vehicles."

A frisson of delight shot through Maggie, *finally*, she thought to herself, *I'm catching a break.* As long as she had the back-up of a vehicle to crawl into in the middle of the night, should her nerves get the better of her, then she didn't care.

She beamed at John.

"Then what are we waiting for?" she announced as she hopped up and started for the door. She swung by the counter first to pay for the coffee but Aunt Bridget was having none of it. Instead she popped the sandwiches she'd just made for them into two paper bags and waved them on their way.

Maggie retrieved her new camping supplies from beside the door and waited for John out on the front porch. She surveyed the cars parked out front and mused to herself how she wouldn't mind spending the night in the sleek black sedan. She was somewhat disappointed then when John walked passed it to a vehicle a few cars down, a vehicle that definitely fell into the vintage category and had seen better days.

"Oh," she said as she came up beside him, "*this* is the vehicle?"

Her emphasis on the word "this" told John all he needed to know about how she felt regarding Sam's old Ford F150 and her attitude irked him, after all Sam didn't have to provide her with a replacement vehicle. He didn't owe her anything, he was just being kind. And it was good enough to get her to Albany or Saratoga Springs and that's all he cared about. He turned to look at her, his brown eyes like a pair of flints.

"Is there a problem?" he clipped at her.

Maggie realized she had come across as ungrateful rather than dismayed. She looked around him into the truck's interior and noticed it had a bench seat. This would make sleeping in it a lot easier and she felt much better. She smiled at him and shook her head.

"Nope, no problem at all," she informed him, "I was just wondering how I'd manage to sleep in it if I need to but it's all good, I can just stretch out on the seat."

She moved past him and it was then John noticed she was carrying items she definitely didn't have with her when he left her at Bridget's Bakery. They looked suspiciously like a tent and camping supplies, then her words hit him "how I'd manage to sleep in it" and he knew, with crystal clear clarity, what her plan was.

Oh no, oh fuck no! he thought, *she is NOT that crazy.*

But one look at her overly enthusiastic expression told him she was *that* crazy and then some. She was just about to climb in behind the wheel when he grabbed her arm.

"Hang on a minute, you ARE planning on driving to the nearest town with an available hotel room aren't you?" he spluttered.

Maggie had known, just known, he was going to object to her camping plan. God but the guy was annoying, predictable but annoying. She shrugged his hand off her arm and squared up to him, well as much as anyone could square up to a man-mountain.

"Listen," she started, "I really appreciate all you have done for me over the past two days, I really do but where I go from here and what I do, really isn't any of your business."

John couldn't believe his ears. On top of what seemed like her intention to camp in the Adirondack wilderness by herself, she was now basically telling him to mind his own business and get lost. He looked into her green eyes, flashing with defiance. He could feel his blood starting to come to the boil. She went to get into the truck again and again he grabbed hold of her, this time with both hands.

"Just a minute there, lady," he ground out between clenched teeth as Maggie tried to shrug out of his grip but this time he wasn't letting her go. "Do you actually have some crazy idea in your head to go camping in the woods by yourself, yes or no?"

Her eyes blazed with anger and her chin was positively pointing skyward as she hissed out her reply, "Yes."

With that she placed both her hands on his chest and tried to push away from him but he was having none of it and pulled her closer. That, however, was a mistake. Immediately he felt the fullness of her breasts against him and desire flashed through him like molten liquid. He looked down into her upturned face and even though he felt like strangling her, he felt like kissing her more.

How a woman could infuriate him and turn him on so much at the same time, he had no idea but as she opened her mouth to say something, he didn't care, as he crushed his lips to hers. He wanted to shut her up, to dominate her, to own her, possess her and most of all he desperately wanted to get her the hell out of his system.

His frustration got the better of him and he kissed her hard, pulling her roughly against him until she could barely breathe. He slid one arm around her back, holding her in a vise-like grip and he placed his other hand on the back of her head, pressing her to him as he ravaged her mouth.

It happened so quickly, Maggie didn't see it coming. Only seconds ago she had been about to launch into a tirade against the man who was now kissing her so thoroughly she thought she might faint, except for the fact her body was on fire.

She knew she should resist, somehow wriggle free of his grip and ask him what the hell did he think he was doing but that would mean this amazing kiss would have to end and she had never been kissed like this in her life and she intended to get as much of it as she could. So she wrapped her arms around his neck and opened her mouth even further to allow him ravage her that bit more.

John felt her acquiesce and a small part of him felt a sense of triumph. It was good to know he had something in his armory to deal with her. He slowed his assault on her mouth and instead of continuing to crush her lips to his and mercilessly invade her mouth with his tongue, he now gently caressed her lips and his tongue languished inside her, making teasing forays inside her mouth.

Maggie thought she was going to lose her mind. God, if this man could send her to another dimension with just a kiss, she didn't dare imagine what all-out sex with him would be like. Each gentle caress of her lips and tease of her tongue sent flickers of desire rippling through her, starting in her mouth and ending between her legs, where they were building into one pulsating throb of need. She moaned into John's mouth and pressed herself against him, communicating in a way words never could just how much she wanted him.

John's anger started to dissipate but this left him with an even bigger problem as it was being replaced by something much more troublesome, raging desire and a hard-on so intense it hurt. She wasn't supposed to kiss him back. She was supposed to get angry and pissed off. She was supposed to scream at him, slap his face and tell him to go to hell, thereby solving his problem. That would have been the reaction of a normal woman but it seemed this particular woman didn't do normal.

He slowed the kiss and reluctantly pulled away, unable to look at her. He felt, yet again, he owed her an apology, so he grabbed himself by his very blue balls and opened his mouth to start to tell her he was sorry but before he got a word out he felt her finger against his lips. He looked down and the sight of her mouth swollen from his kiss and the dark green desire blazing in her eyes was breathtaking. Godammit but if there was an available room in this town right now he'd be dragging her irresistible ass into it and finishing this.

"Shhh," she quietly commanded him, "I know what you're going to say and I don't want to hear it. Don't start blowing all hot and cold on me again. I'm not sorry you kissed me like that, not one little bit but if you do it again you better make sure your lips aren't writing checks other parts of you can't cash."

John was so stunned by her words, he could only watch as she took the keys from his hand, released herself from his grip and climbed in behind the wheel of the truck. It was already running by the time he came to his senses.

Okay, lady, he thought, *you wanna camp in the woods by yourself? Then camp in the woods. See the fuck if I care.*

Maggie couldn't help laughing to herself at the shock registered all over John's gorgeous face and it pleased her no end.

"Are you coming?" she smirked at him.

"Not with you behind the wheel I'm not," came the curt reply.

Maggie groaned to herself, *Jesus does he ever give this alpha shit a rest.*

"What's the problem?" she fired back at him.

"You're not insured until you send Sam your details and a picture of your driving license, that's the problem," he informed her and she couldn't miss the sound of smug satisfaction in his voice.

Something akin to a strangled scream escaped from her lips as she moved along the seat to let him in behind the wheel. Too late, she realized, she was wedged between him and Rock. She squashed the poor dog up against the door in her efforts to put some semblance of distance between her and this annoying but incredibly handsome man, who had her head spinning so much she couldn't remember her last straight thought. She reached for her bag and cell phone as John silently pulled out on to the road.

She took her driver's license out of her purse and took a photo.

"What's Sam's cell phone number?" she asked.

John didn't skip a beat or take his eyes off the road as he recited a ten digit number.

Maggie couldn't help marveling at how he seemed to be a walking telephone directory. She sent her photo and details on to Sam, asking him to confirm when she was covered to drive the truck.

They drove along the asphalt for a while and John's posture made it clear he wasn't up for conversation. Which was too bad because Maggie wasn't comfortable with the heavy silence enveloping the cab.

"So apart from Aunt Bridget, do you have any other family around here?" she tentatively inquired.

She earned a confused glance for her efforts and almost wished she hadn't opened her mouth. Then a wide grin spread across John's face, like he now understood where she was coming from and he chuckled, "Bridget isn't my real aunt. She was one of my mother's oldest and closest friends."

"Oh." Maggie smiled but she guessed from the word "was" that his mother was no longer alive. "Are either of your parents still living?" she asked in a quiet voice and immediately regretted it at the flash of pain which shot across his face.

She wasn't really expecting him to answer her when he replied in a tight voice, "No."

"I'm sorry to hear that," she apologized.

"Don't be," came the quiet reply, "*you* had nothing to do with their deaths."

Maggie thought the emphasis he put on the word "you" was strange. It was almost as if he was saying someone was responsible for their deaths and she couldn't help wondering if he thought that someone was him. She decided oppressive silence was better than conversation littered with emotional landmines and shut her mouth.

John drove on, his eyes fixed steadfastly on the road ahead but his mind was lost in the past, consumed with memories of his parents, the two finest people he'd ever met and who he had loved with all his heart.

His father, ever the military man down to his boots, smiling and playful, throwing a squealing John in the air. Somber and resolute every time he walked out the door to God only knows what troubled hot-spot in the world. A man who John had only really come to fully understand in recent years.

His mother, intelligent, beautiful and accomplished. Oh how he had adored her. He could see her now, her auburn hair, warm brown eyes and loving smile as she gazed into his eyes. A familiar shaft of guilt ran through him as he remembered the last time he had looked into those eyes and seen the pain she had tried to hide from him. The pain he had put there.

Completely lost in his thoughts now, he nearly drove past the turn-off for Old Creek Road and wrenched the truck onto the centuries old track at the last second. The next thing he knew he had a fiery red-head crushed up against him, with one hand on his shoulder and the other on his balls. His reaction, as always with this woman, was instantaneous.

She looked up at him, annoyance and desire flashing dangerously in her eyes.

"You know, if you're going to insist on driving then you might take care to try and keep us on the road," she spat at him as she desperately tried to disentangle herself.

The urge to shut her up, in the most effective way he knew how, was almost too much but then he remembered her warning from the last time he had quietened her and simply threw the word "sorry" at her and drove on. It was time to get rid of her once and for all and be done with this head-wrecking, ball-busting shit.

He didn't care how much her sexy ass bounced on the bench beside him, he hit the throttle and the old F150 rattled across the ten miles to Stillwater Lake in record time.

FIVE

Maggie was relieved to see the end of the road and the sparkling waters of the lake. The late afternoon sun glittered across its surface and she could feel a tingle of excitement rising like a fountain in the pit of her stomach. The forest ran almost to the shoreline but off to the left there was about half an acre of grass. The whole setting was peaceful and serene - just what she was looking for.

"This is perfect," she sighed.

John looked at her and a part of him thawed slightly towards the pig-headed woman who had turned his life so much on its head over the past two days. She was obviously desperate for some solitude and something unpleasant had driven her here, something she wasn't ready to face back in New York. If anyone could understand where she was coming from it was him.

"I'm glad you like it," he smiled at her, "come on let's get you set up."

With that he jumped out of the truck and grabbed her things from the back.

"Follow me," he commanded.

"Er, I can take some of those things," Maggie offered but he was already striding across the grass.

"Or not," she grumbled to herself, as she hurried after him, wondering if there was such a thing as an ultra-alpha male because she was pretty sure she had found one.

She couldn't help wondering exactly where he was going when he rounded the trees at the far end of the grass but her eyes lit up with delight when she spotted the small green area nestled amongst the trees and hidden from view. It was better than she had hoped for as a spot to camp. John deposited her things on the ground.

"You like it?" he asked.

"It's perfect," she beamed back at him, "thank you, thank you very much."

John smiled back.

"Well if you're going to insist on being out here on your own then I reckon a bit of privacy couldn't do any harm."

Maggie was touched by his consideration.

"Thanks, I appreciate that and it's such a beautiful spot."

She gazed out at the lake and a sigh of contentment slipped past her lips. Finally, she was in a place where she could work on getting her head straight.

John looked at her and even though he was worried about leaving her here on her own, he hoped she would find some of the peace she so obviously craved and an escape from whatever was troubling her.

Watching her gaze out across the lake, the sun warming her face and her eyes sparkling with joy, already half lost in thought, he felt almost like an intruder on her private space. She needed to be here and he understood that and he needed to leave before he did something stupid. He understood that too.

"Ok, let's get you set up then," he announced in a voice with a sudden croak in it.

Maggie turned to look at him.

"What?"

"Let's get you set up," John repeated, "you know - the tent and everything."

"Oh, oh that," Maggie replied, "don't worry about that, the guy in the shop told me it practically puts itself up. Please, you have done so much for me already, I don't want to take up any more of your time. Actually, I was wondering if you want me to drive you back to the cabin, Sam sent a text to say everything was fine and I'm fully insured on the truck, so it's not a problem."

John shook his head.

"No thanks, I'm looking forward to the hike back with Rock but I'd really feel a lot better about leaving you here on your own if I knew you at least had the tent up okay."

Maggie was touched by his concern but was confident she could get a little two man tent up by herself. It was clear she had very much intruded on this guy's personal space for the past two days and he had seemed almost desperate at times to be rid of her so she wasn't going to keep him here any longer than necessary.

"Listen, seriously, the guy in the shop showed me how to do it," she lied, "it's a piece of cake. You and Mr. Adorable over there should make the most of the late afternoon sunshine and hike back whilst it's still bright. I couldn't be happier here on my own and I've got all the time in the world to sort myself out and erect the tent."

She tried to inject a note of authority into her voice and put heavy emphasis on the words, "on my own". It seemed to work.

John shrugged his impressive shoulders, "Okay," he agreed, "but can I have your phone for a minute?"

Maggie thought it a strange request but she decided not to argue. She pulled her cell phone out of her bag and handed it to him. Thirty seconds later he handed it back.

"Reception can be patchy out here but a text message usually gets through. That's my number, if you need anything then just contact me and I'll help you out."

Maggie didn't know quite what to say but couldn't help wondering if "need anything" included a booty call. She smiled at him.

"Thanks, I will," she said in a low voice.

He nodded his head at her, called Rock and started to walk away.

He was just about to round the trees when he turned and smiled.

"It's been a pleasure meeting you Maggie," he said and then disappeared.

Maggie's knees went weak at his smile and as soon as he was out of sight she slumped to the ground. God, how could one man have such an effect on her, she wondered to herself.

Well first of all, a little voice trilled inside her head, *as men go, there aren't too many put together as spectacularly as him and secondly, no guy you've ever met has challenged you or simultaneously treated you with such consideration as he has.*

Maggie nodded her head, as if agreeing with her inner voice, and looked in John's direction. If she didn't so desperately need to straighten her head out right now she'd be running after him. It's not that she was looking for a deep and meaningful relationship but she didn't get too many opportunities for mind-blowing sex these days either and she had a feeling the gorgeously bossy man who had just walked away would rock her world in ways she couldn't even imagine.

She looked at the number on her phone beside the word John and made a promise to herself, as soon as she had her head sorted she was going to call it and make sure and get the rest of her sorted too. Buoyed by the prospect, she jumped up and happily announced to the wilderness, "Okay let's make camp."

John had walked about a quarter of a mile when he stopped. He couldn't shake the feeling of uneasiness that had plagued him since he'd left Maggie. He had felt like a complete shit leaving her there on her own, no matter how happy she had seemed about it. Concerns kept running through his mind. Would she be able to get the tent up? Did she have water? A lantern or flashlight? Had she even thought to bring anything with her to eat? He berated himself for not checking these things before he'd left.

He had at least taken the precaution of guaranteeing her safety as much as possible by bringing her to his favorite secluded spot beside the lake and he comforted himself in the knowledge that in all his years hiking and fishing there, he had only ever seen a handful of other human beings. Still, he felt uneasy.

He was also somewhat surprised he wasn't happier at finally being by himself. He'd done the right thing, he was sure of it. He'd walked away from a woman who could mess him up on so many levels and he also needed some time alone to figure things out and get himself straightened out. So why did it feel like he had done something wrong, like he had let something slip through his fingers that he should have held onto as tightly as possible and never let go.

He walked on another few steps but it was no good, he had to go back and at least check she was okay. He took the shortcut through the woods and a few minutes later was about to announce his presence when he stopped. It seemed little Miss City Slicker had everything under control. Hanging from one of the trees was the very latest in outdoors' water filtration. Spread out on a groundsheet, in a very methodical manner, was just about every other thing you'd need for a few days camping in the forest, including food. Sitting beside it all, looking very pleased with herself, was Maggie, munching happily on the sandwich Bridget had made. He noticed the only thing she hadn't yet taken care of was putting up the tent.

He pulled back, obviously she was better prepared than he had given her credit for and he had to admit to being impressed. He also had to admire her balls for wanting to be out here by herself, he didn't know any other woman who would be up for that. If the truth be told, he had never really met a woman quite like the red-haired goddess currently gazing contentedly across the lake and devouring her sandwich in a manner to rival any of his SEAL buddies.

He hadn't really believed such a woman could exist, a woman who drove him nuts in every way but who made him feel so alive, he nearly forgot to breathe. Just a look from her emerald eyes was enough to break through the layers of protective isolation he had wrapped himself in for years. Up until now, he hadn't met a woman who could even make a dent in his carefully constructed barriers, they were made of the finest emotional kevlar after all.

Sure, he knew how to play the game, how to smile and charm and give a woman what she wanted so they could enjoy some mutually consensual one on one but he had kept it all at surface level. The minute a woman had looked for more from him, he had walked.

The day he enlisted in the United States' Navy he'd made a vow to never get seriously involved with a woman for as long as he served and he had strengthened that vow when he became a SEAL. It hadn't been a problem until approximately twenty-four hours ago. He knew instinctively it would be next to impossible to walk away from a woman who got under his skin as much as Maggie but the prospect of what he could have with her was so tantalizing he couldn't help considering it.

He shook his head, *stop it John*, he reprimanded himself, *you have your rules for a reason. Do you really want a woman like that in your head when you go on deployment? And never mind the damage she could do to you, what about the damage you could do to her? Would you really want to subject her to years of heart-ache as she has to watch you walk out the door and, if somehow things worked out between you and you convinced her to marry you, put her through the pain of trying to deal with heartbroken children who can't understand where or why you're gone?*

Would you really want to do that to a woman as fierce and independent as her? Would you want to be the one responsible for putting the fire out in her eyes as she buckles under the strain of your absence and carries all the other responsibilities of your lives on her own? Do you John? Is that what you want?

Would you want to watch her try to stay stoic and strong as she cares for you in the event you come back to her injured and broken. Would you want to be responsible for her devastation should she have to watch your casket being lowered into the ground in the event you come back to her in a box? Do you want that John? Do you want any little bit of that? Damn right you don't! So back the fuck off and leave her to her life. The last thing she needs in it is a Goddamn Navy SEAL.

His words made him shrink back into the woods and he found a perfect spot to conceal himself. He decided he was going to wait until she had the tent up and everything was okay before he walked out of her life for good.

Maggie had to hand it to Aunt Bridget, the woman made a mean chicken and bacon sandwich. She wiped the remnants of it from around her mouth with the back of her hand and washed it down with what she had left of her mineral water. She wondered if it would be the last decent tasting water she would get for a few days as she looked back at the water filtration unit hanging from a tree behind her. The young camping enthusiast back in the shop had assured her the water tasted as good as what she had just slugged out of the bottle but she had her doubts.

She breathed in the fresh air and decided she didn't care, slightly unpleasant tasting water was a trade-off she was more than willing to pay for the peace and solitude of this stunningly beautiful place. She looked out over the lake as the early evening sun warmed her face and sighed contentedly.

"Perfect," she exhaled and sent a silent thanks to John for bringing her to this spot.

She thought about the domineering man who had been in her life for the past two days, about his smile and his chocolate colored eyes that darkened to smoldering pools of ebony after he kissed her. She thought about the five o'clock shadow that accentuated his handsome features and how it had scratched against her skin as he had crushed his lips to hers.

She remembered the feel of his broad shoulders and the taut muscles of his abdomen and caught her breath as a light throb started between her legs. She jumped up in response and thought she'd best get this tent up before she changed her mind and went in search of a cabin in the woods and its very sexy owner.

Twenty frustrating minutes later she was still no nearer to getting the damn thing up as she wiped the sweat from her forehead. She threw her jacket on to the grass and stripped down to her tank top. She looked at the instructions again and cursed them.

"Oh, this tent practically erects itself," she mimicked the young sales assistant. "I don't fucking think so," she gritted out through clenched teeth as she turned the instruction sheet the other way around to see if it made more sense.

John chuckled to himself as he continued to watch Maggie struggle with the tent. He hadn't expected his return to the lake to be this entertaining. He could see exactly what needed to be done and was considering giving her another ten minutes before showing himself and putting her out of her misery. But then she stripped down to a miniscule tank top that barely contained her luscious breasts and the chuckle in his throat died as it was replaced with another response much lower in his body.

"Fuck," he swore to himself, as desire licked deep in his groin, "she can sleep in the fucking truck."

Maggie wiped the sweat from her brow and looked longingly at the cool waters of the lake. The storm hadn't done much to dampen down the heat and humidity of the Indian summer upper New York State was enjoying in the last few weeks. As sweat trickled down her spine Maggie wondered just how secluded her camping hideaway was as she considered cooling off in the lake and remembered she didn't have a swimsuit with her. A little voice whispered inside her mind, *you're on your own in the middle of the wilderness, who needs a swimsuit?*

She grinned to herself, there was no way she was brave enough to skinny-dip, even if she was on her own in the middle of nowhere, and with that she turned her attention back to the Chinese puzzle that was her tent.

Fifteen mind-bending and physically challenging minutes later, the tent was up and she was drenched in sweat. She looked at the lake and it was almost as if it was calling her name. She looked around and, reassuring herself there wasn't a soul for miles, decided she may as well challenge herself completely out of her comfort zone and started to strip.

The tent was up and John had to smile at the tenacity of its owner, she was certainly no quitter. He looked at Rock and then down at his boots as he considered how much he was going to regret his decision to walk away from such a delicious prospect as Maggie but that's exactly what he was going to do. He lifted himself off the trunk of the tree he had been resting on and looked up for one final glimpse of the woman who had found a chink in his defenses, something he suspected it might take him a while to repair. The sight that filled his vision stopped him dead in his tracks. There, on the shores of the lake, was Maggie, standing in only her panties and bra.

John sucked in all the available air surrounding him, "Holy fuck," he whispered as hot tendrils of desire snaked their way through his body and licked mercilessly at his groin. She was looking nervously around her and suddenly it dawned on John what she had in mind.

"Oh no," he groaned, "please don't do it, for the love of God please do not take off the rest of your clothes."

Seconds later she stood naked, a flame-haired vision of female perfection, on the shores of Stillwater Lake.

John clutched at his stomach as something that could only be described as primitive and carnal bolted through him. He knew he should respect her privacy and look away but he stood transfixed, unable and unwilling to take his eyes off her, off the full curve of her breasts, the creaminess of her skin and the perfect arc of her buttocks. One of his hands moved to the zipper of his pants as he tried to relieve some of the pressure on his cock. He was already harder than he had ever been in his life as he watched her step into the water.

Maggie couldn't quite believe what she was doing but stripping off and throwing caution to the wind felt incredibly liberating. She tentatively stuck her toes into the water and nearly changed her mind but knew the only way to do this was in one go, so she took a deep breath and charged into the lake, submerging her hot skin into its cooling waters in one shriek-filled motion.

The feel of the cool water as it swirled around her naked flesh was almost erotic and Maggie relished its chilly caress as she swam further out into the lake. Once she hit deeper water, she dived into the depths and enjoyed the cold rush of the water against her face and its frigid touch on her breasts. She came up for air, exhilarated and feeling lighter than she had for months, as if she had shed a great weight in the hidden depths of Stillwater Lake.

The water was cold enough that she knew she wouldn't be able to stay in it for long so she flipped on her back and floated free and unfettered, letting what was left of the sun's rays warm her as she basked in this new sense of freedom.

John watched as she swam further out into the lake. He watched as the perfect orbs of her ass broke the still surface as she dived into its depths and as her mouth-watering breasts glistened when she came up for air. She was on her back now, floating, absorbing the last of the evening sun, her eyes closed in blissful abandon. The only visible parts of her were her toes, tips of her knees, face and the tops of her breasts, the nipples standing to attention as if they were desperate to escape the water's cold touch.

John didn't know what turned him on more, the sight of those hard buds just begging for the warmth of his tongue or the serene smile on Maggie's face. And turned on he was, in a bad way. He was considering doing something about it in his hideaway but he figured that would consign him to the creepy pervert box and it was a place he hadn't figured on ever visiting. No, he was going to have to take his blue balls and rock hard dick and somehow make it back to the cabin, where he could take care of business in private and not whilst the source of his temptation was only a few hundred feet away.

He was in the middle of re-adjusting himself when he noticed Rock perk up as if he could hear something. John stopped what he was doing and it took him another thirty seconds before he heard it too, the sound of tires moving at speed along the gravel track.

Fuck he thought, *this is the end of the road, whoever it is means to come up here or else they are lost. Either way, they aren't just going to drive by.*

He looked out at the lake, Maggie was still floating on her back, completely unaware she was about to get some company. He thought about shouting out to her, to warn her but then she would know he had probably been here the whole time and he didn't fancy that, especially not after the way he had freaked her out this morning at the cabin.

Maybe they'll just turn around and leave, he reasoned with himself, *after all, who would be coming up here at this time of the day.*

He had just finished that thought when he picked up the muffled thump of music over the noise of the tires. Something in John's gut told him this wasn't good, not good at all and his gut was never wrong, it was, after all, what had saved his life on numerous occasions.

Approximately one minute later a black Escalade braked to a halt at the edge of the lake, Nickelback boomed from its interior and four obviously intoxicated adult males in their early twenties tumbled out of it. Correction, four intoxicated and possibly all high adult males, such was the stink of marijuana that floated on the fresh Adirondack air once they opened the doors.

John swore under his breath, "Fuck, this couldn't be any fucking worse," and looked over at Maggie. He cringed at the look of horror on her face but was happy to see she was quietly making her way back to the shoreline, even if she was headed straight in his direction. He looked over at the bunch of yahoos, two of them now relieving themselves in the bushes, and hoped that's all they were here for and would soon be on their way.

No such luck.

The front seat passenger went around to the trunk and hauled out a case of beer. It was obvious these boys were settling in for a few hours and John only hoped there weren't more on their way.

Once the driver had finished relieving himself, he also went to the trunk and hauled out another case of beer. He was just about to follow his friend when he noticed Sam's truck.

"Oh, hey boys, looks like we've got some company," he shouted to the others.

John checked on Maggie. She was still making her way to the shoreline, slowly and as stealthily as possible so as not to draw attention to herself. He hoped she would make it to the cover of the trees before these guys noticed her.

Nope, no such luck.

"Whoa!" shouted Driver-boy. "What do we have here, looks like we've got our very own mermaid, boys."

John winced and cursed under his breath again, "Stay away from her, you asshole."

Maggie stopped dead. She couldn't believe it. Where the hell had these idiots come from? And why oh why, she wondered to herself, did they have to show up the one and only time she had ever skinny-dipped in her life.

She turned to look at them and thought to herself that maybe they'd prove to be the decent type but the second she set her eyes on them, she knew otherwise. They were obviously a bunch of frat boys up in the Adirondacks for a weekend of drinking and smoking weed. She was now an added attraction and something told her this could get nasty. The four of them were now standing at the same spot where she had entered the water and the ring-leader had just picked up her bra and panties.

"Oh this just gets better," he laughed to the others, who now looked at her like a bunch of starving coyotes.

John couldn't believe what was happening, "Just put her underwear down and walk away, ass-wipe," he growled to himself, "and take your leery friends with you."

He could tell from their accents, clothes and accessories they were a bunch of frat boys from the supposedly upper echelons of Boston society, they screamed money but he knew that meant nothing in terms of their behavior. If America had learned anything in recent years it was what a bunch of frat boys or jocks were capable of when there was enough drink or drugs involved and it was downright ugly.

The thoughts of any of these jerks laying a finger on Maggie thoroughly nauseated him and he could feel the muscles in his stomach clenched tight. It was obvious these dick-heads weren't going to go away, if anything it looked like they intended at best to embarrass Maggie and at worst… well John didn't want to think about it.

He decided it was time to deal with this situation. He looked at Maggie and felt a quickening of his insides at the stricken look on her face. She believed she was out here all alone, naked and defenseless, faced with four drunk and high frat boys and the fact she had no answers to this dilemma was written all over her striking features. And if John wasn't mistaken she was shivering. He suspected she'd freeze to death before she would willingly walk out of the water in front of these jerks. It was time to sort this shit out.

He broke cover but not before ordering Rock to stay. There was every chance this was going to get ugly and he didn't want his dog getting hurt. He then started walking in the direction of the four clowns who were so busy taunting Maggie, they didn't notice him.

"Come on honey, come and have some fun with your new boyfriends."

"Getting cold sweetheart? Come over here and let me warm you up. I've got a red hot poker waiting for you."

"We've got all night so don't stay out there too long now or you'll catch a chill and you're going to need all of your energy, for all of us."

John's blood started to boil at the overt sexual references. How dare these fuckers treat a woman that way. Who the fuck did they think they were? Kicking their asses was going to be thoroughly enjoyable, the only thing was, with four of them against one of him, the odds were stacked unfairly in his favor. He grinned to himself and thought, *oh well, that's just too bad.*

"Hey guys," he called out, "how about we leave the lady alone and give her a little bit of privacy."

Four heads swiveled in his direction and John almost laughed at the look of shock on each face as they tried to figure out where he had come from. The driver and obvious ring-leader, was the first to recover.

"Hey man, it's cool," he replied, "we're just having a bit of fun, so why don't you keep moving your sneaky ninja ass right along and get outta here."

John grinned, *sneaky ninja ass eh? I like that one,* he thought. So, Driver-boy was feeling all brave with his three pals, no surprise there, classic modus operandi of the type of jerk who'd taunt and threaten a woman on her own, naked and defenseless in the middle of nowhere. The other three jostled in behind him in a show of support.

"Not gonna happen I'm afraid, I'm here to make sure the lady gets out of the lake okay and the only people who are leaving are you guys."

Driver-boy laughed and was quickly joined by the three stooges.

"You know what man, you're a funny guy, thanks for the laughs, now fuck off."

Maggie looked on in horror from the lake. Where the hell had John suddenly come from and what was he doing taking on these guys? It was clear they were up for a fight. He looked like he could handle himself but four against one meant he was going to get hurt and badly. She needed to put a stop to this but hadn't a clue how, she was so cold at this stage she couldn't feel her toes.

Then it occurred to her, she should just get out of the water, it would be embarrassing but it was nothing compared to the prospect of John getting hurt. She was sure, now he was here, the threat of anything else happening was greatly decreased, after all it was one thing a woman reporting a rape but it was another matter entirely when there was a witness and she was sure these guys didn't fancy a few years behind bars.

"Hey, you know what assholes," she called out, "it's no big deal, I'm sure even you guys have seen a woman naked before." Then, she tried to put one of her frozen feet in front of the other.

John groaned inwardly, he should have known she wouldn't have been able to keep her smart mouth shut. What the hell was she thinking? He turned to look at her and in that moment Driver-boy decided to take his shot.

"See asshole, even the lady is up for showing us what she's got," he sleazed before stepping up and slugging a punch into John's solar plexus.

John had to grin as shock registered on the idiot's face when his fist connected with a solid wall of muscle. Contact had been made. Now it was time to end this charade.

If Maggie was ever asked to describe what happened next, she wouldn't be sure quite what to say. She could only ever confirm there was a flurry of kicks and punches, which resulted in four frat boys lying flat on their asses, before the man who had laid them all out threw them back in their Escalade, quickly followed by their cases of beer, and told them never to show their pig-ignorant faces in The Adirondacks again.

She watched as the Escalade threw up dirt and stones in its wake as its four occupants hightailed it out of sight. She looked at John as he watched them go. Then he turned to look at her. She was still in the water. She hadn't moved since the first punch had been thrown and now she was shaking so badly from the cold, she thought she might fall over if she tried to walk.

John raced over to her rucksack and emptied its contents out onto the grass, he grabbed her towel and started running towards her. She tried to voice her objections but her teeth were chattering too much. He came towards her in the water and she inched in his direction. As soon as she was arms-length away he grabbed her and pulled her towards him. She tried her best to cover herself but her efforts were useless and she thought it ironic how her face should be flaming in embarrassment as the rest of her literally froze. He enveloped her in the towel, lifted her into his arms and carried her towards the tent.

Oh God, Maggie thought, *I'm being carried, no guy has ever carried me before, this is way past embarrassing.*

When they got to the tent, he gently put her standing on the grass.

"Are you all right to stand for a few seconds?"

She nodded as she watched him stick his head into the tent.

When he re-emerged he had the brand new sleeping bag in his hands. He unzipped it, removed his wet boots, socks and pants, got into it and then pulled her down to him. He put her sitting between his legs, removed the towel and pulled her naked form against his chest. He zipped the sleeping bag up as far as it would go and then enfolded her in his arms and held her shaking body against him as the very last vestiges of daylight disappeared behind the mountain at the far end of the lake.

Maggie sat there and let the heat from his body suffuse through her as she tried to process everything that had happened in her life in the past few days which had culminated with her shivering, naked, in a stranger's arms on the shores of a lake in the Adirondacks. And she realized she'd happily go through all the unpleasant parts again, just so she could end up here because it felt so incredibly good.

The warmth of his body, the strength of his arms and the rock-solid feel of him made her want to snuggle into him and forget the worries of the world. Slowly the realization came over her that she'd never had that in any of her relationships. She'd always been the one to carry the concerns of the other party, the one with the open arms providing comfort, many times battling through exhaustion to smile and provide her support. Never had any of her boyfriends returned a fraction of it.

She'd been the safe place for all of them to fall but all she'd ever had in return was the equivalent of a brick wall. She didn't dare snuggle but she allowed herself to fall back against John just a tiny bit further as it dawned on her this man could give her more than she even knew she needed.

John felt her relax into him a little bit more and smiled. The shivers were starting to abate and he could feel the ice in her veins beginning to thaw. He was sure it wouldn't be too long before she had something smart to say and would be pulling away from him but he hoped it wouldn't be too soon as he didn't want this silent connection between them to end.

The feel of her curves against him was intoxicating and he wanted nothing more than to kiss all the stress of the last half hour out of her body. He wanted to hold her and feel her, listen to the rise and fall of her breath and relish being with her whilst all her defenses were down. As he sat there in the forest with the darkness of night closing in upon him he could feel the chink in his armor widening to a gaping hole and sent a silent prayer heavenwards that he may be granted the strength to resist the temptation enveloped perfectly in his arms, for both their sakes.

For the first time in her life Maggie didn't want to break the silence. She could quite happily spend the rest of the night in John's arms and fall asleep to the twinkling of the stars but he'd gotten wet coming into the lake to help her and he couldn't have made it back to the cabin yet, so probably hadn't eaten, therefore he had to be getting cold and on top of that had to be starving. As much as she wanted to selfishly remain where she was, her concerns for him far outweighed her own desires. However, she knew instinctively he wouldn't release her until she assured him she was okay and so it was with great reluctance, she opened her mouth.

"I'm feeling much better now, thank you so much," she whispered.

John didn't move and continued to hold onto her. She wondered if he'd heard her and she tried to turn in his arms but he tightened his hold.

"I heard you," he informed her, his voice low and husky, "just let me hold you for another few minutes. It's okay Maggie, I've got you. Let go. You don't have to worry about you or me, you don't have to be strong or in control. Let it be. Let me be here for you, even if it's just for a few minutes."

With that, Maggie felt something crack inside her. Her whole life had been about striving, pushing, achieving and proving herself. She always had to have the answers, anything less would mean she was weak and weakness was not what was going to take her to the top of her profession.

She'd watched as close colleagues had taken other options in their careers, options she'd considered easier than the path she had chosen. She always accepted that was okay for them but not for her, she was Super-Maggie and she was going to be Super-Doctor.

She'd watched as her female colleagues, in particular, had traded career opportunities against the demands of marriage and children. She'd watched and she had neatly packaged all those parts of herself away that might have wanted any of that. She had packaged them away and literally put them on ice.

Now, a man she had only just met was holding her in his arms and melting more than just the frozen blood in her veins. She relaxed into him, telling him more than words ever could just how right he was and she felt a warmth move through her body that went far beyond her bones.

John smiled and held her to him, gently brushing his lips across the top of her head. In that terrible moment when he had seen her emotionally stripped bare and the fear and uncertainty glistening in her eyes, he had realized just how much she felt the need to always be strong and have all the answers. She had reminded him of another woman who'd been a pillar of strength and carried so much for others. There was nothing more he could do for his mother but he could at least give Maggie a place to put aside her cares, a place where someone else could be strong for her, even if it was for just a few minutes inside his arms.

Maggie was so blissed out, she wasn't sure when the shivering had stopped. She still felt a chill but as the intensity of her emotions started to subside it dawned on her she was totally naked and she hadn't a clue how to wriggle out of this particular situation to spare herself any further blushes. In addition, it occurred to her she most certainly didn't want to camp in the forest on her own anymore but she didn't know what to do about that either.

John could almost hear the cogs of her mind clicking into gear and he was sure he could guess what was bothering her; being naked and being on her own in the forest. He could help her out on both counts.

"Okay, I suppose it would be a good idea to get some clothes on you and get you in front of the fire back at the cabin."

Maggie couldn't help the gasp of relief that escaped from her lips. There was nowhere else on earth she would rather spend the night than in the safety and warmth of this man's sanctuary in the woods.

"If you just let me wriggle out first, I'll rustle up some clothes for you and we can pack up and go."

Seconds later John released his hold on her and started to unzip the sleeping bag. An ache so intense rippled through Maggie at the loss of his touch that she shuddered. Immediately concerned, John took off his shirt and put it around her shoulders.

"Here, I'll get your things and then you should put this on," he advised, a look in his eyes that said, *and don't argue with me.*

She didn't. The sight of him standing there in his boxers and a white tee-shirt stretched across his impressive chest had just liquefied her insides, rendering her speechless.

"Thank you," she managed to croak in reply as she watched him walk over to where her clothes, including her panties and bra, were lying beside the lake. She pulled his shirt tightly around her and inhaled the heady combination of sandalwood, amber, bergamot and John. She closed her eyes and savored the unique scent of a man, who, she was quickly coming to realize, was just as unique in so many ways.

John shouted a command and Rock came bounding out of the trees. She watched as man and dog made a mutual fuss over each other and somewhere in one of the dark woman-caves of her mind a warning bell clanged and a wary voice whispered, *be careful Maggie, falling for this guy might be a fall you can never recover from.* Rock came running over to her and she promptly ignored the annoying voice as she happily snuggled into John's shirt and his dog.

Ten minutes later she was cuddled up to Rock as John steered the old F150 along the road and was still smarting at how quickly he had managed to dismantle the tent. She was surprised at how soon they arrived at the cabin and squinted her eyes in suspicion at John.

"Oh, look how close my secluded camp-spot was to the cabin," she exclaimed, "what a coincidence."

John turned and grinned at her.

"What a coincidence indeed, just because I allowed you to go off into the forest by yourself doesn't mean I wasn't going to keep my eye on you."

Maggie was incredulous, "Allowed me" she repeated, "did you just say 'allowed me'?"

John laughed. There she was, little Miss Spitfire was back and he was surprised at how good it made him feel.

"Stay here," he ordered, "in the warmth of the truck, until I get the fire going."

In truth he also wanted to get into the bathroom to have a look at the cut on his arm before she noticed it. One of those yahoos had managed to whack him with a log which had a sharp edge sticking out of it and he now had a jagged gash on the inside of his left forearm.

"No need," she announced, "I'm perfectly fine, I'll come and help you."

With that she started to slide along the seat.

Frustration got the better of him, as always with this woman, and he turned to her with his hands raised to his ears in the classic frustration gesture. He watched as a look of horror came over her face and too late, he realized his mistake.

"You're hurt!" she exclaimed and immediately reached for his arm.

He put both arms down and grappled for the door handle.

"It's nothing," he protested, "just a scratch."

"Scratch, my ass," came the retort as he heard her jump out of the truck behind him, "we're dealing with that straight away."

He was taken aback at the note of authority in her voice and decided it was probably best not to argue with her and just let her have a look at it. If she was a nurse or paramedic, as he suspected, then it would save him the bother of having to try to stitch it.

Five minutes later, by the golden glow of a paraffin lamp, he watched as what was obviously a very experienced medical professional went to work on his arm. First she cleaned it, then she removed a number of splinters, stitched it and covered it with a dressing.

As he watched her, he couldn't help noticing how good she looked in his shirt. He knew she only had the scrap of a tank top on underneath it and he remembered how her breasts had looked practically tumbling out of it back at the lake. Her proximity to him, the scent of pine, cedar and earth coming from her and the heat of her touch on his arm all combined to ignite a spark in his abdomen, a spark of desire that was very quickly building into a flame.

When she looked up into his eyes and happily announced, "All done," the effect was explosive. The look of care and concern shining in her eyes, care and concern just for him, was his undoing and it incinerated all his carefully constructed defenses in one fell swoop. He couldn't hold back his need for her any longer.

He reached for her and crushed her to him. He claimed her lips with a kiss, long and deep and with a ferocity he didn't know he possessed. And incredibly, she came right back at him with a passion and hunger that was mind-blowing.

She twined her arms around his neck and pulled him even closer. He groaned as he felt the swell of those incredible breasts soften against his chest, those instruments of torture he just couldn't resist for a second longer. Securing her to him with one arm around her waist, he let his other hand travel up and under her tank top until his palm was filled with the curved perfection of her breast. He took the tantalizing bud at its tip between his thumb and finger and rolled and squeezed it to life until it swelled to the point where it was begging to be kissed.

Maggie groaned, a groan so feral and full of need it sent him tumbling over the edge. All sanity was gone now, any last shred of armor he'd had left was obliterated by that groan and the hunger this woman so obviously had for him. He was a man ablaze with lust, desire, carnal need - call it what you will but the devil himself and all the hounds of hell couldn't stop him now.

Somewhere in the back of his mind he hoped Maggie was able for the demon she had unleashed. With an animalistic growl he pulled his shirt from her body and ripped her tank top over her head before claiming the swollen nipple of her breast with his mouth. He sucked and played with it mercilessly between his teeth. His other hand came around and grabbed her other breast, the nipple readily engorging to his touch. He lavished the same attention on it with his mouth and sucked hard.

Maggie cried out and he stopped. He looked down at her and what he saw nearly caused him to come there and then. Her lips were swollen from his kiss and the tips of her breasts, a deep rose-colored red from the attentions of his mouth, stood out as if begging him for more but her eyes, oh God her eyes were two emerald pools of need, want and hunger that screamed, *don't you dare fucking stop.*

And in that instant he was consumed by what could only be described as a delirium of desire, the only cure for which was the woman before him. He pulled her to him and subjected her to a kiss so savage, it left him breathless. He thought she might stop him and a part of him almost hoped she would as he had never felt so out of control in all his life but no, she came at him with a savagery of her own and he was done.

Maggie had never believed the stories about women coming from a guy just fondling and sucking their breasts but when John had sucked hard on her she had almost exploded into orgasm. Her legs had buckled and she'd cried out in desperation, she wanted him so badly the ache between her legs was becoming unbearable.

There wasn't a part of her body that wasn't aflame with need for him. No man had ever made her feel like this and she had well and truly lost her mind around about the time his mouth first connected with her nipple. Her body was now acting in a way it never had before and she loved it.

She pressed herself against this incredible man and reached for his belt. He broke their kiss, as if in desperate need of air and perhaps scrambling for a scrap of sanity. The memories of the morning came flooding back, *oh no, oh no you don't mister, you ain't backing out on me this time,* she thought as she ground herself mercilessly against his crotch. Then she took his tee-shirt and ripped it from his body. She grinned to herself, *ha, two can play at that game.*

She wrapped her arms around his neck and pressed her desire-filled breasts to his chest, skin to skin. A low growl came up from his throat, his hands claimed her breasts and his lips crushed hers once more.

John could feel a pressure building in him that he knew he wasn't going to be able to control for much longer. This woman drove him insane with need and he could feel his control slipping on many levels, both physically and emotionally. He had to get inside her now whilst he still had an ounce of sanity left. With his tongue still dominating her mouth he scooped her up and carried her over to the bed. He sat her on the edge and removed her pants, gasping when he saw she was wearing no panties and as the full naked glory of her lay before him.

Maggie reached up and unbuckled his belt. The ache between her legs was now a throbbing agony and she was desperate for him. His jeans fell to the floor and the evidence of his desire was barely contained by his boxers. She pushed them down and gasped at the size and beauty of the man before her.

Something quickened deep inside her and a liquid heat pooled between her legs. She looked up into his face and saw a man barely holding it together, such was his need for her and Goddamn if she didn't nearly come on the strength of that look alone. But she didn't, instead she lowered herself back onto the bed and spread her legs wide, her invite explicit.

John simply couldn't take anymore, he slipped the condom he'd grabbed from the first aid kit over his painfully engorged penis and lowered himself towards Maggie and what he hoped would be his salvation. God help him but his need for this woman was overwhelming and he hoped what he was about to do next was something he could come back from.

Slowly and gently he probed her opening with his cock and he could feel how ready she was for him. He intended to try and take it as slow as he could but it seemed her need for him was just as great as his need for her and she moved down the bed lowering herself onto him whispering, "Take me John, please, just take me."

Those words were the catalyst that obliterated any semblance of sanity and control he was grasping onto and with an almighty roar he surged into her. She screamed his name and lunged forward, clawing at his shoulders and then they started to move in unison, each thrusting with a primal need to assuage the yearning and carnal hunger they had sparked in the other.

John thrust mercilessly into Maggie as a volcanic pressure started to build in his groin and she pulled him to her demanding more. He let rip with everything he had in him, holding nothing back and suddenly she was falling apart beneath him, shuddering in ecstasy and screaming his name. That was all it took to send him into the stratosphere. He came so hard he nearly blacked out and as a primal roar ripped from his throat with a power and intensity he'd never experienced before, he knew he was never going to be the same again.

As he adjusted his weight onto his uninjured arm John considered what he had just experienced came pretty close to an out of body experience. He understood now why the French called it "le petit mort", the little death. Damn it, he felt as if a part of him was still floating around the heavens somewhere.

However, as wonderful as it had been for him, he was almost afraid to look at Maggie. There was no doubt she had experienced a "petit mort" of her own but at what cost? He had never taken a woman so hard before and now shame and embarrassment were starting to creep over him.

He looked down at her and softly gasped at the beautiful sight before him. Her hair was spread out on the bed like a flaming fan behind her head. Her eyes were closed, a soft blush colored her cheeks and her lips, swollen from the passion of his kisses, rested in the most luxurious of smiles and he could swear her skin was glowing, like she had been lit from within.

Her smile widened and she chuckled before opening her eyes.

Okaaay, thought John, *she seems fine.*

"Are you okay?" she asked him.

John couldn't believe his ears. She was asking *him* if *he* was okay?

"I..I've possibly never been better," he stuttered "but what about you? I didn't hurt you did I?"

Maggie looked up into the eyes of the man who had just taken her to the moon and back, the man who still remained fused to her body in the most perfect way and she couldn't believe the fear and concern she saw in his eyes and if she wasn't mistaken a touch of embarrassment.

Hurt her? God nothing could be further from the truth. Sure, she had never had a man as well endowed as him before and he had filled and stretched her in ways she could never have imagined but he hadn't *hurt* her.

She smiled and cupped his cheek in her hand.

"No, John, you most certainly didn't hurt me. Hurt is not a word I'd use to describe what you just did to me and I'm so glad the rest of you cashed the checks those lips of yours were writing all day."

He smiled at her and a butterfly skittered across Maggie's tummy. Then he dipped his head and kissed her, gently and slow. The solitary butterfly was joined by a host of others and Maggie knew she was in trouble.

You haven't hurt me yet she thought *but there's a strong possibility you might.*

An involuntary shudder rippled through her body at the thought and John immediately stopped kissing her.

"Shit, you're freezing," he announced, as he silently berated himself for selfishly caving to his overwhelming desire for this woman before properly looking after her. Grabbing his penis, he gently eased out of her, making sure to secure the condom.

"No," Maggie protested, "I'm fine, that's not it, really. I was just thinking about something...."

Her voice trailed off as their physical connection was broken and she felt inexplicably empty. She reached for him but it was too late, he was already out of her grasp. He grabbed a soft fleece throw off the couch and handed it to her.

"Here, wrap yourself in this until I get the fire going," he commanded and with that turned and headed for the bathroom.

Maggie watched his naked magnificence move across the room and considered if she had been mistaken or if there had been a slight change in his demeanor.

Oh God, she thought to herself, *that was the most amazing sex of my life, I hope he doesn't regret it because that would gut me.*

John disposed of the condom and looked at himself in the mirror. Looking back at him was a thirty-four year old man who had just had the most incredible sex of his life. He had hoped by sating his need for Maggie that he might get her out of his system. He had hoped she was simply an itch he had needed to scratch. But as tiny after-shocks of pleasure continued to pulse low in his abdomen, he knew she was more like the sexual equivalent of crack cocaine. He could feel the need for his next hit of her already starting to build. Fuck!

He took a few calming breaths and told himself to get a grip. The first thing he needed to do was look after her rather than look after his need for her. She, after all, had cared for him as soon as they had made it inside the cabin. He went back into the living room and smiled at the sight of her wrapped in the aqua-marine colored throw. Damn if it didn't make her eyes seem other worldly.

"I'm sorry Maggie," he apologized, "I shouldn't have...." he trailed off at the look of hurt and anger that flashed in those incredible eyes.

She jumped off the bed and stalked over to him, her temper evident now in every move of her body.

"Don't," she spat at him, "don't you dare tell me you're sorry you had sex with me. I happen to think what happened between us was pretty fucking amazing and I'd rather remember it for the wonderful event it was without having it tainted by your regrets thank you very much. So, whatever you were about to say, just can it and keep it to yourself."

It amazed him how a woman as sexy, vibrant and beautiful as her could have such a low opinion of herself when it came to men. Why did she always assume the worst, in relation to herself, when it came to his motives? It amazed and infuriated him.

He could feel his blood starting to heat and his anger rising as he looked down into her upturned face.

Her chin jutted towards him in defiance and her eyes seethed with temper and the effect, of course, was simply breathtaking. A heat of another kind started to chase the anger from his system and he could feel himself getting hard again. Christ but he had it bad. However, this time he swore he wasn't going to do anything about it, at least not until he had looked after her in other ways.

"Maggie," he sighed, "I don't regret what just happened between us either and I'm at a loss as to why you'd think I would. I was simply going to apologize for not lighting the fire and looking after you first, making sure you were warm. I let my needs selfishly get in the way of that and I'm sorry."

Maggie couldn't believe he was apologizing for not lighting the damn fire but as she looked into his chocolate colored eyes she couldn't mistake the sincerity shining there. Sincerity and perhaps frustration and she felt slightly foolish. She shook her head as she looked down at the floor.

"I'm sorry," she said in a small voice, "it's just, you always seem to be trying so hard to resist me and even though your body tells me you want me in the most fundamental and natural of ways, your words say otherwise."

John pulled her to him and encased her in those iron-like arms. He let out a long, slow breath.

"Maggie," he breathed, "I want you like I've never wanted a woman in my whole damn life and that terrifies the living shit out of me. I'm used to control in all things and I'm damned if I can control myself around you. On top of that I'm a man who comes with a whole lot of baggage and complications and I'm not interested in inflicting those on anybody, especially someone as vital and alive as you. So, yes, I've tried to resist you but you and this unbelievable body of yours would test the limits of a monk."

He ran his hands down her body, leaving delicious tingles of heat in their wake. He cupped her ass and ran his hands back up over her buttocks, into the small of her back and brought them to rest on her shoulders. He looked into her eyes, like he was looking into the depths of her soul. Her breath caught in her throat as he lowered his head and kissed her, a kiss so thorough and intense it made her head spin. He pulled away and she fell against him.

"And now, I'm going to light a fire and look after you properly before I lose control of myself again."

Maggie could feel the evidence of his desire jutting against her stomach and considered shrugging out of the throw and seducing him into changing his mind thereby easing the ache that had already sprung up again between her legs. However, there was an unspoken plea hiding in his eyes and she suspected his need to grapple back some control was of greater importance at that moment in time than his need for her. She smiled and stepped back. Fine, she'd let him off the hook this time but he needn't think she was going to respect his inner control freak going forward, after all, her newly discovered inner sex addict wasn't going to settle for that.

"That'd be nice," she hummed against his ear as she slipped out of his arms. She pulled the throw tight around her and sat on the couch, not once releasing him from her gaze. Then her eyes dropped to his very erect penis and she smiled, a slow, languid smile so full of intent he had to move away from her before the demands of his body overthrew the objections of his mind and he found himself tossing her over the back of the couch and having her again.

He grabbed a pair of boxers and a shirt, threw them on and marched out the door.

The chilly evening air was like a slap back to reality. John stood on the veranda for a moment and let the events of the past hour sink in. He'd done it. He'd had no-holds barred sex with a woman who had driven him insane with desire for the past twenty-four hours, a woman who he had tried to resist with everything he had in him and failed. He'd known they'd be spectacular together. He'd known she would get under his skin unlike any woman he'd ever met. He'd known he had nothing to offer her except, at most, a few days together in the Adirondacks and still he'd gone ahead and given in.

You knew all that, he said to himself, *smart-ass bastard you are, then how is it you don't know how in the hell you are going to walk away from her?*

With that he stalked off to the side of the cabin to pick up some kindling and logs for the fire. On his way back a noise from the truck caught his attention and he could just make out Rock's soulful eyes peeping out at him. God, this woman drove him so crazy he'd even forgotten to let his dog out of the truck. He walked over and opened the door.

"Come on buddy," he soothed, "everything's all right, just your pal here has lost his mind but I'm sure I'll be okay eventually."

Rock looked at him, cocked his head to the side and then shook it before bounding up to the door of the cabin. John laughed.

"Or maybe not eh?" He said to Rock as he opened the door.

Both dog and man stopped dead in their tracks at the vision that met them as they entered the cabin. Maggie was curled up on the couch, cocooned in the throw, her head on a cushion with her sunset colored hair spread out around her, and quietly snoring. But it was the look of peace and contentment upon her perfect features that caused John's heart to skip a beat and the unbidden thought occurred to him at just how natural it was to have her there. He shook his head in denial and crushed the thought to dust because thinking like that was dangerous.

He moved over to the fireplace and went about setting a fire. Moments later the kindling crackled into life and John turned once more to look at the woman on his couch. One of her legs had escaped the cocoon and was stretched out in languorous abandon. He had to fight the urge to trail his finger up its ivory length.

The fire burst into life and the reflection of the flames in Maggie's hair was almost mesmeric. He could see how red-haired women had come to be viewed with superstition in so many societies in the past as he felt as if this particular red-head had woven some sort of spell over him. A spell he was hoping he would be able to break sometime soon.

For the moment he needed to eat. He went to the kitchen, grabbed a beer and rustled Bridget's sandwich out of his backpack. He grinned as he took the first mouthful, God that woman knew how to make a mean chicken and bacon sandwich.

He smiled to himself as he remembered the unspoken question in her eyes on being introduced to Maggie. His mother's old friend never missed a trick and he imagined it would be killing her right about now to know just how much of a "friend" Maggie was. He wouldn't be surprised if she had even gone as far as phoning his sister.

The familiar pang of sorrow and regret pinged through him at the thought of his only sibling and how things still remained strained between them. They had done a lot of work to repair the damage over the years and relations had improved at surface level but he knew she still blamed him for their mother's death and he knew she still hadn't really forgiven him. He knew this because he still hadn't forgiven himself.

Memories floated before him now, long-ago memories of them all in happier times. He remembered hiking with his parents to Stillwater Lake and spending idyllic days there exploring the shoreline with his sister, staring at an endless blue sky whilst cuddling with his mother on a picnic blanket and jumping off his father's shoulders into the cool waters of the lake.

He remembered toasting marshmallows with his sister before the very same fire he sat at now, the two of them giggling themselves to sleep on camping cots in the corner. He loved his sister and he loved his niece and nephews as if they were his own. He missed her but he accepted he had created the distance between them and he accepted he had to live with that. Maybe one day in the future he could try to redress things properly and make it up to her but that would take time and commitment and for the next few years the United States Navy had first call on all he had to offer in those departments.

Which brought him back to the woman stretched out on his couch, a woman he would dearly love to entertain the idea of a relationship with but didn't dare. He was contracted to the Navy for another year and looking at signing up for another seven after that. In the coming months he'd have to make up his mind as to what he was going to do.

Until recently he wouldn't even have questioned whether he was going to sign up for those seven years or not. He'd be forty-three years of age when he came out, entitled to a full pension and still young enough to do other things with his life. If he was still alive of course and in one piece and mentally stable.

Okay, he reasoned with himself, *if I'm dead then I won't have anything to worry about.*

He realized it was strange to worry less about being dead than injury or mental instability but there it was and he knew the rest of the guys thought pretty much the same, except maybe for the ones with wives and kids. The ones with kids especially would take serious injury any day over death and never seeing their kids again.

He'd been certain beyond a doubt of his future path on entering the Navy and even more convinced when he got accepted into the SEALs but he was twelve years in now and things were starting to look a little different.

Those years had seen him deeply involved in the Afghanistan and Iraq campaigns, some of the hardest and dirtiest campaigns in the history of the U.S. military, dealing with an enemy that was everywhere and nowhere and didn't care about the rules of engagement and was more than willing to play their own rules against them. Things weren't so black and white anymore and so often he and his team-mates seemed to be constantly operating in murky grey areas.

Then there was the increasing involvement of politicians in their work with social media and the dominance of the internet adding an extra layer of scrutiny but always without context. The job had intensified so much on one level and changed on so many others since he had become a SEAL that in recent times he had started to wonder if he really was able for twenty years of it, especially when he had sacrificed so much and continued to do so.

He realized his decision not to engage in a serious relationship and forge a life for himself outside of the teams was his decision alone and he knew guys who had made the same decision and other guys who had followed their hearts.

Some of those guys had ended up with their hearts broken, some of them had died at least having met and followed through on the love of their lives.

Over the years he had seen very few marriages survive the teams and he had seen the devastating emotional carnage resulting from the wreckage. Of the marriages and relationships that survived, he was in no doubt their survival came at huge personal and emotional cost.

He thought of some of those marriages now and he had to admit the guys who had managed to pull those long-term relationships off had something very special and if he was honest, something he was more than a little envious of. However, he was at a loss as to how they had managed it and he doubted if he had what it took to pull it off and he certainly hadn't ever met a woman he believed would be able to withstand the challenges of being married to a SEAL, at least until....

"Fuck," John swore under his breath. It was time for a whiskey and time to kill this particular line of thinking.

He went to the kitchen and poured a generous measure of the twelve year old Jameson into a mug. He went back and sat on his bed and looked at the woman stretched out on his couch.

God but she was a beautiful sight.

He smiled and chuckled to himself. She was to his life what a photo-bomber was to a photograph. She had literally landed into his existence and was now filling it in every way and the crazy thing was, as much as she infuriated, challenged and tormented him, he had to admit he liked having her there.

"Fuck," he swore again, "I'm in fucking trouble."

He knocked back a healthy measure of the whiskey. Maggie sighed and moved on the couch. The throw fell away and John's breath halted in his throat at the amazing vision of female perfection before him.

She wasn't skinny by any stretch of the imagination but had curves in all the right places and his hands itched with the need to explore her luscious landscape. She sighed again and the breathy sound caused a rush of blood to his groin. He slugged the rest of the whiskey, got up and pulled the covers back on the bed.

He returned the mug to the kitchen and then bent down and picked Maggie up off the couch. She groaned and snuggled into him, which made it all the more difficult to deposit her onto the bed. John smiled to himself as he considered how, of course, she wouldn't make it easy for him.

He gently eased her onto the side of the bed nearest the wall and then stripped out of his shirt and boxers and climbed in beside her. She immediately crawled into him and flung her arm across his chest. He smiled. She felt good. She felt right. And just for tonight he was going to take that. He closed his eyes and let the night, and all it had to offer, take him.

***

Maggie could feel a wonderful heat soothing its way through her body and strangely enough its source seemed to be made of something hard and unyielding. In her semi-conscious state she shifted closer into the source of the heat and then she realized she was encased by what felt like two strong arms, one flung over the top of her and one under her, in the crook of which she rested her head.

Slowly she started to rise to consciousness as if floating up from a comforting dream and realized she was lying in bed, on her side, and all around her was the man who had turned her world upside down over the past two days.

She could feel the relaxed rhythm of his breath against her hair and loved how his hard muscularity molded perfectly to her curves. She thought it was sweet how he had obviously lifted her to the bed and was now holding her in his arms. She remembered him holding her at the lake and not only warming her but giving her permission to let go of all her troubles and fears, reassuring her she was safe in his arms.

She'd never had anything like that before, someone else willing to carry her burden even if just for a short while. She knew he had seen her fear as she'd stood naked in the lake. He had seen it and hadn't thought any less of her, on the contrary, he had invited her to hand it over to him, to let him carry it for a while.

A warmth of a different kind started to diffuse itself around the perimeter of her heart. For all his bossy and domineering ways, John was a special kind of guy and she knew the more time she spent with him, the more walking away from him would only be achieved with great difficulty.

On that thought she snuggled into his sleeping form just that tiny bit more and drifted off in the blissful knowledge that for the first time in her life, someone else, literally, had her back.

SIX

What in all that's holy is that smell? Maggie thought as she identified the combined scents of cinnamon, vanilla and possibly homemade bread wafting across the cabin. She opened her eyes and looked in the direction of the kitchen and the sight she found there caused her to smile in disbelief as she watched John happily flip a pancake in the air and do a little victory dance as he managed to successfully catch it in the pan.

God, the man can cook as well, she thought to herself as she stretched awake, wistfully running her arm across the still warm space where John had lain beside her.

"Good morning, sleepyhead," his rich tones greeted her from the kitchen, "I hope you like pancakes."

She smiled and looked over at him. "Good morning to you too, Jamie Oliver," she laughed, "and yes I do like pancakes, especially when they smell that good."

And especially when they are cooked by a guy whose ass looks as perfect as yours in a pair of jeans, she thought to herself.

She was just about to hop out of the bed when she remembered she was naked. She was well aware John had seen her in all her naked glory but for some inexplicable reason she felt shy about sauntering around the cabin totally nude.

She looked around and spotted his shirt from the night before lying beside the bed. She reached down and put it on, its hem coming to just above her knees. She felt like a silly cliché in a movie as she walked over to the kitchen but felt a little better when she spotted the heat in John's eyes as they appraised her.

"You seem to have everything under control," she observed, "but is there anything I can do?"

He grinned at her and handed her two plates and a small butter dish.

"You can put these on the table and then sit your pretty ass down and get ready to eat the best damn pancakes of your life."

Maggie laughed. "Whoa there Jamie, I'll have you know I've eaten some mighty fine pancakes in my time and so far ain't nobody has ever beaten Grandma O'Brien's."

John cocked his head in the same manner as Rock did when he was being totally adorable, and looked at her.

"Is that your surname?" He asked.

Maggie smiled, realizing what he had just realized, that the two of them didn't even know each other's last names.

"Yes it is. What's yours?"

"Sullivan."

"Ah, sounds like the two of us share the same sort of heritage," Maggie observed.

"My father was third generation Irish and my mother was French," John informed her. "What about you?"

"Both parents are second generation Irish."

"Hmmm," John mused, "explains a few things."

"And what's that supposed to mean?" came the retort.

"The green eyes and the red hair of course," John smirked at her and just as she was about to sit down, he added, "along with the quick temper and smart mouth."

"Well I suppose we have your French blood to thank for your cockiness and domineering manner," she quipped.

John leaned back in his chair and laughed.

"Touché," he announced as he deposited a mountain of pancakes on the table.

They were so mouth-wateringly delicious that, after wondering if someone was coming to breakfast, Maggie was glad nobody had shown up as she helped herself to pancake number three. She washed it back with her second mug of coffee and looked up to see John grinning at her.

"I'm thinking they're at least as good as Grandma's," he chuckled.

Maggie considered how she had just polished off three pancakes in front of this man, barely pausing for breath. They weren't as good as Grandma's, not by a long shot, they were far, far better and quite simply the best pancakes she had ever eaten but she was never going to tell him that.

"Yes, they're at least as good as Grandma's," she giggled and then laughed outright as he cocked his eyebrow at her in such a way that invited her to admit they were, in fact, better than Grandma's. Never.

"As good as," she re-iterated, "and that's all you're getting."

He laughed as he pushed himself away from the table and got out of his chair, reaching for the plates.

"You and that mouth never disappoint," he smiled.

"You seemed to like my mouth enough last night," Maggie quipped and for the life of her she didn't know why she referred to the big invisible elephant in the room, the one neither of them was talking about. The "what happens now?" elephant.

There was no mistaking her remark had instantly changed the atmosphere and she wished she could take it back as John put the plates back down on the table. He moved closer until he was standing over her. She looked up and gulped as she saw raw lust burning in his eyes.

"You're right," he husked, "I thoroughly enjoyed it." And before Maggie could get her wits about her he swooped and started to thoroughly enjoy it again. But he didn't stop there as he slid his hand inside his shirt and cupped her breast.

Pleasure seared through Maggie at his touch and she moaned wantonly into his kiss. She went to get up and enfold herself in his arms but he held her in the chair. He stopped kissing her and his two hands moved to the buttons on the shirt but he never took his eyes off hers. Quickly and deftly he undid each button until the shirt was hanging open, just about revealing the perfect curves of her breasts. He pushed each side of the shirt aside and inhaled sharply as he looked down. Then suddenly he was down on one knee and feasting on her as he fondled, sucked, nipped and licked each breast in turn.

Maggie squirmed and thrust against him, moaning his name in need as the unbearable ache started to build again between her legs. It was almost as if he read her mind because, with his mouth firmly attached to her nipple, his hands moved lower and within seconds he slid two fingers inside her and started to massage her swollen bud of desire with his thumb.

Maggie gasped as her body became consumed with all the overwhelming sensations John was assaulting it with. Then, in one swift movement, his mouth left her nipple and his head was between her legs, his tongue and mouth taking over from where his thumb had been. His fingers continued to ram into her and the pressure built and built until she was crying his name and bucking against his mouth in pure ecstasy.

She was still floating somewhere in another dimension, her body liquid and weightless when she had the sensation of being carried and realized John was carrying her to the bed. He lay her down across it, face first and she realized he wasn't finished with her.

She heard him undo the buckle of his belt and his jeans fall to the floor. She heard the tear of a condom wrapper and then she heard him groan as his cock gently pushed at her entrance. She knew he was asking for permission and she was only too delighted to grant it as she positioned herself on her knees, her ass pointing more in an upwards position so she could take him deep. And she did. As his hands came around to claim her breasts, he surged into her with a feral roar and filled her like no other man had before.

He moved slowly at first, still fondling her breasts and breathing heavily into her shoulder but then she urged him to go faster and it was like releasing a prized stallion from his leash. His hands gripped her by the hips and he pounded into her like a man losing his mind and as her own orgasm ripped through her and she howled out his name, she felt him convulse into her as he rode out an orgasm so powerful it left him gasping for breath.

When it was over he collapsed on top of her and then rolled onto his side bringing her with him so as to stay inside her. The two of them were silent, content to try and catch their breaths. He slid his arm around her waist and pulled her close. And then what he said next had her laughing so hard he couldn't stay inside her any longer.

"Betchya Grandma can't serve up a side of scorching hot sex with *her* pancakes."

As John's orgasm continued to pulsate deep within his groin, intensified by the vibration of Maggie's laughter, he pulled her close and wished they could hide away from the world forever. But he knew that wasn't going to happen and a sadness he'd never experienced before settled upon him.

He pulled her even closer and moved the two of them up onto the pillows until she was lying with her head resting on his chest. It felt good to have her there. No woman had ever felt as perfect lying on his chest as Maggie did and as much as he wanted to think of her lying there a lot more in the future he knew it would be unfair to give her the impression that was going to happen.

Maggie sensed the change in him and wondered what it was that bothered him so much and why he tried so hard to resist her. Then a terrible thought occurred to her, *goddamn it, he's married!*

He didn't wear a ring but that meant nothing, hardly any of the doctors at the hospital wore one either. Anger and indignation flared through her and she shot out of his arms into an upright sitting position. She twisted around to look at him and felt a slight sense of satisfaction at the stunned look on his face.

"What the f..." he started to say but she cut him off.

"Are you married?" She hurled at him, her eyes flashing with all the anger that told him she thoroughly believed he was.

John could not believe his ears.

Was he what? Married! What the fuck?

He stared at her, incredulous. What the hell had given her that idea? And the way she was looking at him.... Actually, the way she was looking at him was kinda funny, her face was a picture of anger, righteous indignation and horror at the prospect she may have unwittingly had sex with a married man.

His shock quickly turned to amusement and within seconds he was laughing so hard he couldn't speak. Her indignation increased and he laughed some more, great big belly-laughs that reverberated off the walls of the cabin.

"I'm glad I'm such a source of amusement to you," she spat at him as she made an attempt to move past him and get out of the bed.

John was torn between letting her get out of the bed and flounce away from him, as he was sure she had some pretty impressive flouncing planned, or to grab her and set her straight. Behind the fury of her last comment he had detected a tiny amount of hurt and embarrassment so he opted to set her straight, well at least as much as he could. He wasn't in the habit of telling a woman he'd just met he was a member of the special forces of the U.S. military.

He stopped laughing and his hand flashed out and grabbed her.

"Why on earth would you think I'm married?" he asked.

She looked into his eyes and could see the mirth still lingering there but as always with John there was a sincerity she couldn't deny.

She dipped her head, feeling a little foolish and somewhat apprehensive. Mentioning his emotional volatility meant opening the door for a discussion about what this was between them and where it was going, if anywhere, and she wasn't sure she was ready for that and she suspected he definitely wasn't. She felt like she was about to step on an emotional landmine that could blow this thing up between them before it even had a chance to get started.

"Maggie?" he pressed, placing a finger under her chin and raising her head up so he could look into her eyes.

Damn it, she thought, *why couldn't I have just kept my big, dumb mouth shut. Okay, I started this conversation so I need to face up to it and see it through.*

"You blow so hot and cold," she said in a low voice, "I can feel it. Even now that we've.... er we've....."

God, what do I say here, she thought, *had sex? Fucked? Made love? What was the appropriate term?*

She decided on the first.

"Had sex twice, you still seem to have some sort of problem with me, like you want me and yet, you don't want me or at least you regret having me. So, I've come to the conclusion a guy who acts like that must have a reason and the only logical explanation I can think of is that you are married. I mean, what else could there be?"

John smiled, a slow languid smile. She was scarily perceptive and he could see how his behavior would cause her to think crazy thoughts. He felt a twinge of guilt and knew he had to lay some of his shit out on the line for her, not all of it but some of it and he had to be honest with her about where this was going for him, which wasn't much past the next few days even though he was man enough to admit to himself he wished it could go further.

"Maggie, I'm sorry. I don't want you to feel on any level that I don't want you, believe me nothing is further from the truth and I can assure you, I most definitely am *not* married but I do come with a shit-storm of complications and I have no idea how to reconcile those against what this is between us. "

The growing confusion in her eyes was hard to watch. He dipped his head and looked at his hands instead.

"I'm not in a position to offer you anything past the next few days. When your car is fixed, I'll take you into Little Creek and as hard as it will be, I'll say goodbye. I think for both our sakes that would be the best course of action. I'm planning on a hike up to Widow's Peak today with Rock and I'd love it if you'd come with us and stay here for a day or two but a few days are all I'm in a position to offer you Maggie. A few days of memories with a guy you met once in the woods and that's it, after that the two of us have to walk away."

Maggie was shocked. She hadn't quite expected this response. His certainty unnerved her and she wondered what the hell the deal was with him but there was something in his tone, a hint of regret and an echo of sorrow that made her think this decision cost him, that he wished things could be different but was absolute in his belief they couldn't.

"If you want to take Sam's truck and leave here today then that's okay too Maggie," he said quietly, "I'll understand. Take a few minutes to think about it."

With that he got up from the bed and went to the bathroom.

Maggie was stunned. She'd never had such a proposition before and she hadn't a clue what to think. The most annoying, domineering and amazing man she'd ever met, who'd given her the most incredible sex of her life, had just told her there was no hope of more than a few days with him. And he had absolutely meant it.

So, now she had to choose between spending more time with him or walking away. Of course she wanted to spend as much time as possible with him but that presented her with a slight problem because she already liked him way too much. The alternative was to stay, lose another tiny piece of her heart to him each day and then walk away, lick her wounds and try to forget him.

Well, she'd never seen this one coming when she'd left New York two days ago. She looked at Rock, who was watching her from where he was stretched out on the rug in front of the fireplace.

"Any advice?" she asked.

He just kept staring at her.

"Thanks," she announced to his soulful gaze, "you're a great help."

So, I can stay here she thought *and enjoy this intriguing man and have some incredible sex or I can leave, be by myself and hope I have sex like that again sometime in my lifetime. Okay, so my heart is going to take a battering but maybe I should prioritize other parts of my body on this occasion. And a few days of sizzling sex with a smokin hot guy in the woods is always a good memory to have in the bag for the rocking chair days......*

She looked around the cabin, at a place where she'd found peace, safety and ecstasy. The decision was a no-brainer. She'd trade another day or two of this place, with its owner and everything those days promised, against the probability of months of heartache.

John sat on the closed toilet lid with his head in his hands.

What the fuck are you doing John?" he asked himself. "*What the fuck are you doing?*

He didn't like the confusion he'd put in Maggie's eyes and he most definitely didn't like the guilt he felt at putting it there. This "thing" between the two of them was already affecting him emotionally and that was more than he wanted to be affected and now he had just gone and invited her to join him for the day when he should be telling her to get the hell away from him.

He had made his lack of availability clear and left her in no doubt that a few days, at most, was all they could have together. He'd thought those words would make him feel different, make him feel strong and help him to compartmentalize his attraction to Maggie into a nice, neat, little box. Instead he felt like a selfish piece of shit because those words meant he was weak, too weak to just call this now and walk away before either of them got hurt. He'd said those words but he hadn't meant them.

The truth was he *wanted* to spend the next day or two with Maggie. He *wanted* to make her smile and laugh and scream his name in pleasure. He *wanted* her to infuriate and torment him, to turn him on and take him into her hot, inviting core. He *wanted* her to tell him more about herself and to make him laugh like no other woman had ever made him laugh. He *wanted* to spend more than another day or two with her because if he was being completely honest with himself, he *wanted* Maggie like he had never wanted any other woman before.

He knew he should tell her to go but he didn't want to. It was that simple and it made him a selfish coward, unwilling and unable to man up enough to do what needed to be done because no matter how much he might wish things to be different, they weren't. In a way she was right, he was married, to his job, to the teams, to the United States Navy and almost as unavailable to her as a married man.

He'd tried his damn best to resist her and failed, so now he was going to enjoy a few days with her and then walk away. Whenever her car was fixed would be a natural parting point for them, he wouldn't have to spell things out to her, and they could go their separate ways. He only hoped months of rigorous training and a difficult deployment or two would help him forget how much he wanted her.

He jumped into the shower and allowed the guilt and regret he was already feeling to strengthen his resolve. If he felt like this now, he didn't want to think about how he would feel if he spent any more than a few days with the flame-haired temptress.

For now it was as if her fingertips were placed lightly around his heart. He couldn't let it get to the point where she had his heart firmly in her hands and he didn't want to face the prospect of carrying hers in his. The hot water stung where her nails had left their mark on his back, and it occurred to him if they were the only marks he was left with when he came out of this then he would consider himself lucky.

He turned off the water, wrapped a towel around his waist and walked out into the living area. Maggie was in the kitchen, cleaning up after breakfast. She turned to him and with a dazzling smile asked, "How far is it to Widow's Peak?"

SEVEN

Maggie figured they had walked about four miles already. Most of it had been on dirt roads but for the past mile or so they had been following a narrow track through the forest which was now starting to thin out and give way to rock and scrub. The Indian summer looked like it had no intention of abating and whereas Maggie had started out enjoying the sunshine on her face, she was now starting to feel decidedly hot. She stopped and caught her breath. John marched on. She removed her back-pack and started to unzip her hoodie. Rock stopped and looked back at her. It was comforting to know the dog had, at least, noticed she had stopped.

The hike had started out with the two of them engaged in small talk but as the miles had passed and the trail narrowed John had pulled ahead and become increasingly silent. She would even go so far as to say pre-occupied and she wondered what his story was.

From some of the scars on his body she couldn't help wondering if he was in law enforcement or maybe on the wrong side of the law. She'd seen enough guys come through the E.R. to know about things such as the underground fighting scene and she was curious if it was his involvement with something like this that made him secretive and insistent on things going no further between them than a few days together.

He certainly had the body of a fighter and her stomach clenched with desire as she remembered how he had put it to devastating use only a few hours before. She also remembered how he had laid out those fools at the lake. She'd only ever seen anything like that in a movie.

However, as she watched him continue along the trail, she considered how there were things about him that didn't quite fit the profile of other fighters she had come across. If she had to guess she would say he was educated to at least University level. He also didn't have the hard spiky edge to him she had experienced with the fighters she'd treated in the E.R. You knew some of those guys didn't care too much about other human beings and she often wondered to what extent they cared about themselves, as so many of them seemed dead inside.

No, John cared, she could see it in his eyes and in the way he interacted with people. If anything, she would say he was protective and honorable. He'd only just met her but he had been willing to take on four guys to protect her.

As she tied her hair up behind her head and watched him continue up the trail she wondered even more what played on his mind to the extent he hadn't yet noticed both she and Rock were no longer anywhere near him.

John thought about the text he'd received from Snake just before they'd left the cabin.

"Yo big man. News on Wolf not good. Piece of shrapnel lodged near base of spine. Inoperable. Paralyzed. Best hope is shrapnel moves over time and damaged tissue etc heals."

He'd known Wolf's injuries were serious but he'd hoped they were ones he could recover from. A fresh wave of guilt swept over him as he recalled them approaching the compound in Somalia, the compound that was supposed to have minimal operatives present at the time of their last rescue mission. So much for that shit. Wolf had been a step ahead of him, scanning and scoping for possible threats. John, a step behind, had been covering his six when all hell had broken loose but Wolf had taken the brunt of enemy fire, inadvertently (or maybe not) protecting John.

"Fuck!" John swore to himself as he charged ahead on the trail. The op had been a disaster from the outset and he had known it. Nothing had been right. The intelligence had been sketchy and poor but for reasons that had only become apparent since the completion of the op, they were ordered to go ahead anyway.

They believed they were going in to rescue a journalist and her cameraman. It was only afterwards they'd found out the so-called journalist was self-appointed and the real reason they'd been sent in to get her was because she'd had an affair with a high ranking CIA official in Djibouti and the powers that be were afraid she'd reveal sensitive information to the Somalians in order to secure her release. However, no-one had suspected that her and the cameraman's capture were merely a ruse to achieve a bigger goal, to ambush a SEAL team.

Whether they had been fed incorrect intelligence or whether their informant was discovered after they had put their rescue plan together, they would never know but within seconds of boots on the ground they had all realized they were in big trouble after ten times as many insurgents as they were told to expect had started to shoot at them. Thankfully a lot of them couldn't shoot for shit but then the IEDs and grenades had entered the equation and it had become a defensive rather than an offensive operation. It was only because they were able to call in air support that they were not totally fucked. Somehow, they had managed to rescue the hostages and get the hell out of there but the casualty count had been high with Freezer and Wolf coming off the worst.

He thought about his two buddies and even though his body was on a trail in the Adirondacks in upstate New York, his mind was very much back in the inky black waters of the Somalian coast as he and his team-mates made their approach towards the beach, their only light that of the crescent moon. The whole swim in to the beach he had pondered the pre-op briefing, unable to shake the feeling of it being incomplete, like the chief had wrapped it up before he had given them all the info they needed. Usually he had a pretty good visual in his head of what they were facing into but this time the image in his mind had gaps in it like an unfinished jigsaw puzzle.

He quickly slipped out of his diving gear and took up his position within the team as they prepared to advance on the small coastal outpost a mile and a half inland, where they believed the hostages were being held.

He adjusted his NVGs and moved swiftly across the sand. Fifteen minutes later he was looking at the small white-washed houses of their target and his gut was screaming there was something wrong but he couldn't place it. The moon ducked behind a cloud and he thought he caught movement out the side of his eye on one of the roof-tops but when he zeroed in on it there was nothing there. Then it hit him - shouldn't there be someone, somewhere? He stopped in his tracks. This was a compound under the control of a local militia group. They had hostages and even though they weren't supposed to be expecting an attack, wouldn't they have at least one guy on guard, just in case? Freezer came up beside him.

"John, what's up?" He asked.

John started walking again, trying to dismiss his concerns as paranoia. He fell in just behind Wolf and shook his head.

"It's too fucking quiet," he responded, barely able to hear himself over the pounding of his heart.

Freezer never got a chance to respond as the silence shattered all around them and the first bullet ripped through his leg.

John looked up to see where the bullets were coming from and shock shot through him as he looked at the rooftops which were now covered in insurgents. Within seconds more started pouring out from the buildings and they were mired in the fire-fight of their lives.

He started running for cover when something whizzed past his head and then the ground opened up behind him. Grenades. Fuck! He pushed on, determined to get out of the main line of fire and that's when Wolf went down. He grabbed his team-mate and dragged him with him. He hit the wall of one of the buildings, his heart pounding out of his chest and his mind on fire with what was happening.

Maggie looked up the trail and wondered just how she was going to catch up with John or if she should even try. He seemed lost in another world, not even looking back to check where she or Rock were. His pace had increased since she had stopped to tie up her hair and now he was looking left and right of the trail as if searching for something. She was just wondering if she should call after him when he started running. She knew instinctively something was wrong and she shouted his name. He didn't look back. It was as if he hadn't even heard her. He ran on and again she shouted his name but he disappeared around a bend in the trail and she figured the best thing to do was to chase after him.

"John!" In the middle of all the chaos someone was calling his name. Something flew over his head again. He looked up. The sky was blue, not black and full of stars. He blinked and realized he wasn't in a village on the Somalian coast, fighting for his life but hiking a trail in the Adirondacks.

"Shit," he exclaimed, as he looked around him, wondering where Maggie and Rock were. He closed his eyes and grabbed his head with both hands and shook it as if trying to clear it but images of Wolf bleeding out at his feet and Freezer crawling towards him in the blood-soaked Somalian dirt were all he could see.

Maggie rounded the bend and stopped dead. There, about fifty meters ahead of her on the trail, was John, holding his head in his hands and shaking it vigorously from side to side. Then his hands fell to his sides and he looked around him, his eyes wide, as if he was trying to clear something from them. She thought about yesterday after he had kissed her at Dr. Matt's place and how he had confessed to having a lot on his mind.

No shit, thought Maggie, as she wondered what it was that was ripping him up inside. She decided to approach him with caution in order not to startle him.

Rock, however, had no such concerns and bounded up to his owner as if he hadn't seen him in days. By the time Maggie caught up with him John was laughing and fussing over the dog but she could tell the laughter wasn't the carefree sort, as it had been in the past forty-eight hours. No, this laughter had a pitch of nervousness and relief to it that made her anxious. Then he looked up at her and even though he was smiling he couldn't hide the pain and torment in his eyes. Maggie's heart squeezed at the thoughts of him hurting so much.

"John, are you...?" she started to ask him if he was okay but he cut her off.

"Hey, I'm sorry about that," he said in a sheepish voice, "I kinda got lost in my thoughts and fancied running off a bit of steam. Are you ready for a bit of a climb?"

She knew he had cut her off deliberately and was using each word as a brick, trying to build a bridge back to some sort of normality between them. She sensed he was embarrassed at her seeing him in anything less than total control and suspected he was here in the wilderness so he could find a release from whatever it was that troubled him. She suddenly felt like an intruder in his private space, an interloper on his bruised emotional landscape and she considered whether she should leave him alone.

She smiled back at him, nervous and unsure.

"You know John, I can make it back to the cabin from here, maybe you'd prefer to head on up to the Peak without me."

John felt like a fool for what just happened and was touched by her consideration and sincerity. He wouldn't have asked her along today if he hadn't genuinely wanted her with him. He thought how he only had another day or two with her at most and he stepped towards her, took her hand and started to lead her along the trail.

"You're not getting out of a climb that easy," he joked as he guided her along the narrowing trail.

"Oh you think I'm some sort of lightweight," she flung at him as she dropped his hand and powered ahead of him, "well, see if you can keep up."

John stood there and laughed as he watched her sexy as-all-hell ass swing past him and flounce up the trail. He loved it when she flounced, she did it so spectacularly well.

Maggie smiled to herself as she charged ahead, now that laugh had been genuine and carefree and she felt good knowing she had caused him to laugh like that, after all his laughter was currently her second most favorite sound in the world. Number one was the way he moaned her name just after he came.

Just the memory of it from a few hours ago was enough to set off a tingle between her legs and she figured that kinda thinking wasn't going to get her to the top of Widow's peak, so she tucked her chin into her chest and set off at a challenging pace.

She might love the sound of his laughter but his taunts still annoyed the unholy hell out of her and she intended to make him eat his words. That was until the trail started to climb and she began to get short of breath. She started to slow and hoped he wouldn't notice.

The trail became practically vertical and she knew she had to stop before she hyper-ventilated. She stopped and pretended to adjust her backpack. A chuckle sounded behind her and then a large warm hand enveloped her own as John's strong fingers intertwined themselves between hers.

"Come on," he purred into her ear, "as much as I'm enjoying the view back there, I think it would be nice if we could hit the peak together."

She looked at him, all ready with a retort but the words died in her throat at the sight of his smile, a smile that lit up his whole face and shone out from his eyes, its warmth and sincerity wrapping around her like a cloak of the finest silk. All she could do was squeeze his hand and smile back and hope he mistook the wobble in her legs as strain from the climb and not the devastating effect of that smile.

"Almost there," he re-assured her as he gently pulled her along behind him.

Minutes later they were at the top and the view was breathtaking.

"Wow," Maggie exclaimed as she looked down at the peaks and valleys below that stretched on for as far as the eye could see. A late morning mist hung low amongst the forests anxiously awaiting the sun's touch so it could disappear.

John came up behind her and went to put his arms around her but stopped himself. Sex was one thing but that kind of intimacy was another matter entirely. As much as he'd like her to be his girlfriend, she wasn't and he had to guard against giving her any sort of impression there was even a remote chance of that because it wasn't going to happen. Instead he stood beside her and enjoyed the expression of awe on her face.

"It's beautiful," she breathed.

John had to agree, except he wasn't looking at the landscape.

"You hungry?" he asked and Maggie nodded her head.

"Come on," John urged her, "there's a nice spot over here where we can sit down and eat."

Just a few feet over from the top of the peak was a small grassy area. John removed his backpack and pulled a small check tablecloth out of it, whereupon he proceeded to place a rustic loaf of bread and three generous slabs of brie, camembert and roquefort cheese. He then produced two wine glasses and a bottle of Chablis that was being kept perfectly chilled in the cooler pack he had it encased in. Maggie looked on in astonishment.

"Where did you get all this?" she gasped.

John looked up at her and smiled.

"Well the cheeses I already had and I baked the bread this morning whilst you snored away over in the corner," he grinned.

Maggie's mouth dropped, so she *had* smelled freshly baked bread this morning. God the man was incredible, not only was he an amazing lover but he could cook too, pity he was only available for the next day or two.

John laughed at her and poured a glass of wine.

"Take a seat Madame," he smiled, as he directed her to sit on the grass beside the tablecloth, "I hope you like French cheese."

Maggie laughed back.

"I love it," she announced, as he handed her a slice of bread with brie so ripe it was in danger of running right off it. She quickly put it into her mouth and couldn't help groaning at how good it tasted.

The muscles in John's stomach clenched at the sound and he slugged back half his glass of wine in an attempt to quench the flames of desire once again licking at his groin. Fuck but this woman had an effect on him he just couldn't fathom.

"So, how did your parents meet?" Maggie asked, wondering if it was a good idea to bring up the subject of his parents again but she figured the subject of how they met was much safer than her last enquiry.

John smiled as if remembering fond memories.

"My mother was studying English in Paris and wanted to improve her language skills, so she decided to spend a semester in America at Columbia University in New York and that's where she met my father. She never left and the rest, as they say, is history."

Maggie smiled. "It sounds like a beautiful love affair," she remarked.

"They loved each other very much," John replied with a half-smile but she didn't miss the hint of sadness in his eyes.

"What about your parents, how did they meet?" John asked.

"Med school," Maggie replied, "as my father tells it, he fell in love at first sight but my mother wasn't so convinced. However, the incurable romantic won her round in the end and they just celebrated their fortieth wedding anniversary."

"Forty years, that's impressive," John observed as he looked out over the mountains.

"Hmmm…" Maggie mused, "I suspect they had their ups and downs but nothing that myself or my brothers and sisters were privy to, well the downs anyway."

John continued to look out over the faraway mountains and she sensed his thoughts were even further away.

She reached for some more bread and cheese and he turned and smiled at her.

"You like it?"

"It's freakin delicious," she informed him, "where the hell did you learn to bake bread like that?"

John grinned again. "I told you, my mother was French. When she couldn't get the bread here that she wanted, she simply baked it herself, plus I spent many summers with my grandparents in France and what my mother didn't teach me about cooking my grandmother made sure she did."

"Wow," exclaimed Maggie, "that explains those pancakes, just as well I'm only going to be here for another day or two or I'll be rolling back to New York."

Maggie hadn't meant anything by her words but she immediately regretted them upon spotting the stung look on John's face. God he was right, her mouth never failed.

He turned to look at her and she didn't know how to read his expression. She held her breath, afraid of what he was going to say.

"Maggie," he started, his voice low and husky, "I'd love nothing more than to stay up here for a hundred days with you and see where this thing takes us but I have commitments I can't get out of, serious shit I'm not prepared to drag anyone else into. I'm not saying you'll have to leave tomorrow or the next day because I don't care about you. I already care about you too fucking much."

Yet again Maggie was stunned and utterly confused by his words. Had he just admitted he had feelings for her? And what the hell was going on in his life that had him so convinced he couldn't act on those feelings?

She looked over at him and was surprised to see him looking at her, his eyes a pair of dark clouds issuing their own silent plea for understanding.

She wasn't sure what to say but felt she had to try and say something.

"John, I'm sorry, I didn't mean anything by what I just said. It wasn't a dig at you, I promise. I'd love nothing more than to stay here with you too and see where this thing between us goes. However, I have some pretty heavy commitments of my own that I have to get back to. And I respect where you're coming from but I have to admit it would make it a lot easier to understand if you would share your reasons with me for insisting we can have no more than a few days together because to be honest I'd like to see you again."

There, she'd said it. It may have all come out in a rushed jumble but she'd admitted to wanting to see him again in the near future even though he was telling her it wasn't going to happen. She took in a deep breath. Putting herself on the line like this was a new departure and it had the butterflies in her tummy doing the equivalent of Riverdance.

John drained his glass, stood up and looked down at her, the sadness and regret in his eyes tugging at her heart.

"I'm sorry Maggie," he said, his voice heavy, "I'm going to hike a little further along the trail, I'll be back in about an hour or so. Will you be okay here on your own?"

Maggie knew it wasn't a question and it was now her turn to be stung. She looked out over the peaks and valleys and in a quiet voice of her own replied, "Yes, I'll be fine, thanks."

"Okay," he murmured and with that he called Rock and set off on the trail in the opposite direction to which they'd come.

Maggie tucked her backpack behind her head and lay back, letting the afternoon sun warm her face. She couldn't believe she'd just told a guy, who had done nothing but tell her he wasn't up for a relationship, that she wanted to see him again. What the hell was wrong with her? It was the equivalent of begging a guy for a date.

Dammit! she cursed to herself, *when I get back to New York, I'm getting out more.*

If the past few days had taught her anything it was how she needed to get back to having some kind of life for herself and that included dating. There was only one problem with that plan. When she left the Adirondacks she would know a man existed who was more perfect than any man she could have ever dreamed of and she wondered how she was supposed to find a man to top that? She closed her eyes, sighed and thought to herself, *how indeed?*

John charged along the trail, anger and frustration powering each stride.

"Fuck," he swore to himself "why the fuck didn't I just stick to my guns and leave her the fuck alone?

Because she's unlike any woman you've ever met," a small voice whispered in the back of his mind *and you want her and you want to believe you can have the same something with her that those other guys have who figured out a way to navigate a life in the teams along with the woman they love. Other than your job, your life is empty John, you're empty and you're dying inside.*

He stopped and shook his head. *No*, he thought to himself, he couldn't think like that. He was going to stick to the plan and say goodbye to her in a day or two but she was right about one thing, she at least deserved some sort of explanation of where he was coming from. He took off running down the trail. Maybe if he ran hard and fast enough he wouldn't feel the ache in his soul, he wouldn't feel the sadness, regret, guilt and doubt gnawing away at him like a pack of rats with blunt teeth.

He needed to feel nothing other than his lungs straining for air and his legs screaming for relief. He turned right and headed straight up the trail for Widow's Rest, a much smaller but seriously steeper peak than Widow's Peak.

***

Maggie stirred and realized she'd fallen asleep. She sat up and looked around, there was no sign of John or Rock. Instinctively she looked at her left wrist to see what time it was and to figure out how long she'd been asleep but remembered she'd left her watch back in the cabin. She didn't have her phone with her either. She felt, however, she'd been out for quite a while as she attempted to shake the last vestiges of deep sleep from her mind.

She wondered where John could be. She packed up the remains of the picnic and took a walk around. She was sure the sun was much higher in the sky than it had been before she'd fallen asleep and she started to worry. What if something had happened to him? She decided to wait a while longer before taking a walk along the trail as she was sure he wouldn't be impressed if he came back and she wasn't there.

Twenty minutes later, tamping down her concerns, she decided to take a walk along the trail to see if there was any sign of him. The trail quickly narrowed and dipped and after about ten minutes curved sharply to the right whereupon it snaked through some trees before opening out onto a clearing in front of a small lake. It then veered off to the left but Maggie no longer needed to follow it as she'd found what she was looking for and oh how she had found it.

Walking out of the lake was John, completely naked, his magnificent body glistening in the sunlight. He ran his hands through his hair and then proceeded to sit down on the grass with his back to her.

Maggie held back in the trees, she'd confirmed he was okay and he had made it clear to her when he left he wanted some time to himself, so she figured the best thing to do now was to double back down the trail and wait for him at Widow's Peak. She'd just taken the first few steps when she heard his voice.

"You may as well come out, I know you're there."

"Shit," Maggie cursed under her breath, this guy seemed to have some sort of supernatural antennae. She turned around and started to walk over to where he sat on the grass, still facing towards the lake. Rock bounded up to her and she laughed at the dog's obvious delight at her presence. She dropped down beside John and asked him how the hell he had known she was there.

He turned and smiled at her. "I believe I'm a sneaky-assed ninja, as our friend so eloquently put it yesterday."

Maggie laughed. "He may have been an asshole but he may also have had a point."

John smiled again and Maggie's insides turned molten.

Tiny droplets of water continued to run along the surface of his skin, dipping in and out of the contours of his muscled arms and torso. She reached out and traced one as it ran the length of his arm.

A shiver ran through John at the heat from her touch. He looked over at her and the scorching desire burning in her eyes set his skin on fire. The air between them suddenly ignited with sexual electricity and he felt uncharacteristically nervous. Before anything else happened between them he wanted to tell her why he believed this thing between them couldn't go any further than the next few days. He opened his mouth to speak but Maggie placed her finger on his lips and told him to shush.

"I don't want to hear it," she whispered, "I only want you and I'm going to have you now John and no power on this earth is going to stop me."

With that she fused her lips to his in a kiss so fervent with need he forgot everything except satisfying the primal urge that tore through him. He clamped his arms around her in an iron-like grip and pulled her to him but it seemed she had other ideas.

Maggie pushed him to the ground and pulled her lips away from his, she smiled down at him before placing her tongue at the base of his ear and then slowly trailing it down his neck and chest to his nipple. She took the erect tip into her mouth and sucked hard, only releasing it on his sharp intake of breath. She then proceeded to play with it between her tongue and lips, once or twice nipping it with her teeth.

John groaned beneath her and Maggie smiled to herself, it felt incredible to have a man as powerful as him losing it to her touch. A fresh wave of visceral lust surged through her. She scraped her nails lightly down his torso and her tongue wasn't long in following. Her hands rested on the hardness of his hips and she placed feather-light kisses along the wall of muscle stretched between them. She didn't move her hands and she knew he wasn't expecting her next move as she swiftly took his engorged penis into her mouth. John bucked beneath her.

"Jesus, Maggie," he hissed as his hand came up to caress the back of her head telling her he liked what she was doing. She smiled to herself, she was only getting started. She sucked him, licked him and swirled her tongue around the head of his cock without stopping and the moans of pleasure coming from him were the greatest turn on she'd ever had. She increased her pace and took him as deep as she could as he started to thrust.

John's body and mind were on fire and he felt delirious at all the sensations coursing through him. He was desperately trying to hang on to some semblance of control but then he looked down and the vision of Maggie lavishing all her attention on his cock pushed him over the edge and his body started to thrust involuntarily.

Fuck, he thought to himself, *if she keeps going like this I'm going to come.*

As tempting as that prospect was, he was uncomfortable at the prospect of coming in her mouth and he was also desperate to be inside her, to be able to let go completely and fully experience the orgasm he knew was going to tear through him very soon.

"Maggie," he tried to say her name but it came out in a strangled whisper.

"Maggie," he tried again and this time there was more power behind it.

"Mmmmm...." she replied, not pausing for breath.

"Maggie, for Christ's sake I'm going to come, you need to stop."

She kept going.

He wrapped his hands around either side of her head and tugged gently but she didn't budge.

He groaned. Dammit he wanted to let rip but there was no way he was going to let loose in her mouth. He needed to be inside her - now.

"Maggie, please," he pleaded, "I need to be inside you now, I need to fuck you hard and I don't want to do that to your mouth."

His words were the equivalent of a sexual lightning bolt straight to Maggie's core, she lifted her head, straddled this incredible man and kissed him mercilessly on the lips.

"Do it," she husked into his ear, "get inside me now."

John didn't need to be told twice. He flipped them both over so she was underneath him. He disposed of her boots, jeans and panties in thirty seconds, grabbed his backpack, sourced a condom and powered into her in under a minute.

The sense of relief that surged through him at being inside her was mind-bending and as he called her name out to the Adirondack wilderness he couldn't help feeling there was no other place on this earth he was meant to be. She was like being lost in a storm and suddenly finding shelter.

Her hips lifted off the ground in a silent invite to take her more and he immediately obliged as he slammed into her again and again until the lines between reality and bliss became blurred to the point of insanity and his body was rocked by an orgasm so powerful he thought it would never end.

Maggie clawed into John's back as an orgasm so intense seized her that for a moment she was nearly sure she had an out of body experience. She certainly felt like she was floating back to earth as John lay on top of her catching his breath. As she lay there looking up at the endless blue sky, feeling the cool earth beneath her and her body a boneless mass of post-orgasmic bliss she realized there was no way she was ever going to meet a man who could top the one in her arms. She hadn't found one in thirty-six years, so why did she think she could just go back to New York and find one now?

Shit, she cursed silently to herself but then John raised himself up on his arms, looked into her eyes, tenderly swept the hair off her face and placed a gentle kiss upon her lips and she felt herself losing another piece of her heart to this enigmatic man. She squeezed her eyes shut because the last thing she needed was for him to see she was falling for him. She'd already put enough of herself on the line earlier and she wasn't prepared to reveal anymore.

John didn't miss the fact she closed her eyes and knew she was shutting herself off to him. He knew they were getting perilously close to a turning point where it would make it much more difficult to walk away.

He'd never had a connection with any other woman the way he had with Maggie. Despite her quick-fire temper and pig-headedness he instinctively knew he could say anything to her because it felt like he'd known her his whole life and no woman had ever caused him to physically lose control the way she did and he loved the way she could handle that. Of course it wasn't the only thing he loved about her and therein lay the problem, he was already falling for her in so many ways he was losing the ability to think straight.

He only hoped in time he would figure out a way to handle it and, when he told her the truth about what he was, she would make the decision about how to end things easy for him and walk away.

He gently pulled out of her and grabbed a plastic bag from his backpack into which he disposed of the condom, making a mental note to replenish supplies when he was next in Little Creek.

Maggie rolled over onto her stomach and he couldn't resist giving a playful slap to her perfect ass.

"Now you've had your wicked way with me I think we'd better start making tracks back to the cabin, after all I didn't come all this way for wild garlic only for it to go to waste."

Maggie giggled. "Watch it with the ass-slapping there big boy, I'll have you know I have some ninja moves of my own."

John laughed, her feistiness was perhaps one of the things he loved most about her. He was looking forward to seeing her face when she realized she'd told a U.S. Navy SEAL to watch it. Then again, as he felt his shirt slide over the fresh welts in his back, she'd left more marks on his body than any other person alive so maybe she could afford a light threat or two.

EIGHT

They got back to the cabin just as the sun started its descent over the tree-tops and Maggie flung herself into one of the chairs on the veranda.

"A little too much exertion for one day?" John laughed, a wicked twinkle in his eyes.

Maggie was too tired to fire back a retort.

"Very funny," she replied, "since you're so chipper, you can get the beers."

He laughed even more.

"Coming right up m'lady," he announced before disappearing into the cabin.

Rock flunked down beside her and she proceeded to remove her boots. She then leaned back in the chair and looked out at the tree-tops darkening against the flame colored sunset and listened to the gentle evening-song of the birds. John came back, popped a cold beer in her hand and dropped down into the seat beside her.

"Looks like we're going to get a perfect ending to a perfect day," he observed as he clinked his bottle against hers.

Maggie smiled over at him and her heart pinged at the warmth of the smile looking back at her. He was telling her just how much the day had meant to him and she felt a bit better about putting herself on the line in the middle of it. She remained clueless as to why he objected to seeing her again but she had no idea how to get past that with him.

The two of them sat there in comfortable silence drinking in not only their beers but also the incredible beauty all around them. Maggie felt like her soul had finally found some peace and she was incredibly grateful to the man sitting beside her. She would probably be gone tomorrow and if what he said was true, she would never see him again, so now seemed like a good time to thank him. She turned to look at him and her breath held in her throat at the sheer beauty of him as he looked out over the Adirondack landscape. God, how was she supposed to forget him?

"Thank you so much, for everything John," she said in a low voice that seemed strangely disconnected from her body and she felt almost like she was going to cry.

John said nothing.

She looked over at him and judging by the strained expression on his face and the way he was looking down at his beer bottle, she guessed he might be struggling with the situation himself. The goodbye in her words was obvious. He looked up at her and she saw the moment he made a decision, she hoped it was a change of heart.

"I'm military, Maggie," he said in a voice so low she almost didn't catch what he said.

A penny started to drop somewhere in the recesses of Maggie's mind but she held her tongue, as she sensed there was more.

"I'm actually special forces, I'm a U.S. Navy SEAL."

The penny clattered to the floor inside Maggie's head. So that was it. That was the reason why he had tried so hard to resist her and refused to take the incredible connection they shared any further. It was quite a revelation and she suspected not an easy one for him to share. She wasn't sure how to respond.

"What? Nothing to say?" he grinned at her.

She looked over at him and couldn't miss the nervousness hiding behind the smile in those caramel colored eyes.

She grinned back. "I'm not sure how to follow that. After all, what does that mean? Apart from the fact SEALs are badass and kill bad guys in different parts of the world, I don't know anything else about them but I'm pretty sure they're not monks."

John laughed. "No, we're definitely not monks but we do travel all over the world and our deployments are long. When I leave here I'm returning to base for two months and then I'll be deployed overseas for a minimum of six months. It's why I don't do relationships, I'm never around long enough to see them through."

"Oh" was all Maggie could manage by way of reply and took another slug of her beer, "well my concerns as to how I would have managed to fit you into my schedule suddenly seem redundant."

John chuckled, so she was finally ready to admit she was something other than a hairdresser.

"I hadn't realized hairdressing was such a time-consuming profession."

Maggie looked down at her feet, it was time to come clean. She turned to John and extended her hand. John took it, smiling.

"Dr. Maggie O'Brien," she announced, "senior trauma surgeon, Hillview."

John was impressed and nodded his head as he let go of her hand.

"I was thinking you patched me up pretty good for a hairdresser," he laughed.

Maggie smiled and then started to laugh. "I'm not sure why I said hairdresser, I barely even go to the hairdressers."

John smiled, he was going to miss the sound of her laughter, the way it bubbled up from somewhere deep inside her and was like an explosion of happiness from her soul.

"So, why not just admit you're a doctor?" he asked, the puzzlement in his voice quite clear. "It's not exactly a profession people tend to deny."

Maggie sobered, remembering the cataclysmic event which propelled her here.

"I've had a tough few months work-wise, culminating in a crisis last Thursday and I came up here to get my head straight and the last thing I wanted to talk about upon meeting you was my job. I came up here to get away from it and I wasn't ready to talk about it. I'm sorry for lying but does that make sense to you?"

John smiled, a sad smile. "Yeah, Maggie, that makes a lot of sense to me," he agreed.

He drained what was left of his beer and got up from his chair. He felt like he needed something a lot stronger but decided to settle for another bottle of amber nectar. "Want another one?" he asked Maggie.

"Please," she replied, as she finished the one in her hand and handed him the bottle.

When he was gone she tucked her legs up underneath her, wrapped her arms around them and rested her chin on her knees. The sky was dark now and a chill nipped at the air. She watched as the first glow of moonlight started to peep through the treetops.

What do I do now? she asked herself, *do I try to convince him to give this thing between us a chance? Do we stay in touch? Friend each other on Facebook? Are Navy SEALs allowed on Facebook? Can they communicate when they are overseas? Email?*

She didn't know anyone who was military, much less special forces and she hadn't a clue how it all worked but she did know men and women of the military somehow managed to fall in love, sustain relationships and create families every day of the week. She was even willing to bet that included a few Navy SEALs. So how come John was so opposed to the idea?

John blew out a deep breath and placed both hands on the kitchen counter. He felt much better for telling her the reason why he wouldn't be able to see her again. He'd heard the goodbye in her thank you and felt the sadness in her voice and knew he owed it to her to be straight.

Now, at least, she'd be able to see the futility in falling for a guy like him and he was sure it would make forgetting him a lot easier. All he had to do was figure out how he was supposed to forget her. He grabbed the beers and headed back out to the veranda.

Maggie thanked him for the beer and he sat down. He just had time to note the appearance of the moon when she asked him a question.

"So, do you know *any* SEALs who have managed to pull off a successful relationship?"

Sarcasm dripped from her every word and he smiled. He'd allow her that.

"Yeah, one or two but for the most part the teams are an emotional disaster zone. The majority of them are fucked up, divorced or both."

Maggie physically flinched at his words.

"I'm sorry, I didn't mean to sound so harsh," he apologized. "We might be badass and kill bad guys but we make piss-poor boyfriends and even worse husbands."

Maggie hugged herself a little tighter at the bite in his words. She took a sip of her beer and watched the moon rise and light up the darkness of the night-sky.

Hmmmm," she thought, *if you're that bad then how come you've shown me more tenderness, compassion and care in a few days than any other guy in my entire lifetime*?

She looked over at him and was surprised to see him looking at her.

"How long are your contracts?"

"Seven years."

"How much longer are you in for?"

"Eighteen months and then I'll probably sign up for another seven, which will bring me up to my twenty years service."

So, he's in for another eight and a half years, she thought to herself, *I suppose that's the end of the conversation.*

She stood up. She suddenly needed to go to the bathroom.

As she went to go past him he took her hand and she looked down into his sad eyes.

"I'm sorry Maggie," he whispered, "I wish things were different."

"Yeah," she croaked, "so do I."

She dropped his hand and hurried to the bathroom where she rested her head on the cold mirror.

"Congratulations Maggie," she breathed to her reflection, "congratulations on falling for a guy who isn't even in the country most of the time. It would take you to pull this one off. Outstanding job Doctor O'Brien."

When she came out of the bathroom John smiled at her from the kitchen.

"I thought I'd better get dinner started," he informed her and she realized he too had decided their previous conversation was over. Annoyance flashed through her and she knew it was completely irrational, but she felt the feelings they had for each other deserved a little something more than to be dispensed with in the cold face of reality.

However, she kept her irritation in check as she felt there was nothing to be gained by a show of petulance. She was about to ask if there was anything she could do to help with dinner when her phone beeped. She checked the screen and saw a message from an unknown number:

"Hello Miss O'Brien. A cancellation has come up for tomorrow night, please let me know if you are interested, sincerely yours, Gerard Dewey, General Manager, Little Creek Hotel."

She looked up and saw John watching her.

"Everything okay?" he asked.

"Yeah, everything's just fine," she replied, as she texted back her acceptance of the room. "A cancellation has come up at the Little Creek Hotel for tomorrow night, I'm just texting Mr. Dewey back to let him know I'm taking it."

She thought she saw him pause what he was doing for a few seconds but he quickly continued.

"Hey, that's great," he announced in what she presumed was supposed to be a cheery voice but it sounded strangely hollow.

"Yes, it is," she agreed through a smile as fake as his voice and the room suddenly felt like a cavern in which both of them seemed empty and lost.

"If you don't mind I'm going to take a shower," she said and grabbed her things and fled to the sanctuary of the bathroom.

She let the hot water run over her body, remembering the feel of John's hands and lips throughout the day and felt sad at knowing how much she was going to ache for his touch in the coming months.

So, this was it, tonight was the last night she would get to spend with a guy who she could so easily fall in love with. Tonight was the last night she would have a man make love to her who set her body aflame with desire, almost to the point of delusion. Tonight was the last night she would lie in that same man's arms and feel safe from the cares of the world.

"Fuck," she cursed under her breath, "then you'd better get out there and make the most of it."

She pulled on a pair of yoga pants, a bra and a soft cotton tank top much like the one John had ripped from her body the night before and she felt the heat pooling in her lower abdomen just at the memory. She opened the door and went out into the main part of the cabin. It was illuminated with the soft glow of the paraffin lamps and the fire crackled in the hearth. It really was too romantic for words. John was over near the bed and turned to look at her.

"Need anything?" he asked.

"Just my jacket," she replied.

He turned and picked up a fresh shirt off one of the shelves.

"Here," he said, offering her the shirt, "put it on, I like you in my shirts."

Maggie blushed as she remembered what had happened the last time she'd worn one of his shirts. She looked up into his face and judging by the heat burning in his eyes he was remembering it too.

"Thanks," she smiled, as she shrugged into it.

"My pleasure," he replied, his voice low and husky.

"So what's for dinner?" Maggie chirped, eager to ease the sexual tension that had suddenly engulfed the cabin.

John smiled as he made his way over to the kitchen.

"Tonight, m'lady, we will be dining on lamb, marinated in olive oil, a dash of lemon, rosemary and wild garlic, served with a side of baby new potatoes and green salad. It will be accompanied by a particularly good Syrah from the south of France, should the lady wish to join me in a glass or two."

Maggie laughed.

"The lady most certainly does," she informed him and accepted the glass he now held towards her.

The dinner was delicious and afterwards the two of them sat on the couch and proceeded to finish off their glasses of wine. Rock stretched out in front of the fire and sighed contentedly. Maggie envied the dog, at least he would get to come back here. She wondered when John would get the chance to come here again.

"How often do you come up here?" she asked

"As often as I can," John answered. "I especially like to get up here if we've had a particularly difficult deployment or tricky op."

She remembered what he'd said to her at Matt's place about having been through a tough time recently.

"Like the one you were on recently?" she probed.

John looked at her and she could see he wasn't sure how much to share with her.

"Yeah, like that," he agreed.

"What happened, did someone die?"

"No, but it came pretty close. Two of my best buddies are in pretty bad shape and one of them will probably never walk again."

She couldn't miss the shaft of pain that shadowed across his handsome features.

"I'm sorry," she whispered, not really knowing what else to say. If fifteen years in medicine had taught her anything it was never to blurt out some trite phrase in order to relieve your own discomfort in the face of another's pain.

John looked at her, his eyes two dark pools of sorrow and if she wasn't mistaken, guilt.

"Comes with the territory," he replied and she couldn't miss the extra edge of warning in his voice.

A shiver snaked its way down Maggie's spine. She couldn't imagine a man as powerful as John crippled in a wheelchair but she supposed the friends he spoke about were just as powerfully built as him.

She reached out and placed her hand on his arm. He reached over with his other hand and intertwined his fingers with hers. He looked into her eyes and she knew the time for talking was done.

He pulled her to him and placed a kiss of such exquisite tenderness on her lips she could feel tears gathering at the back of her eyes. She wrapped her arms around him and pulled him closer.

They were two souls who had been brought together whilst trying to escape the troubles of the world. For tonight they had this sanctuary in the Adirondack wilderness and each other to find solace in and she intended to make the most of it.

John felt Maggie's arms curve around him and pull him closer but more than that he felt a quiet sadness within her he hadn't been aware of before and instantly felt guilty at being the one who had put it there.

In all his years of being a SEAL he had never regretted his decision to stay single, until now. Watching Maggie walk away was going to be tougher than anything he had endured in those years but he would do it, for both their sakes.

But tonight he planned to do his best to kiss all that sadness away, as he intended to mark every inch of her voluptuous body with his kisses and brand her with his desire. She might meet and fall in love with some other guy in the future but tonight she was his and he was going to make love to her sweet and slow and ensure the memory of him burned bright in her mind for a very long time.

He broke their kiss and buried his face between her neck and shoulder and her palm came up to cradle the back of his head. He pulled her up from the couch, took her hand and brought her over to the bed. He looked into her eyes and slid his shirt down one of her shoulders, exposing her bare flesh. He placed his lips where the shirt had been and kissed her, causing goosebumps to scatter down her arm. He then moved to the other arm and repeated his actions as the shirt fell to the floor.

He hooked his fingers under the edge of her tiny tank top and lifted it over her head exposing her amazing breasts. He reached behind her, undid the clasp of her bra and watched it fall to the floor. He took her right breast in his hand and fondled her as she moaned into his touch. His hands slid down over the delicious curve of her waist and tugged at her pants as he bent his knees and kissed his way down. Her pants fell to the floor and she stepped out of them, causing her to part her legs.

He swiped her panties to the floor in one quick movement and his tongue darted in between her legs, hungry to taste her and intent on making her moan his name.

She convulsed into him, grabbing onto his shoulders and exclaimed, "Jesus Christ, John!" He stood up as he ran two fingers from her entrance to the bud of nerve-endings now throbbing with the need for his touch.

"You'd best lie down Maggie," he husked into her ear, "this is going to take a while."

Multiple orgasms later she grinned into his face as he took her into his arms and put her lying on his chest. The fire had burned low, leaving nothing but the glowing embers.

"You sure weren't kidding about that taking a while," she laughed into his rock-hard chest.

"Is that a complaint?" he smiled, as he tightened his arms around her.

"It most certainly is not," she laughed, "even if I did feel at one point like you were trying to kill me with death by orgasm."

John exploded into laughter. "Death by orgasm?" he laughed. "Now there's a way to go."

Maggie chuckled. "If I were to die, then I'd certainly like to die by orgasm."

John laughed again, "If?" he asked. "Have you figured out a way to dodge the bullet?"

His words and the image of the bullet hit Maggie right between the eyes and brought his reality home to her with laser-like focus.

She stopped laughing and raised herself up off his chest. She looked into his eyes and whispered, "How many SEALs have been killed in action over the past few years?"

John looked away. "Too many," he answered, his voice low and full of sorrow.

Maggie rested her cheek back on his chest, and could hear his heart beating powerful and strong.

"Let's suspend reality for a few minutes John and forget about the real world. If things were different, would you be calling me for a date when I get back to New York?"

John smiled.

"In a heart-beat. Would you take my call?"

Maggie smiled a watery smile into his chest.

"In a heart-beat."

NINE

Maggie wasn't sure what woke her but she was glad it did as it gave her a chance to savor the vision of male perfection lying beside her in the bed. Even though the rhythm and depth of his breathing told her he was sound asleep, she still resisted the urge to run her hand over his gloriously muscled torso for fear of waking him up. She knew what she had to do and as much as it pained her, she knew it would be easier if she was gone when he woke up.

Bit by bit she inched her way out of the bed and started to get dressed. She packed the rest of her things into her back-pack and located the keys to the truck in the kitchen. All the while Rock watched her from his position on the rug in front of the fireplace. A lump formed in her throat as she went over to whisper goodbye to him and kissed him on his head. He sat up and cocked his head to the side in that adorable manner he shared with his owner and then he looked over at John, still sleeping. Maggie followed his gaze and her heart squeezed painfully in her chest at the beautiful sight of the magnificent man lying there in the early morning sunlight with all his defenses down.

"Goodbye John," she breathed and walked out the door.

She didn't remember ever feeling so lonely or sad as she drove into the Adirondack sunrise, the glorious shades of orange, red and pink trying and failing to raise her mood. She knew it was way too early to check in to the Little Creek Hotel so she headed over to Stillwater Lake and watched the sun set the sky on fire as it continued its majestic rise. She sat on the shores of the lake and pondered everything that had happened in the past few days and found it hard to believe that was all it had taken to lose her heart to a man who refused to have it.

She decided to send him a text, just to let him know she was okay and to thank him, once again, for all he had done.

"Good morning sleepyhead. Would you believe I woke early, so I decided to hit the road. Thanks again for all you did for me. Stay safe and feel free to call anytime you are in New York xx Maggie."

She'd left the door to her heart open but she knew there was practically no chance of him ever walking through it. It was still early but she decided to go in search of coffee anyway.

Somewhere in the recesses of his sleep-infused brain John registered the sound of his phone buzzing with a message. He reached out and brought it to within a few inches of his face as he opened one eye to see who was texting him at this hour of the morning. Both eyes flew open and he sat straight up in the bed when he read the words on the screen.

He looked over to where their sender had spent the night lying beside him and realized she really was gone. He flopped back down onto the pillows and read the text again. She'd certainly kept it light and breezy but the fact she had slipped away at sunrise told him all he needed to know and he was glad she had spared both of them the unpleasantness of an awkward goodbye. He rolled over to where he could still smell her on his sheets and his heart lurched in his chest as he realized just how much he missed her already.

He swung his legs over the side of the bed and sat there with his head in his hands, consumed with a heartbreaking loneliness. He looked for Rock and found him lying in front of the door, looking at it mournfully. He pulled on a pair of boxers and walked over to him.

"Yeah, I know pal, I miss her too," he said in a low voice as he patted Rock on the head.

Rock got up and scratched at the door as if desperate to get outside and see if Maggie was there. John opened the door and watched as he bounded out and ran to where the truck had been parked the night before. He sniffed all around the area before looking back at John, his head cocked to the side as if saying, "where is she?"

"She's gone," was all John could say as he sat on the top step and rubbed at the ache sitting heavy on his chest, wondering how long it would last. The sky was full of the pinks and purples of the sunrise and he thought of her sitting on the veranda the night before, happy and content before he had dropped his bombshell.

"Dammit," he swore to the surrounding wilderness as he decided the best way to get through the day was to tackle the toughest trail in the Adirondacks.

***

Maggie drove through Little Creek and of course the only place open was Bridget's Tea House, and as much as she wanted a mug of coffee right now, she wasn't desperate enough to brave Aunt Bridget and the questions Maggie was sure she would have about her relationship with John.

"Relationship? Ha! Fat chance," Maggie snorted to herself. She continued to drive on through the town in the hopes there might be a diner or a truck-stop on the outskirts. Sure enough she wasn't disappointed as she spotted Big Al's Little Diner about half a mile outside of town.

She opened the door and the smell of freshly brewed coffee was like manna from heaven. She ordered a mug from the young Goth behind the counter, who looked like she could do with a bucket of caffeine herself, before she sat down in one of the booths that lined the window. She picked up the menu and a pang of something close to heartache shot through her at the first item listed on the menu, "pancakes".

Memories from the morning before flooded her brain and she closed her eyes in an effort to shut them off. She definitely wasn't having pancakes this morning and opted for a BLT instead. The Goth princess ambled over with her coffee and she had just submitted her order when the door rattled open. Something akin to a spark of life twinkled in the dead eyes of the Princess Of Darkness and seconds later Maggie understood why as the gorgeous physique of Sam Taber slid into the booth opposite her.

"Good morning," he grinned, his sky-blue eyes gleaming with mischief, "dining on your own this morning?"

Maggie grinned back, she figured he was an incorrigible flirt but behind it all he seemed to be a pretty decent guy.

"Looks that way," she replied.

A fleeting expression of surprise crossed his face followed by what she thought looked like understanding.

"Ah, I see," he observed, "well, I hope you don't mind if I join you?"

"Not at all," smiled Maggie.

"How'd the truck go for you?" he asked.

"Fine," Maggie replied, "she has some quirks but you can't beat her reliability. I really appreciate you lending her to me."

Sam smiled. "Well any friend of John's is a friend of mine."

Maggie smiled too.

The Princess Of Darkness arrived with her food and delivered it with a death glare.

She then turned to Sam and asked, "The usual?"

"Please," he confirmed with a nod, "to go."

She bestowed what Maggie guessed was a smile on him before disappearing behind the counter again.

"I think somebody doesn't like her favorite customer talking to the tourists," Maggie whispered across to Sam.

Sam chuckled. "You might want to check that BLT before you eat it, there's no telling how far Twinkle will go in her quest to eliminate the female competition around here."

Maggie, nearly choked on her coffee, "Twinkle?" she laughed.

"Well, what else would you call her?" he laughed back.

Maggie checked the inside of her BLT, just in case and took the first bite.

"So how long have you and John known each other?" Sam asked.

Maggie took her time chewing her food as she contemplated her answer.

"Not long," she replied in the best non-committal way she knew how.

Sam nodded his head.

"John's a good guy," he told her, his voice solemn now, "he's actually one of the best guys you could ever hope to meet."

Maggie was surprised at his uncharacteristic seriousness.

"How long have you guys known each other?" she asked.

"Since we were kids. He'd come up here with his family every summer and we'd hang together. Then we spent some time in the er...." he hesitated, obviously not sure if he should say any more.

"It's okay," Maggie interrupted him, "I know what John is."

A look of surprise shot across Sam's face before he continued, "navy. We were both in the navy and got accepted into the SEAL training program at the same time."

"Oh," said Maggie, "were you a SEAL too?"

Regret glistened in Sam's eyes.

"No, I didn't make the cut but it wasn't for the lack of help from John, I can tell you that. I busted my knee during hell week and had to quit. John tried to pick up the slack for me for two days and even risked his own shot on the team. He really just wanted to get me over the line but in the end the damage to my leg was too much and I rung out. I couldn't cost him his place on the team."

Maggie could tell from his tone that his failure, as he obviously saw it, still rankled with him.

"Did you ever try again?" she asked.

"No," he replied, "it was all I could do to get my knee back in shape just to stay in the navy."

Maggie was just about to ask him how long ago he had left naval life when "Twinkle" arrived with his breakfast and coffee.

Sam handed her a few dollars, thanked her and got up to leave.

"John's one in a million," he informed Maggie and she was touched by the sincerity of his tone, "but his decision to become a SEAL cost him and he's made some pretty tough choices. I hope if there is something real between you two then you can work it out."

Maggie wasn't sure quite how to reply to that so she just nodded.

Sam smiled. "I'm expecting the parts for your car to be delivered today, so I'll call you when I have it fixed. Where are you staying anyway?"

"The Little Creek Hotel," Maggie replied. "I look forward to your call."

After he was gone Maggie ordered another mug of coffee and nursed it whilst she gazed out the window. The diner filled up with its early morning patrons but she was lost in her thoughts.

She pondered Sam's words, about how John's decision to become a SEAL had cost him. Had he lost someone? Is that why he was so vehement in his belief they should go their separate ways? She shrugged her shoulders, *well it's all water under the bridge now*, she thought to herself, *I'll never see him again*. Just thinking about it sent a shaft of sadness through her and she got up, paid her bill and bade farewell to Twinkle.

***

The Little Creek Hotel was open for business and the front lobby was buzzing with fishermen eager to get out on the water for the day. Old Twinkly Eyes was delighted to see Maggie but couldn't hide his disappointment at her being on her own.

"Will anyone be joining you later?" he inquired, in that non-subtle way he had as he led her to her room.

"No," Maggie replied in such a tone as to not invite questions.

Old Twinkly Eyes was undeterred.

"Oh that's a pity," he stated as he opened the door.

The room was dominated by a large four poster bed made from solid oak. A pot-bellied stove sat in the corner with two high-backed armchairs on either side of it and three long windows featured along the wall to Maggie's left.

Old Twinkly Eyes, or Gerard as he had asked her to call him, opened the middle set of windows and stepped out on to a small balcony which had two chairs, an occasional table and fabulous views of the river.

Maggie smiled. "This is perfect."

Old Twinkly Eye's smiled back. "It's a pity you have to enjoy it all by yourself."

Maggie couldn't help laughing at him. "You are impossible."

He smiled a knowing smile. "I've seen a few things in my time around here Miss O'Brien and it's not too often I've seen chemistry the likes of which I saw between you and your sailor boy. An attraction like that shouldn't be taken for granted. Not everybody gets to experience that in their lifetime and those who do should at least give it a chance. And on that note I'll let you get on with things. Just dial zero if you need anything or come and see me at the front desk."

With that, he walked out the door and Maggie was left standing there with her mouth open.

***

The sweat trickled in rivulets down John's spine as he clawed at the slab of rock in front of him, grasping for purchase on the smooth surface in order to make the last fifty feet to the top. His legs burned and his breath came in irregular gasps as his body protested at the trial it was being put through but his mind was gloriously blank. He hauled himself the final few feet and then collapsed on top of a patch of moss.

He felt the sting of perspiration in the fresh welts on his back and his mind flooded with memories of the day before. He groaned as he lay there thinking about the woman he had all but thrown away and he desperately wished he could turn off his thoughts and regain the mental blankness from moments before.

He sat up and looked out at the incredible vista before him. It felt good to be here, his body stretched and sore from the climb, with the rugged beauty of the Adirondacks at his feet but he knew it would be infinitely sweeter with a certain red-head by his side.

He smiled to himself at how he was sure he would get a hundred chances to tease her along the trail and how he would be guaranteed a spectacular flounce or two. Something tightened in his chest and he winced at the realization of just how much he missed her. He lay back on the moss and gazed up at the blue sky.

"You did the right thing," he whispered to himself, as the memory of her taking him inside her yesterday at Widow's Peak sliced him in two.

***

Maggie opened her eyes. She'd lain on the bed for a few minutes and remembered being seduced by its softness and comfort. She'd obviously fallen for its charms more than she realized as it became clear the light outside the window had changed dramatically and she guessed it was no longer morning-time but early afternoon.

She checked her phone and was shocked to see 13:45 displayed on the screen. She was also disappointed there was nothing in her message inbox. It seemed John meant, in addition to not seeing her again, that there would be no further contact. She felt more than a little hurt as she swung her legs off the bed and headed for the bathroom.

Buck up Missy, she told herself as she proceeded to pee, *you played with some scorching hot fire and now you deal with the burns.*

She washed her hands and splashed some water on her face, put on her trainers, grabbed her backpack and headed out the door. She figured a vigorous walk along the river was just what she needed.

***

The trail was dark now as John picked his way along but the lack of light didn't bother him as he was on the home stretch and just under a mile away from the cabin. What did bother him, however, was the lack of urgency in his stride and the fact he was trudging. He tried to tell himself it was because he'd trekked over forty kilometers of tough terrain and his body was tired but in his heart he knew the real reason he was delaying his return to the cabin.

She wouldn't be there and he was dreading facing the night without her. He shrugged and sneered cruelly to himself, *ha, you couldn't wait to be rid of her and now you're dreading being without her. Make up your mind, asshole.*

Ten minutes later he trudged up to the cabin and let himself in. He threw his backpack on the floor beside the door and grabbed a beer. He sat on the couch and gulped back the honey colored liquid, surrounded by shadows. He stared over at the crumpled sheets of the bed and could just about detect the faint scent of coconut and jasmine. Desire, hot and liquid coiled itself around his abdomen.

"Dammit," he swore to the empty room as he slugged back the rest of the beer.

He stood up and headed to the bathroom, where he stripped and subjected himself to a cold shower. Images of Maggie standing in the bathroom doorway desperately trying to preserve her modesty with a tiny towel played throughout his mind. He dried off and went back into the main part of the cabin.

After pulling on a pair of boxers, jeans and a tee-shirt he reached for the shirt at the end of the bed when he realized it was the one she had worn the night before. He raised it to his nostrils and inhaled the intoxicating smell of her and a need so intense clawed at him that the muscles in his stomach clenched as if there were a thousand tiny bear traps biting into his skin.

An ice-cold loneliness trickled over him, chilling him to the bone and he sank onto the bed staring empty-eyed into the dark corners of the cabin. In that moment he questioned every decision he'd ever made and none more so than the one to walk away from a woman who made him feel more alive than he had ever believed possible.

Desire and need crackled along his skin much in the same way an addict craves his next hit and John knew exactly what he was going to do. Like a moth drawn to the flame, as long as Maggie O'Brien remained only a few miles away there was no way in hell he was going to be able to stay away.

"Fuck it," he swore to the room as he pulled on his socks and boots, shrugged into the shirt and stalked his way over to the kitchen. He grabbed a set of keys out of the cupboard, called Rock and walked out the door.

Thirty seconds later he fired up the black Ford Raptor, parked at the back of the cabin, and powered his way towards Little Creek. Eminem blasted from the speakers as he drove, obliterating any rational thoughts. He didn't want to think. What he was doing was madness, he knew that and he was sure he would have plenty of time in the future to wonder about what came over him. Tonight he was acting on instinct, pure and raw and for tonight that was all that mattered.

***

Maggie had covered the last mile back to the hotel, in the darkness, wearing only a light top and jeans and was feeling the early evening chill by the time she walked into The Little Creek hotel. She made her way up to her room as fast as she could, dumped her clothes on the floor and hopped into the steaming hot shower.

The walk along the river had been beautiful and afforded her the opportunity to do some straight thinking. She'd decided as much as she loved her job, she needed to cut back on her hours a little and use the extra time to have more of a life. She also realized she wanted to travel more and expand her horizons.

However, of all the things she had thought about, she'd thought about John the most and how meeting him had thrown the spotlight on the lack of a significant other in her life.

She would dearly love him to fill that role but he had made it crystal clear he wasn't prepared to entertain that idea and as much as she itched to drive back out to the cabin to try and convince him otherwise, her pride kept her within the safe confines of the Little Creek Hotel. She rinsed out her hair, turned off the water and wrapped her curves in the soft cotton of the bathrobe.

***

John found a quiet spot to park the Raptor, poured some water in a bowl for Rock and put a blanket on the front passenger seat for him. "Hopefully I'm going to be a while," he murmured softly as he gave his buddy a pat on the head and tickle behind the ears before walking off to the Little Creek Hotel.

Gerard Dewey was standing behind the reception desk and just hearing about Hank Beresford The Third's big catch of the day when he saw the enormous form of John Sullivan fill the doorway to the hotel and there was no doubt in his mind but the man was on a mission. Gerard couldn't help the mega-watt smile that lit up his face as John marched towards him. He looked over Hank Beresford's shoulder and happily announced, "She's in room thirteen."

John didn't falter but merely nodded his thanks and made straight for the stairs. Gerard turned to Hank, still smiling from ear to ear, and cheerfully informed him, "You may want to use your ear-plugs tonight."

Maggie was just about to start drying her hair when there was a knock on the door. She considered quickly getting dressed before answering it but then decided it was probably just some lady from housekeeping so she was okay to answer it in only the bathrobe. Three seconds later she stood, transfixed and in total shock at the vision of John in all his alpha male masculine glory as he filled the doorway.

And then he was reaching for her.

"Don't ask me why I'm here," he growled into her ear, "because I'll be damned if I know but all I do know is I want you Maggie and as long as you're here in Little Creek I can't stay away."

Her mind was desperately trying to catch up with the reality of him actually being in front of her when he savaged her mouth with a kiss so thorough it sent her head into a spin. He raked his hands through her hair and crushed her to him as his lips left a trail of fire down her neck.

She gasped in a breath of air and a sudden rush of oxygen to her brain snapped her back to reality and as much as her body throbbed with desire for him, she needed a moment to gather her thoughts. She placed her hands on his rock-hard chest and gently pushed against him, creating a tiny crack of space between them.

"John," she croaked and he immediately stilled and stopped kissing her. His arms fell away and his hand came up to his forehead as he stepped away from her.

"Shit, Maggie, I'm sorry," he started to apologize, "I hoped you wanted this, wanted me...." His voice trailed off.

Maggie took his hand. "John, it's not that I don't want you but I'm confused. You made it very clear there couldn't be anything between us and yet here you are. I've spent the day trying to rationalize things. I thought I'd never see you again and now here you are standing in front of me. What am I supposed to think?"

John looked at her and her heart squeezed at the torment building in his eyes.

"I don't know," he answered her, "to be honest I don't know what's happening to me, I thought I could do it, say goodbye to you and move on, I've done it plenty of times before. But when I got back to the cabin this evening, I missed you and there was no way in hell I could stay away from you knowing you were only a few miles down the road. I don't want to want you Maggie but I do and it's driving me crazy. But if you'd prefer me to leave, then I'll respect that and be on my way."

Maggie dropped his hand and reached out to the open door. She knew the wisest thing to do would be to ask him to leave but she only had one response to the anguish in his eyes. She closed the door, loosened her bathrobe and pressed herself against the man who she very much feared was going to break her heart.

"I'm pretty sure I know what's happening to me," she whispered into his ear before she let the bathrobe slip to the floor and placed her lips on his in a kiss which, she was certain, sealed her fate.

Relief surged through John and he launched what could almost be classified as an assault on her lips and body. He craved her to the point of madness and wanted his hands and lips in as much simultaneous contact with her body as was possible.

He kissed her, caressed her, licked and explored her till he didn't know which way was up. He was lost in the feel and scent of her, in the way she moaned into his touch and the grind of her body against his. His head was spinning when she husked into his ear, "Get naked John."

He obeyed her command immediately and moments later he watched her eyes darken with raw lust as she reached out to touch him. Fuck but his balls nearly exploded at that look.

"Jesus, John," she whispered, "has anyone ever told you, you're a fine specimen of a man?"

John laughed. "Is that a purely medical opinion Dr. O'Brien?"

Maggie smiled back at him, slow and sexy.

"No, that's the opinion of the woman who needs you inside her right now."

"I've gotta warn you," he replied, "you keep looking at me and talking to me like that and I ain't gonna last long."

With that he pulled her to him and proceeded to worship her body with everything he had in him. Somehow, they made it to the bed and Maggie was no sooner on her back than he was at her entrance. She might need him inside her now but he needed to be there hours ago and he couldn't wait a second longer. He was quite literally out of his mind with need for her. He slipped the head of his cock inside her and a feeling he could only liken to dying and coming back to life again washed over him. She felt *that* good. He pushed in further and the guttural way she moaned his name practically pushed him over the edge.

"Oh God," she moaned again, "you feel sooooo good," as she proceeded to move her hips to take him deeper. Then she froze.

"John, are you wearing a condom?" she asked, a slight hint of panic in her voice.

"Fuck and dammit," John roared as he yanked out of her.

He was so crazy for her he had forgotten the basics about taking precautions. Godammit but this woman drove him insane. He had never forgotten to use a condom before and now the worst of it was, he remembered he didn't have one. He'd been so desperate to get here, he'd left them in the backpack at the cabin.

"Shit, Maggie, I'm sorry," he apologized as he turned away from her. God but he felt stupid.

"Hey," she called to him as she sat up, "it's okay, there's no harm done, we can just continue with one on."

"That's the problem," he croaked, "I don't have any protection with me, I left them all back at the cabin."

Maggie couldn't help the giggle that escaped her.

John whirled around, incredulous she found the situation funny.

"You think this is funny?" he asked.

"Oh yes," she laughed, "you have to admit there's something amusing about a U.S. Navy SEAL getting caught without protection."

With that, she collapsed into a fit of giggles on to the bed. John might have joined her if his dick didn't hurt so much.

"Ok, Sweetheart," he smirked at her, "I can have my little sailor down here dealt with in about thirty seconds but what are you going to do?"

Maggie looked up at him with a slightly confused expression on her face.

"What do you mean, what am I going to do? Us girls are made a little differently to you boys. I might be a bit frustrated but I'll cope."

John grinned and there was something positively wicked about that grin and the sparkle in his eyes.

"Oh really?" he asked, as he wrapped his hand around her ankle and lifted her foot to his mouth. He proceeded to kiss it and then slowly sucked on each of her toes. He then took the tip of his tongue and starting at the inside of her ankle, ran it up the inside of her leg, stopping just at the apex of her thighs.

He looked up at her and she could see the grin was stretched right across his face now and pure mischief twinkled in his eyes. She was sensing a backfire to her teasing. He dipped his head and ran the tip of his tongue down the inside of her other leg and proceeded to kiss and suck at that foot until her body quivered with desire. Then his fingers stroked up between her legs and she gasped at the thrill of pleasure that rippled through her body.

"John, what the..." she started to say but in one swift movement he silenced her with his lips. His fingers, however, didn't stop and continued to play her like a master violinist might command a fine violin. She writhed under his touch and he kissed her harder and moved his fingers faster. She reached up to his shoulders and pulled him towards her. Her breasts pushed against his chest and he groaned as he dragged his lips away from hers. For the first time in her life she was actually considering breaking her golden rule regarding condoms.

He looked down at her, a peculiar mix of laughter and frustration in his eyes.

"So, what I meant was, what are you going to do when the only thing you want in this whole world is me inside of you Maggie? What are you going to do when I have you so senseless with need for me and you're already moaning my name and clawing at my back that you'd give anything to have me inside you. You see, that's the way you make me feel and I believe it's only fair we have a level playing field here Maggie. So, now, what are you going to do?"

She looked up into his dark eyes and behind the laughter and the mischief she could see something else hiding there, something that looked a bit like desperation, as if he was struggling to keep his emotions in check. She had no idea what they could do about this situation except to relieve each other.

"I suppose we'll have to get creative," she breathed as his fingers continued to touch and tease her to the point where she was actually considering coitus interruptus, which meant she wasn't far from being completely senseless, as he had warned.

She reached down between his legs and ran the palm of her hand along the length of his cock. He groaned into her touch and for some inexplicable reason an image of her driver's license flashed into her mind, which she thought was very odd until another, hazier image of something tucked in behind her driver's license presented itself.

"Oh my God!" she announced as she slipped out from underneath John and scurried across the room.

"Maggie, I hope to God there is a good reason why you just did that," John rasped.

She turned around to face him, a look of jubilation on her face and something between her forefinger and thumb.

"Ta-dah!" she exclaimed as she skipped back to the bed and when John realized what she was holding in her hands, he thought he'd never seen a sight so amazing in all his life.

"Where in hell's name did you just get that from?" he asked.

She grinned at him like a mad-woman.

"It's been in my purse for ages and I'd forgotten all about it but I just remembered I saw it the other day when I got my driver's license out for Sam. It's not the freshest but I'm sure it's good, after all condoms hardly go off do they. But I only have the one so we'd better make the most of it."

John pulled her to him and kissed her so hard she thought she might pass out. Then he dipped his head and sucked on her left breast and played with the nipple on the other one until the first orgasm shuddered through her body.

"Oh, I intend to," he whispered into her ear as his head moved lower.

Hank Beresford the Third thought he heard a pounding noise and a woman's scream. He took his earplugs out and listened but the only noise in room twelve was the gentle swooshing of the river coming through the open window. He put his earplugs back in and wondered why on earth old man Dewey had told him to wear them in the first place.

***

John raised himself up on his forearms and tried to catch his breath. Even with a condom on, the sex he'd just had was mind-blowing. He couldn't remember ever having sex as intense with any other woman. It was as if they were two fireflies lost in the darkness of the night, each carrying their own spark but when they connected, those sparks combined to produce an all consuming inferno.

He looked down at Maggie and she smiled up at him, her eyes shining with post-orgasmic satisfaction and his heart flipped in his chest. He liked that smile and he loved putting that look in her eyes.

"I'm so glad you didn't sort your little sailor out all by yourself," she chuckled, "it would have been a terrible waste."

John laughed. God but this woman made him laugh, even as much as she could drive him crazy, she made him laugh more. She was an addictive combination and he wasn't quite sure how he was going to handle things between them now he had broken all his rules regarding seeing her again.

"So am I," he smiled down to her, "but I'd better take care of him right now or things could get messy."

He secured the condom against the base of his cock and gently slid out of her, already missing her white-hot caress. He carefully removed it and headed for the bathroom. For a millisecond, just before he disposed of it, he thought it felt slightly lighter than the ones in recent days but then his phone rang and he dismissed his thoughts as foolish as he made a dash for the phone. He scrabbled it out of his jean's pocket just as it stopped ringing and the missed call display read, Juliette. He smiled to himself, sure in the knowledge now that Bridget had most definitely been in touch with his sister and had mentioned a certain red-head.

Maggie watched John from the comfort of the four-poster and couldn't help wondering who was calling that caused him to break out into a wide smile. A niggle of jealousy wormed its way through her at the thought it might be another woman.

"Feel free to call back," she said, interested to see if he would.

He looked at her and shook his head.

"I most certainly will not," he laughed. "I'll let her stew for a while."

So it was a woman, Maggie thought to herself as jealousy seared through her and she sat bolt upright in the bed, unimpressed with his attitude and wondering if she had been wrong about him and he was full of shit about not having a girlfriend or even a wife.

"That's no way to treat a lady," she retorted.

John stopped and looked at the sensational vision of womanhood before him. Her hair shimmered around her head and down her back in post-fuck disarray, her lips were still swollen from the attention of his kisses, the sheet she held against herself did nothing to hide her mouth-watering curves and her cheeks still held their post-orgasmic flush.

But it was her eyes that had him rooted to the spot, God help him but those eyes were going to be the death of him. They flashed at him now with anger and contempt, two orbs of dark jade and for the life of him he couldn't understand why until he saw something else lurking in them, jealousy. He grinned, so his sexy firebrand had a jealous streak, he should have known.

He continued to make his way over to her and could see his grin was having the desired effect as her eyes lit up like lights on a Christmas tree.

"Why, Dr. O'Brien, is that jealousy I see flashing in your eyes?" he chuckled and watched as her eyebrows shot up and her back arched in indignation.

"Don't flatter yourself," she spat.

He came to the side of the bed and towered over her, his naked torso flush with her face. He put the phone under her nose and suggested, "why don't you call her back, after all it's you she wants to know all about anyway."

Maggie's head jerked up to look at him, confusion clouding her eyes.

"What?" she asked, her tone less sure now.

"My sister," John informed her with more than a hint of smugness, "I'm willing to bet the jungle drums have been beating fast and furious between her and Aunt Bridget and she wants to know all about the red-head who was with me at the tea shop. Frankly, I'm surprised it's taken this long for her to call."

Maggie wanted to dash underneath the covers and hide until the embarrassment currently flooding through her disappeared. She couldn't believe she had shown her emotional hand like that. She usually wasn't the jealous type but this man did things to her emotional equilibrium she didn't understand. Jealousy meant she cared, a lot, and she didn't really want him to know that just yet.

She resisted the urge to disappear under the sheets and hung her head instead.

"Oh," was all she could manage by way of reply.

Seconds later she felt his finger, long and strong, under her chin as he tilted her head up to look at him. She almost gulped at the warmth, sincerity and slight irritation burning in the dark amber of his eyes.

"Maggie, I don't have a girlfriend or a wife," he smiled, "I told you that. I won't bullshit you Maggie and I know I'm here after everything I said yesterday but you're not so easy to walk away from. As I said, I don't want to want you but I do. I shouldn't be here but here I am and I'm not sure how to handle all that but one thing I can promise you Maggie is honesty. I'll always be honest with you."

With that he bent down and kissed her and unbeknownst to him, stole yet another piece of her heart.

She curled her arms around his neck and kissed him like she could kiss him forever. The sheet fell away and her breasts brushed against his chest. He gasped into her mouth and she smiled to herself, *no, my high and mighty Navy SEAL, I'm not so easy to walk away from.*

John could feel himself growing hard again and in the absence of a condom decided to nip things in the bud rather than torture himself, plus if he didn't get some food soon he might need the flame-haired temptress for her medical skills rather than the other things she could do to his body.

He broke the kiss and smiled down at her, "as much as I'd like to feast on you all over again, I'm afraid if I don't get some food soon, I'm going to need you in a medical capacity."

Maggie smiled back, "good because I'm ravenous and if I don't get some nourishment into me soon then I'll be in need of your brawn just to get me to the bathroom."

"Then why don't you order up some room service and I'll see if I can get this stove lit," he replied.

"No problem, what do you fancy to eat?"

"Steak and fries will do me fine, maybe with some garlic butter on the side and a nice bottle of red. Oh and I like my beef rare."

Of course you do, Maggie thought to herself as she picked up the phone.

Twenty minutes later there was a knock at the door, signifying the arrival of their food. Maggie signed for it and took charge of the trolley but not before noticing the wine wasn't the one she'd ordered. She called the young waiter back and pointed out the mistake. He smiled and informed her this particular bottle had been selected by Mr. Dewey himself and was compliments of the hotel. Maggie smiled, Old Twinkly Eyes really was the last of the great romantics.

When she turned around she realized John had been busy whilst she'd been dealing with the waiter. The small outside table and two chairs were now in front of the stove, with a pillowcase doubling as a tablecloth and a tea-light from the bathroom serving as a centerpiece. It seemed Mr. Dewey wasn't the only romantic around here.

"Impressive," she smiled.

"We aim to please," he grinned as he indicated for her to sit in the chair he'd just pulled out from the table.

He picked the wine up from the trolley and expressed his delight at the vintage, "ah Monsieur Dewey, une bouteille de Bordeaux 2004, merci beaucoup, c'est un grand plaisir pour nous."

He put a glass in front of Maggie and proceeded to pour the wine he was obviously impressed with.

"Madame," he said with a flourish of his hand and Maggie decided she liked it when he called her that and she definitely liked him talking French. It was hot as hell. She took a sip and had to agree it was pretty good.

He placed her plate of food in front of her and whispered in her ear, "bon appetit."

He sat opposite her and proceeded to make a 16oz rib eye disappear along with what looked like a million fries.

She chuckled. "You really weren't joking about being close to starvation, were you?"

John grinned at her. "Hiking some of the toughest terrain in the Adirondacks for the day and rounding it off with some pretty energetic sex will give any man an appetite."

Energetic sex? Maggie mused to herself, *yep, that pretty much sums it up.*

She grinned back. "So that's what you did today?"

"Yeah," replied John, "figured it was the best way to work a few things out of my system, especially after waking up on my own."

Maggie ducked her head. "Yeah, sorry about that, I just thought it was a good idea at the time."

"Well, considering all I had to say last night, I suppose I couldn't blame you," John admitted. "How much longer do you have in the Adirondacks before you have to head back to New York?"

Maggie lifted her head and a flicker of something he couldn't quite place skipped across her face.

"I'm working Sunday night, so I suppose early Sunday morning or even Saturday night."

There was something in her expression that caused him pause, as if she didn't want to face the prospect of going back.

"Do you like your job?" he probed.

Maggie stared at him as if the question were preposterous.

"Of course I like my job. I love my job," she replied but her eyes suggested she had other feelings about her job, ones she wasn't sharing with him.

"Why do you ask?"

"It just seems to me you don't seem too enthusiastic about going back to New York."

Maggie looked away, at some far point in the room and sighed.

"The night before I left, there was an incident. I lost a patient. A little girl. She came in as an accident but it was clear within seconds of treating her that she was an abuse case. We were making progress with her when her mother showed up with the man I suspect of inflicting her injuries. We didn't allow access and they caused a scene, shouting and becoming violent. Kayla, the little girl, heard the man's voice and was so terrified she went into cardiac arrest. She died in my arms."

Maggie said the last sentence so quietly John barely heard it. When Maggie looked at him again he could see a lone tear trickling out the side of her right eye.

"I've seen too many cases like Kayla's in the past few months John and I don't know what to do about it. Yes, I love my job but lately it seems to be coming at a very high price. Do you know what I mean?"

John got up from the table and, taking Maggie's hands in his, pulled her up from the chair and enfolded her in his enormous arms.

"I know exactly what you mean," he murmured into her hair and then he led her over to the bed, where he laid her down beside him and held her close.

Maggie melted into the giant of a man lying beside her and breathed in his unique scent. God but it felt good to have someone to share her burden with. She couldn't admit to anyone else that at times her job wore her down, she couldn't let the super-doctor mask slip but John had a way of stripping her bare and exposing the things that troubled her.

She dreaded the next Kayla and knew she needed to get herself together, to fortify herself before she had to face a situation like that again. And then there was the matter of her reaction to Kayla's death. That hadn't been good, not good at all and she was sure it had a lot to do with Professor O'Keefe advising her to take some time off. There was a lot waiting for her back in New York.

She sighed into John's chest and he pulled her closer to him.

"When do you have to leave?" she asked.

"I have to report for duty on Monday morning, so I'm leaving early on Sunday."

Maggie nodded into his chest. She wasn't sure why she was nodding but she couldn't think what else to do. She had no idea where things stood between them now but yet again, as if reading her thoughts, John spoke.

"Maggie, I know I have no right to ask after everything I've said but would you consider spending the next few days with me back at the cabin?"

Maggie couldn't quite believe what she was hearing and her heart skipped a beat as her breath held in her chest. She'd spent the day trying to accept she would never see him again and here he was, holding her in his arms and asking her to spend the rest of her time in the Adirondacks with him.

John felt her go still and a sliver of nervousness trickled down his spine. He wasn't sure about them spending the next few days together but he was certain he didn't want to go back to the cabin without her. He was definitely sailing in uncharted territory.

He wanted to move on, to forget her but she was like an invisible vine in his blood and as long as she was within a hundred mile radius, he knew he was incapable of staying away. The vine thrived and blossomed whenever he was around her and made him feel alive, wanted and cared for and he realized now, he hadn't felt like that for a very long time.

He realized part of him was dying due to the choices and decisions he'd made and maybe it was time to face up to the fact he could make other choices. Maybe. Or maybe leaving her would just be easier if he was facing into a long deployment.

She shifted beside him and raised herself up on her elbow. Her green eyes penetrated the depths of his own and he shifted slightly under the intensity of her gaze.

"I don't know John," she replied in a voice that had as many questions as answers. "I don't know what that means. I don't know what you being here means. I already care for you a great deal and I'm afraid another few days with you would mean caring for you too much."

And going past the point of no return, she added to herself.

"To be honest Maggie," John replied, "I'm not sure what it all means either. I'm not up for a spot of psycho-analysis right now but I do know I want you and I like being with you and I like the way I feel when you're around and you seem to have done something to my cabin because it doesn't feel the same without you in it."

He stopped to smile at her. She grinned back.

"Circumstances haven't changed. I still have to report for duty on Monday morning and in another few months I'll be deployed. I'm still not long-term relationship material but if you're up for making this week one that we can both take special memories away from, then so am I. Actually, there is nothing in this world I'd rather do than spend the next few days with you but I'll understand if you'd rather walk away in the morning."

Maggie smiled to herself. Even if she said no, this sweet, gorgeous man was still planning on staying the night, not storming off in a huff. She looked at him and saw a shadow of vulnerability concealed deep within his eyes. She guessed this was the closest he'd ever come to revealing how much he cared about a woman and a part of him was obviously afraid she would throw it all back in his face.

Just as she knew the wisest thing to do earlier would have been to ask him to leave, she knew, for her heart's sake, she should now refuse his invite to spend the next few days together. She was rapidly approaching the point of no return with him but she was like a wild horse running towards a precipice that knew it should slow down but enjoyed the feeling of running wild and free too much to stop.

She couldn't remember a time when she had felt as peaceful and happy as she had in the last few days. She feared a huge emotional precipice was waiting somewhere down the line but God help her she couldn't stop.

She looked into his face, her eyes like emerald lasers.

"I'd love to spend the next few days with you John but I have one condition."

His eyes widened as the vulnerability was replaced by fear, fear she would ask him for something he couldn't possibly give.

"Maggie, I...." he started to say but she placed a finger on his lips, silencing him.

"John, don't worry, I'm not going to ask you for something you can't give me but you're a man of honor, are you not?"

John nodded his head, "For sure."

Maggie smiled, he looked even more afraid now. "And you would never break a promise?"

John squirmed. "Never."

Maggie chuckled at his obvious discomfort.

"Then I'll accompany you back to the cabin for the next few days, if you promise me, after we leave, we stay in touch. I don't necessarily mean seeing each other but the odd text would be nice and an email or even a phone call now and then. And if you and your sexy ass are ever in New York, you'll give me a call. I'm not the type of person who can take someone into my life and then cut all ties with them, that doesn't sit easy with me John."

John let out a sigh of relief. Staying in touch was definitely something he could do. He'd never done it with any of the other women he'd slept with but he could certainly do it with Maggie.

He smiled at her. "Staying in touch is not a problem, as long as you understand when I'm overseas my communications will be sporadic."

Maggie grinned. "Understood. I just need to know you're... um.... okay."

Comprehension flooded John's brain and he was both touched and alarmed at the realization as to how much Maggie already cared about him. He tamped down the panic rising in him at the thought.

She's a doctor, he told himself, *she's the caring type who probably follows up on patients, of course she's going to care about a guy she has spent an intimate week with.*

He hoped for her sake that's all it was as the thought of her falling in love with him brought him out in a cold sweat. He could handle his own heartache but Maggie's would be too much to bear.

He pulled her closer.

Don't fall in love with me Maggie, he whispered silently to himself, *dear God, please do not fall in love with me. I come with far too high a price.*

Maggie leaned into him and placed a gentle kiss upon his lips.

"Well that's it then," she announced, "the deal is sealed with a kiss."

John grinned at her, a devilish grin much like the one he had treated her to earlier.

"Oh I think we can seal it with a bit more than that," he husked into her ear as his hands loosened the belt of her bathrobe.

Some time later, after a number of "creative" make-out sessions, he held Maggie's naked body close as she breathed softly into his chest. He'd told her earlier he didn't know what was happening to him and he wasn't up for any psycho-analysis but in the heart of the night, surrounded by darkness and shadows he couldn't escape it. He was falling for the woman in his arms and falling for her in a big way. And he was fucked if he knew what to do about it.

TEN

Maggie snuggled in closer to the beautiful man lying beside her. She felt the gentle rhythm of his chest fall and rise beneath her cheek and the hard muscularity of his thigh between her legs. Her hand started a slow exploration from his left nipple into the dip at the top of his sternum, down along his ribcage and down further still to the ridged muscles of his abdomen. Her index finger explored each ridge in deliberate detail sending messages of appreciation back to her brain. Her hand moved lower and she couldn't help wondering what time the drug store opened.

Their creative make-out sessions last night had been wonderful but she was horny as hell from it all and had an almost desperate need to get John inside her as soon as possible. She had a gnawing ache deep inside her that only he had the cure for.

As her hand cupped his balls there was no mistaking the increase in the rhythm of his breaths and she felt him smile as he placed a kiss into her hair.

"Good morning," he murmured, his voice deep and throaty.

"Good morning," Maggie replied as she ran her hand along his now rock-hard cock and smiled seductively up at him, "I wonder what time the drugstore opens around here."

"I'm not sure," chuckled John, "but if you keep going like that I might be forced to use some of my lock-picking skills."

Maggie laughed. "Can you really pick locks?"

John smiled back at her. "Well knocking doors down kinda starts to wear on you after a while and eliminates the element of surprise so picking a lock saves a lot of hassle, so yes, I really can pick locks."

She rubbed her hand along his impressive manhood and whispered into his ear. "Then what are you waiting for?"

John was about to reply when there was a knocking at the door and the phone started to ring at the same time. His spidey senses immediately told him something was off, it was too much of a co-incidence to have both events happen at the same time. He looked at Maggie, whose expression told him she was somewhere between confused and pissed off.

"Are you expecting anyone or a phone call?" he asked.

Maggie shook her head.

"No," she answered but by now she was already out of the bed, pulling on her bathrobe and heading towards the door.

A feeling of dread coiled itself around John's stomach and he was just about to warn Maggie against answering the door, when she turned the handle.

Too late.

The door opened to reveal two police officers, a male and a female.

The male officer spoke.

"Are you Doctor Maggie O'Brien, Senior Trauma Surgeon at Hillview Hospital, New York?"

Maggie couldn't speak. Her first thought was something had happened to her parents but she quickly dismissed that idea as she knew if that was the case then one of her siblings would have called her on her cell phone. No, it took her a few more seconds to realize why the officers were here but it didn't mean she was any less shocked.

It was something she had feared might happen as a result of the events of last Thursday night but she had dismissed her fears as crazy thinking. It seemed they hadn't been so crazy after all.

The young female officer spoke this time with a defined edge to her voice. "Ma'am, we need you to confirm if you are Doctor Maggie O'Brien?"

Maggie nodded. "Y....ye.....yes, I'm Doctor O'Brien," she stammered, her heart racing now at the prospect of what was going to happen next.

The male officer spoke, in a kinder tone to that of his colleague. "Doctor O'Brien, you're under arrest for assault on Frank Baker of Hunt's

Point, The Bronx, New York city on October sixteenth last at approximately twenty-two hundred hours in the trauma unit of Hillview hospital and you are requested to accompany me and my colleague to the local police station."

Maggie had feared this was coming and yet couldn't believe her ears. She could feel the adrenaline spiking in her system as her fight or flight reaction uselessly kicked in because she could do neither. The room started to spin and she grabbed the door frame as she heard John explode from the bed, "What the fuck?"

The next thing he was beside her and the young female officer's mouth was on the floor as she took in the vision of masculine perfection standing just a few feet away.

"Sir," the male officer spoke, "I'd appreciate it if you could step away from Doctor O'Brien and put some clothes on."

John ignored him and wrapped his arms around Maggie.

"Hey," he spoke softly into her ear, "hey, are you okay?"

Maggie looked up into his eyes and wanted to say so much, to explain but all she could do was nod.

"Sir," the male officer said again, much more sharply this time but before he could say another word John fixed him with a glare so menacing he immediately softened his tone and said, "please sir put some clothes on, you can accompany Doctor O'Brien to the police station if you wish but only if you are dressed."

Maggie started to shake as the effects of the adrenaline flowing through her body took hold. She was so embarrassed at this happening in front of John and yet, at the same time, she felt incredible comfort in having his arms around her.

The young female officer spoke. "Ma'am, you're going to have to put some clothes on too."

The phone stopped ringing.

Maggie nodded.

The male officer proceeded to mirandize her and she realized it was really happening. She was actually being arrested. *Oh God.*

Somehow she managed to use the bathroom and get dressed. She started packing up her things but the male police officer told her they needed to get going. John put his arm around her and said he'd look after everything later.

"The sooner we get out of here, the sooner we can get this thing sorted," he re-assured her in a calm voice. She nodded. She couldn't look at him.

"I'm sorry you've got tangled up in this, " she whispered into his chest.

He placed his finger under her chin and raised her face up to look into his.

"Hey," he soothed, in a low voice full of confidence she didn't share, "it's going to be all right, we'll get it sorted. I'll make a few phone calls and have a lawyer for you before you get to the police station."

The female officer approached, handcuffs in hand.

John looked at her, incredulous.

"I don't think there's any need for those, " he snarled.

The female officer looked at her colleague and he shook his head. "If you could just accompany us to the cruiser Dr. O'Brien," he said, "we'll take you with us to the police station and your boyfriend can meet us there."

Maggie shot a look at John. He smiled in return, as if he didn't mind in the least being called her boyfriend.

Maggie was grateful it was still early morning and there were hardly any guests around to witness her humiliation. Gerard Dewey, however, was another matter. He came running out from behind the reception desk, his ancient features set with worry and his eyes glassy with concern.

"Dr. O'Brien," he called, "is there anything I can do for you?"

Maggie shook her head, she was so touched by his concern she could hardly speak.

"I'll be fine, thank you Gerard," she managed to choke out.

He ran up and stopped dead in front of her, his eyes wild with worry and something in his hand.

"Here, take this," he said, "this is the business card of a new attorney in town. She's good, just got here from New York where she was a kick-ass prosecutor but she's a defense attorney now. She'll have you out of there in no time."

He shoved the card into her hand and stepped out of the way.

"Don't worry about your things or the room," he called after her, "I'll look after all that."

Maggie nodded, "thank you," she smiled, struggling to hold back the tears fighting to escape from her eyes.

The officers shuffled her out the door and the next thing she knew she was looking out the back window of the cruiser as John and Old Twinkly Eyes watched her being driven away. She looked down at the card and took in the name printed in the center in glossy black letters. Gina Gallinaro, Attorney at law.

I hope you are as good as he says you are, she said to herself, *because you are my only hope.*

John let out a long breath and turned to Gerard, "I suppose that was you on the phone?" he asked.

Gerard nodded his head, a look of resignation on his face. "Yes, I was trying to warn you, give you a heads up but damn they were fast up those stairs."

"Well, thanks for trying, " John said.

"What the hell have they arrested her for anyway?" Gerard asked. "She's a fiery one for sure but she's a decent human being, you can tell that from her in the first five minutes."

John shook his head. "I don't know what's going on but they've charged her with assault."

Gerard's eyebrows nearly shot off his face. "Assault? Well, all I can say is she must have had good cause."

John thought back on what she'd told him about her last night at work, the same night she was being charged with assault and considered how the two events must be related.

"I suspect she might have had more cause than most," he said in a voice so low Gerard barely heard him but there was no mistaking the anger stiffening his jaw.

"Well you'd better get down to the station and see how you can help her out," Gerard announced, "but first I'll get the kitchen to rustle you up some coffee and a bit of breakfast you can take with you. I suppose you'll be needing to see to your dog."

John looked over at his truck and could see Rock's face peeking out the passenger side window.

"See you in ten minutes," he said to Gerard as he started to walk away, "oh and by the way, I'll pack up her things, when she's released, she'll be coming with me."

Gerard smiled, now those words had just made his morning a lot better.

***

John took Rock down to the river and watched as he went nuts on an early morning sniffathon following invisible trails into bushes and around trees. He sat on one of the riverside benches and holding his head in his hands, let out a long, slow breath.

He sure hadn't seen this morning's events coming and one thing you could definitely say about life with Dr. Maggie O'Brien, it certainly wasn't boring. Assault was a serious charge though and he therefore hoped it was totally bogus. He'd only known her a few days and there was no doubt she was quick-tempered but he couldn't see her inflicting serious harm on another human being. Unless someone had posed a threat to a member of her team or one of her patients, then he could see her turning into a full on wildcat.   After all, Maggie O'Brien's emotions never ran far below the surface.   He smiled as he got up and called Rock.   She was what his grandfather would have called a "helluva" woman.

ELEVEN

John followed the young female officer as she led the way to Maggie's cell and mused to himself how it was obviously a slow day for crime in Little Creek. Only one other cell was occupied and it looked to John like it was a case of a young guy in need of sleeping off a big night. Thankfully, Maggie was in the end cell so this afforded them some privacy to talk.

His heart twisted a little at the sight of her sitting on the floor, her knees pulled up to her chest, her arms wrapped around them as if she were trying to literally hold herself together. But it was her eyes, as usual, that got to him the most. He could see the strain of unshed tears as she stared disconsolately at the wall. She barely looked at him as he left the coffee and paper bag down in front of the bars.

"Officer Caldwell here has kindly agreed to let you have some coffee and something to eat, compliments of Gerard Dewey," he informed her, trying his best to muster up a smile, "he seems to have taken quite a shine to you."

Maggie didn't move. She didn't look at him and didn't respond.

Officer Caldwell shifted uncomfortably before announcing, "I'll let you two have some time together," as she turned and walked off.

"Maggie, come on, have something to eat and some coffee," John cajoled, "it could be a long day."

She looked at him, as if he was speaking from somewhere far away, her eyes not exactly focused on him.

"Thanks for the food and coffee John," she said in a low, flat voice, "it's okay, I'll be fine from here, you can go now. I don't expect you to wait around a jailhouse for the day with a woman you met only a few days ago in the woods."

She attempted a smile but the best she could pull off was a grimace.

John stood up against the bars.

"Hey, I'd appreciate it if you'd let me make my own mind up as to how I'd like to spend my time. Right now I want to be here and I want to see you drink that coffee before it goes cold. Then I want to see you eat some of that BLT your friend Gerard had specially made for you and then I want you to tell me what these assault charges are all about. And I am not going anywhere till all three of those things have happened."

Maggie couldn't help a half-smile at Mr. Bossy-boots reaming out his demands. God but the man was domineering and also sexy as hell as he glared through the bars at her as if they were mere plastic pipes he could bend out of the way if he so chose.

"That's better," John smiled, "now get your ass over here and do as you are told, for once."

Maggie smiled more now and moved over to where he had left the food and coffee. He sat down on the floor just on the other side of the bars and she sat opposite him. She took a slug of the coffee and couldn't believe how good it tasted. She wasn't sure how much of the BLT she would manage, as it turned out getting arrested didn't do much for her appetite but she would give it a go just to keep him happy.

She'd managed a few bites and drunk most of the coffee when she looked into his eyes and began to explain how she was under arrest for assault.

"You remember last night I told you there was an incident where I lost a patient, a little girl?"

John nodded.

"You remember I told you the mother and her boyfriend showed up and caused a scene, becoming violent and how the sound of the boyfriend's voice affected the little girl and literally scared her to death?"

Again, John nodded.

"Well, what I didn't tell you was how I reacted. I didn't tell you how I've been working crazy hours for months now, how we've seen a huge increase in these types of cases. Broken and battered children turning up at all hours of the day and night, supposedly victims of accidents but we all know within minutes of treating them that's bullshit. We even see some of them come in again a few months after we've fixed them, victims of yet another 'accident'. Did you have any idea kids were becoming more accident prone?" she asked John, her voice laced with bitterness and storm clouds in her eyes.

He said nothing but took a hold of her hand.

"We inform child protective services when we suspect a child is in a dangerous situation and I think they do what they can but it's hard when you see a child back in the trauma unit who you treated only a few months ago. I've had a lot of these cases in the past eighteen months and when Kayla flat-lined on me, something deep inside me snapped.

She had a boot mark imprinted on her back where the bastard had obviously kicked her. I looked over to where the mother and the boyfriend were fighting with the two police officers and I saw that piece of scum kicking one of the officers. I saw the sole of his boot and I saw it had the exact same pattern as the boot-mark on Kayla's back and I knew, I knew every punch, every kick, every cigarette burn and every slap he had put on her tiny body and I became enraged.

I don't remember much but all I can tell you for sure is I wanted justice for Kayla and I wanted to wipe that bastard off the face of the earth. I can recall being dragged off him by some of the staff. Apparently, I even had a pair of surgical scissors in my hand. "

She said the last part in almost a whisper and with her head dipped, looking at the floor.

"I wanted to kill him John, I wanted to kill him so bad."

John squeezed her hand. He wasn't sure what to say, he, after all, was a trained killer.

She glanced sideways at him as if trying to gauge his reaction.

"I'm sorry I didn't say anything. The guy was arrested that night on suspicion of murder and I didn't think anything would come of my regrettable behavior. The head of the trauma department suggested I should take some time off and I gladly complied and accepted Matt's offer of a place to stay in the Adirondacks. I think you can see now why I was so desperate for some time on my own, I needed to think, to try and work things out. I never imagined matters would take this direction and I'm really sorry you're caught up in all this. Seriously, I don't mind if you go, the attorney should be here any minute now and by the sounds of her I don't think she'll be very long sorting things out."

She tried to smile at him but her effort lasted only a millisecond. Smiling was not coming easy to her at the moment.

John ignored her telling him to go, yet again. It was beginning to irk him.

"Did you call the one on the card Gerard gave you?" he asked.

"Yes, she sounds super-efficient."

John smiled. "Well both Gerard and Sam agree she is the best attorney in town so hopefully you'll be out of here in time for me to cook you up something special tonight."

Maggie couldn't believe what she was hearing. Instead of running for the hills, this gorgeous man was planning on cooking her dinner. It was too much and she could feel the tears building behind her eyes like floodwaters threatening a dam. She squeezed his hand, willing herself not to cry but it was too late. Tears edged out the sides of her eyes. She bowed her head in an effort to hide her face. She hated crying but she honestly felt as if she was falling apart. Her life had become a roller-coaster of highs and lows in the past week and now it was completely out of control and she didn't know which way to turn.

John's heart twisted some more on hearing the first sniff of Maggie's tears. She refused to look at him and he knew she was using her beautiful gold-flecked red hair like a curtain, hiding the sad spectacle of her tears.

"It's going to be okay, Maggie," he soothed, "you'll be out of here in no time. I've seen how these things go, believe me, I can't count the number of times guys from the teams have been involved in punch-ups and nothing ever comes of them. You're a good person, any judge will see that."

He squeezed his arm as much as he could through the bars and tried to get it around her shoulders. He wanted to take her into his arms and hold her till all her fears and doubts vanished, until she didn't have to worry about the world anymore. At the same time he wanted to drive to New York, track down the piece of scum known as Frank Baker and finish the job Maggie had started.

Maggie felt John's arm slide around her shoulders and allowed herself to lean ever so slightly into it, hoping he wouldn't notice. It amazed her how she'd only known him for a few days but it was as if she'd known him forever. She knew instinctively she could rely on him for anything and just that thought alone brought a warmth to her soul.

He brushed a kiss against her hair and she couldn't hold back the sigh which escaped her. Getting through today's nightmare would be one thing but walking away from this dream of a man was an ordeal she didn't want to contemplate. At least this time she knew she would hear from him again which gave her hope that maybe they could work something out in the future, not that hers was looking exactly peachy at the moment.

John was just about to ask her if she was feeling better when the sound of heels clickety-clacking against the tiled floor could be heard approaching at considerable speed. The door at the end of the corridor opened and Officer Caldwell entered with a woman who was little over five foot but exuded confidence far in excess of that.

"I think your attorney is here," John murmured to Maggie. They both stood up and watched as the two females approached.

Officer Caldwell spoke first. "This is your attorney," she informed Maggie, "Gina Gallinaro."

Gina reached out her perfectly manicured hand and shook Maggie's.

"It's good to meet you Dr. O'Brien," she said, "don't worry we'll have this unfortunate mess cleared up in no time."

Before Maggie could reply, she turned to John and asked, "Who are you?"

John couldn't help smiling at her directness, he liked her already.

"John Sullivan, Dr. O'Brien's, *friend*."

He put special emphasis on the word friend as if to let her know he was definitely more than that but Maggie couldn't help the twinge of disappointment she felt that he hadn't said he was her boyfriend. That would have been a ray of sunlight on what had, so far, been a very grey day.

Gina let her eyes roam freely over John and Maggie didn't miss the sparkle of feminine approval at what she saw. But when she spoke her voice was all clipped professionalism.

"Well, John, Dr. O'Brien will be accompanying me to one of the interrogation rooms to make her statement and I'd say that will take about an hour, so if you want you can wait at the main desk until we're done and I'm sure after that Officer Caldwell will let you have some more "friend" time together."

Maggie couldn't help smirking at her emphasis on the word "friend", letting him know she was under no illusions as to what type of "friends" she believed they were.

John squeezed Maggie's hand.

"It looks like you're in good hands," he smiled, "I'll see you in a little while."

Maggie managed a small smile and nodded her head before watching him walk away.

Officer Caldwell unlocked the cell and Maggie accompanied her and Gina to the interrogation room.

Once there she recounted the details of why she was under arrest to Gina, who nodded her head, took notes and asked questions throughout. When Maggie was finished she furiously scribbled down a page of notes before lifting her head, sending her wavy black tresses floating around her perfect features like an ebony colored head-dress and announced, "Okay, so this is the way I see it, this charge is completely bogus and is merely a ploy by Frank Baker's attorney to see if he can get a deal for his client."

Maggie was confused. How did her being charged with assault on Frank Baker help his case?

Gina didn't miss the confused expression on Maggie's face.

"Basically," she started to explain, "by his lawyer getting him to press charges against you, he is hoping the prosecutor in New York will cut a deal if Frank Baker agrees to drop the charges against you. So, the charges are simply a strategy. From what you are saying he will have marks on his body to try to prove his claim but they are more likely to have come from his interaction with the security officers than you and he'll have a hell of a time trying to prove otherwise. I presume there are security cameras all over the hospital?"

Maggie nodded. "Yes of course."

Gina beamed. "Excellent," she announced as she got up from her chair, "I'm sure the footage will show how you came to the aide of the officers who were engaged in a violent struggle with Mr. Baker and how your actions were motivated by your concerns for the security officers and members of your staff. I need to go now and inform Judge Carter just what a nonsense this whole thing is. I should have you out of here by lunchtime."

Maggie couldn't believe her ears and yet she had every reason to believe Gina Gallinaro meant every word she said because there wasn't a scintilla of doubt in her voice.

"That would be great," Maggie said wide-eyed, as if she couldn't quite believe her luck could change on this horrible day.

Gina smiled and extended her hand, "don't worry Maggie, this will all go away and you and your "friend" can make up for lost time."

Maggie dipped her head, blushed and simply said, "Thank you."

TWELVE

It took longer than she had promised but Gina Gallinaro was as good as her word and at ten minutes past three Maggie was released on her own recognizance from Little Creek Police Station. She had to report to the seventy-second precinct in Brooklyn on her return to New York but for now she was free to go and was relieved. Sam had kindly delivered her car to the police station earlier in the day so she was somewhat confused when John led her in the opposite direction to her Prius once they got to the parking lot.

With all that had happened in the past twenty-four hours, she hadn't really considered how he had made it to the Little Creek Hotel last night or how he'd been getting around today. For all she knew the man had walked everywhere as she hadn't seen so much as a bicycle at the cabin. It came as something of a shock then when he pointed what was obviously a remote security device at the biggest truck in the parking lot and it blipped to life.

"What the hell is that?" Maggie asked, slightly in awe of the sleek black machine.

John grinned. "That, Dr. O'Brien, is the wonder of automotive engineering known as the Ford F150 Raptor."

Maggie shielded her eyes from the late afternoon sun as she looked up into his face and couldn't miss the male pride shining in his eyes. This Raptor thing was obviously his pride and joy.

"But I should really drive my own car," she objected.

John stopped his march across the parking lot and took both her hands in his, causing her to turn and look up at him.

"Maggie, you've had the day from hell, let's just get back to the cabin. We can come and collect your car another day, for now let's just get back to base and chill."

His words were kind and spoken softly but there was an underlying edge of something. Frustration? Anxiety? She wasn't sure but she realized spending most of the day in Little Creek and especially the jail house probably hadn't been high on his list of things to do for the day. Guilt and shame burned through her and she dropped her head at the same time as she let go of his hands.

"Yeah, you're right," she replied, "driving the back-roads of the Adirondacks seems too much like hard work for me right now."

John noticed the subtle change in her body language and was surprised at how much he missed the defiant rise of her chin. She looked beat down and he was overcome with a need to enfold her in his arms and keep her there forever, protecting her from the evils of the world. His job was tough but he'd never had a child die in his arms and now she'd been arrested for understandably losing it and attacking the piece of shit she believed responsible.

She started to walk away from him towards the Raptor but he reached out and caught her by the shoulder. She turned, a look of confusion on her face but before she could say anything he wrapped her up in his arms and kissed the top of her head. He held her to him as tightly as he dared without restricting her air supply.

There was so much he wanted to say, to tell her how he felt about her but he knew it would be wrong. He was going to have to walk away from her in another few days and he didn't want to make her life any more complicated than it already was but dammit he needed to hold her, he needed to try and communicate on some level how much he cared about her.

Maggie melted into John's arms. She hadn't been looking for anything remotely resembling human interaction during her stay in the Adirondacks but she was so grateful, in so many ways, for meeting John. He had made today, in particular, bearable and now here he was holding her in his arms as if his life depended on it. For a fleeting moment she wished she could stay here with him forever and not have to go back and face her life in New York. He kissed the top of her head and she smiled into his granite-like chest.

"Thank you," she whispered as she slid her arms around him and enjoyed a brief moment of peace.

A muffled bark sounded from behind them and a chuckle rumbled up from somewhere deep inside John. He released Maggie and turned around. There, at the passenger side window of the Raptor was Rock going nuts with excitement.

"Looks like someone can't wait to say hello," he laughed.

Maggie's face lit up in a smile and she rushed over and opened the door. Rock immediately launched a love-bomb of licks, barks and yelps. Maggie laughed and John felt a warmth steal through him at seeing a genuine smile on her face again.

"Do you think he'll share the front seat with me?" she asked.

"I think he'd ride the tow-bar with you," John laughed as he helped Maggie up into the cab and closed the door.

He went around to the driver's side and was about to get into the truck when he was stopped in his tracks by the scene before him. Rock's face was turned up towards Maggie who was rubbing him vigorously behind the ears. Maggie's face was a picture of joy matched only by the intense delight on his dog's face and in that moment a feeling so fierce and strong rocked him so hard he had to hold onto the door of the truck. He was floored by the intensity of emotion and could no longer deny that at some point over the past few days he had lost a large piece of his heart to this beautiful woman and so, it seemed, had his dog.

THIRTEEN

Most people dreamed of five star resorts on a tropical island as their idea of paradise but Maggie had never been so happy to see John's tiny cabin hidden away in the middle of the Adirondack wilderness. She was sitting out on the veranda now with a glass of wine in her hand and a light blanket wrapped around her shoulders. She couldn't be sure if it was her body's response to stress or if it really was considerably cooler this afternoon.

John was in the kitchen putting things away and prepping the dinner. He'd seemed pre-occupied since they got back. She supposed that was to be expected, after all it wasn't every day the woman you were sleeping with got arrested. He'd insisted she sit out on the veranda and "relax". It had been more of a command than a suggestion but she had happily obeyed and accepted the glass of wine he'd brought her.

She sipped on it now as she looked out at the beauty of the wilderness surrounding her. It seemed as if the leaves had changed color overnight and blazed in all their flame-colored glory under the touch of the late afternoon sun. She pulled her knees up to her chest and released a long breath.

Her life was completely unrecognizable from what it had been only a week ago and her head hurt from trying to reconcile all that had happened. She sipped again at the wine and let its relaxing effect run in unseen rivulets all over her body. Her shoulders loosened and she could feel the tension seeping out of her bones and into the cool Adirondack air. There was nowhere on earth where she had found such a sense of peace and contentment as she had here at John's cabin. She had no idea what awaited her back in New York or what, if anything, the future held for her and John and she was simply too exhausted to wade through the mental fog enveloping her to think about it.

John slugged his beer and grabbed a knife. He placed an onion on the chopping board and plunged the blade into its pungent white flesh. He hadn't been able to stop thinking about the strange surge of emotion that had come over him back in the parking lot.

He wasn't quite sure what it had been or what to call it, just as he didn't have a word for exactly how he felt about Maggie. Seeing her down and defeated had felt like a blunt knife being dragged across his gut and her tears had felt like small paper cuts to his heart but her smile lit him up from the inside out, every single time. He had no words for what any of that meant and the depth of emotion he felt for her.

He supposed other people would use the love word but he wasn't going to do that because there was no way he could be in love or falling in love with anyone, especially Maggie. Loving her would mean making her his and that was simply too much to ask.

Like, I'm in like with her, he told himself, *okay, I'm in big like with her. Okay, all right, I'm in big, big like with her, the biggest fucking like I can be in like with her but that's it.*

He threw the onions in the pan, took another slug of beer and as the translucent little squares started to sizzle, he swore yet again.

"Fuck."

The sun dipped lower and Maggie pulled the blanket closer as she wondered what culinary delight John had planned for this evening as the delicious smell of onions, garlic and bacon wafted past her on the veranda. She considered offering to help but he had given her the distinct impression he wanted to have some time to himself.

She thought about all he had told her regarding his last deployment and what had happened to his friends and guilt rippled through her again. He had no doubt come up to the cabin to deal with the unpleasant events in his own life and had been unwittingly sucked into the drama of hers. She wished she could turn back the clock and give him his day back but she supposed if she was going to do that then she would go back to last Thursday night and completely change the course of events.

Then the thought struck her if she hadn't reacted the way she did she would never have found herself in the Adirondacks and would never have met John. She smiled ruefully to herself, he was quite a reward for losing her temper.

"Penny for 'em."

John's low voice hummed in her ear as he bent down and refilled her glass. He lowered his enormous frame into the chair beside her and half-smiled at her in that adorable way he shared with his dog, his head cocked to the side and his eyes bright with inquisitiveness.

Maggie smiled back but John didn't miss the fact the smile didn't reach her eyes.

"I was just considering how I've kinda gatecrashed your party for one up here and I suppose you don't get much time off in your line of work. I've cost you a whole day out of your holidays and for that I'm truly sorry."

John couldn't believe his ears. With everything she had been through today and all that lay ahead of her once she got back to New York, she was worrying about him. He was speechless.

The silence stretched between them like an elastic band about to snap and Maggie became increasingly uncomfortable. She sipped at her wine and stared straight ahead, afraid to look in John's direction.

"Maggie," John said in a low voice, "have you ever been spanked?"

Wine sprayed from Maggie's mouth as she sputtered in shock and her head swiveled around at such a speed there was a distinct danger it might detach from her neck.

"Whaaaaat?" she screeched, her eyes wide with astonishment. Of all the things she had expected him to say, asking her if she'd ever been spanked certainly hadn't been one of them.

"I asked you if you'd ever been spanked?" he repeated and from the look on his face and the tone of his voice he was deadly serious.

Maggie shook her head. "No, I've never been spanked, why.... why would you ask such a thing?"

"Because I want to know if I'd be the first."

Maggie looked at him like she was seeing him for the first time. "Why would you want to spank me?"

John smiled. "I didn't say I wanted to but if you say sorry for what happened today one more time then I will go all Christian Grey on you and put you over my knee and spank you till you can't remember the damned word. I'll admit, meeting someone hadn't been part of my plan when I came up here but I'll never regret meeting you Maggie and having this time with you, so please don't apologize for any of it."

It was Maggie's turn to be speechless.

He reached out and took her hand in his.

"Now get over here and put that mouth of yours to some good use."

Maggie put her glass down and lowered herself onto his lap. He enfolded her in a rock-hard caress and she touched her lips off his in a whisper of a kiss. Then she smudged her lips against his, taking his lower lip into her mouth, sucking it gentle and slow. He groaned and she released it as she looked into his eyes and what she saw there in that unguarded moment caused her heart to soar, for there, in the dark amber of his eyes, were John's feelings for her, raw and exposed. The sight was mesmerizing.

She expected him to try to look away or disentangle himself but he didn't. He remained underneath her, his face turned up to hers, all his emotions laid bare, his vulnerabilities unmasked and on show - unhidden and unprotected. No words passed between them but so much was said. Maggie swallowed past the lump in her throat and felt her heart swell in her chest as a host of butterflies danced across her tummy. Without breaking eye contact she lowered her lips and kissed him again.

"Maggie, Jesus Maggie, what the fuck have you done to me," John whispered as he finally closed his eyes and kissed her as if he wanted to possess her heart and soul.

Somewhere inside the cabin a timer rang out and John smiled into the kiss. He managed to drag his lips away from Maggie's and announced, "Dinner is ready."

"Thank God," Maggie smiled, "or I thought I might have to eat you."

John laughed.

"Oh I'm all yours for dessert baby."

***

After finishing yet another delicious meal cooked by a man who seemed to be a master chef masquerading as a U.S. Navy SEAL, Maggie insisted on cleaning the kitchen. Once the plates were put away, she grabbed a beer for John and joined him on the couch. The heat from the fire and the extra glass of wine she'd had with dinner meant her bones felt like molten lava. John reached out and threw his arm around her, pulling her into his body and she was only too glad to take shelter there. He kissed the top of her head and she smiled as her head spun. She'd had the day from hell but here she was, as happy as she had ever been. She leaned into him and a small sigh escaped her.

John chuckled. "I'm thinking you like my cooking."

Maggie looked up into his laughing eyes.

"Can you tell me what that delicious concoction was?" she asked.

"That, my food-loving friend, was the ultimate in French comfort food known as Tartiflette and just what I thought the doctor might need this evening."

Maggie smiled. "The doctor can't imagine anything more perfect and may have eaten just a bit too much, I suppose it has a thousand calories."

John laughed again. "A gazillion but it's said the best way to work them off is to have wild sex with the chef."

Maggie laughed at the mischief twinkling in his eyes. "Is it now?" she asked

John nodded his head. "Uh huh," he husked as he lowered his head and kissed her.

White-hot desire flared through Maggie at the instance of his touch and she twisted herself around into his arms. She linked her hands together at the back of his neck and pulled him to her as she straddled his lap. His fingers dug into her buttocks as he pressed her against him and the large bulge of his desire caused her to groan with unashamed need into his mouth.

His breathing became ragged as he whispered, "Maggie," against her tongue.

Desperation devoured John and his hands reached for Maggie's breasts which seemed to swell with desire at his touch. Maggie was kissing him like there were no tomorrows and he could barely breathe through his need for her. He pulled her top over her head and yanked the bra down from her breasts, there was no way he could wait until he had the clasp undone. He took her nipple into his mouth and the world fell away as he licked, nipped, sucked and played with it between his teeth. Maggie arched into him as she called out his name and John knew he needed to be inside her as soon as possible or there was a distinct possibility he would come in his boxers.

He slid his hands to her hips and tugged at the zip on her jeans. Maggie wiggled agonizingly on his lap and soon the jeans were lying in a pile on the floor, swiftly followed by her panties. Switching his attention to her other breast, he looked up into her face and the fire burning in her eyes nearly stopped his heart.

Her hands left the back of his head and focused their attention on the buckle of his belt. Seconds later his cock throbbed under her touch and he couldn't wait any longer. He reached down to where his back-pack sat at the side of the sofa, and grabbed the box of condoms.

Maggie took one from the box and with a gaze that could have melted ice, she slid it over his cock. She then smiled as she raised herself up and lowered herself onto him.

John's head fell back in ecstasy as she slowly started to move, taking him deeper with each dip of her body. She gripped the back of the sofa, placing her arms on either side of his head and proceeded to increase her pace, writhing and grinding against him.

John felt his last shred of control slip away as he dug his fingers into her hips and pounded into her like a man possessed and for a split second he considered maybe he was.

"John, oh God John," Maggie screamed as she arched back into a pre-orgasmic movement much like a ballet dancer primes herself before soaring across the stage in one graceful leap. John slammed into her and she exploded around him. The incredible sight of her losing it to his touch robbed him of all rational thought as he plummeted after her into a chasm of orgasmic bliss.

Maggie was glad John's arms were around her as she felt she might float away. His chin rested on the top of her head as her cheek lay upon his heart. She listened to it beat frantically underneath her as their breathing started to normalize in the wake of the astounding high they had simultaneously hit just moments ago. John stroked her hair and held her to him like he never wanted to let her go. She was happy to lie against him and let the world turn, content to stay in his arms forever. She closed her eyes and breathed into him, almost tasting his unique scent of sandalwood and amber. The rhythm of his breath soothed her and she could feel herself drifting deliciously off into a world where she would never have to leave him.

John held Maggie in his arms as his heart desperately tried to steady itself. He didn't understand how he could feel the way he did about this woman who had only been in his life for the past five days but there was no denying it, he may have dated other women for months but his feelings for Maggie were way past anything he had felt for any of them.

The rational part of his brain argued he'd hand-picked those women exactly because he knew there was very little chance of forming a deep emotional attachment with any of them and to further ensure that would never happen he had kept contact to a minimum.

Maggie had unintentionally hi-jacked him from the outset. She'd slipped unseen past all his defenses and found a way into his heart. He closed his eyes and thought, *what if? What if I let her in? What if I give this a chance? She's strong, independent, feisty. Just the sort of woman who can handle me and all my baggage.*

For a moment he let himself imagine Maggie waiting for him post-deployment. He saw her in the hallway of his house in Virginia Beach, running towards him as he opened the front door. He smiled. How fucking good would that be? The smile had barely formed though when another image floated into his mind, an image he was all too familiar with and the presence of which caused a sharp stab of pain to his heart.

He was eight years old and back in the house in Virginia Beach. Dawn was just starting to break but the house was still swathed in the grey hues of the pre-morning light. He hid in the shadows on the stairs, clutching Blue, his favorite teddy bear and peered through the balusters at his parents as they held each other in a tight embrace. His father was suited and booted, ready to go. His mother wore a dusty pink nightgown, the one with the tiny white flowers on it. Her hair was loose and falling in chestnut colored waves down her back. His father pulled back, "Jeanine, I've really got to go," he whispered into her eyes before bending his head and kissing her.

"It's okay. Go," his mother replied, her voice tight and torn. "don't worry about us, we'll be okay here."

His father opened the door, took one look back and was gone.

The door closed. His mother fell against it, her arms dragging along its cold, uncaring surface as she slid to the floor. As her hands connected with the dark timber she curled into a ball and all John could hear were strange choking noises as she desperately tried to stifle her sobs.

He wondered if he should go to her when something warm splashed onto his hand. He swiped at his eyes and realized he was crying. He clutched Blue tighter, crept back up the stairs and hid his tears under the covers of his bed. Daddy had asked him to look after mommy but he didn't know how to do that when he was crying more than her.

Back in the cabin John's eyes flew open as he drew in a ragged breath, willing the memory away. He thought of his mother, independent and strong and he remembered the toll his father's choices and subsequently his, had taken on her and he let it galvanize his resolve.

No. No way am I going to ask that life of Maggie, he told himself, *she deserves better than that.*

With his decision made he brought his attention back to the only woman who had ever made him question his decision to stay single. Her breathing had slowed considerably and he could feel tiny puffs of breath against his chest. He suspected she was asleep and he smiled to himself, she really was unlike any woman he had ever met.

He slowly eased out of her and threw the used condom on the fire. He brought her legs around so they lay across his lap. He covered her with the fleece from the back of the sofa and cradled her in his arms. He sat like that with her for some time, breathing her in, kissing her coconut-scented hair and generally savoring every heart-rending moment of her. He thought of the endless nights that lay ahead of him in some God-forsaken dust-hole and knew the memories of this week with Maggie were all he was going to have to sustain him.

She burrowed into him and curled her arm around his neck. He looked down and saw her lips stretch into a lazy smile and he felt something shift deep within him. He couldn't imagine never seeing her again but he knew he had to let her go. The very thought of it had him pulling her closer and he held her tight for a long time. At some point he nodded off and was only awoken by the late night chill as the fire, the sole source of heat in the cabin, was reduced to dying embers. With Maggie in his arms John got up from the couch. She murmured something in her sleep.

"Shhhh," John soothed into her hair, "I got you."

She let out a contented sigh and he gently deposited her onto the bed. He stripped out of his clothes and lay beside her. He undid the clasp of her bra and gently removed it, whereupon he molded his naked form to hers. Skin to skin. Heartbeat to heartbeat. He snaked his arm around her waist and pulled her tight against him. In a few days he'd have to let her go but tonight she was his and he intended to hold her close.

FOURTEEN

Maggie opened her eyes and stared into the pre-dawn darkness. John's arm was slung lightly around her waist and his breath warmed her shoulder. She thought back over the three days since she had been released from Little Creek jail and how they had been three of the most wonderful days of her life. She'd spent every moment with John and when he hadn't been teaching her how to fly-fish or leading her along a trail, he'd been creating some culinary delight in the kitchen.

The nights and even the mornings had been taken up with delights of another kind and Maggie relished how her body hummed from the after-effects of his touch. She felt like a guitar which had been left in the corner of a bar, dusty and forgotten until one day a master guitar player wandered by and played the most wonderful tunes upon it.

She squeezed her eyes shut at the prospects of soon finding herself back in a dark corner, wondering when she would ever find herself in the hands of a master musician like John again. She twisted around and looked into his face. His breathing came in deep, regular beats and was that of a man immersed in sleep, free of the worries of the world. She was tempted to kiss him, only gently and on the forehead but she didn't dare. Her plan was to leave under the cover of darkness and she didn't want to risk waking him.

She knew he wouldn't like her sneaking off again but she didn't know what else to do. He'd been quiet and pre-occupied the night before and she knew the situation between them played on his mind but he hadn't broached the subject. He hadn't asked to see her again.

He didn't deploy for another few months and she knew his schedule was just as busy as her own but she would be willing to try and find the time to see him, so she didn't understand why he steadfastly refused to entertain the prospect of seeing her again.

She knew if she waited till the morning she would not only get upset when it came time to leave but there was a high probability she would blurt out what was on her mind and demand an answer. She suspected this was something he wouldn't be happy with and the last thing she wanted to do was part on a sour note.

John obviously believed there was nothing for them to discuss, so, when all was said and done she had decided it would be best to leave in the middle of the night. She was due to start the night-shift at Hillview at eight o'clock the next night so this way she could get back to New York in time to have a pre-shift nap.

This dream of a week was over. The cold and cruel talons of reality reached for her and ever the pragmatist, she knew the best thing to do was to just face it.

She closed her eyes, turned to John and inhaled his unique scent, then she lifted his arm and gently set it upon the sheet. She looked upon his perfect profile as the night-shadows played upon it and she dragged her heart out of the bed and tiptoed across the floor.

She dressed as quietly as she could and her heart leapt in her chest as John stirred and rolled over in the bed. She grabbed her back-pack and took out the thank you card she'd bought yesterday in Little Creek along with the bottle of eighteen year old Jameson Special Reserve Whiskey. She placed them both on the kitchen counter and pulled on her boots.

Careful not to jangle her keys, she walked very quietly to the front door only to find her exit blocked by Rock, who was lying across it as if he'd known all along what her plan was. She grinned at his sad, stubborn face and swallowed past the lump in her throat. She was going to miss this dog almost as much as his owner. She crouched down to pet him and he responded immediately to her touch. Bit by bit she coaxed him away from the door and when she could open it enough to squeeze through, she took her chance.

As soon as she was on the other side she could hear his tiny whimpers and her heart fell into her boots. Partially blinded by the tears suddenly clouding her vision she stumbled to her car in the dark and let it roll down the hill before turning the key in the ignition. She clicked her seat-belt, hit the gas and didn't look back.

***

John could feel the warmth of the first rays of sunlight upon his face but there was a chill he couldn't quite account for. He turned over onto his side and sent his arm out in search of the wonderful curves that had kept him warm throughout the night. Nothing. His hand connected with the cold, rumpled sheet and before he even had his eyes open a horrible sense of deja-vu crept over him. He opened one eye first and then the other to confirm what he already knew, once again Maggie had used the cover of night to make a clean getaway.

"Fuck!" he announced to the stark emptiness of the cabin.

He knew he'd been distant the night before. He knew he should have had the balls to have a discussion about where things stood between them but he had left it because, in truth, he was torn. He'd felt his resolve to not see her again slipping with each moment he'd spent in her company. The past three days had been three days of perfection and no woman had ever made him happier. He wanted to try and find a way to make things work between them but memories, both distant and recent, haunted him and he still believed he came with too high a price for Maggie to have to pay.

So, as much as he felt like they owed it to each other to at least say a proper goodbye, in a way she'd probably done them both a favor because if, this morning, she'd asked to see him again, he would have asked where and when.

He lay there looking at the ceiling, waves of desolation washing over him. Maggie had given him a glimpse of what life could be like if he just let her in and fuck, if it wasn't a tempting prospect. This past week was like a wonderful mirage but now the desert landscape of his life lay before him in all its arid and lonely glory. He rubbed at his chest and realized he was rubbing over his heart, trying to ease the dull throb of pain. He knew he was going to miss her but if how he was feeling right now was anything to go by then the coming months were going to be a new form of agony.

Rock whimpered at the door and John dragged himself from the bed and let him out. Just like before the dog ran to where Maggie's car had been parked and sniffed all around as if by the power of sniffing alone he could will her back. He then looked at John and John could swear his eyes were full of angry accusation.

He turned to go back into the cabin but stopped and stood in the doorway, shocked and disturbed at how different the place felt without Maggie. He didn't understand how one woman could make such a difference in so short a time but the tiny space seemed empty and deserted and he could only compare the way he felt to the first time he, his sister and mother had come here after the death of his father. It had taken him a long time to feel at ease in the place after that and he wondered how long it would be before he would be able to come here and not feel Maggie's absence as sharply as it cut through him right now.

He went to the kitchen and stopped when he saw the bottle of whiskey and the card. His heart rate increased and a heightened sense of anticipation, mixed with a trickle of foreboding, quickened through his bloodstream as he picked up the card and opened it.

Dear John,

thank you so much for an amazing week. I am taking the most wonderful memories back to New York with me. Thank you for all you did in relation to my car, protecting my modesty at the lake and just being there for me on the day of my arrest. I'm sure you hadn't imagined consorting with a felon during your time here in the Adirondacks.

I'm sorry to yet again leave without saying goodbye. However, if the truth be told, I'm a little sad at the prospect and whatever about saying goodbye to you, there is no way I can face Rock. Your dog has completely stolen my heart.

Actually, since I'm telling the truth here, I may as well admit you have stolen a bit of it too. I don't normally put myself on the line like this but then again, I don't normally run into guys like you every day either. Actually, I've never run into a guy quite like you in thirty-six years..... But now I'm rambling, trying to put off what I have to say. Big breath.

You're a great guy John and I think you deserve somebody in your life. I understand your reasons for not letting anyone in but this has to make for a lonely life for you. I don't like to think of you being lonely like that.... Even though we have only known each other for just over a week, I believe there is something between us that could develop into something special if given the chance. (God, I'm dying here writing this...) I could never imagine writing something like this to any other man, only you. I think you know there is something between us too. You deserve to have someone to come back to John. I'd like if that someone could be me.

Take care,

Maggie.

John released the breath he didn't realize he'd been holding and whispered to the cold morning air, "Where and when Maggie? Where and when?" as he closed his eyes and shook his head.

He made a cup of coffee, sat on the veranda and watched as the glow of the autumn sunrise warmed the landscape around him. An hour later he was gone. The Raptor chewed up the road as he headed back to reality. Eminem, Guns n Roses, ACDC and a host of other rappers and rockers kept him company along the way, blaring from the speakers as he desperately tried to leave the memories of the past week behind and blast away the loneliness that threatened to swallow him whole.

FIFTEEN

New York

Maggie rubbed at her eyes as the alarm on her phone beeped furiously beside her. Instead of a nap she'd fallen into a deep sleep and currently felt like something from the zombie apocalypse. She fumbled out of bed, made a mug of very strong coffee, had a shower and an hour later, finally feeling somewhat perky, she presented herself for the night shift at the emergency room of Hillview Hospital. Memories of her last shift played on her mind and she prayed it would be a quiet night without any major incidents.

Her distracted thoughts were the only reason she could think of as to why it took her a while to notice the staff were a little bit off. Actually, it seemed they were only a little bit off with her, not each other. Those who usually greeted her with a cheery hello merely half smiled and said, "Hi Maggie," as if they didn't expect to see her there.

Jesus, I've only been gone a week, Maggie thought to herself.

However, when she rocked up to the E.R. Manager's desk she knew something was seriously wrong as she looked into the confused face of Diane Byrne.

"Maggie, what the hell are you doing here?" Diane asked.

Now it was Maggie's turn to look confused.

"I work here, remember?" she replied with a slight edge to her voice.

She watched as a frown marred Diane's beautiful Jamaican skin.

"Maggie, didn't you receive the letter? Have you checked your emails since you left?" Diane asked, her voice a melody of concern.

Maggie noted how she had said "the letter", not, "a letter" but "the letter." She knew this wasn't good. "The letter" lent weight and significance to whatever this piece of correspondence was and she didn't like the sound of that.

"Maggie?" Diane prompted.

"No," Maggie replied, "I only just got back today and I was exhausted and had a nap and then came straight here. What's the story? What letter are you talking about?"

Diane pursed her lips and dipped her head at the same time and Maggie held her breath.

"The letter that informs you of your suspension whilst an internal inquiry is undertaken into your behavior on the last night you worked. You can't come back to work until the inquiry is concluded Maggie. All the details are in the letter. I sent you an email to say how sorry I was and hoped to be welcoming you back to work soon.

"What?" Maggie almost shouted, "inquiry? What freaking inquiry?"

Her outburst drew a number of curious glances but Maggie didn't care, she couldn't believe her ears, *she was being investigated by the hospital?*

Diane watched as her friend and one of the finest physicians she'd ever had the pleasure to work with, tried to digest the news that no doctor ever wants to hear. Maggie's face contorted into a mask of confusion, hurt and disbelief. Diane's heart went out to her but there was very little she could do. Maggie grasped the counter with both hands, as if to steady herself and Diane was out of her seat in seconds. She knew she'd take the news hard, after all not too many people came as committed to their job as Maggie.

She put her arm around her and guided her to a small assessment room that, mercifully, was empty.

Maggie sat on the treatment bed and stared at the floor.

Diane was at a loss as to what to do.

"Can I get you anything?" she asked.

Maggie shook her head.

Diane sat in the chair in the corner.

"I'm sorry Maggie, you don't deserve this," she soothed, her voice rich with sympathy.

Maggie raised her head. "How long is it going to take?"

Diane shook her head. "I don't know. Typically these things take six to eight weeks but it could take longer with Thanksgiving and Christmas. I think it's probably best to see it as a chance to take a much deserved break and do some things you've always wanted to do but never had the time."

Maggie turned and looked at her and Diane had to fight back the tears at the hurt in Maggie's eyes.

"Are they aware of my arrest?" Maggie asked.

Diane nodded. "Yes, it's what spurred them on to suspend you and launch a full inquiry into the events of that night. I'm so sorry Maggie, it's not fair but there's nothing you or I can do about it. I'd say, go home, get some rest, take a holiday and get the best legal representation you can afford and fight this thing."

Maggie nodded.

Diane could hear the phone ringing on her desk.

"I've got to get back to my desk and answer the damn phone. Wait here, I'll be back in a few minutes."

Five minutes later Diane walked back into the small assessment room but Maggie was gone.

***

Virginia Beach

John threw his sports bag into the back of the Raptor and climbed into the driver's seat. It was Friday and he'd completed his first week back at base. Their next deployment was scheduled for mid-January and due to increased terrorist activity in Somalia, they were headed to Djibouti.

The pirates and warlords that once preyed on commercial tankers up and down the Somali coast had diversified and were now in the hostage taking business with their efforts focused on aid agencies and NGOs in Somalia and neighboring Kenya. This was bad enough news in itself but it was made worse by the fact they could negotiate a "quick sale" of captives with Somalia terrorist groups who wanted nothing more than to parade foreign hostages in front of a camera and threaten all manner of heinous acts.

His team had been informed their next deployment would be focused on hostage rescue and terrorist apprehension or elimination. This meant their training and preparation in the coming months would be specific to infiltration, execution and extraction, which translated into lots of hard physical training and this suited John perfectly. The harder he drove himself during the day, the less time he had to think at night. And there was only one thing uppermost in his thoughts, Maggie.

He had a weekend of almost torturous physical activity mapped out for himself but tonight he was going to meet some of the guys for a bite to eat and a few beers. Twenty minutes later he rocked up to Cody's Bar, possibly the most unglamorous bar in Virginia Beach with a few booths along one wall and just enough room for two pool tables but it was owned by an ex-SEAL and served the best steak in town and was a place where guys from the teams could eat and drink in peace. SEAL-baiters and frog-hogs knew better than to darken its door.

A few hours later, mellow from a few beers and laughs with the boys, he climbed into the Raptor and faced into the same challenge he had faced for the last five nights - not thinking about Maggie.

Apart from a text he'd sent to make sure she'd got back to New York okay they'd had no contact. And it was killing him. He missed her voice and her laugh. He missed the spark and fire in her eyes and God help him but he missed the silken feel of her skin under his fingertips. He pulled up outside his house with a semi-hard cock just thinking about her.

"Fuck," he exclaimed as he opened the front door and marched through the house. Rock bounded up to him in his usual over-enthusiastic style and John had to smile at his dog's affectionate antics.

He went straight to the kitchen and grabbed a crystal tumbler and the bottle of Jameson Maggie had bought him. He half-filled the glass with the amber liquid and sat out on his deck, breathing in the salty air. The night was fresh and reminded him of the last night in the Adirondacks with Maggie.

So far he had managed to distract himself from thinking too much about her during the day but the nights were driving him crazy. Every night, right about this time, he craved her. His dreams were full of the scent of coconut and jasmine and he would wake in the middle of the night with his arm outstretched, looking for her, only to find a cold and crumpled bed-sheet. He wondered if she was the same? Did she miss him? He thought about her card. It was pretty much all he thought about.

"you deserve someone to come back to. I'd like that someone to be me."

The prospect to give this thing between them a chance was tempting and he suspected it would be a hell of a lot easier than trying to figure out how he was supposed to forget her because if he was honest with himself he wasn't doing very well on that score. His craving for her only intensified as each night passed.

He slugged back the whiskey and mused to himself how much it reminded him of the woman he was trying to forget - fiery and full-bodied. He refilled his glass and made a decision he was later to blame on the Irish fire-water. He picked up his cell phone, scrolled through to Maggie's number and started a text:

"Hey, how's it going back in NY?"

His thumb hovered over the send button as he tried to decide whether to send it or not but then he reasoned to himself, *Fuck it. It's Friday night, I'm just checking in with a friend.*

He pressed send as a voice in his head told him he had just tried to sell himself the greatest bullshit story of all time. He was no "friend", he was more like a drowning man in need of a lifeline.

He was just about to take another drink of whiskey when his phone buzzed, telling him he had a message.

"Hey you, NY not so good. Good to hear from you :-) How's VB?"

John tried to tell himself the warm, fuzzy feeling he felt at the appearance of the words on the screen were the effects of the whiskey but another part of him knew it was because the lifeline he so desperately needed was at his fingertips.

"Exhausting but good. What's up with NY?"

The phone remained silent and after a few minutes John started to wonder if texting on a Friday night was such a good idea. He had stupidly and arrogantly assumed she would be on her own but what if she was with someone? At eleven o'clock on a Friday night it was more than a possibility. The mere thought of another man's hands or lips anywhere near Maggie sent a shaft of something through him so intense he could hardly breathe. He jumped up from his seat and dragged his fingers through his hair.

"Fuck," he exclaimed to the cool night air, "fuck."

Of all the things he had tried not to think about, Maggie being with someone else hadn't been one of them but now he couldn't get the image out of his mind or the accompanying twist of jealousy out of his gut.

He grabbed the bottle of whiskey and was just about to take a slug from the bottle when his phone buzzed. He snatched it up from the table.

"Suspended from job. Hospital inquiry into events of fateful night. Not sure what to do with myself now. Kinda bummed. Might just split, take a road trip, go see a friend in Florida. On the upside my apartment has never been so tidy."

Shit.   John couldn't believe what he was reading.   Maggie suspended from her job? Crap. Anger rushed through his veins. How could it be that someone like Maggie ended up under investigation? She was one of the good guys! He thought about how upset she must be and without hesitation pressed the dial button.

She picked up on the second ring. "Hey, how you doing?'

Just the sound of her voice was enough to tie his stomach up in knots.

"Hey, yourself. More to the point, how are you doing?"

"All things considered, not too bad, I've caught up on a lot of sleep and my apartment is spotless. I'm up to date with all of my bills and my laundry's done so, you know, go me."

John wasn't fooled by her chipper words or tone. He could feel her hurt coming through the phone and cursed the fact he was hundreds of miles away. His arms ached to hold her and he wanted to soothe her whilst holding her against him, feeling her breath against his chest.

"Maggie, I asked how're you doing not what you've been doing."

A few seconds silence passed, then her voice, low and strained, sounded through his phone.

"I've been better John. To be honest, I never thought I'd be suspended from my job, a job I've given my all to and which I love. It's probably going to take a few months to resolve and I'm not sure what the outcome will be but I don't know what to do with myself."

Her voice trailed off and the uncertainty and dejection in it tore at his heart. He didn't know what to say.

"A road-trip sounds like a good idea. You're thinking of driving to Florida?"

"Yeah, a friend of mine, Ruby, is working down there at the moment and has been pestering me for the past few months to come down and visit. Of course, I never had the time but that's not something I can complain about now."

John listened and couldn't miss the edge of bitter regret in her tone. God but he wanted to see her, to hold her, to kiss her.... He shook his head, the whiskey was starting to take hold.

"Virginia Beach is on the way to Florida."

The words were out before he had time to think them through but he knew in his soul he needed to see her. The words from her card, the words that haunted him, ran through his mind.

"you deserve someone to come back to. I'd like that someone to be me."

Silence.

He looked at the phone to see if he had lost the connection. He hadn't but still there was silence.

"Maggie?" he prompted.

He heard a sharp intake of breath and then she spoke.

"John, I'm not sure what you're saying to me. If you're asking me to stop off to see you in Virginia Beach on my way to Florida..... I don't know. I'm a bit of an emotional mess right now and you've made it clear how things stand between us, so to be honest I'm not really up for any more emotional roller-coasting at the minute."

Her voice fell to a whisper.

"I miss you John and I'm not in a place right now where I can put myself through much more emotionally, so whereas I'm sure Virginia Beach is a real nice place with lots to see and do, it's not really on my itinerary."

John winced at her words and the way her voiced cracked at the end.

He knew this was it, he needed to call it, to make his mind up. Was he going to give his feelings for Maggie a chance and let this incredible connection between them grow or was he going to walk away for good, hang up the phone and never speak to her again.

There was only one option. There had only ever been one option. He'd thought it was a choice but it was no choice at all. He needed her as sure as he needed air to breathe and he needed to give them a chance, to see if they could make it.

"Maggie, I've been thinking about your card and what you said about me deserving someone to come back to. I'd like the chance to talk about it if you could bring yourself to stop off in Virginia Beach because I don't think I deserve you but I'd like that someone to be you."

He heard a soft gasp and smiled to himself. He held his breath as he waited for her response.

"I'll think about it John, as long as Rock is okay with it."

He could hear the smile in her voice and couldn't help the stupid grin that cracked up half his face.

"Oh he's rolling out the welcome mat as we speak."

She laughed. "Well that's nice to hear. I'm going to go now, I have a long drive planned for tomorrow and I need to get some sleep. It's good to hear your voice John."

John's face scrunched up in confusion. Did that mean she was coming to see him or was she going straight to Florida?

"Well do I get the guest room ready or not?"

A few seconds silence.

"I'll let you know. Goodnight John and give Rock a kiss from me."

With that she was gone and he was left wondering where he stood, which, he supposed, was all he deserved.

SIXTEEN

New York

Maggie couldn't believe the phone call she'd had with John the night before. It had been a shining light in what had proven to be a very dark week and she'd gone to bed in considerably brighter form. He'd actually thought about what she had to say in her card and wanted to give this thing a chance between them. She hadn't been prepared to commit to anything on the phone but she had spent the night thinking about it. Her mind wasn't fully made up, after all, he blew so hot and cold and she wasn't in the best frame of mind for that right now but the logistics of spending time together just got a whole lot easier since time was something she now had an abundance of.

She dragged her suitcase across the hallway and knocked on her neighbor's door. It was probably a bit early for Andy but she had no choice, she wanted to get on the road early. She heard a bolt being pulled on the other side and the words, "who the hell is up at this time of the mawning."

She chuckled to herself, Andy was not a morning person.

"Oh come on Andy," she laughed, "cheer up, it's only me."

The door opened.

"Maggie, what the fuck?"

Andy stood there, all five foot three of him, his black hair under the dubious control of a hairnet and his body encased in a red silk kimono with perfectly painted scarlet toenails peeping out at the bottom.

Maggie smiled at the vision before her. Andy was an institution on the New York club scene and could command up to ten thousand dollars a night for his unique cabaret act. He'd come to America from Thailand over twenty years ago as some designer's plaything but he had made this city his own. As a rule, he never got out of bed before midday.

"I'm going on a road trip and I want to make sure you still have spare keys for my apartment and mailbox. I need you to keep my plants alive and I may need you to open some mail for me as I'm not sure how long I'm going to be gone."

"Whey the fuck ah you going?" he asked, as if he should have been consulted.

"I'm not sure, I'm planning on going to see Ruby in Florida but I might take a detour to Virginia Beach on the way."

Andy perked up at the sound of Ruby, she was one of his favorite people on the planet after all but his eyes narrowed suspiciously at the sound of Virginia Beach.

"What's in Veeginia Beach?" Whenever Andy dropped the "r" sound from a word he tended to overcompensate with the pronunciation of the remaining letters.

Maggie hadn't had a chance to fill him in on what had happened in the Adirondacks and with everything else that had happened she hadn't felt like talking about it but she knew she wasn't going to get away without telling him something about what was in Virginia Beach. She smiled.

"A sexy as hell navy SEAL who I met on my trip to the Adirondacks, that's what's in Virginia Beach and if things work out you might just get to meet him."

Andy's eyes widened with delight.

"Well what the hell ah you waiting here foh," he announced, "go get that beast and don't think about yo plants, they ah safe with me. All I ask is foh some updates."

He winked in that camp style he had, all hands on hips and pouty lips. Maggie laughed, enveloped him in a bear-hug, turned around and jumped in the elevator.

***

Virginia Beach

John was wondering if he should bother with the five mile soft-sand run he had planned. After the two hours he'd spent in the gym this morning and the three mile open water swim he'd completed this afternoon he was thinking it might be an idea to conserve some energy, just in case Maggie decided to accept his invitation. However, if she decided to drive straight to Florida he was going to need more than just a five mile run to tire him out and calm him down.

He'd done nothing but think about his invitation since she'd hung up the phone and he'd spent half the night and most of the day second-guessing and tormenting himself. The decision to give this thing a go between them had seemed so simple after a few beers and half a bottle of whiskey but now in the harsh light of day he wasn't so sure. He wanted to, there was no doubt about that and hearing Maggie on the phone last night had only served to underline how much he missed and cared about her. He just wasn't so sure he could actually *do* it and he was both excited and nervous all at the same time.

He looked down the beach. The sun was shining and a light breeze was coming off the ocean, perfect running weather. He checked his watch. Three thirty pm and he still hadn't heard from her.

Fuck it, he silently swore to himself. It looked like a ten mile run was more of what he was going to need. Rock barked beside him, eager to get to the beach.

"Come on buddy," he said as he crossed the boardwalk and let him off the leash. Rock shot off across the sand, delighted to be free. John grinned to himself.

"Don't overdo it there champ, we've a few miles to cover," he laughed, as he tucked his head into his chest and started to run.

He was about two miles down the beach when he felt his phone buzz in his pocket. He took it out and the number one sat on top of the message icon. He pressed it and a message from Maggie popped up.

"*So, Virginia Beach looks nice.*"

He smiled. He liked how he smiled a lot more since Maggie came into his life. He tapped in a quick response and pressed send.

"*Whereabouts are you?*"

Seconds later his phone buzzed again.

"At the beach, watching a really cute guy running with his even cuter dog."

John laughed and looked up towards the boardwalk. She wasn't hard to spot, her flame-colored hair blowing in the wind. She waved and he smiled as he started to run towards her.

He thought he was keeping a good pace until Rock shot past him like an RPG and made a beeline for Maggie. By the time he reached her his dog was making a complete fool of himself, jumping, squealing and barking with joy. Maggie was doing her best to pet him and laughing her head off.

The sound of her laughter set off a strange tingling in his abdomen and he suddenly felt like an awkward sixteen year old in the presence of his teenage crush. A shyness he didn't understand crept over him and instead of taking Maggie in his arms and kissing her like he had imagined, he simply stood where he was and said, "Hey you."

Maggie looked at him, her eyes still shining with laughter.

"Hey," she said, her tone asking the question she didn't put into words.

He understood. That was the thing about him and Maggie, there seemed to be this current of communication constantly running between them that neither of them had to figure out.

He smiled. "I'm really glad you're here."

Maggie smiled back and damn if that smile didn't light him up like a fucking Christmas tree.

"I'm glad I'm here too. I really missed this damn dog."

John laughed. "Not as much as he missed you. Come on let's get you settled in at Casa Sullivan and Rock."

***

John noticed Maggie's look of surprise as soon as she entered the house.

"What? Not what you expected?" he asked.

Maggie looked at him, not sure what to say, so she opted for the truth.

"No. It's more like a family home, not a bachelor pad."

John grinned. "That's because it was my family home. This is where I grew up, well mostly, once we stopped moving around."

He dropped her suitcase at the bottom of the stairs.

"Come on through, what can I get you, wine or beer?"

"If you've got the same kinda wine in Virginia Beach as you had in the Adirondacks then I'll take a wine please."

Maggie took in the beautiful decor as she followed John through the open plan house. It was classic American meets what she presumed was Provence, from her limited knowledge of France, and she was struck by the feeling of warmth. This house was very much a home.

She smiled to herself when she saw her card taking pride of place on the dining table. John handed her a glass of wine but didn't refer to the card.

"Come on, we can sit out on the deck," he suggested.

Practically the whole back part of the house was glass which afforded spectacular views of the beach and the Atlantic Ocean. The part leading off the dining area was divided into panels which folded into each other as John pushed them along a hidden rail. He stepped out onto the deck and sat in one of the two Adirondack chairs. Maggie sat in the other one.

"This is beautiful," she announced, her voice low and husky.

"Thanks," John agreed, "it's not a bad place to spend my time, when I'm in the country."

Maggie took her eyes off the ocean and looked at him. "How long do you have before you have to go overseas again?"

"We're scheduled to ship out mid-January."

"And you'll be gone for six months?"

"Minimum."

Silence.

Both of them looked at the Ocean as if its depths held a solution to their unspoken dilemma. They had time but was it enough time to make a go of this thing between them or would they just be getting to know each other when they'd have to part? John reached across and intertwined his fingers between Maggie's. Maggie looked over at him, put her glass down and got up from her chair.

"I suppose there's no time to waste then," she declared, her voice thick with lust as she lowered herself onto John and connected her lips to his. To say this was a kiss would be an understatement, this was a claiming. Maggie didn't just kiss him with her lips but with her entire body.

John's response was swift and powerful. He pulled her to him and devoured her like a man who hadn't had sustenance in over a week. His head spun as he lost himself in the kiss and surrendered to her touch.

"Maggie, Maggie, Maggie, what the fuck have you done to me?" he whispered into her mouth as she paused to pull his tee-shirt up.

She pulled back, smiled and looked into his eyes.

"I don't know John, what have I done to you?" she asked. "Or would you rather find out what I'm going to do to you?"

He didn't have a chance to respond before she pulled his tee-shirt up and took his nipple between her teeth. The effect was electric and desire, hot and fluid, crackled through him. His body's response was instantaneous and he jerked in a reflex-like movement whilst gasping for breath at the same time.

Maggie pushed him firmly back against the chair with one hand whilst the other moved lower to caress his already rock hard cock.

"Easy there tiger," she laughed, "just sit back and enjoy the show."

She then reached inside his boxers and John knew he wasn't going to last long against this Maggie onslaught.

"I suggest we take this show inside," he whispered into her ear.

Maggie laughed. "I suggest you might be right."

They made it as far as the couch when John couldn't hold himself back any more. He pulled Maggie to him and crushed his lips to hers. He dragged her sweater over her head and tried to control his ragged breathing as he took in the sight of her standing in front of him in only her jeans and a black lace bra. A sound, low and guttural, escaped from his lips as he slid the bra-straps down her shoulders.

Maggie reached behind her.

"Allow me," she offered, her voice heavy with desire.

The bra fell away and for a moment John had to close his eyes as he fought to keep some semblance of control. She slipped her arms around his neck, pressing her incredible breasts against him and whispered in his ear.

"I want you John."

That was it. He lost it. The rest of it happened in a blur of hands, lips, tongue, fingers, breasts, skin and mind-blowing orgasm.

Afterwards he held Maggie against him on the couch. He loved the way her curves melded into him, as if they were a perfect physical match, the product of two molds in heaven that said, "this goes with that." Her hair was spread across his chest and he couldn't resist the urge to stroke it.

"So do all first-time visitors to Virginia Beach receive this sort of welcome?" Maggie chuckled into his chest.

John laughed. "Only the special ones."

Maggie smiled. "I'm certainly feeling very special right now."

It was John's turn to smile. "Well I hope you're not in any rush to get to Florida because I aim to make you feel very special for as long as you're here."

SEVENTEEN

Maggie lay in bed and thought to herself just how much John had kept his promise since the night she'd arrived. Apart from eating and bathroom breaks, they'd spent the rest of that weekend in the bedroom and he'd made her feel very special indeed. It was now just over a week since she'd arrived and it had been a week of laughs, sunset walks, great conversation and scorching hot sex.

The one thing they hadn't talked about though was how long he wanted her to stay. She couldn't help wondering what he'd meant when he'd said he wanted to give this thing between them a go. Did he mean for her to come for a week and then go on to Florida and then stop by again on her way back to New York, where he intended to come and see her at weekends? Or did he mean for her to stay here in Virginia Beach and see where things went? She hadn't a clue.

She shifted onto her side in the bed and could just make out the beginnings of daylight peeping through the gap in the curtains. John's bedroom looked out across the ocean and she thought how amazing it would be to see the sun rise across the Atlantic, after all it wasn't something she could treat herself to in New York.

She smiled as she lifted his heavy arm from around her waist and silently made her way to the window. Pulling the curtain back just enough to see the sun start to warm the ocean, she gasped at the beauty of the colors as she watched the grey of the early morning ocean turn pink, purple, orange and gold.

John reached out his arm and instead of connecting with warm curves, it connected with a rumpled, cold sheet. His eyes flew open.

No. Not again, he thought as he sat straight up in the bed.

He immediately spotted Maggie over by the window, the sweet curves he had searched for perfectly silhouetted against the early morning light and relief flooded through him. They hadn't discussed what the plan was in relation to seeing each other now they had agreed to give this thing a go between them but the past week had been amazing and he wasn't ready for her to leave yet. If he was totally honest with himself he was starting to think he never would be.

He'd thought he might find it strange having her here for more than a night or two, especially since she was the only woman he had ever brought into the house, but just like back at the cabin, it was almost as if she belonged here.

He loved walking in the door and being met with her smile. He loved the faint scent of her around the house and making love to her every night. He loved how she hungered for him and how her hunger never seemed to wane, if anything it seemed to increase by the day. To be wanted like that was the biggest turn-on he'd ever known.

Maggie was so entranced by the beauty of the sunrise she didn't hear John get out of bed but she was glad of the warmth of his body as he slid his arms around her waist and enveloped her into his heat.

"Has anyone ever told you, you're the sexiest woman alive," he murmured into her ear.

Maggie chuckled. "I hear it all the time."

John smiled into the nape of her neck before placing a feather-light kiss just below her ear. "I'm not sure how I feel about that."

Maggie pressed herself into him and raised her arms so they coiled around his neck. "Too bad. You hang out with a sex bomb like me and you've got to accept other guys are gonna notice."

He knew she was only teasing him but her words caused a tightening in his abdomen all the same. The thought of another guy running his hands over her sensational curves, like he was doing right now, quickened his pulse and set his nerves on edge. The possibility of some other guy bringing her to orgasm and watching her face as she exploded into bliss had his balls in knots.

No fucking way, a voice, he barely recognized, raged in his head, *no way, it's not happening. Ever.*

He pulled her against him as his hand trailed up from her hip, dipped into her waist and cupped her breast.

"You're mine, Maggie," he growled into her ear, "all mine.

Maggie surrendered herself to the wonderful sensations John's touch released into her body and tried not to think too much about what he'd said.

The possessive growl of, "you're mine" was the first indication she'd had that they were in an exclusive relationship, or they were in a relationship at all. He continued to kiss the back of her neck and now his fingers teased her nipples. Frissons of desire warmed her body and she knew she was only seconds away from the point of no return. She didn't want to ruin the moment but she needed to know more about how he saw things between them.

She squirmed under his touch and rubbed herself against his hard length. John groaned and moved one of his hands lower. Maggie shivered as it slid between her legs.

"You know if you keep this up, I won't be able to leave for Florida tomorrow," she said in a husky voice overflowing with need.

John stopped everything he was doing. Actually it felt more to Maggie like he froze.

"What?" he asked, a tightness in his voice. "Why the hell would you be leaving for Florida tomorrow?"

Maggie smiled to herself. It didn't sound like he was too crazy about the idea.

"That's where I was going when I decided to stop off and see you Sailor Boy, remember?"

John still didn't move. "Yes, I seem to remember you had some sort of road-trip planned all right but I thought me and my little sailor boy here had done a pretty good job of convincing you to abandon that idea."

Maggie laughed and turned around in his arms. She looked up into his face and was struck by his dismayed expression.

"Well I don't want to overstay my welcome," she smiled up at him.

John smiled back and looked down at the space between them, where the hard evidence of his arousal nudged her stomach.

"Does it look like you've overstayed your welcome?" he grinned.

Maggie laughed. "No but you know what I mean, I don't want to make any presumptions about staying here. I'm afraid of things being too much too soon."

John sighed and rested his forehead against Maggie's.

"Well, I was kind of hoping to get past the welcome stage and move on to the "getting to know you" stage and I think that's going to take a while. I know you miss your job and hanging around Virginia Beach waiting for me to come home probably isn't your idea of fun but when I said I wanted to give this thing between us a go Maggie, I meant it. I'm not making any promises about being perfect boyfriend material but I want to try. You could get a call back to work tomorrow and I deploy in ten weeks and the one thing we won't have then is time, so I say we make the most of it and spend as much time together as possible."

He paused and a devilish grin broke out across his face before he continued. "Besides, tomorrow wouldn't be the best day for travelling, I've heard there's been an invasion of giant leprechauns in North Carolina and the Department of Defense are advising people not to travel."

Maggie pulled back and stared at him, then she caught the glint of mischief in his eyes and threw her head back and laughed. But this was no ordinary laugh, this was a "from the bottom of her soul" gigantic belly-laugh that shook her whole body.

John marveled at the wonderful sound reverberating throughout his house and how the vibration of her laughter caused a tingling sensation to run in unseen channels all over his body.

"Giant leprechauns?" Maggie asked, her tone telling him she didn't believe a word of it.

He smiled and pulled her closer. "Trust me on this, I'm Special Forces, I know these things," he half-laughed and half-whispered into her mouth.

His lips descended on Maggie's and her last conscious thought before surrendering to total bliss was, *looks like Florida can wait.*

EIGHTEEN

The following weeks passed in pretty much the same manner as the first and every Sunday evening Maggie would joke that she'd best be off to Florida and John would respond with some equally outlandish reason as to why she should stay in Virginia Beach. An alien invasion in Georgia, snow drifts in Florida and the discovery of dragons in South Carolina were all risks he couldn't possibly let her take.

Of course, the biggest risk of all was the man who kept her in Virginia Beach. Each week had seen him take another piece of her heart and she knew she was tumbling into love, free-falling helplessly and there was nothing she could or wanted to do about it.

She hoped he felt the same way but she couldn't be sure. At times his eyes brimmed with so much emotion he looked like he was about to shatter from the pressure of trying to keep it all in. At other times he was remote and closed-off and these were the times she feared they weren't on an equal emotional footing.

She put most of these withdrawn episodes down to the pressures of his job and concerns for his two team-mates who still struggled with their injuries. However, she was taking it as a positive sign that he was taking her to his sister's house for Thanksgiving.

His sister lived in Richmond, was married to George, a corporate attorney, had three children and taught English and French at the University of Richmond, just like her mother before her.

She was John's closest living relative and Maggie was nervous as hell about meeting her and to compound matters, she hadn't exactly packed for a semi-casual thanksgiving weekend in Virginia. Her suitcase of jeans, sweaters and tee-shirts didn't quite cut it and she'd told John to go without her but it seemed his sister wasn't taking no for an answer when it came to meeting the only woman her brother had let into his life in twelve years.

They were on their approach to Richmond now and John steered the Raptor off the highway. Maggie looked over at him and marveled at how he looked like he had just stepped from the pages of a men's fashion magazine in his beige, chino-style pants, light blue cotton shirt and navy sweater. She had managed to cobble together a decent outfit of black jeans and a dark green tunic-style sweater from a last-minute shopping expedition but still felt self-conscious.

John looked over at Maggie. The closer they got to Richmond, the less she spoke and she hadn't said anything at all in the last five minutes, which had to be some kind of record. He reached over and placed his hand on her thigh.

"It'll be fine, Maggie," he assured her.

She looked over at him and smiled. "That's easy for you to say, you know these people."

John laughed. "Yes, I do and that's all they are, people, not girlfriend-eating monsters."

Maggie laughed. She supposed he was right but she still couldn't help being nervous.

They passed the university and were soon driving through the affluent neighborhood of Westham. A few minutes later John turned off the main road and drove along a secondary road from which he steered the truck onto a private driveway. Rock was going nuts with excitement and pacing along the back seat. Over the past few weeks Maggie had successfully trained him, with the liberal application of treats, to sit in the back. She reached behind her to pet him, wishing she could share his excitement.

A few seconds later the picture perfect colonial style home of a successful upper middle class family came into view. Maggie drew in a sharp breath. John squeezed her hand and smiled.

"I promise I'll be by your side the whole time."

Maggie smiled weakly and was just about to reply when the air was filled with a high pitched squeal.

"Uncy Don! Uncy Don! Wocky, wocky, I'm here."

John burst out laughing. "They've sent their most evil emissary as the welcoming committee."

Maggie looked out the window to see the most adorable two year old girl jumping up and down with excitement, her dark brown curls bouncing around her chubby cheeks and her caramel colored eyes gleaming with excitement.

She laughed. "She might not be able to swallow me whole but she looks like she could take a fair chunk out of me."

John got out of the truck and scooped his niece up into the air, which resulted in more high-pitched squeals. Maggie got out and released Rock before he combusted. John had explained this is where he stayed when John was on deployment, so it was like his second home. He had also warned her she could expect to take a back seat in his affections as the dog adored the three kids. Judging from the way Rock was licking Sophie's face, she didn't doubt it.

"Uncle John!"

A young boy of about eight years of age burst from the house and hurled himself at John.

John laughed. "Hey buddy," he said as he reached down to ruffle his nephew's hair.

A few seconds later an older boy appeared. She knew from what John had told her this was Marc, his oldest nephew but she wasn't prepared for how much he looked like his uncle. John's house was full of family photos of when he and his sister were children and it was as if Maggie was watching one of those photos come to life in front of her.

Marc was a much cooler emotional prospect than his siblings and approached with his hands in his pockets and the practiced nonchalance of a pre-teen but his smile gave away his absolute delight at seeing his uncle John.

John high-fived him as Maggie reached into the back of the truck for the flowers and post-dinner treats. When she turned around, a carbon copy of John's mother was making her way towards them, a huge smile on her face. She and John took each other into a warm embrace and then she turned her attention to Maggie.

"Hi, I'm Juliette," she said, her eyes brimming with kind curiosity and her hand extended.

Maggie shook her hand.

"Maggie," she replied, "I'm pleased to meet you."

Juliette's smile widened.

"Oh these are for you," Maggie said as she placed the flowers in Juliette's hands.

"Thank you," Juliette said and then motioned towards the house, "come on let's get inside and rescue George from the kitchen."

The two year old cherub known as Sophie had both her arms encircled around John's neck and his youngest nephew, Luc, held onto his hand.

Marc fell into step beside Maggie, his hands now safely back in his pockets and his eyes focused on the driveway. Maggie could almost feel his shyness.

"Hi Maggie, I'm Marc," he said in a quiet voice.

Maggie smiled over at him and said, "I'm very pleased to meet you Marc."

Marc glanced sideways at her and smiled and again she was struck at just how like his uncle he was.

Sophie waved from John's shoulder. "Hi Aggie, my name is Sophie, I'm peesed to meet you too."

Everybody laughed as they went into the house and that set the tone for the whole day. The next few hours were a happy mix of laughter, teasing and easy conversation. Maggie was touched at the closeness between John and his sister and amazed at the loving relationship he had with the children.

She hadn't really thought about this side of him and she felt another piece of her heart slip away as she watched the easy affection he shared with them. Juliette's husband, George, seemed to pick up on her nerves and had gone out of his way to make her feel comfortable which had eased her stress levels considerably and she'd found herself enjoying the day much more than she'd thought possible.

They'd taken a break from eating after the turkey and Maggie, John, Rock and the kids had all gone for a walk but now everyone was seated back at the table as Juliette approached with a stunning looking cake.

Maggie wondered why there were a number of candles on it and figured maybe it was George's birthday. Sophie bounced up and down with excitement on John's knee and Maggie turned to laugh at him but the laugh died away in her throat as she noted his strained expression.

"I'm not sure if John has told you Maggie," Juliette spoke, "but today is also our mother's birthday."

Maggie looked at Juliette and glanced quickly at John, who was staring steadfastly at the cake.

She turned back to face Juliette.

"No, he didn't mention it," she said quietly, as she sat there very much wishing he had and wondering why the subject of his mother seemed to bring him so much pain.

Juliette half-smiled and looked at John but he didn't meet her gaze either.

"I blow, I blow," exclaimed Sophie as she ratcheted up the bounce factor on John's knee.

"No! Me, I want to blow," shouted Luc.

Juliette laughed. "All the children have to blow out the candles together, you know that," she admonished her youngest son as she set the cake down in front of John and Sophie. Marc and Luc crowded around.

"Bonne anniversaire Maman," Juliette said in a quiet voice that splintered slightly at the end.

The children blew out the candles all at the same time and their happy faces were in stark contrast to the tight jaw and unsmiling face of their uncle John. Maggie continued to stare at him, willing him to look at her. She reached under the table and searched for his hand. She found it and laced her fingers between his. He turned to look at her and the pain in his eyes washed over her like a shockwave.

She wanted to take him into her arms and soothe it all away but even if she could get past Sophie, she knew it wasn't going to happen. He had been very careful all day not to be overly physical. Maggie wasn't sure why, maybe he was shy about showing his feelings in front of his sister or maybe he wanted to keep the heat factor under control. Either way, Maggie found it a bit strange, as back in Virginia Beach he could never keep his hands off her for more than five minutes and it wasn't always in a sexual way. Whether they were sitting on the couch or out on the deck he would have his arm thrown around her or take a hold of her hand. It was one of the things she loved about him, amongst a long list of others.

Love. There was that word again and as she repeated it in her head, she knew she was totally in love with the man beside her. Seeing the pain in his eyes had caused her heart to swell with a need to take his hurt and ease it, to make it her own and free him of it. If that wasn't love she didn't know what was.

He turned to her and passed Sophie into her arms.

"I need the bathroom," he told her in a tight voice as he walked past her in the direction of the hallway.

Juliette handed George a knife and followed her brother.

Maggie looked questioningly at George as he sliced into the cake.

His expression was one of grudging acceptance as he passed her a piece.

"Their mother's death is still something that doesn't sit easy between them," he explained to Maggie.

Maggie was just about to ask how she died when Sophie dropped her slice of cake on to the floor and went into the kind of meltdown only a two year old was capable of.

Juliette came running back into the dining room when she heard the screams of her daughter and Maggie could see the tears hiding in her eyes.

"John has just taken Rock out for a few minutes," she informed Maggie before she scooped Sophie up into her arms and tried to console her over the cake that was now splattered all over the floor.

"Okay," Maggie nodded, wondering what it was about their mother's death that caused such pain for the two of them.

***

John watched Rock disappear into the trees and let out a long breath.

"Fuck," he exclaimed and the words formed a small breath-cloud on the cool Virginia air.

He dragged his hands through his hair in a vain attempt to calm the emotions swirling through his body. All the familiar ones were there, guilt, regret, sorrow and grief but they were overlaid with the ones he wasn't so familiar with, happiness, contentment and joy. He'd been having one of the best days of his life up until Juliette had produced that damn cake. It wasn't that he didn't want to observe their mother's birthday, he'd just have preferred it to be more of a private moment between him and his sister. He'd known the minute he'd seen the candles that the cake wasn't just dessert and he'd been completely unprepared for the juggernaut of emotions it had released. And all that in front of Maggie.

Maggie. Watching her interact with the kids and engage in easy conversation with Juliette and George had done something strange to his heart. It was as if the bindings he hadn't realized he'd wrapped it in had been loosened and he'd felt a happiness he barely remembered flowing through his veins.

"Fuck," he swore again as he started to climb back up the hill to the house. He'd promised he would stay by her side throughout the day and here he was out in the woods caught up with the pain of his past when he should be focusing on the new-found happiness of his present.

He entered the front door only to find Maggie coming out of the downstairs bathroom.

"Hey," she said, "you okay?"

He smiled at her and took her hand.

"Yeah, I'm fine, Rock just needed to go out" he told her, brushing off the concern in her eyes and continuing to walk in the direction of the dining room.

Maggie didn't move, forcing him to stop.

"What's up?" he asked

She took her hand from his and crossed her arms across her chest, protective and wary.

"I think we've just stepped into the 'getting to know each other' stage John but for that to happen, we've got to actually talk to each other. You and I both know it wasn't Rock who needed to go out, it was you and you can try to hide what's really going on with you as much as you want but at some stage you've either got to open up to me and tell me what's going on or maybe we're best rethinking this whole thing before it goes any further."

John was taken aback at the depth of emotion quivering in her voice and the hurt smoldering in her eyes. He was so used to keeping his feelings to himself, to clinically compartmentalizing them and storing them away in a shiny safety deposit box in his mind, he hadn't realized his actions had affected Maggie. How could he? He wasn't used to having someone like Maggie in his life, someone who cared primarily about him and he most certainly wasn't used to sharing his innermost thoughts and feelings. He stood in front of her now, not sure what to do.

She walked past him.

"Think about it John," she whispered, as he watched her disappear into the dining room.

***

The rest of the afternoon passed with a particularly riotous game of Monopoly with Sophie insisting her and Uncy Don were the winners. No-one was brave enough to argue with her, especially since her two year old nerves were becoming frayed around the edges as her bedtime approached.

John had just come back down the stairs from reading her bedtime story when the boys dragged him into the sitting-room to watch the football game. Maggie took a seat and smiled at the sight of the two boys either side of John on the sofa, shouting and cheering between glances of sheer idolization at their uncle.

She thought she could sit there and watch them all night but not half an hour into the game a wave of exhaustion came over her so fierce that she thought she might pass out. She struggled to get it under control for about ten minutes but finally she made her excuses and explained that she needed to go lie down.

John extricated himself from his nephews and accompanied her upstairs.

"Hey," he said in a soft voice as soon as he closed the bedroom door behind him, "are you okay?"

Maggie flopped onto the bed and looked up into his face. She was immediately touched to see the concern burning in his eyes.

"Yes, I'm fine," she told him, "just incredibly exhausted. I hope you don't mind but I need to lie down for a while."

John looked at Maggie and from the tired look on her face, doubted she would be re-joining him and his family this side of breakfast.

"Hey, no problem," he assured her, "do you want me to stay up here with you?"

Maggie smiled. "And have to face two very disappointed boys in the morning? No way. You go. Your family are going to be much better company than me. I'll come back down just as soon as I'm feeling better."

John looked at her and at how she could barely keep her eyes open. He bent down and took her face into both his hands before placing a tender kiss upon her lips.

"Okay," he said in a low voice, "just let me know if you need anything."

"Will do," she smiled, her eyes half closed.

***

John spent the next few hours watching the football and enjoying time with his nephews but his mind was on Maggie and what she'd said to him earlier. As suspected, she didn't make an appearance back down the stairs and not long after the boys went to bed he made his excuses to George and Juliette and joined her in the bedroom.

She lay on the bed, fast asleep, two pillows and one hand tucked underneath her head. At some stage she had kicked off her boots and they lay on top of each other on the floor. He stood watching her, not wanting to disturb her. The moonlight played on her skin and he marveled at how beautiful she looked.

He went to the bathroom and when he came back he sat in the window seat, content to just look at her. He watched the rise and fall of her chest and listened to the gentle exhalation of breath on her lips.

He thought again about what she'd said, about him opening up to her and he wondered how he would do that. He questioned if he even could, after all he preferred to keep his emotions in lockdown but then her assertion from earlier rang in his ears, "*maybe we're best rethinking this thing...*" and he knew he was going to have to damn well try.

Maggie moved on the bed and her eyes flickered open. She looked around the room and for a moment she seemed slightly panicked as if she didn't know where she was. Then her eyes fell upon him and she smiled, a smile of such joy and pleasure at his presence in the room that his heart flipped in his chest.

"Hey," she said in a slow, sleepy voice.

"Hey," he husked back.

"What you doing all the way over there?" she drawled.

"Watching my girlfriend's face in the moonlight," he replied.

"Well why don't you come over here for a closer look?" she invited.

John got up from the window seat and slowly crossed the room. With every step he took he resolved to try and reveal a piece of himself to this woman who was causing chaos in his heart and in his soul.

He sat on the bed beside her. "You feeling better?"

She smiled. "Yes thanks, still tired but not as much as before. I'm thinking everyone is probably in bed by now."

John nodded as he brushed the hair away from her cheek.

"I hope your sister and George aren't offended by my early exit."

John shook his head and smiled. "No. I think they realize it was a pretty big day for you."

Maggie smiled back. "I can usually last a bit longer, I have even been known to tire my nephews and nieces out but I'm not sure what came over me this evening, turkey over-load maybe. What about you? How are things between you and Juliette?"

He didn't mean to but he tensed at the question. He instinctively knew she was deliberately opening a conversation where he could tell her about why he had reacted the way he did earlier.

He took a deep breath, time to give this "opening up" thing a go.

"We're fine."

He paused.

She waited.

Another deep breath.

"My sister has never really forgiven me for my mother's death."

Maggie looked puzzled but said nothing.

John continued. "Both of us watched the toll my father's career and ultimately his death took on my mother. She begged me never to join the army or the navy and for a long time that was fine with me, my father's boots were big and I figured there was no way I could ever fill them anyway. However, after 9/11 everything changed for me and I knew I couldn't deny what was in my blood any longer and I wanted to serve and protect my country. Juliette was furious when I enlisted and refused to speak to me after I joined the SEALs."

He stopped. Memories unbidden and unwanted attacked him from all quarters, memories of Juliette's fury and his mother's tears. A sharp pain shot across his chest. He could hardly breathe. He got up from the bed and started to pace the room. Fuck, this was way harder than he thought.

Maggie came over to him and took both his hands in hers.

"It's okay John, it's just me here."

He looked down at her and a feeling of something close to panic came over him and then he felt it, a tsunami of guilt and grief, unstoppable and unwavering washed over him so powerful it nearly took his legs out from underneath him.

Memories blurred before his eyes of him standing in front of the team Commander being told about his mother's death and him being unable to comprehend it. Returning home for the first time and his mother not being there and the consequences of his choices hitting him like a freight train.

He gasped for breath.

Maggie's eyes flared with concern.

"John, it's okay, if it's too much, you don't have to tell me now, you can tell me some other time."

John looked down at her and saw the concern in her eyes and knew she would give him an out but now he had opened this particular floodgate he needed to tell her all of it.

"My mother died from a massive heart attack the day I deployed with the SEALs. She waved me off and closed the door. Juliette found her a few hours later. She died there behind the door, all by herself, no-one to comfort or hold her in her final hours. Juliette believes her heart broke, that she simply couldn't face losing her son to war, just as she had lost her husband. Juliette blamed me and to a certain extent still does."

He said the last part in a voice so low Maggie barely heard him but his anguish was all too plain to see.

She wanted to take him into her arms and ease his pain but she sensed there was more. He stood before her as his fingertips grazed hers but she sensed his mind was far away in the past.

"John?" she prompted, "John."

He looked at her and the agony in his eyes caused her heart to skip a beat because in that moment she realized what it was he wasn't saying. Juliette might blame him for their mother's death but no-one blamed him more than he blamed himself.

He pulled his hands away and walked to the window. He felt raw and exposed and not at all comfortable with Maggie seeing him like this.

He struggled to control his breathing and placed one hand on the wall in an effort to steady himself. Fuck but this hurt. His chest felt tight like his heart had swollen with pain and his lungs no longer had any room to expand. He rubbed his hand over his heart but it did nothing to ease the anguish.

Then he felt Maggie's arms come around him, warm and strong.

"I'm sorry John, so sorry. I had no idea your mother died in those circumstances."

She reached a hand up over his heart and let it rest there as if she knew the pain that radiated from it.

John said nothing. He didn't trust himself to speak.

"Thank you for telling me. I know it wasn't easy."

She slid around to face him but he couldn't look at her.

She reached up and cupped the side of his face, applying the smallest amount of pressure.

"John please look at me."

He reluctantly turned his head and looked into her eyes and was surprised to see fear and apprehension there and something else, something he didn't quite recognize.

"I'm sorry I put pressure on you to talk to me and tell me what's going on with you but you see I have this little problem. I've fallen in love with you John and it's really hard for me to know where I stand with you emotionally at times and after I had my little realization today I kinda panicked."

She smiled a wry smile up at him. "So there you have it, all my emotional cards are on the table."

John looked at her and saw the beautiful woman before him but also saw so much more. Loving a guy like him was a big ask and yet she was brave enough to embrace it. Admitting her feelings left her exposed and vulnerable and yet again she was brave enough to tell him. Getting him to look into her eyes as she revealed how she felt meant he witnessed the raw honesty of her words as she offered them to him, leaving her with nowhere to run or hide as she laid herself emotionally bare before him. He didn't know if he could ever be that brave and a lump rose in his throat as he realized the extent to which she also trusted him.

Her honesty completely disarmed him and he couldn't speak. The raw beauty of her as she stood there framed by the moonlight was almost too much. She was in love with him. She was his. She was offering herself to him and him alone and he was pretty sure he didn't deserve her.

Maggie watched the maelstrom of emotions play out on John's face and started to worry if perhaps she had revealed too much or if now had been the wrong time.

"Penny for em?" she whispered into the darkness.

John said nothing but pulled her to him and held her close.

She didn't expect him to tell her that he reciprocated her feelings, at least not right away but she hoped he would at least give her some indication as to how he felt and if they were on the same emotional page or not.

He kissed the top of her head and she pulled back a little to look up into his face.

He smiled down at her. It was a beautiful smile of happiness and quiet joy but still he didn't say anything.

"John, you're killing me here. I just told you I've fallen in love with you and you're leaving me flapping around in a very cold wind."

He smiled again, slow and languid and then finally he spoke. "I'm just considering what's the best thing to do about your 'little problem' as you call it."

Maggie smiled back. "I'm looking forward to hearing your suggestions."

John leaned down and brushed his lips against hers. "I'm not so good with this love stuff Maggie and I'm not going to admit to anything tonight but what if I told you I think I might have a little problem of my own."

Maggie smiled. "Then I'd tell you to let Dr. Maggie O'Brien treat you for that."

John chuckled as he bent to kiss her. "I think my treatment needs to be intensive and also needs to start straight away."

NINETEEN

It had been two weeks since Thanksgiving and despite receiving lots of 'treatment' for his suspected problem, John still hadn't told her if he was in love with her or not. He certainly acted like he was and Maggie had to smile at the huge bouquet of roses taking pride of place on the dining room table and the antique heart-shaped locket around her neck, in which he'd put a photo of her "one true love," Rock.

She smiled at the dog now as he lay at her feet on the deck. They were just back from an epic walk on the beach and he looked exhausted. She sipped her coffee and thought some more over the last three weeks.

They'd come back from John's sister's house the day after Thanksgiving and spent the rest of the weekend together. John's training schedule had intensified significantly but thankfully he'd still had the weekends off. They'd mostly spent them in the environs of Virginia Beach and had run into a few of his team-mates who had been only too delighted to introduce themselves to her.

She smiled to herself, she had no doubt they were all well aware of her presence in John's life and that he was in no hurry to introduce her but it hadn't stopped them coming up to her in the restaurants and bars of Virginia Beach. They all seemed like real nice guys, which was just as well as she was due to meet all of them again tonight along with the rest of the team.

Tonight was the annual Christmas party at Cody's Bar. The "party" ran over the whole weekend to facilitate numbers and tonight happened to be for SEAL Team Eight.

Maggie was almost as nervous as she had been going to John's sister's house at Thanksgiving. She knew how he felt about these men, especially those he was closest to in his own platoon. They were closer than brothers, their bonds forged through hardship and endurance and she feared if they didn't like her then it could have serious consequences for her relationship with John. Of course she'd feel a lot better if she knew for sure he felt the same way about her as she felt about him. She supposed she should consider it as a positive indicator that he was taking her tonight as he'd explained only wives, fiancées and serious girlfriends were allowed.

As she drained the last of her coffee she realized her nerves were starting to get the better of her and her thoughts were starting to run amok so she decided to go and get ready. John would be here in an hour and she figured the least she could do was make herself as presentable as possible.

***

John opened the door and was immediately hit with the scent of coconut and jasmine floating down the stairs. The second thing to hit him was the sound of Whitney Houston's, I Will Always Love You, being strangled to death. He smiled, his girl couldn't sing for shit but she loved to try.

He took the stairs two at a time in the hopes of finding her singing into the hairbrush. Fuck but he loved coming home to her. He thought again about her revelation in his sister's house that she had fallen in love with him. It was practically all he had thought about in the past few weeks. She hadn't said it again and he suspected she wouldn't until he told her how *he* felt. He had admitted that night to maybe having fallen a little in love with her too. His feelings for other women he'd dated didn't come anywhere near the way he felt about Maggie. He laughed, even the very idea was absurd. But could he say what he was feeling was love?

He slowed as he approached the top of the stairs. Love. What the fuck did he know about it? He'd never been in love before. What the hell was love anyway? He thought about all the guys in the teams who'd thought they'd found the one, only to discover afterwards, they hadn't.

But if love meant you couldn't stop thinking about someone, couldn't wait to get home to see that same someone and your heart stuttered in your chest when they smiled at you, then he supposed he could be in love.

If the thought of that someone in the arms of another turned your guts inside out and if the prospect of her not being in your life felt like a knife to the heart then he supposed he could be in love.

He waited at the door and smiled as Maggie's version of Whitney's song hit an ear-splitting crescendo.

If you smiled more in a few short months than you had in an entire lifetime, he guessed you could be in love.

He gave a quick knock and entered but the sight that greeted him caused him to stop in his tracks and gasp.

Standing in the middle of the room was Maggie in a black dress that hugged all her curves and made her look sensational. She'd put on some make-up which highlighted her most striking feature, her eyes. On her feet were four inch black heels upon which she sashayed towards him. The overall effect was pure sex-bomb and for a fleeting moment John considered skipping the party but that would only mean the guys would end up bringing the party back here as they were all intent on meeting Maggie.

He thought about the love thing again and supposed if your girlfriend took your breath away at least once a day then you just might possibly be in love with her.

She twined herself around him.

"Well hello sailor," she breathed into his ear and it was all John could do to not throw her on the bed and have his wicked way with her. He was rock hard just looking at her. Fuck but with her looking like this it was going to be a nightmare trying not to embarrass himself in front of the guys.

"Couldn't find anything sexier to wear?" he smirked at her.

"I'm glad you like it," she said, as she traced the tip of her tongue along his neck up to the lobe of his ear.

John inhaled sharply. "Maggie, if you keep that up, we ain't gonna make it to no party."

She laughed as she pulled his head down towards hers. She kissed him, nice and slow and just when he thought his balls might explode she stopped and looked into his eyes.

"Then I suppose I'd better go downstairs and leave you to get ready."

As much as he wanted to rip the dress from her bones and sink himself into her as far as he could possibly go, he had to agree, he needed to shower and change.

"Then you'd better go quick," he growled at her.

He watched her walk out the door and he figured if you could imagine only making love to the same woman for the rest of your life and still not getting enough of her then maybe you were in love.

***

The party was in full swing, which was no surprise as a lot of the guys had come straight from work. So far Maggie was holding her own amongst the good humored banter and not so gentle ribbing between his team-mates and he couldn't be more proud of her.

They'd all wanted to meet the woman who had caused him to rethink his attitude towards relationships but he had held them off, he hadn't wanted to put any pressure on what this thing was between him and Maggie. In many ways he wanted to keep whatever it was just between the two of them, to mind it and keep it hidden and not let anything touch it. That way, nothing could hurt it. But he'd known he wasn't going to keep these boys at bay much longer so he'd decided to bring Maggie here tonight. This way he didn't have to spell it out, how he felt about her was implicit, she was the one he would be coming back to.

Maggie watched John go to the bar and marveled at how in a room full of brawn, he was still the biggest guy there. As nervous as she'd been, she was glad she had come. The guys were a lot of fun and some of the other wives and girlfriends were really nice.

She thought it was particularly sweet how the guys had brought along Karen and Maria, the wives of their two injured team-mates and had gone out of their way to dance and laugh and joke with them so they could have at least one night off from their troubles.

One guy was doing an outstanding job, as far as she could recall John had called him Joker. She smiled as he approached her now, all six foot something, sandy hair, brown eyes, coiled muscle and pent up mischief.

She sensed he'd been waiting for a chance to get her to himself and with John on his way to the bar he'd seen his opportunity and pounced. Maggie smiled as he stood in front of her, one arm across his very taut abdomen and the other held out to the side in the classic invitation to dance pose.

"Would the lady care to join me in a dance?" he grinned at her.

Maggie laughed. "The lady would," she replied as she took his hand and joined him.

Jason Derulo's, Want To Want Me, came on and Joker went into full on dancing king mode. Maggie laughed at the incongruity of this badass Navy SEAL pulling some pretty cool hip hop moves and could see how he'd gotten his moniker. She tried to hold her own in the dance department but she didn't hold a candle to this guy.

John felt the tingling in the back of his neck almost before he heard the sound that caused it. He turned around and saw Maggie on the dance-floor with her head tilted back and belly-laughing at the antics of Joker. The fucker had obviously been waiting for his chance to get her to himself and all John hoped was that he would keep things like embarrassing stories and nicknames to himself too, not to mention his hands.

John looked back at the bar to see if his drinks were nearly ready. The music changed to Ed Sheeran's, Thinking Out Loud and John knew, even before he turned around, what he was going to see. Yep, Joker had Maggie in his arms and was holding her curves far too close against that hard-ass body of his. And the fucker was grinning from ear to ear. Classic Joker move. The guy just couldn't help himself when it came to pushing peoples' buttons and he loved to find everyone's line in the sand.

"Fuck the drinks," John swore to himself as he started to make his way back to Maggie.

Joker was about to find out when it came to Maggie, there wasn't even a line.

An arm shot out of the crowd, a long muscular arm with a dark tattoo of an angel stretched across its forearm. It sliced across John's abdomen like a bolt across a barn door.

"Don't," a voice warned and John looked to his side into the black, fathomless eyes of Snake, who shot him a rueful grin.

"You know it's what he wants, to get you all riled up," Snake observed.

John stopped.

"Yeah, I know that Snake," he replied, "but Maggie isn't some frog-hog to play games with, she's *my girlfriend.*"

He put heavy emphasis on the words "my" and "girlfriend" so Snake would understand the extent to which he cared about Maggie. Girlfriend was a word none of the guys had heard him use much.

Snake retracted his arm.

"You know if you go over there all riled up he's gonna ride your ass about it for the whole deployment. It's not worth it. Come on back to the bar, I'll help you with the drinks and we can go over there together. I'll get him away from Maggie and you can act like nothing's happened. Play the fucker at his own game."

John smiled, he liked the sound of that.

Snake took the beers for the boys and John grabbed the drinks for Maggie, Karen and Maria. He turned around to walk back in Maggie's direction and stopped dead. Joker had her flush against him and his hand was moving dangerously close to the delicious curve of her ass. Something primitive took hold deep inside John and he started to move.

Fuck you and your games Joker, he thought to himself as he cut his way through the crowd. His eyes never left Maggie as Joker continued to hold her close. And then they turned and Maggie's emerald eyes were looking straight at him. He stopped. She smiled and raised an eyebrow as she nodded her head in Joker's direction as if to say, "Get a load of this guy."

John smiled. She was onto him. His beautiful, smart girlfriend knew exactly what the prick was up to and he loved her for it.

And that's when everything came to a grinding halt. He was pretty sure the world kept spinning but the air around him seemed to thicken and everything in his immediate vicinity felt like it was happening in slow motion.

He loved her.

The truth of those words hit him so hard he felt like his heart might slam out of his chest.

Who had he been kidding with all his dumbass shit about love back at the house. He could duck and dive around it all he liked but he'd fallen in love with her the moment she'd threatened him with her imaginary tire iron and he had only fallen deeper and deeper every wonderful moment since.

She was coming towards him now, having disentangled herself from Joker who was grinning at him with an evil glint in his eye knowing he'd lost his own game. John grinned back and flipped him off. Joker laughed and raised his beer in acknowledgement of John's victory.

Maggie stood before him, a questioning look on her face.

"You okay?" she inquired.

John looked at her, at how beautiful she looked and the words he wanted to say wouldn't come. He was speechless.

She was his. The woman he loved was standing before him, her face slightly flushed from her exertions with Joker and her eyes full of love and concern for him and he had no idea how he'd gotten so lucky.

He held out her drink.

"I'm fine," he croaked.

Understatement of the century. He felt like the king of the world right now and he needed to get Maggie back to the house to show her just what that meant.

He put his free arm around her and guided her back to the others. He handed Karen and Maria their drinks, then turned to Maggie and asked her to dance.

Jamie Lawson's, Wasn't Expecting That, came through the speakers and Maggie draped her arms around his neck.

"You dance almost as good as Joker," she teased.

John looked down into her laughing eyes.

"And he dances almost as good as he winds people up."

Maggie laughed. "He was doing a pretty good job to you, I thought I saw steam coming out of your ears at one point."

John smiled. "That had nothing to do with the dancing dickhead and everything to do with my smokin hot thoughts watching you in that dress all night and I'm not going to be able to watch you in it much longer."

Maggie looked up into his eyes and the hunger he saw there had him hardening in his pants.

"I'm ready to leave whenever you are," she whispered into his ear.

He didn't need any more encouragement. He took her hand and started heading towards the door but Joker wasn't quite done.

"Leaving so soon?" he asked as he stepped into their path, his eyes glinting with devilment.

John glared at him. "Just as soon as you get out of the way."

Joker smiled, his evil fucking smile and John just knew he was up to something. "Not before I get a goodnight kiss from the lovely Maggie," he smirked, not taking his eyes off John.

John could feel his patience start to slip. Joker liked to push it but tonight he was walking a very thin tightrope, fuck it, he was dancing on a razor-blade.

Maggie laughed. "It would be my pleasure," she said as she leaned over and placed a peck on his cheek, "merry Christmas."

Joker smiled. "Merry Christmas Maggie, thanks for the dance and enjoy the rest of the night."

He moved out of the way to let them pass.

"Night, Dickhead," John tossed at him as he walked past.

"Night, Horse," Joker tossed back and John kept walking to the sound of the fucker's laughter.

They were in the back of the cab when Maggie asked what Joker had said to him as they left.

"Nothing," John replied as he looked out the window.

"That's strange, I could swear he said 'goodnight, Horse' or something like that," she pressed.

John shifted in the seat and Maggie laughed.

"He did. John? Why did he call you Horse?"

John had been afraid of this. He knew as soon as Maggie started spending any amount of time around the guys that she'd find out his nickname and she would understand better than most why he'd been given it. He could feel the color rising in his cheeks.

"Oh my God," Maggie exclaimed before collapsing into a fit of giggles, "is that your nickname? Is that because of your, not so little, sailor?"

John nodded and silently vowed to kick the shit out of Joker as Maggie laughed all the way back to the house.

She was still laughing as he unlocked the door and Rock bounded towards them. He gave her a few minutes to make a fuss of the dog and then he took her hand.

"And now it's time to get you the hell out of that dress," he growled as he led her up the stairs.

***

Maggie tried to keep up with the gorgeous man in front of her as he practically hauled her up the stairs. He might be anxious to get her out of her dress but it was all she could do all night not to drag him into a dark corner, rip his shirt open and fuck him against a wall.

Maybe it was the effects of being in a room full of alpha male testosterone for the past few hours but she was horny as hell. And then there had been the way he'd looked at her when he'd been walking back with the drinks. Something about that look had liquefied her insides and put every nerve in her body standing to attention. But it was the way he had blushed in the cab that had completely obliterated the last piece of her heart. Her big navy SEAL, fearless, strong and proud, trying to hide his embarrassment in the shadows over his much deserved nickname. She sighed as he led her into the bedroom, there wasn't a part of her heart that didn't totally belong to him.

As soon as they were in the bedroom, John pulled her to him and devoured her in a kiss. He had felt the power of his emotions building in him ever since his realization back at the party that he was in love with this amazing woman and if he didn't give them physical expression soon he felt he might explode.

As his lips and tongue claimed and explored Maggie's mouth, his hands reached back and found the zip on her dress. He smiled to himself as he felt it give and he slid it slowly down her back. He wrenched his lips away from her mouth and turned her around. He placed his lips at the nape of her neck and following the trail of the zip, kissed his way down her back to where it stopped just at the curve of her buttocks. Then he licked his way back up again. Maggie shuddered and let out a gasp of pleasure.

John smiled. He was only getting started.

He took the tip of his finger and ran it under the material of the dress, sliding it down over her shoulder. His lips followed.

He then did the same to the other side.

The dress fell away and he placed his hands where it still sat on her hips. With the lightest touch he slid the dress downwards until it fell into a puddle of black chiffon and silk on the floor.

He placed the tip of his finger at the top of her spine and slowly snaked it down to the base. He gripped her hips and placed feather-light kisses along her shoulders, back into her spine and then down to her buttocks.

Maggie writhed against him and whispered his name as she reached up and twined her arms around his neck. She made a move to turn around but he held her in place.

He didn't want her looking into his eyes just yet. He didn't want her to see the truth of him until the right moment.

He unclasped her bra and teased it down her arms.

Then his hands cupped her breasts and Maggie arched into and away from him like a prima ballerina. Her breasts pushed into his hands and the nipples hardened to his touch.

He groaned and kissed the back of her neck. He teased her nipples as he scraped his teeth along her shoulder and then he slid his fingers into her black lace panties. Maggie pressed herself against him in undeniable need.

"John," she whimpered into the darkness, her voice a husky note of raw desire.

He hooked his fingers into the black lace as he slid them down over the delicious arc of her buttocks and then down her endless legs. His mouth followed, kissing and licking all the way down to the back of her knees.

She stepped out of her panties and stood before him in only those gorgeous fuck-me heels.

She turned around.

This time he didn't stop her.

Everything about her screamed white-hot desire but especially her eyes that blazed like a pair of fiery emeralds.

She stepped closer to him.

He picked her up and deposited her on the bed and he could tell from her face, he had taken her by surprise. She reached for the buttons on his shirt but he took her hands and secured them above her head.

"Ah, ah," he said as he shook his head.

"John, what are you doing?" she asked.

"You'll see," he smiled as placed his lips over hers and kissed her into silence.

He took one of his hands away and caressed her breast, bringing all the blood supply to its erect tip before claiming it with his mouth. Maggie stretched and writhed underneath him in a desperate attempt to control the need he knew was surging through her.

"John."

His name fell from her lips like a ragged plea and he heard the feral lust dripping from her tongue but he had a plan and he had to deny her just a little longer in order to carry it out.

His mouth stayed on her breast but his hand moved lower and quickly found the swollen bud between her legs.

She was so ready for him he nearly changed his mind about what he was about to do but then she bucked against him and tried to loosen his grip on her wrists and he knew the prospect of what he was about to see was so beautiful there was no possible way he could stop now.

He sucked on her, hard, and she cried out. His fingers increased their tempo between her legs and she began to move in the way he knew she moved when she needed to climb towards release.

"John," she breathed, her voice raw and breathless, "let me go, I need....I need to touch you."

John smiled against her breast.

Not happening, he thought to himself as he took her nipple between his teeth and flicked his tongue across it mercilessly.

Her eyes flew open and she writhed furiously under him as her hips fell into a frantic rhythm beneath his hand.

He could feel she was close.

"John....please...."

He released his mouth from her breast and looked into her eyes.

He didn't think his cock could get any harder but when he looked into those eyes, raw and vulnerable and full of desperate need for him, he thought he was going to shoot his load right there.

"Trust me, Maggie. Let go. Come for me honey."

She looked at him, questioning and confused.

"Trust me, Maggie," he whispered as he set his fingers to merciless.

He could feel her start to come, could feel the small rivulets of ecstasy joining together into one overwhelming wave and he knew this was it.

"Look at me, Maggie. Look at me," he commanded.

She looked at him just as she was poised at the precipice of bliss and it was obvious she didn't understand what he was doing but she trusted him and it was all there in her eyes laid out for him to see, her trust, her need and her love.

He had to squeeze the words he wanted to say out past the lump that suddenly formed in his throat.

"I love you Maggie. I love you," he whispered as her eyes flew open and her body convulsed into rapture. John had never seen anything as exquisite in his entire life.

He didn't give her any time to come down from her orgasmic high before he sheathed himself with a condom and powered into her, totally surrendering himself to this woman and all that she promised.

TWENTY

John reflected on the past ten days as he watched Rock chase down the beach like a bird-seeking missile on his endless quest to catch the seagulls that constantly tormented him.   He smiled to himself as he considered how the past ten days had been the happiest of his life.

His admission of love to Maggie had seen her open up to him like a beautiful flower, one stunning petal at a time. He hadn't known a human being was capable of such a huge capacity for love but Maggie certainly was and he loved her all the more for it. When Maggie loved she loved with her heart and soul and held absolutely no part of herself back.

He smiled as he recalled her jumping for joy around the kitchen when Gina had phoned to say all charges against her had been dropped and how her celebrations had ended with her taking him inside her on the dining room table.

The inquiry at the hospital was still ongoing but the dropping of the criminal charges would undoubtedly help her case, it just wasn't clear when it would be resolved. She'd shared her concerns with him about her job and they'd talked about her plans for the future, which included working less and living more.

John had liked the sound of that. He liked talking about the future with her and he figured he'd like it even more if it didn't have a great big cloud hanging over it called deployment. Usually he relished getting back into the action and bringing months of training and preparation to bear on whatever operation they were sent on. However, the last op still left a bad taste in his mouth and now there was the added issue of leaving Maggie.

He broke out into a cold sweat just thinking about it as dread, cold and grey, clogged its way up his throat.

"Damn it," he swore to himself. He had no idea how the guys with wives and long-term girlfriends did it, deployment after deployment. Leaving her was going to be torture and he didn't even want to contemplate how he was going to get through six months without her.

Maybe he'd ask Freezer for some tips when he went to see him tomorrow. He'd been with Karen forever and they'd come through too many deployments to count. John's heart sank at the thought of his friend. He still remained in hospital and some complications had arisen regarding his injuries. John had no idea what they were but he was hoping to find out more tomorrow.

A niggle of something tugged at his subconscious and he tried to shake it off but it wasn't so easily denied. He knew what it was and it was something he'd refused to think about in the past few weeks.

He had asked Maggie to come to Virginia Beach to give the amazing connection between them a chance and it had developed into something incredible. But that didn't mean all his fears and concerns had simply dissolved and turned to dust. He had consigned them to the recesses of his mind and refused to think about them but they festered there all the same.

He felt they had no place in this new life he was trying to forge with Maggie. He felt it wasn't fair to bring them out into the open and face them as he knew they had the potential to derail him but there were times like today when he couldn't help thinking about the what ifs. What if he was injured? What if he was captured? What if he was killed? How would any of those things impact Maggie's life?

He shook his head.

Stop it, he admonished himself, *the time for thinking like that is over and is counter-productive. You agreed to give things a go with Maggie and it's resulted in this amazing relationship so let all that shit-thinking go.*

He whistled out to Rock and switched his pace up into a jog. He needed to leave the gremlins of fear and doubt on the beach and get back to the woman who had opened up his world in more ways than he could ever have imagined.

The sun was just going down when he slipped through the gate from the beach onto the deck and the sight awaiting him caused his heart to explode in his chest.

She hadn't been feeling well when he'd left her sitting in one of the chairs. She was still in it but now she was all wrapped up in a blanket, her hair blowing lightly in the early evening breeze and her eyes closed in sleep.

A small smile played about her lips and her breathing was even and deep. She looked the picture of beauty and peace and so many powerful emotions washed over him in that moment he was overcome and had to lower himself into the other seat.

The love he had found with Maggie had set off a sort of emotional chain reaction in the past few months and so much of himself that he had shut down had sparked back into life. But now it was as if all those emotions had suddenly ignited into an uncontrollable blaze and he gulped in great big chunks of air in an effort to get it under control.

He loved this woman beyond all reason and whereas he recognized his life was all the richer for having her in it, he was also aware it brought fears and concerns that he'd never had to think about before.

How would she cope with his deployment? What if something happened when he was away, like her losing her job, and he wouldn't be there to console her? Would she find comfort in the arms of another? How would she cope every night for six long months without him in her bed? Would the loneliness eat her up? Would she decide this way of life wasn't for her?

The mere prospect of that possibility sliced through him like a knife, to the extent he winced as if in physical pain.

Love, he thought to himself, *the most wonderful feeling in the world and at the same time, the most terrifying.*

***

Maggie had been watching John for the past two minutes and couldn't help wondering what he was thinking about to the extent it had him so consumed he hadn't noticed she was awake.

"Hey," she said but even as soft as her voice had been it still startled him.

"Hey," he replied, his eyes looking at her but his attention very much taken up with what was on his mind.

"You okay?" she asked.

"Yeah, sure," he replied, too quickly.

Maggie straightened herself in her chair.

"John," she fired back, a warning note in her voice, "what's wrong?"

John sat there and considered fobbing her off with a "nothing" answer but he knew she hated it when he tried to avoid talking about things that were bothering him. He looked down at his hands, he really didn't want to have this conversation but he supposed they had to.

"John?" she prompted.

He looked at her. "How do you feel about me going on deployment?"

Her face crumpled and he could see her pulling back into herself, as if she was sorry she had asked the question but then he saw the moment she rallied and prepared to answer him. That was one of the things about Maggie, she never shied away from a difficult conversation. She looked down before she answered though.

"I'm dreading it." Her voice was low and soft like she was saying words she didn't want to hear. "How about you?"

John's voice wasn't any better. "Dreading it."

She looked at him and smiled a watery smile. "This is it, isn't it?" she asked. "The reality of our situation. I suppose we just have to focus on July and being together again rather than on all the months we'll be apart."

John tried to smile but couldn't. "I love you Maggie. I never thought it was possible to love another person the way I love you but God help me I love you with every living cell in my body. This is the first time I'm leaving my heart behind when I deploy and I'm asking you to please look after it."

Maggie was out of her chair in an instant. She'd heard his words but more than that she'd heard the cold fear they were wrapped in.

She knelt in front of him and placed her hands on either side of his face so that he had to look into her eyes.

"Hey," she said, her voice low and full of meaning, "you don't have to worry about your heart, it's safe with me and I'm going to take extra special care of it."

John half-smiled and pulled her up into his arms.

He kissed her, gentle and slow but Maggie didn't miss the undercurrent of desperation.

He pulled the blanket over them and they stayed there for a while looking at the stars and listening to the ocean.

Maggie laid her head on his chest and listened to the strong beat of his heart. She didn't want to think about January and having to watch him go. She could feel the sadness in him tonight and by a process of emotional osmosis it wasn't long before her own heart was heavy.

"I love you John," she whispered into his chest, "and I promise you, I'll keep your heart safe, always."

John said nothing but pulled her closer and said all he couldn't say with a gentle kiss to the top of her head.

TWENTY-ONE

Maggie stretched in the bed and was surprised to find an empty space and not the delicious wall of muscle she had become accustomed to. She reached out to grab her watch and nearly dropped it on the floor when she saw the time was 8:45 am. She scrambled herself together and after a quick trip to the bathroom, made her way downstairs. John was nowhere to be seen but there was a note waiting for her on the dining-table.

"Morning sleepy-head, I thought, since you weren't feeling too good yesterday, I'd let you sleep. Hope you're feeling better. I'm heading over to the hospital to see Freezer and Wolf. Not sure how long I'll be but I should be back in time to take you for a nice Christmas Eve lunch so don't go overboard on the pancakes. I'll call you when I'm on my way back.

Love you, John."

Maggie smiled, he loved to tease her about the morning in the cabin when she had devoured three of his pancakes without pausing for breath. She blushed as she remembered what had followed.

She read the last line again and held the note to her chest as she felt a heat radiate from it into her heart and spread through her bones.

"Love you, John."

If she lived till a hundred, she would never tire of him telling her he loved her.

***

John thought it strange that Brunhilde, the Guardian Of The Gate, wasn't at her usual post as he entered the ward where Freezer was currently housed. Of course that wasn't her real name but it's what he and the guys called Nurse Schmidt, who was built like a male discus thrower and obviously came from solid Germanic stock. She seemed to delight in intercepting them and kicking their asses out on a regular basis to the extent they all tried to time their visits to when she was off duty.

He thought it equally strange to find a "fasting" sign at the end of Freezer's bed but was so delighted not to find Brunhilde in the room, he didn't think much more of it.

Freezer was sitting up looking at something on his phone.

"Hey Horse, how you doing?" he asked, a twinkle in his eye.

John smiled. The twinkle told him Freezer had obviously heard about Joker's stunt at the party.

"I'm good. What's the story, are they starving you now too?" he asked, nodding towards the fasting sign.

A strange look came into Freezer's eyes before he answered.

"Yeah, looks that way but let's not talk shit about me. I wanna hear all about this lady, Joker's real smitten with her."

"Fuck you, asshole," John laughed as he took a seat beside the bed.

Freezer laughed. "Please tell me you've at least got a picture of her on your phone."

John smiled. Ordinarily, he wouldn't be so quick to share anything about his relationship but he figured if him sharing a few details with Freezer cheered the guy up then he was all for it.

He took out his phone and showed Freezer a photo he had taken of Maggie on the beach. It was his favorite photo. She'd been walking just ahead of him and he had called her name, camera at the ready. She'd turned, not expecting to have the camera on her and he had caught her completely unawares as she had smiled at him, the sun shining behind her head and the wind teasing her hair around her face. It was a beautiful photo of a beautiful woman.

"Hey, I can see why Joker likes her," Freezer laughed and John swiped the phone out of his reach.

"That dickhead has no idea how close he came to getting pulverized," John half laughed and half growled.

"Yeah, Karen told me all about it, " Freezer smiled, "just as well we all know and love him."

John smiled. "Yeah, to know him is to love him and to hate him in equal measure. But never mind about that asshole, what gives with you?"

Freezer's head dropped and he looked away. John thought he saw a flicker of pain flash across his face but he couldn't be sure.

Freezer was just about to answer him when the door opened and its frame was filled by the imposing build of Brunhilde.

"What the hell!" she shouted. "How the fuck did you get in here?"

That was the other thing about Brunhilde, she swore like a sailor, it was actually one of the things the guys liked about her.

John groaned and looked at Freezer who just smiled back, a weird smile of resignation.

John started to get up from the chair but she wasn't waiting for him to make his own exit. She pulled at his jacket.

"Come on, you gotta go. You can't be here, especially not today."

She had him almost half-way to the door when it occurred to him something was off. The fasting sign, her absence, Freezer. Her words rang out in his ears like warning bells, "*especially not today.*" Why not today? What was so special about today?

He looked back and saw Freezer bent over in the bed, his head in his hands.

What the fuck?

"Freezer?" he called but his friend didn't look up or acknowledge his words.

Brunhilde had him at the door.

"Hey," he said as he tried to swat her away, "all right, I get it, you want me out but what the fuck is going on?"

She opened the door and gave him a shove.

God but the woman is strong, thought John as he found himself in the middle of the corridor.

Brunhilde squared up to him.

"We're just about to take him down to surgery," she announced, "Professor Carmichael has a window in his schedule and flew in this morning from Walter Reed. There's nothing more they can do, today they are going to amputate his leg."

John was pretty sure she hadn't moved her hand but he staggered back as if she had sucker-punched him anyway.

"What?" he gasped and watched as Brunhilde's professional mask momentarily slipped to reveal a human being.

"I'm sorry," she said as her eyes left his and she looked at a spot on the floor just in front of her feet. "I thought you knew. There is nothing more can be done for his left leg. They have to take it off."

She reached out her hand in a gesture of comfort but John flinched away from her touch and stumbled another few steps backwards.

He was hearing her words but he couldn't process them.

Freezer losing his leg? No. Not possible. Not happening.

He made a move to go back into the room and Brunhilde immediately blocked him.

"No," she said, her voice stern but with an underlying echo of compassion, "you'll only make it worse for him."

John looked into her eyes and saw the eyes of a woman who had to bear witness to the worst of what war brought home on a daily basis. Eyes full of pain she carried for all the men and women who had come through her care, for those who were broken, like Freezer, and couldn't be put back together again.

He stepped back and nodded his head.

He tried to speak but his throat suddenly seemed full of razor blades and he realized tears were threatening to spill out the sides of his eyes.

He turned and walked away but he only got as far as the nurses' station when he had to grab onto the wall for support.

"I'm sorry," Brunhilde said in a soft voice from behind him.

He nodded again before bringing his hand up to his face and squeezing at his eyes in a desperate attempt to bring them back under control. One lonely tear defied him and slid precariously down his cheek. He quickly brushed it away as he strode towards the double doors at the end of the endless corridor.

He was just about to push them open when he heard a strangled sob coming from the waiting room. He looked and saw Karen sitting all alone on the floor with her back against the wall, her knees bent up to her chest and her head in her hands. He was in front of her in seconds, his hands reaching for her.

"Hey," he managed to squeeze out past the razor blades.

She looked up and the look in her eyes sliced through him more than any bullet ever had.

"Oh John," she sobbed as she threw herself into his arms, "what are we going to do?"

John sat back on the floor and held Karen close as her sobs cut through each of their hearts. He didn't answer her question. He couldn't. He had no answers, only overwhelming sorrow for his friend and the warrior who had fought beside him in too many battles to count, a warrior who prided himself on his physical prowess and who was about to have his leg removed from his body. John felt sick at the thought and pushed down the bile that had crawled up from his stomach.

He closed his eyes and images assailed him from the night back in Somalia. The sound of gunfire ricocheted through his mind and the image of Freezer, wounded and bloodied, crawling through the dirt, tore at his soul.

***

Maggie knew instinctively something was wrong. Twelve o'clock had come and gone and there had been no sign of John. One o'clock had rolled around and he had failed to show. By two o'clock she'd sent a text but there had been no reply. It was now nearly three o'clock and she was both worried and annoyed. She couldn't imagine what might have happened that would have prevented him from sending a quick text but then again she told herself maybe that's what it was like being involved with a special forces guy.

No, she told herself, *no matter how crazy it is at work I can usually find thirty seconds to send a quick text.*

He wasn't even working today so she couldn't imagine what might have happened that resulted in complete radio silence. She was only glad she had decided to have something to eat.

She was just putting on her jacket to take Rock for a walk when she heard the Raptor pulling into the driveway. She thought it strange how John didn't come in straight away and even though her intuition told her something was off, her head reassured her everything was okay, he probably just had some last minute Christmas things he needed to get out of the trunk.

John looked at his front door and thought back over his career in the navy, especially his time as a SEAL, and considered any number of things he'd had to do that were unpleasant and unpalatable to him. He stared at the glossy black paint and thought how none of those things compared to what he had to do once he opened that door.

Maggie heard the door open and placed her jacket on the back of the couch. John's familiar footstep sounded, soft and slow on the polished timber and Maggie's breath caught in her throat.

His huge frame filled the entrance to the living-room and in that instant she knew. Everything about him screamed pain and for reasons she couldn't yet define, her blood chilled at the possibility of what was to come.

"Hey," she said, her voice a nervous tremor. He still hadn't looked at her.

"Hey," he replied, his voice broken and full of sorrow.

Maggie felt her pulse quicken. "What is it John?"

He raised his head, slowly, so slowly, as if looking into her eyes was the hardest thing he'd ever had to do. "I'm sorry, Maggie," he started but his voice faltered and he looked away.

She took a few steps towards him and then stopped.

His eyes were black pools of agony and she was glad he had looked away because it pained her to see them.

"John what's happened?"

He took in a ragged breath and dragged his hand down his face.

"Things with Freezer aren't good. They amputated his leg today. How's that for a fucking Christmas present."

She heard the sadness in his voice and immediately wanted to go to him to offer the comfort of her touch but something stopped her. Was it the seething anger she'd heard there too?

She stood looking at him, not knowing what to say. She also felt there was more, much more.

"I'm sorry," she finally whispered.

Still, he didn't look at her, just nodded slightly in acknowledgement of her comment.

They stood there. Neither of them moving. Both silent. Each listening for the high-pitched scream of an incoming bomb.

Maggie didn't move. Her first instincts were to go to the man she loved and envelop him in her arms to ease his distress but another instinct kept her rooted to the spot.

The silence clawed at her nerves but she did nothing to break it.

Rock barked out on the deck, demanding to be let in.

Maggie turned to go to him when John shouted, "No!"

Shock shot through Maggie and she whirled around to look at him. She'd never heard him raise his voice before.

He looked at her now and his stormy eyes brimmed with an apology.

"I'm sorry," he said, his voice an empty husk, as if all his energy had dissipated with the shout.

Maggie moved towards him.

He put up his hand, warning her to stay away.

Maggie's blood turned to ice.

When John opened his mouth to speak his voice was deathly quiet.

"I have something to say and it's probably best if he's not jumping around us making his usual commotion when I say it."

He looked away.

"Do you know how your mother was upset that you wouldn't be home for Christmas.... well I've been thinking maybe you should go home and be with your family. Maybe that's for the best."

His voice trailed off at the end and Maggie didn't miss the spasm of pain that contorted his beautiful face.

She stood there trying to process what he was saying. Her head already knew but her heart refused to hear it.

"John, what are you saying?" she asked, her voice tentative as if she didn't want to ask the question but she knew she had to.

He swung his head to the side and looked up at the ceiling.

"Maggie, you know what I'm saying. Please don't make me spell it out."

She grabbed on to the couch as the full realization of his words sledge-hammered their way through her heart.

"You're breaking up with me?" she gasped.

He let out an agonized sigh.

"It's for the best," he said and his voice cracked as if it couldn't cope with the words.

Maggie tightened her hold on the couch as a white-hot fury surged through her. "So let me be clear. You're breaking up with me. You're fucking breaking up with me on Christmas Eve! What sort of asshole does that!"

John's head dipped and he stared steadfastly at the floor. He'd known when he'd walked in the door this was going to be the worst day of his life, second only to hearing about his parents' deaths.

He'd known a woman as passionate as Maggie was never going to take a break-up lying down. He'd known she would be furious and he didn't expect anything less from the woman he loved. He knew she wouldn't hold back and he braced himself now for the onslaught and prayed he would survive it.

"I'm setting you free, Maggie," he tried to explain in a quiet voice which he hoped would have a calming effect. "I'm releasing you from this life with me, you deserve better. Get the hell out of here and don't look back."

He dared to look at her then and instantly wished he hadn't. Disbelief, shock and heart-breaking anger glared back at him. He felt his resolve slip a little and he looked away before the force of her emotions drilled their way through his defenses and caused his resolve to collapse completely.

She deserved better than a life with him, a life of loneliness, fear and heartache and he loved her too much to shackle her to him, to have her waiting for his return, a return that might never come and even if it did, there was a high probability it would come with too high a price for her to pay.

He looked away and his gaze fell on a picture of his mother, smiling and seemingly carefree but John knew better, his mother had never been carefree.

Maggie's voice lashed at him like a whip from across the room.

"Setting me free. Oh how gallant of you. And what about the guy who asked me to come here, to give things a chance between us. Where is he? Where is the guy who only this morning wrote in a note that he loved me? Where's the guy who made love to me last night like I was the only woman on this earth, who moaned my name into the night like it was a salve to his soul? Tell me where's that guy?"

Her words were like well placed daggers and each one of them landed a direct hit on his heart. He closed his eyes as if to shut out the pain.

"That guy was a fool who thought love was everything, like a super-power that made you immune to all the shit in this world but today he realized it doesn't. Love leaves you vulnerable, it leaves you having to deal with things you shouldn't and I won't have that for you Maggie."

Maggie looked at the man in front of her. The beautiful, glorious, most amazing man she'd ever met, who she loved to the depths of her soul. The man, who until a few minutes ago, she had been planning a future with but who now stood across from her broken and in pain.

Her fury waned.

"Well what if you don't have a choice in it John?" I love you and I know you love me and I believe love can see us through whatever challenges we might have to face."

She took a step towards him and reached out her arm but he recoiled from her touch. She stopped, her hand frozen in mid-air as the pain of his rejection lanced through her.

A matching agony seared through John as he watched Maggie's face twist in pain but there was no way he could let her touch him. He was desperately trying to maintain control and do what needed doing but if she made any sort of physical contact with him he knew he would be done.

"Love is enough for most people Maggie," he said, his voice raw, "but in the world I live in it's a liability. I won't take advantage of your love for me. I'm sorry I brought you into this world but it's better to break up now after a few months than down the line. You'll meet someone else, someone who can be there for you and give you a life you deserve but that won't happen if you're still tangled up with me."

Maggie stood there incredulous, listening to his words, and her anger came back ten-fold. She couldn't believe he could dismiss all that had happened between them over the last few months and talk about discarding it like it was some sort of make-believe game they'd been playing.

"Fuck you," she threw at him. "Fuck you if you think I can walk away from what we have, just forget about it, like it never happened and find someone else. I haven't found a man in thirty-six years that comes anywhere near you. I never believed a man like you even existed and now you want me to walk away from you, forget about you and move on with some other guy? Fuck you John. Fuck you because that's never going to happen and even if you came back to me injured and broken, you'd still be more of a man to me than any other man out there."

Her voice broke and she knew she was dangerously close to tears and she'd be damned if she was going to reduce herself to a blubbering mess in front of him.

He stood across the room, his head bowed, staring at the floor and she could feel small fissures starting to tear at the outermost edges of her heart.

"And what about you?" she fired at him. "Do you intend to stay single for the next eight years and then cruise the singles bars in your forties, a washed up warrior looking for something he was lucky enough to once have. Do you think you can just pick up a love like this at the local seven-eleven?"

John stood in silence letting the pain of her words wash over him like acid rain. He didn't care what happened to him as long as he never had to face the prospect of becoming a burden on her or being returned to her in a body bag.

Silence.

He looked up and Maggie was holding her head in her hands.

A sliver of fear, ice-cold, wound its way around the knot in his stomach.

She raised her head and her eyes were two fathomless pools of agony. She looked broken and it took every shred of resolve he had to stay where he was and not take her into his arms. He looked away but there was no escaping the anguish in her voice.

"I get it. I understand now. This has all been some sort of game for you, a dipping of your toes into the waters of love and now you want out. You don't love me. You've never really loved me, this was all just a charade."

Her words were like a scalpel to his heart and John's head whipped up in shock. He started to move towards her. She couldn't believe that. He wouldn't have her believing that. Everything he was doing was because he loved her. He loved her beyond reason and that was part of the problem.

He'd lost perspective and the love he felt for Maggie had caused him to lose sight of reality but today had been a reality check beyond any other, brutal and unforgiving. He wouldn't have her sobbing, like Karen, in someone else's arms over him. He wouldn't become a burden on her. But there was no way he would have her believe anything other than he loved her.

He stood in front of her now and she looked up into his eyes.

He crossed his arms and dug his fingers into his biceps in an almost superhuman effort to stop himself from holding her.

His voice shook with emotion as he spoke.

"Do not interpret my intention to set you free of me as meaning I don't love you Maggie. It's only because I love you to the extent I do, that I can do this. My life was an empty shell before you came along and you filled that shell with the sound of the ocean. An ocean of laughter and happy times. These past few months have been beyond anything I could ever have dreamed of. I was dying a slow death before I met you and I don't know how I'm going to survive without you but please don't ever say I don't love you and please don't destroy the memory of what we've had because those memories are all I'm going to have to keep me going."

She reached out her hands then and placed her fingers on his arms as if she wanted to prise them open. He steeled his resolve and not an inch of him moved. She let her fingers rest on his arms as she looked up into his eyes.

"Then why do this John? Why tear us apart? Why destroy the both of us? You've had a bad day. You got a shock when you saw the outcome for Freezer today. I understand you're upset and how seeing your friend having to go through that has rocked you to your core but it's no reason to end things between us. You once promised me you'd always be honest with me but what about being honest with yourself. What's really going on here John?"

He looked down at her, confused by her words. Hadn't he made it clear what was going on here? Hadn't he made it clear he loved her so much he was willing to sacrifice his happiness and his future so that she could go on and eventually have some in hers?

"You don't get it, do you?" she whispered, her voice a barely audible croak, "here you are the big Navy SEAL, the mighty warrior, prepared to put his life on the line, fearless and strong but you're not prepared to face what scares you most of all."

His confusion grew.

Maggie's face twisted into a sneer, his least favorite expression.

"Love, John. Love. It terrifies you."

He stepped back then, anxious to put some distance between them. She stepped towards him and her hands reached up towards his face. Tears slipped treacherously down her cheeks.

"Don't do this John, please don't do this. I'm not beyond begging you. Don't break both our hearts."

Her hands connected with his face and her fingers stuck like velcro to the dark stubble along his jaw. She turned his head to look into her eyes and the despair he saw there was too much. She went to kiss him and he cracked. He dragged her hands away and twisted out of her reach.

He needed to get away from her before she stripped away all his defenses. He had always been defenseless against her touch. He turned his back and took a few steps. His voice was brittle when he spoke but he didn't care.

"I'm going now Maggie and I think it would be best if you were gone by the time I get back."

He started to walk away but she grabbed at him.

"John, please don't do this," she pleaded but he shrugged her arm away and kept walking.

The last sound he heard before he left his house was a soft whimper like that of a puppy which has given its heart to its new owner and has just received its first kicking.

TWENTY-TWO

In the ten years Cody Roberts had been running his bar, he'd seen more broken-hearted SEALs than he'd cared to count but if there was one SEAL he hadn't expected to fall into this category it was Lieutenant John Sullivan. The man had been in his bar now for a number of hours and had gone through a quarter keg of beer and half a bottle of Jameson, the Irish whiskey he was so fond of.

Cody had known there was something up from the minute he'd entered the bar but had also known better than to ask. As the alcohol had taken effect though, John had revealed his day in dribs and drabs of conversation, informing him of Freezer's terrible news and finally confessing his catastrophic decision to end things with Maggie.

He sat now at the end of the bar staring into his whiskey like it had all the answers. He held his head in his hands and looked as broken and defeated as any man Cody had ever seen. Some of his team-mates approached him, knowing something was wrong but he shrugged them all away and Cody knew it was only a matter of time before he started throwing punches.

The guy was in a world of pain and Cody knew better than most how a man like John Sullivan would eventually try to find some release from his inner agony. He watched as John stumbled to the bathroom and his mind was made up. He took out his cell phone, selected two names and sent a quick text:

"*Need your ass here asap. Horse is here - shitfaced. Cut up over Freezer and the dumb fucker broke up with Maggie. He's not pretty and needs to go home now before he starts to break up my bar.*"

Snake was surprised to hear his phone beep with a text message at eleven thirty on Christmas eve night and was even more surprised when he saw who it was from and what it said. Still, he was in his Mustang and heading towards Cody's Bar in thirty seconds flat.

Joker was just throwing the last few things into his overnight bag, getting ready to hit the road in the morning, when he heard his phone buzz with a text message.

"Fuck," was all he had to say when he saw what was written across his phone's screen as he grabbed his keys, jumped into his Jeep and headed into town.

John steadied himself before he opened the door of the bathroom to go back out into the bar. He knew he should probably go home but he couldn't face it. He couldn't face going back to the house knowing Maggie wouldn't be there. He also knew Cody would kick his ass out at some stage, so, until then, he was quite happy to keep drinking.

The alcohol was doing an outstanding job of numbing his pain and he intended to drink himself to the point of paralysis because he knew once he sobered up a shit-storm of agony awaited him. He just needed to be left alone to get on with his drinking and he was getting fed up with the assholes who kept coming up to him suggesting he'd had enough and offering to take him home.

"Not fuckin goin home," he muttered to himself as he swayed back to his spot at the bar.

He was half way into his second whiskey when he looked to his right and saw the tattooed arm of Snake appear beside him. In fairness to his brother, he didn't make any half-assed suggestion about taking him home but ordered three whiskeys instead. John was wondering who the other one was for when he felt a hand on his left shoulder and looked around to find Joker.

"Thought you could use some company," Joker said calmly into his ear and John couldn't speak past the lump in his throat.

They were here, of course they were here. They didn't just look out for each other on the battlefield but in the trenches that were their lives when they weren't deployed which were full of all sorts of unseen landmines.

Snake raised his glass.

"To Freezer."

Both John and Joker raised their own glasses and repeated Snake's words before knocking back the Irish firewater. John slammed his glass on the counter as the emotions of the day washed over him. Having

Snake and Joker here pushed him over the emotional precipice he had been clinging to for the past few hours and he could feel it crumbling away under his feet. He was falling. He grabbed the edge of the bar and tried desperately to stem the tidal wave of emotion that threatened to wash him away. A sob tore from his throat as the hands of his brothers caught him.

"Come on," Snake said in a quiet voice, "let's take this party back to your place."

Cody handed two bottles of Jameson to Joker over the counter.

"Think you're gonna need these, happy fucking Christmas," he rasped, as the sight of yet another SEAL paying the heavy emotional price for doing his job tore at his heart.

They were half-way through the second bottle of whiskey when John finally passed out. Joker and Snake looked at each other. Joker took a coin out of his pocket.

"Heads I get the spare room, tails you get the couch."

Five minutes later they deposited John on his bed and Joker headed to the spare room as Snake headed downstairs.

John briefly opened his eyes and smiled, he was home and back in his bed and for a moment, through the magical effects of alcohol, he forgot about the tumultuous events of the day. Maggie was here and that meant all was right with his world. He reached over to pull her warm curves into him but all he was met with was an empty space and a cold sheet. Then it all came crashing back in high definition, her tears, his agony, the heart-wrenching whimper. He fell back against his pillow and a lone tear trickled out the side of his eye as he felt his heart crack and shatter into a million tiny pieces and he prayed for the night to take him.

TWENTY-THREE

The drive back to New York had taken nearly ten hours due to the amount of times Maggie was forced to pull over. She'd endured a storm of emotions whilst trying to steer her wheels back to Brooklyn, from anger to despair to overwhelming sadness. It had been the latter that had forced her to pull over to the side of the road more times than she could count, accompanied as it was each time with a flash-flood of tears.

She looked at her red and blotchy face now in her bathroom mirror and the raw puffiness of her eyes. She'd never cried as much in her life and hadn't known your eyes could physically hurt from crying. But the hurt in her eyes was nothing compared to the pain in her heart. She physically ached all over and a sharp shaft of sorrow sat heavy on her chest.

She took some small comfort in the fact she was in her apartment and she even managed to raise a half smile at how Andy had tidied it up. He was a complete neat freak and she could only imagine how horrified he had been on walking in the door after she'd left.

Her stomach growled with hunger but the thoughts of eating anything made her feel decidedly queasy. She made herself a cup of cocoa instead and sat on the couch, sipping the hot drops of comfort and wondering how on earth she was going to sleep.

Her thoughts kept slipping back to Virginia Beach and the man who had broken her heart. She couldn't help thinking back over the past few months and dissecting their time together. She remembered his reluctance in the beginning to enter into a relationship and how she had feared her heart might be in danger but then she had dismissed those fears when he had asked her to come to be with him in Virginia Beach. She had wholeheartedly believed he was as fully invested in the relationship as her. Bitterness, cold and cruel, sluiced its way through her veins and she shook her head at how stupid and naive she had been.

She knew she should stop thinking about him, to try and move on as quickly as possible to accepting the situation. The doctor in her told her exactly what she needed to do, the steps were logical; accept, move on, forgive, or at least forget, and heal. However, the woman in her remembered his touch, ached for his kisses and longed for him to turn up at her door, to tell her it had all been a stupid mistake and beg her to take him back.

Fresh tears welled in her eyes and plopped unceremoniously into her cocoa. She considered drinking something stronger but her stomach heaved at the very thought. It was three o'clock in the morning and a wave of exhaustion washed over her. She knew she should get up and go to bed but the thoughts of lying on her own, with no wall of muscle to cuddle up to, caused fresh tears to fall and her heart to squeeze in agony.

"Oh John," she whispered to the empty space of her apartment, "why? Why did you have to do this to us?"

She wondered about him and how he was doing and as much as she wanted to hate him, she hoped he wasn't in the same sort of anguish as her because it was something she wouldn't wish on her worst enemy.

She leaned her head back onto the arm of the couch and lay there as sob after sob tore from her throat. There was nothing she could do to stem the flow of pain so she just succumbed to it like a stick thrown into a river that bounces helplessly against the banks and is lacerated by the sharp, jagged edges of unseen rocks. She hoped by the time she came to the river's end she wasn't just a collection of splinters.

***

Hours later, Maggie cracked half an eye open as the smell of freshly brewed coffee wafted teasingly up her nostrils. For one glorious moment she thought she was back in Virginia Beach and John was brewing a pot as he normally did in the morning but then she looked up and saw the antique ceiling fan that dominated the living area of her apartment and her reality came crashing down on her. She looked over to the kitchen to see Andy pottering away. He didn't even look in her direction when he spoke.

"I'm thinking the fact you ah heah and not in Veeginia Beach means it is not a happy kisstmas."

Maggie opened her mouth to speak but the words wouldn't come out. Instead, the sight of her wonderful friend in her kitchen, making her coffee and cooking her breakfast caused her lower lip to tremble uncontrollably as she desperately tried to hold back the fresh wave of tears threatening to spill out her sore eyes. God but she was a mess.

Andy looked at her then and the look of concern that came over his face caused her to crumble.

She buried her face in her hands and cried unashamedly in front of her friend. He was by her side in an instant.

"What happened?" he asked, a note of anger in his voice as if he'd already guessed the answer.

Maggie lifted her head.

"It's over. He dumped me."

The words were no sooner out of her mouth than a fresh wave of agony washed over her. Andy took her into his arms and held her against him as he wondered what kind of man was stupid enough to let a woman like Maggie go.

Maggie hiccupped into Andy's chest and wished she could stop crying. Her eyes stung and her throat hurt and she could hardly breathe. She pulled away from him and apologized through her hiccups for slobbering all over his t-shirt. Andy laughed.

"Don't mind about that," he said, "just tell me what happened."

Maggie relayed the whole sorry tale over copious mugs of coffee and Andy's delicious eggs benedict. By the time she was finished she felt slightly better and managed to hold back the sobs that threatened to engulf her again.

Andy stayed with her for most of the morning until he had to go to a private gig he had lined up somewhere on the Upper East Side. She closed the door after him and turned to her empty apartment wondering how she was going to get through the day.

One thing she wasn't going to do was return her mother's calls. She had called twice during the time Andy was here and Maggie had no doubt it was to wish her a merry Christmas in Virginia Beach. She had been pretty annoyed that on the rare Christmas her daughter wasn't working, she'd chosen to spend it with a man her mother had never met instead of with her family in Brooklyn. Of course John had been invited but Maggie had declined the invitation, sure in the knowledge he wasn't ready for the onslaught of the O'Brien clan. Bitterness choked her as she ruefully acknowledged to herself how he hadn't even been ready for just little old her.

Her phone vibrated with a message as she tidied up the kitchen. Hope flared in her heart as she went to pick it up that it might be from John but her head told her to steady herself as it was more likely a text from one of the O'Briens. Sure enough it was a selfie of her nephews Dylan and Patrick with some of their Christmas goodies. She smiled. They looked hyper. For a split second she considered driving out to Brooklyn, the kids would be a perfect distraction after all but she quickly dismissed the idea at the prospect of them seeing her cry and there was no doubt she was going to cry. The waterworks might be turned off for the moment but she could feel the pressure building.

God, how she wished she could go to work right now and lose herself in it. Instead, she showered, went through her mail, checked her emails, flicked through the TV channels and eventually sat on her couch staring into space. She wondered what John was doing and couldn't help reflecting on how differently the day had turned out to what she had been expecting.

She felt empty, like a part of her soul had been ripped from her. She wondered if that was what it was like once you had met the love of your life, your soulmate, and you were no longer with them, like you were missing part of your soul.

A physical ache, like paint being stripped from her skin, started in her arms and seeped into her chest and down into her stomach. She longed to hold his hard body in her arms and pull him close against her. She missed his heat and the tingle of anticipation whenever any part of their bodies connected. She missed his smile and the way it turned her insides molten and the huskiness of his voice as he whispered her name.

The tears started to fall as she'd known they would. She let them drip from her eyes and run unchecked down her cheeks as an agonized groan escaped from her lips.

"I love you John, God help me but I love you," she croaked to the cold walls of her apartment.

TWENTY-FOUR

Even before he opened his eyes John knew he was going to have the mother-fucker of all hangovers. His phone had been buzzing on and off for the past ten minutes and he was tempted to pick it up and throw it against the wall. No matter how much he might want the calls and texts to be from Maggie, he knew she would burn in hell first before she contacted him. No, he suspected the reason for his phone's constant buzz was his sister and the kids who, no doubt, wanted to wish him and Maggie a merry Christmas.

"Well fuck that," he groaned as he rolled out of the bed.

He had to stop mid-roll as his head struggled to keep pace with the rest of his body and a lightning bolt of pain flashed behind his eyes.

"Fuck," he exhaled to the room, it was going to be a long, mother of a day.

He made his way to the bathroom and sent a stern warning to the contents of his stomach to stay the fuck where they were.

Tempted as he was to crawl back into bed he decided coffee and painkillers might be a wiser choice as he made his way down the stairs.

There was no sign of Joker or Snake or, for that matter, Rock and he figured maybe the boys had taken the poor dog for a run. He made a coffee, popped two of the strongest painkillers he could find, threw on a sweater and went out on to the deck.

It was a beautiful crisp morning without a cloud in a flawlessly blue sky. He sucked in the salty ocean air and tried not to think about how much he wanted to look over at the other chair and see Maggie sitting there. Instead, he set his eyes on the ocean and wondered how he was going to get through the day and every other day after it.

He felt empty and half-dead like a room that had once been painted in the most beautiful colors and had hosted the most wonderful parties filled with laughter and joy but now was abandoned, the paint peeling from the walls, revealing the cracked plaster beneath, its only companion, the deathly silence.

He would never be sorry for the time he had with Maggie but he had no idea how he was going to get this aching loneliness under control. Right now he felt like it could engulf him.

A noise to his left caught his attention and he half-smiled as his dog came barreling towards him.

"Whoa there," he said as Rock nearly knocked the mug of coffee from his hand.

Snake laughed. "He sure is in lively form this morning."

John looked up at Snake. "Thanks for taking him out and thanks for getting me home last night."

Snake grinned as he walked past him and gave him a hard pat on the shoulder. "Not a problem," he said, "thanks for making a pot of coffee, I don't mind if I do."

Two minutes later he was sitting in the chair John so wished was occupied by someone else and sipping Costa Rica's finest from the biggest mug he could find.

"Fuck but that's good coffee," he exclaimed.

John smiled. "You know I don't fuck around when it comes to food or drink."

Snake nodded. "Nope, no-one could ever accuse you of being anything less than a connoisseur," he agreed as he took another slug and looked over at his platoon leader.

"You feel as rough as you look?" he asked.

"Worse," John replied.

"Figures," Snake observed.

"Yeah, rough day," John said in a quiet voice.

Snake said nothing and just drank the coffee. It was one of the things John liked about Snake, he never felt the need to fill a silence.

"So, I guess I should wish you a happy fucking Christmas," John said dryly. "What are your plans for the day?"

"Ain't got any," Snake announced "'cept for joining some of the boys at Cody's for his Christmas day lunch."

Every Christmas, Cody had a lock-in and invited those who had nowhere else to go to join him for the day.

"You should come," Snake suggested.

John shook his head. "I don't have an invite."

Snake grinned. "That's only because Cody thought you had other plans. Come on, you can come as my plus one, bitch."

John had to laugh, being Snake's date wasn't quite how he had seen his Christmas turning out. He wondered where Joker was, the three of them would make quite the threesome.

"Where's pretty boy?" he asked.

"Had somewhere he had to be," Snake replied, "you know Joker, he's never big on the details."

John nodded, as much as anyone knew Joker he often wondered if anyone actually really knew him. It seemed to John he kept himself well hidden behind all the pranks, wind-ups and general goofing around.

Snake drained his coffee.

"I'm just gonna go back to the house, freshen up, grab the guitar and then I'll swing by and pick you up."

John nodded again. "Sounds good."

Snake gave John another clap on the back before he left, saying all he needed to say with that one wordless gesture.

John leaned back in the chair, closed his eyes and let the sun warm his face. He only wished its effects could reach the ice-cold loneliness of his soul.

TWENTY-FIVE

Maggie traced a drop of rain as it trickled down the glass at JFK airport and remembered another drop of water she had traced along John's skin in what seemed a lifetime ago. Despite New York being shrouded in grey cloud there was still a decent view of the Manhattan skyline and as Maggie stared at its lights twinkling in the distance, she couldn't help wondering if she was doing the right thing.

The past few weeks had seemed never-ending as the inquiry at Hillview continued to drag on, meaning she still couldn't return to work. She had tried to fill her days as best she could to distract herself from the constant heartache that ate away at her but the nights had proven much more difficult to navigate.

She'd thought the flow of tears would stop after the first week and to be fair she had managed to grapple them under control during the day. However, the nights saw her emotional buttresses collapsing and if, somehow, she managed to fall asleep without crying, she would inevitably wake up during the night with wet cheeks. Her pain hadn't eased at all but instead had settled on her like a heavy cloak that she wondered if she was ever going to be able to discard.

There hadn't been a word from John, not a text or a whisper. Her heart squeezed anew at the irrevocable nature of their split and she placed her forehead against the cold glass as a rogue tear slipped down her cheek. She'd hoped he would have changed his mind once he'd had a chance to consider things rationally. She'd hoped he was as miserable as her and couldn't face life without her and she'd waited for his call or a text but there had been nothing except cruel silence. And that was why she was now in JFK airport waiting to board a plane to Kenya.

There was no way she could sit around for the next few months nursing her broken heart, especially knowing John was thousands of miles away on deployment. She needed to do something and Ruby had come along with the perfect opportunity, an eight week placement on a United Nations medical outreach team based in Daadab, Kenya.

She'd promised herself back in the Adirondacks she was going to travel more but she wondered now if going to Kenya to work in the largest refugee camp in the world was the best place to start. It was no good sharing her misgivings with Ruby as this is what her friend lived for.

She looked over at her chatting to some of the other members of the team and smiled. From her tattered boots, worn jeans, faded hoodie, dreadlocked ponytail and nose ring, no-one would ever guess she was an accomplished doctor. She looked more like a roadie for a rock band. Her shabby attire also hid her collection of tattoos and did a pretty good job of disguising the fact she was a trust fund heiress.

Ruby Obermeier of the Obermeier Banking Dynasty was a very wealthy lady indeed but Maggie didn't know anybody who was less interested in money. In typical Ruby fashion she had shunned the trappings and expectations of her family and decided to become a doctor and devote her life to the care of the less well off. She worked for a number of overseas agencies usually in some of the worst places in the world, affected as they were by war or disaster. She worked on rotation, flying into crisis hit areas on a few hours notice and it perfectly suited her adrenaline junkie nature. Maggie was starting to wonder just how much it suited hers but she consoled herself with the fact it was only eight weeks. She could survive anything for eight weeks.

The flight attendant announced the boarding of their flight. She picked up her onboard bag, took one final look at New York and said a silent goodbye to the man who had broken her heart.

TWENTY-SIX

John cracked open another beer and sat out on the deck. The wind was picking up and storm clouds were starting to move in but he didn't care. The sound and smell of the ocean were the only things that had brought him any measure of comfort in the past few weeks. He'd thought the initial pain he'd felt on breaking up with Maggie would subside and somehow ease into a manageable ache but he had been wrong. Instead it had intensified into an almost unbearable agony. Thankfully he had work to distract him from it during the day but the nights were a nightmare he just about managed to endure.

He missed her more than he thought it possible to miss another human being but he also missed the person he was when she was around. She was like a song to his soul and her absence in his life left him bereft and on the brink of despair.

He longed to hear her voice, see her smile and feel the touch of her fingers upon his skin. Every night he yearned to pull her curves against him and lose himself in her arms, to bury himself deep inside her to the point of belonging solely to her.

A fresh blade of pain stabbed at his heart as memories of her moaning his name flashed through his mind. He slugged back the beer and had just decided he needed something stronger to get him through the night, when his doorbell rang.

Rock went nuts. Every time someone had rung the doorbell in the past few weeks he had zoomed to the door at warp speed, sure it was Maggie, only to slink away when it turned out to be somebody else. If John was honest, the dog wasn't the only one who had been disappointed, as stupid as he had to admit that was.

He opened the door and was surprised to see Cody standing there.

"Evening John," he said as he patted Rock on the head.

"Hey," was all John could manage to squeeze out past his surprise, Cody didn't do house calls.

"Think I can come in?" he asked. "That wind blowing up my ass ain't getting any warmer."

John nodded as he opened the door wider. "Yeah, of course, come on in. What can I get you to drink?"

Cody marched past him and John had to marvel at how the guy immediately looked like he owned the place.

"Some of that Irish whiskey you're so fond of will do."

John poured a generous measure into a glass and handed it over, wondering what the hell was going on.

He didn't have to wait long. After all, small-talk wasn't Cody's style.

"You look like hell, John."

John nodded. "I've had better times."

Cody fixed him with one of his soul-piercing stares. "You talk to her?"

Even as accustomed as he was to Cody's straight-talking, he was still shocked at the direct nature of the question. "You mean Maggie?"

Cody raised an eyebrow. "Unless there's another lady in your life, I don't know about, then yes, I mean Maggie."

John looked away from Cody's intense gaze. "No."

Cody made a strange sound like a cross between a huff and a snort. "You think it might be a good idea to pick up the phone or maybe go see her?"

John's head flipped up. He didn't really want to talk about what he thought was a good or a bad idea in relation to Maggie. "No offence, Cody but I don't really want to talk about it."

Cody snorted. A definite snort this time, unmistakably full of contempt.

"I don't care about what you want lieutenant, I'm here to talk about what you need."

Even though John technically outranked him as an officer and Cody was no longer a serving Navy SEAL, he knew Cody's use of his military rank meant the man was serious and John had best listen up.

"Have a seat," John said as he grabbed the bottle of whiskey by the neck and placed it between them on the dining table.

Cody eased himself into a chair and spoke in a slightly softer tone.

"So, if I understand it correctly you're planning on deploying on Monday and leaving the best thing that ever happened to you behind without so much as a word. And I'm assuming you think you'll get over her in time, that the shattered pieces of your heart will someday fuse back together, maybe not in the same way they used to be but you think that's an okay price to pay for setting the woman you love free from a life with you. Is this your plan?"

John nodded. "Something like that."

Cody poured them both some more whiskey.

"Shit plan, John. Shit plan."

John went to speak but Cody raised his hand to silence him.

"Let me tell you what in actual fact will happen... You will leave on Monday with your heart in a million more tiny pieces than before. You'll be in so much pain for the duration of your deployment you won't be able to think straight. If, due to this lack of straight-thinking, you manage to somehow come back alive and uninjured you will spend the rest of your days looking for the missing piece of your soul."

He took a gulp of his whiskey.

John remained silent but couldn't miss the pain in his old Master Chief's eyes. He'd seen the same type of pain in the mirror every day since Maggie had left.

"You're a helluva warrior John and one of the best goddamn SEALs I've ever seen but you've been at the coal-face of this fucking war now for twelve years and that's a long time. You boys who joined up after nine-eleven have been constantly involved in a conflict the likes of which we've never seen before. And I know you've made decisions and put your life on hold but I'm here tonight to tell you to take your finger off the pause button John and to live your life. Don't let the woman you love slip through your fingers. I know after what happened with your mother, the thoughts of having to deploy and leave Maggie behind must be terrifying to you but there are bigger things to be afraid of..."

His voice trailed off and he seemed to John to be lost in memories.

"Let love into your life John and live the best possible life you can live. You've already given so much for your country, don't end up a hollowed out shell, a casualty of battle, miserable and empty for the rest of your days. Talk to her. Go see her. Beg her to take you back. Grovel if you have to but do not get on that plane on Monday without doing all you can to get her back. Trade some of your loneliness for a bit of happiness, John. God knows, you deserve it."

He picked up the rest of his whiskey and threw it down his throat. John was speechless.

Cody stood and John went to get up.

"No, stay there," Cody said, "I'll let myself out. You just think about what I had to say."

With that he marched out of the house and left John to pick his jaw up off the floor.

***

John looked at his watch. The time said 11pm. It had been three hours since Cody left and John hadn't been able to stop thinking about what he'd said. He'd finally gone to bed about an hour ago in the hope he could fall asleep but was starting to realize that wasn't going to happen.

He looked over to Maggie's side of the bed and reached out his hand. He wondered how she was doing and if she was as miserable as him. God what he wouldn't give to have her beside him. Cody's words tormented him, "*beg her to take you back.*"

Would she?

He had no right to ask but he wondered if he should let that stop him. There had been conviction behind Cody's words tonight, as if he'd known exactly what he was talking about and John had to admit he was right about the pain not going away. He shuddered at the thought of it getting worse and he didn't want to think about being stuck in Africa wishing he'd tried to contact Maggie before he left and having to live with the regret of not having done so.

He reasoned with himself that asking her to take him back would be too big a jump after all he'd done but maybe he could ask her to let him back in. He'd destroyed her trust and broken her heart but maybe if he could just re-establish some communication between them, he could start to get her to trust him again.

He'd been an idiot, he realized that now. He'd hit the first major wobble in their relationship and instead of turning to her to help him get through it, he'd pushed her away. He winced at the memory as a fresh wave of yearning washed over him. He needed to put things right between them and he needed to start doing that tonight.

"Fuck it," he announced to the empty room as he reached for his phone.

He found her number, typed in the word "Hey" and pressed send before he had a chance to think about it.

Once the word "sent" appeared on the screen he flung the phone on the bed and said, "Fuck it," again, only louder this time. He didn't know what he was doing but he knew he had to do it.

He waited for a response but none came.

Fuck.

He decided to grab himself by the balls and call.

Her phone went to voicemail. It felt so good to hear her voice he forgot to leave a message.

He called again and this time he spoke.

"Hey, I understand if you don't want to talk to me but I deploy on Monday and I'd really like to talk to you before then so if you can call me back that would be pretty fucking amazing. I know I have no right to say this but I miss you."

He thought of everything else he wanted to say but left it at that.

He waited for a call or a text back but none came. Anxiety chewed away at him and by midnight he couldn't take any more. He picked up the phone and called again.

"Maggie, I know I have no right to ask this but please call me. I'm sorry, so fucking sorry and I'm begging you to call me back."

He hung up. He didn't care how pathetic he sounded, he needed to talk to her.

One o'clock in the morning rolled around and his phone's resolute silence taunted him. He'd picked it up twice to check if it was working properly. It was.

At 1:05am he threw the duvet off him and jumped out of bed. If she wouldn't pick up the phone then there was only one thing left for him to do and that was to go to New York because there was no way in hell he was leaving for Africa on Monday without begging her to forgive him and maybe even consider letting him back into her life.

TWENTY-SEVEN

The thoughts of seeing Maggie had given him a heavy right foot and he'd made it to New York in record time. Gaining entry to her building was easy due to a minimal security system and he was now standing outside her apartment door. Excitement and nervousness coursed through his veins, each battling the other for prominence.

He knocked on her door.

Nothing.

He waited.

He knocked again, harder this time.

Nothing.

He called her name.

"Maggie."

Silence.

"Fuck," he said to the empty hallway.

Of course he'd considered she might not be here but going on the law of probability he'd figured there was a high chance she would be. He knew the hospital's inquiry wasn't due to be concluded yet so he knew she wasn't at work.

A sense of desperation gripped him. He didn't want to think about leaving on Monday without seeing her. He turned to the door and banged on it.

"Maggie, if you're in there please open up," he begged, his voice considerably louder this time.

Nothing.

He considered picking the lock but figured he'd better try one more time to get her to open the door voluntarily.

Fear ran like ice through his blood, there was no way he wasn't going to see her.

No way.

He pounded the door.

"Maggie," he shouted, "please, I'm begging you, open the door."

He heard a click and his heart jumped into his mouth but then a voice with a thick Asian accent sounded from behind him.

"What the fuck? Who the fuck ah you and what the fuck ah you doing making all this noise and banging on Maggie's doh."

John twirled around and was greeted by the sight of an Asian man in a pink kimono, his jet black hair sticking out at various angles to his head and his finger and toe-nails painted a very glossy bright blue. He knew immediately it was Andy, Maggie's neighbor and close friend.

"I'm looking for Maggie," John replied, "do you know if she's inside or where I might find her?"

Recognition flashed in Andy's eyes.

"Foh fuck's sake, you ah John," he said as he stepped back and carefully perused John from toe to head, "so that's what an idiot looks like."

John let the barb go, after all, he couldn't argue. "Maggie?" he repeated, "is she in there? If not, do you know where she is?"

"Why do you wanna know?" Andy asked.

John tamped down his frustration, getting angry with this guy would get him nowhere. "I need to see her," he admitted.

"Well too bad," Andy replied, "she's gone."

John's eyes narrowed at Andy's words. "What do you mean she's gone? Gone where?"

Andy looked at him like he was the dumbest fuck on the planet. "Gone!" he announced and threw his hands in the air for emphasis, "to Kenya."

John looked at the girl-guy in front of him and shook his head. He was sure he'd said Maggie was gone to Kenya but that couldn't be because that would be crazy.

"Kenya where? What do you mean Kenya?" John asked.

Andy raised an eyebrow as if to say he thought John was stupid before but he now realized he was dealing with a whole other level of stupid.

"Kenya, Af-ee-ca," he said in a tone so scathing John almost checked to see if he had lacerations on his skin.

"What the hell is she doing in Kenya?" John asked, hoping the guy was going to tell him she was gone on safari.

"Woking," Andy replied, "in a camp."

Disbelief rocked John.

Fuck no, he thought to himself, *please do not let this be true.*

"Like a refugee camp?" he asked.

Andy nodded.

"Which one?" he asked.

Andy shrugged his shoulders.

"I don't know," he said, "a big one foh the United Nations."

John leaned back against Maggie's door for support.

"Daadab," he whispered.

Andy nodded his head.

"Yes, that's the one."

John exhaled.

"Fuck."

There was increasing evidence the Daadab refugee camp was a hive of terrorist activity and was just one of the threats he and his team would be looking at once they landed in Djibouti.

"Fuck," he said again.

Andy resented John's obvious disapproval of Maggie's choice.

"Well fuck you," he said, "she wouldn't have gone only foh you. She sat around long enough waiting foh you to call."

John winced. The guy was right.

"How long is she gone for?" he asked

"Eight weeks," Andy replied.

Disappointment clawed at John's gut and he slumped against the door. He'd come all this way and driven through the night in the desperate hope of seeing her but he'd left it too late.

Andy watched the huge guy opposite him slump against the door as bitter disappointment washed over him and he almost felt sorry for the guy. Almost. From everything Maggie had told him over the past few weeks, he hadn't been able to decide if the guy was a player or a man who had genuinely wanted to save Maggie from greater heartache down the line. Looking at the haunted expression on this big Navy SEAL's face he figured there was no way the guy was a player and he warmed to him a little.

"You wanna come in foh a coffee?" he asked.

John looked at the vision in pink before him and thought of the long drive back to Virginia Beach.

"No thanks, " he said, "I'm going to hit the road but if you have contact details for Maggie then I'll gladly take them."

Andy smiled at John's self-assured manner, as if he would just hand Maggie's contact details over to him if he had them. He shook his head. "I don't have any. She is going to send me an email when she gets a chance."

John bit his lower lip in frustration. "When she does, can you please tell her I was here and ask her to send me an email?"

Yes, I can do that," Andy replied, "but I can't say that she will. She is not the same Maggie as she was befoh she met you."

John winced. "Yeah, I know," he said as he pushed himself away from the wall, "I want to try and fix that."

Andy nodded as he made his way back into his apartment.

"Good luck," he said, as John started to walk away.

"Thanks," John replied, "I think I'm going to need it."

Six hours later as he pulled up in front of his house in Virginia Beach he had to admit how right Cody had been. It felt like his heart had broken all over again and its tiny pieces were scattered on the wind. He felt empty and yet a great weight sat on him causing his every movement to feel heavy and labored. He fell into his bed and pulled the sheets to him as despair flooded through him at the thought of not seeing her, touching her or hearing her voice for six months or maybe ever again.

"I love you Maggie," he whispered into the coconut and jasmine scented sheet, "fuck it but I love you."

TWENTY-EIGHT

John watched as the early morning sun slowly brought the horizon to life with a mirage of pink, purple and blue. He pushed one leg in front of the other as he put on a last sprint towards his imaginary finish line and thirty seconds later sucked in big chunks of the Djibouti air as he checked his time.

His attention was pulled away from his watch by the thwunk, thwunk of yet another incoming helo, the second one in the last twenty minutes and he wondered if something was going down. He certainly hoped so, the last few weeks had dragged by and despite their intel regarding increased terrorist activity along the Somalian and Kenyan border, there had been no request for the use of their unique skill set.

In some ways being deployed had helped with his heartache over Maggie in so far as he wasn't surrounded by constant reminders of her but in other ways he was finding it harder to cope. Not having any contact with her was killing him and he bitterly regretted not getting Andy's email address before he left New York so that he could follow up with him to see if he had heard from her.

The days in Djibouti were long, filled with a sense of waiting for something to happen and then it never did but the nights were longer. He hated the fucking nights. The nights left him with nowhere to run from his regret and self-loathing. He'd had the most amazing woman in his life and he hadn't just pushed her away, no, he'd delivered the emotional equivalent of a knockout. He cringed as he remembered how hard and unrelenting he'd been.

"Fuck," he swore to the early morning air as he wondered when, or if, he'd ever get a chance to tell her how sorry he was.

***

"Spooks to spare this morning," Snake murmured into John's ear as he took the seat beside him in the operation's center for their morning briefing.

"Yeah," John replied, as he cast his eye over the four newcomers who stood in the shadows at the top of the operation's center, "looks like something is up."

Judging by the edgy body language of the three guys and one woman, all of them definitely CIA, something was going down.

Seconds later, Commander Saunders stood and immediately had everyone's attention.

"Morning all," he started in his southern drawl, and John knew, just from the tone of his voice, something serious was on the agenda. A photo of what looked like a Somalian national appeared on the main screen behind the Commander.

The Commander looked at the screen and spoke.

"The person you see on the screen is Yusuf Ali, a former Somalian pirate who has retired from the piracy business and recently diversified into the lucrative hostage taking business."

Another photo filled the second screen. Commander Saunders moved closer to the second screen and jabbed his index finger at the second photo.

"This here is Mohammed Al Hussein, former Somalian warlord and leader of the recently formed El Mumita, an off-shoot of Al Shabaab. El Mumita is Arabic for The Bringers of Death, and unfortunately this particular bunch of assholes intend to bring as much death and destruction as possible to anyone who doesn't follow their particular brand of Islam. In recent months El Mumita have forged a close alliance with ISIS."

John and Snake exchanged curious looks, this was an interesting development.

The photos disappeared from the screens.

Commander Saunders cleared his throat before continuing.

"Two weeks ago on 24th January, Yusuf Ali and his men conducted a cross-border raid into Kenya."

Another photo of what looked like a small aid camp filled screen one. There were no people pictured but lots of blood and bullet-holes.

The Commander continued.

"The target was a U.N. out-reach camp providing medical treatment to Kenyans affected by the recent drought and also some Somalian refugees."

John felt a prickle of something he couldn't quite identify make its way along his skin.

"A number of Kenyan nationals were taken hostage along with five U.N. staff who all happen to be American."

John sat that little bit straighter in his seat.

A photo of a guy in his mid-forties came up on the screen.

"Doctor Gary Allen, pediatrician."

Another photo flashed up. A guy in his thirties this time.

"Doctor James Harding, expert in tropical diseases."

The prickle of something along John's skin morphed into a sense of unease and lodged itself firmly in his gut.

Another photo.

"Doctor Frank Stillman, retired cardiologist."

John exhaled the breath he didn't realize he'd been holding.

The next photo was of a woman and thankfully she didn't look anything like a doctor.

"Doctor Ruby Obermeier, trauma surgeon and specialist in women's health."

John sat bolt upright. Maggie had gone to Kenya with someone called Dr. Ruby.

The last photo came up on the screen and in that instant his world fell apart.

"Doctor Maggie O'Brien, senior trauma surgeon and newest member of the medical outreach team."

Commander Saunders paused for breath and it seemed to John as if he was looking directly at him when he next spoke.

"Doctor O'Brien is also believed to be about three or four months pregnant."

Shock, brutal and hard-hitting as a wrecking-ball slammed through John. His body flooded with adrenaline and his immediate instinct was to jump out of his seat and run but he felt two heavy restraints on his legs. He looked down and saw Snake's hand on his right thigh, pinning him to his seat and Joker's on his left.

"Shhhh...." Snake whispered out the side of his mouth, "react and you'll find yourself grounded for the rescue op."

John looked up and even though he observed a subtle tension in the body language of all his other team-mates, to their credit, none of them moved or turned around to look at him. All of them focused straight ahead on the words coming out of the Commander's mouth, words he couldn't process. Words he couldn't believe.

Maggie was in the hands of Somalian pirates and if he understood correctly, Yusuf Ali intended to "sell" her and her colleagues to a bunch of killers who were in league with ISIS. And she was pregnant. Pregnant! Nightmares didn't come any worse than this.

"Intel is fluid at this time," Commander Saunders continued, "report back here at 13:00 hours for a further update. That's all."

He immediately left the operation's center, closely followed by the spooks.

The whole team turned and looked at John, disbelief, pity and sympathy coloring their expressions.

John got up from his seat and bolted. Exactly thirty seconds later he emptied the contents of his stomach into the dirt at the back of the op's center. He held onto the wall for support and managed to stagger a few feet before collapsing and sliding down the wall.

He sat there in the Djibouti dirt and tried to process what he had just heard. Maggie was captured and soon would be in the hands of barbarians who prided themselves on the sadistic things they could do to another human being. And she was carrying a baby. His baby. His stomach heaved again. He shook his head. Fuck but this could not be happening. Fuck. Fuck. Fuck.

And then a further realization hit him and his blood ran cold. He had done this. He had driven her away. A bitter laugh sliced like broken glass across his lips. Oh the irony. He had finished with her to protect her, to keep her safe from hurt and heartache and he had only succeeded in putting her in perilous danger.

"You fuckwit," he cursed at himself as his body started to shake.

Damn it but he needed a drink.

As if by magic Joker appeared in the dirt beside him and offered him a silver hip-flask. John looked at him in disbelief.

Joker grinned.

"For emergencies," he said, as he offered it to John, "it's not Irish but it'll do and this situation definitely constitutes an emergency."

John grabbed it and chugged three mouthfuls back in quick succession. He felt it burn its way down his throat and dispel the death-like cold in the pit of his stomach. He took another two slugs for good measure and handed it back to Joker.

Joker took a slug and then spoke, his voice ice-like and calm. "We're gonna get her back John, you know that. Those fucks are not going to get their filthy paws on her."

Snake came around the corner. "Hell no. It's not happening, not while we live and breathe."

John looked at his two team-mates, his brothers, and knew, just like him, they would do everything in their power to get Maggie back, or die trying.

***

Exactly one hour later he found himself outside the door to the Commander's office. He had been summoned and John hoped he wasn't about to be sidelined off the op. His mind had exploded in the past hour and he wouldn't be able to handle that sort of order right now. He needed to be on the team.

He knocked on the door.

"Come in," the Commander barked.

John walked in.

"Lieutenant," the Commander greeted him, "have a seat."

John sat in the seat in front of the Commander's desk and waited for him to speak.

"I've given you an hour to digest the intel from the briefing Lieutenant, anything you want to tell me."

John wasn't quite sure how to respond so he erred on the side of caution.

"I'm not quite sure what you mean, Sir," he replied.

The Commander treated him to a slightly raised eyebrow.

"Lieutenant, I may only have been at Cody's party for an hour but it was long enough to see you with a red-haired lady who bears an uncanny resemblance to Dr. Maggie O'Brien. So don't fuck around with me Lieutenant, is there something you have to tell me."

John's head fell.

"She was my girlfriend, Sir."

The Commander shifted in his seat.

"Was?"

John looked up.

"Yeah, was. I finished it before we deployed, Sir."

The Commander looked unimpressed.

"And the baby?"

John winced as a whole new brand of pain stabbed at his heart. He was still finding it hard to believe Maggie was pregnant with his baby.

"I didn't know she was pregnant, Sir. Not until an hour ago."

The Commander let out a long breath.

"Fuck, Lieutenant, it's a helluva way to find out you're going to be a father. Is it definitely yours?"

John was in no doubt the baby was his, he just wondered if Maggie had known she was pregnant before she left. He looked his commanding officer in the eyes.

"I'm one hundred percent certain, Sir. I'm not sure if Maggie knew she was pregnant when she left. I can't imagine her keeping something like that from me."

Unless she intended to tell me at a later date, he thought ruefully to himself.

The Commander let out a sigh.

"Fuck it Lieutenant. What a clusterfuck of a situation. Why did you end things?"

John didn't feel comfortable discussing his private life with the Commander but he guessed he was trying to get a feel for where his head was at so he decided to tell him the truth.

"I was trying to protect her, Sir. I reacted badly to the news about Freezer and I panicked and I thought it would be best if I set her free of me so she could find someone else who didn't come with so many complications."

The Commander huffed.

"I'm thinking Somalian pirates weren't exactly who you had in mind. You love her?"

John nodded. "Very much."

The Commander didn't say anything and John's heart sank as he feared he was about to receive an order side-lining him.

He got up out of his seat and started to pace back and forth behind his desk. John could see he was struggling with his decision. Then he spoke.

"Ordinarily, I'd sign you off the op but you're one of my best men John, especially at this sort of thing. But I need to know your head is in the game. Lives depend on it, so if, on any level, you aren't up for this then sign yourself out."

Relief surged through John. He couldn't believe he wasn't being side-lined.

"My head is straight sir, you don't have to worry. Having a personal stake in this only makes me more focused on the details, not less so."

The Commander looked happy enough with his answer and half-smiled.

"Okay, so far the plan is for a two-pronged attack. Intel suggests a meeting is to take place over the next few days, with Mohammed Al Hussein and his men planning on travelling to the small village where Yusuf Ali is holed up. We believe the transaction is to take place at this meeting and the hostages will be leaving with Hussein and his men. It is imperative they do not leave the village as it will be almost impossible to track them after that.

The mission will have two objectives. Objective one will be to liberate and secure the hostages and get them the hell out of there.

Objective two will be to capture or kill Mohammed Al Hussein and capture as many of his men as possible. You will lead the team responsible for the rescue of the hostages. Lieutenant Mayhew and his platoon will be responsible for the capture or otherwise of Hussein and his men."

John nodded. "Sounds good, Sir."

The Commander pursed his lips.

"I'm glad you think so. You and your men will insert tonight approximately ten miles from the village. From there you will hump it in to the surrounding hills from where you are to observe and report back. As soon as you spot Hussein and his men you are to call it in. We expect the exchange to take a few hours, we're even hoping he will stay the night, thereby enabling us to undertake our mission at our preferred time of day. However, we have no idea what will happen. If it looks like they are moving the hostages then you are to engage immediately, with your primary objective being the safety of the hostages."

John nodded again. "Understood, Sir."

The Commander looked long and hard at John. "Don't make me regret this decision to put you in charge of the hostage rescue Lieutenant."

John returned his commanding officer's stare. "I won't, Sir."

The Commander grabbed a folder off his desk and marched towards the door. "Good. Come on then, let's go inform the others of the plan."

TWENTY-NINE

Maggie watched as the last of the evening shadows turned into the blanket darkness of night. The small outbuilding she and her colleagues were being kept in only had one window and it was positioned high up in the wall so it simply afforded them a view of the sky and not the village itself or their surroundings. They'd been here nearly two weeks now and had only been allowed out when one of them was ordered to empty the slop bucket. Apart from the initial contact of their abduction, the leader and his men hadn't come near them. They seemed to be suspicious of them and had kept their distance, most especially from her.

Saleemah, the girl who was tasked with their care, seemed to think this was because they thought she and her colleagues had "the sickness" as she called it. Maggie stroked her tummy. She had something in there that had made her sick all right but it was no "sickness".

As soon as she'd landed in Daadab she'd begun to feel unwell and within a few days was suffering from debilitating nausea and tiredness that had quickly escalated to vomiting and exhaustion. Ruby had run a few blood tests and the shocking truth had been revealed, she was pregnant!

Even now, a few weeks later, she still found it hard to believe. She'd missed at least two periods but she'd put that down to stress and a broken heart. She'd never imagined she would be pregnant with John's baby. A wave of anguish washed over her as she thought about the man she loved and missed with every beat of her heart and wondered if she would ever see again.

What was to happen to her and her colleagues was unclear. Saleemah had alluded to "bad men" coming and Maggie hadn't liked the look of abject fear in her eyes when she had mentioned them.

"Stay sick," Saleemah had said, as she'd put her hand on Maggie's tummy, "baby will protect you."

Maggie thought it ironic how a young Somalian girl had figured out her condition with no medical training whatsoever and it had taken a blood test to show her, the doctor, what was going on with her own body. However, she was very grateful for the young girl's kindness. Along with the rations she was sanctioned to deliver to them each day, she often smuggled extra bread or fruit in under her clothes.

"For baby," she would say.

Maggie did her best to share the extra bit of food out amongst them all as she knew the baby would take what it needed from her.

She caressed her tummy again. A baby. John's baby. It was almost inconceivable to her but the small rounding of her tummy told her it was true. A tear slipped quietly from her eye as she considered her situation and how being a captive in a village in the hills of Somalia wasn't quite what she'd envisaged in the event she ever became pregnant.

She wondered who the bad men were Saleemah referred to and how they could possibly be any worse than the brutes who had captured them. Then it occurred to her that apart from their brutality during the abduction, at least they hadn't harmed them since. Were the men who were coming known for their cruelty and what did that mean for her and her colleagues? Would they be moved? Split up?

Terror and panic overwhelmed her and suddenly she was fighting for breath. As bad as things were now, the thoughts of being on her own with a bunch of barbarians terrified her. And the baby? What would happen to her baby? Would they hurt it? Kill it? She placed both her hands over her little bump. No, she thought, Dear God, no, please don't let anything happen to my baby.

She hated crying in front of the others as she knew each one of them was struggling to stay strong and keep a grip on their sanity but tonight the desperation of their situation was proving too much for her. The darkness of the night mirrored the grim nature of her thoughts and huge, agonized tears fell heavily onto her cheeks.

She turned into the wall as she succumbed to the sobs wracking her body and thought about John and how much she ached for him. She wondered if he knew about her situation and if so was he going crazy with worry or was she simply another hostage caught in an unpleasant situation that he had more than just a passing interest in? Chances were she was never going to find out.

Despair, fathomless and un-relenting consumed her and she fought for breath between the sobs.

Seconds later she felt Ruby's arms around her.

"Hey Maggie, come on, don't lose hope, we're getting out of this, you know we are."

Maggie looked up and could just make out her friend's face in the darkness. Of all of them Ruby remained the strongest. Each one of them had cracked at various points and Ruby had been there offering comfort and words of encouragement. Maggie knew her friend and knew she was struggling too but so far had managed to hold herself together and not break down. Maggie couldn't help wondering when it came if it was something Ruby was going to be able to come back from as she suspected her friend's strength stemmed from her steadfast belief in the fact they would be rescued. If that didn't happen soon, she feared Ruby's breakdown would be the most spectacular of them all.

"Are we?' she asked. "How can you be so sure Ruby? How can we know anybody even knows where we are?"

She could feel Ruby bristle in the darkness.

"We're Americans, Maggie. We've got the biggest, most badass army in the world. They will send some of those boys to get us and even if, for some reason they don't, my family are obnoxiously rich and they'll send a private army to get us anyway. So, believe me, we are getting out of this."

Maggie leaned into her friend's arms a little more and allowed herself to grasp onto the sliver of hope she was offering. It was that or sink further into the black hole of despair that was already threatening to devour her.

She looked out the window and could just make out the twinkling of the stars. She pictured John in her mind and pretended it was his arms enfolding her and it seemed as if the stars twinkled that bit brighter as she let the tiny bud of hope take hold in her heart.

THIRTY

John looked through his binoculars at the village approximately two klicks away. It was early morning and only a few of the women were up and about, which wasn't surprising considering the men had spent most of the night getting high on khat.

He had counted thirty-five adult males in all and ten juveniles. The village was small and consisted mostly of traditional style mud huts with tin roofs. The women, of whom he estimated there were about fifteen, did most of the cooking around a communal wood fire which was located in the center of the village and around which the men sat in the evening.

Security was non-existent and it was obvious to John these guys thought the remoteness of their location was protection enough in itself. He smiled.

You're in for a helluva surprise, assholes, he thought to himself.

He scanned the village again, this time specifically looking for the teenage girl who was tasked with looking after the hostages. There was no sign of her and his stomach dropped with disappointment. In the two days he and his team had been watching the village there had been no sighting of Maggie.

They had determined the hostages were being held in a small outbuilding on the edge of the village which struck John as odd. Each morning they'd observed a hostage being tasked with disposing of a bucket of what looked like human excrement. He didn't like to think of Maggie having to perform the most basic of human functions in front of her colleagues but he'd rescued enough hostages to know what the deal was. He consoled himself with the fact that at least they had a bucket.

So far they'd confirmed the presence of Dr. Ruby Obermeier and Dr. James Harding. He was hoping this morning he might get a sighting of Maggie. Just the prospect of it had his heart soaring in his chest.

The temptation to infiltrate the village, under cover of darkness, liberate Maggie and the other hostages and walk them out of there to a point where they could be safely extracted was almost too much. But he knew there was more at stake here than just rescuing the hostages and having

Maggie back in his arms and he had promised the Commander his head was in the game. He had to remember the dual objectives of the mission. However, watching the village and knowing Maggie was down there and not being able to do anything about it, not being able to help her, was stretching his mental and emotional capacity to near breaking point.

Joker fell into the dirt beside him.

"See her yet?" he asked.

John shook his head.

"Negative."

Joker looked through his own binoculars.

"Hmmm... looks like the ladies are cooking up a storm this morning. Wonder if they're expecting visitors?"

John trained his binoculars on the women around the fire.

"I sure fucking hope so, " he replied, "and I hope the intel for this op is better than the last one."

Boots, the big Texan, who had taken Freezer's place in the team, came up behind them.

"There's a vehicle approaching from the south-east, from what I can see there are four bogeys on board."

John swung around and trained his binoculars on the approaching vehicle. Sure enough a Toyota Hi-lux was moving at speed across the dirt-road and John could see four adult males. The driver, a guy in the passenger seat and two in the flat-bed portion in the back. None of them were Mohammed Al Hussein or even recognizable to John.

He watched as they continued on to the village. On their approach there was much commotion amongst the women. One of them ran to the building where John knew Yusuf Ali slept and within minutes he was outside greeting his guests.

"Who are these fuckers?" Snake murmured beside him.

"I'm not sure," John replied but I'm gonna get pics of their ugly faces and send 'em back to base, maybe the spooks know."

Yusuf Ali was joined by some of his men and they, and the four visitors, sat near where the women were cooking over the fire.

The women brought them all food and drink.

Within five minutes of John having sent the photos back to base he had confirmation of the Driver, Khaleem Al Mujarab, third in command to Mohammed Al Hussein.

John smiled. It looked like today was going to be the day and if Hussein had only sent four guys to take possession of the hostages then this shit was going to be too easy.

A few minutes later the girl who was responsible for the care of the hostages was brought before the men by one of the older women and obviously given an order by Ali.

She went in the direction of the building where John knew the hostages were being kept, accompanied by two of Ali's men with guns.

John could feel the blood surging through his veins and he almost felt light-headed at the prospect of getting a visual on Maggie.

The girl opened the door and beckoned for the hostages to come out.

One by one they came out, slowly and each with their hands shading their eyes from the glare of the sun.

John quickly took photos.

Dr. James Harding, confirmed.

Dr. Gary Allen, confirmed.

Dr. Ruby Obermeier, confirmed.

Dr. Frank Stillman, confirmed.

John's heart was in his mouth and he could just about draw the Somalian air into his lungs when the last of the hostages came through the door and was instantly recognizable by her red hair.

Dr. Maggie O'Brien, confirmed.

He quickly took her photo and then slowly exhaled in relief.

He passed the camera off to Joker and grabbed his binoculars.

He zeroed in on her and the sight of her was at once heart-warming and heart-wrenching.

She didn't appear to be injured in any way but her face was gaunt and her hair, the hair he loved to watch as it slipped through his fingers, was dull and matted in parts. But it was her eyes that ripped his heart out of his chest. Her eyes were clouded with uncertainty and fear.

"Hang on Maggie," he whispered, "just hang on, I'm coming for you."

***

Once Maggie and her colleagues were paraded in front of Hussein's men they were quickly returned to the building where they were being kept.

Al Mujarab seemed to take a personal interest in Dr. Ruby which made John nervous.

The safety of the hostages was the primary objective of his mission and he didn't want it complicated by one of the hostages being separated from the rest of the group due to the unwanted attentions of one of Hussein's dickheads.

He reported the morning's activity back to base and wondered what was going to happen next.

In the event Al Mujarab decided to leave with the hostages, he decided him and his squad should move closer to the village.

They were just in their new position when he noticed Al Mujarab walking to the outskirts of the village and making a call on his cell phone.

Nothing much happened for the rest of the day but at 3:10 pm Joker called a heads-up. There were three vehicles approaching from the south-east along the same dirt-road Al Mujarab and his men had travelled earlier.

John looked through his binoculars and confirmed the three vehicles with three adult males in each and he smiled to himself as he recognized the passenger in the second vehicle as being Mohammed Al Hussein. Finally, this shit was going down and soon he would be getting Maggie the hell out of there.

He radioed in to command.

"Be advised, Valentine is confirmed," he informed the Commander and the support team back in Djibouti.

Valentine was the pro-word they had agreed for Mohammed Al Hussein and his men. Some smart-ass had decided to call the rescue mission Operation Lovestruck due to the fact in the western world it was Valentine's weekend.

Whatever, John thought, if I get Maggie out of here safe and sound, that's the best Valentine's Day present I am ever going to get.

***

Hussein got out of his vehicle and John was immediately struck at how much the guy acted like he owned the village and everyone in it. Yusuf Ali did his best to assert his authority but John could tell he was nervous.

They all sat down and Hussein and his men were brought food and drink by the women who seemed frightened of them.

Ali and Hussein chatted for about an hour and then their conversation turned intense and quickly became heated.

John wasn't happy with this development. He could only imagine they were trying to hammer out a deal for the hostages.

All he wanted was for them to agree the deal, have some food, chew some khat, go to sleep and then not know what hit them in the middle of the night as he and his men launched their assault.

Any sort of disagreement between Ali and Hussein could see the op going squirrelly.

Yusuf summoned the girl who looked after the hostages and, just like before, she was dispatched with two armed men to the outbuilding where they were being kept.

Maggie and her colleagues were paraded in front of Hussein and John noted all of them were smart enough not to make eye contact.

However, something about Maggie and Ruby upset Hussein and he called the girl over. He shouted at her for a few seconds and then slapped her hard in the face before pushing her away.

Dr. Ruby's head shot up and a look of venom darted from her eyes.

"Noooo," John whispered quietly to himself, "look back at the ground."

He didn't like the direction things were going in.

Ruby decided discretion was the better part of valor and adjusted her gaze to an unidentified spot on the ground but it was too late.

Hussein marched over to her and grabbed her face in his hand and viciously wrenched her head up to look into his eyes. He shouted something at her but she didn't flinch. However, Maggie lifted her head as if she was going to say something.

"No. Fuck, no, Maggie. Don't say anything." John hissed between clenched teeth as he felt his heart about to burst from his chest.

Hussein looked at Maggie, said something and in one swift movement back-handed her across the cheek.

"Fuck!" John exclaimed, "that fucker is dead-meat."

Snake put his hand on John's shoulder.

"Easy, John," he soothed, "we're gonna get him but we need to stay calm."

John sucked in big breaths of air in a desperate effort to calm himself down and nodded. His men needed to know he was in control.

"Yeah," he agreed, "I just don't like where this is all going."

Snake nodded. "Yeah, I hear ya, Lieutenant."

Hussein had now turned his attention back to Ruby and was circling her like a cat might circle its prey.

John could see Ruby was nervous as hell but to her credit she didn't move and just kept staring at the ground.

Then in a lightning swift movement Hussein ripped her hoodie from her body.

All she was wearing underneath it was a short-sleeved tee-shirt and her tattoos were immediately visible in all their colorful glory. They seemed to enrage Hussein.

He lifted her arms and shouted in her face. Then he jabbed at her nose-ring and flicked her dreadlocked hair.

She stood, unflinching and John had to admire her balls but Hussein wasn't finished.

He twisted his fingers around her hair and yanked mercilessly, pulling Ruby's head back so she was now looking at the sky. His face twisted with menace and he whispered something in her ear. Whatever it was must have been terrifying to Ruby because fear suddenly flickered in her eyes.

Hussein said something to his men and three of them, including a grinning Al Mujarab, got up and came over. Hussein pushed Ruby towards them and said something else.

Whatever it was upset Maggie and she shouted, "No!" loud enough that John and his men could hear her. She reached out for her friend but Hussein grabbed her by the throat and pushed her back in the dirt.

John could feel his blood start to boil. He couldn't take much more of this.

Snake looked over at him. "I don't like where this is all headed, Lieutenant," he said.

"Neither do I," Joker chipped in.

John looked at Maggie through his binoculars and felt his heart breaking all over again as he watched the tears flow down her face.

All he wanted to do was go down into the village, kill all those mother-fuckers and get her the hell out of there but he was a goddamned Navy SEAL and he had a job to do and even though his heart screamed at him to go down there and get her, his head told him the safest thing to do was to stick to the dual objectives of the mission. As much as he wanted to, he couldn't lose his head over the violence he was forced to watch being inflicted on her. Now, more than ever he needed to stay calm and rely on his years of training and experience.

The first thing he had to do was assess the situation in relation to what was happening to Dr. Ruby. For the moment Maggie was relatively safe but Ruby was a different matter.

He trained his binoculars on her and the three men leading her away towards one of the buildings. This was a situation he didn't like at all.

He was just about to radio this latest development back to base when matters took another turn.

Just as Ruby and the three men got to the building, Ruby lashed out at the captor nearest to her and brought him down with a series of well placed kicks and punches. It was obvious she'd had extensive martial arts training. She then turned on one of the others but Mujarab was too quick for her and grabbed her by the hair and in an instant had a knife at her throat.

In that moment John knew there was a high probability Dr. Ruby was never going to come out of that building alive. Whatever these guys had planned for her she intended to fight them all the way and his gut told him that would only have one outcome.

This wasn't exactly how they had planned the op to go down but he knew they needed to move now.

He radioed back to command.

"This is Alpha One of Operation Lovestruck. We have a rose in trouble and need to engage. "

In keeping with the theme name of the operation, they had decided to call the hostages, roses.

The Commander's voice crackled over the radio.

"Roger that, Alpha One. Assault Force Two are on their way. ETA, fifty minutes. "

The original plan had been for the two assault teams to engage at the same time, with John and his team focusing on the hostages and Lieutenant Mayhew and his team focusing on the apprehension or elimination of Hussein and his men.

He now needed to come up with a plan to save Dr. Ruby, keep Maggie and the rest of the hostages as safe as possible and keep the enemy engaged until Assault Force Two arrived.

He turned to his men.

"Okay, this is what we're gonna do. We need to keep these fuckers busy until Mayhew and his cavalry get here. We need them to think there's way more of us, so we need to spread ourselves as widely as possible. Snake, from this distance you should be able to pick 'em off. I need you to shoot out the tires on as many of the trucks as possible first. As soon as they know we are here there's a good chance Hussein will make a run for it and try and take the hostages with him. Then I want you to cover the building the hostages are in. I want those fuckers to very quickly realize, trying to open that door means certain death."

Snake nodded. "Done, Lieutenant."

John looked down at the village. Maggie and the three male hostages were back in the outbuilding but Dr. Ruby was in Al Mujarab's clutches. He had her arms secured behind her back and was sadistically dragging the knife down across her chest.

The insurgent she had knocked into the dirt had just gotten up and now walked over and punched her hard in the stomach.

John wanted to go there and then but knew he needed to wait as long as possible. Every minute they held off would make a big difference to the outcome of the operation.

He could hear the sharp intakes of breath of the others and knew it wasn't easy to watch. However, as long as he had a visual on her, he knew she was okay. As soon as the bastards got her behind that door he knew they had to engage as he suspected the nature of their violence would then become life threatening.

Dr. Ruby was slumped forward, obviously winded and Al Mujarab capitalized on her distress, pushing her forward towards the door.

Suddenly she came to life and proceeded to fight him every step of the way but this only seemed to please him in some sick kind of way and he laughed as he told the other two guys to help him with her.

Thirty seconds later John and his men watched as a still struggling Dr. Ruby disappeared behind the door.

***

Snake had already shot out the tires of four of the vehicles before Hussein and Ali's men realized what was happening but when they did, all hell broke loose.

The first thing Hussein did was to dispatch some of his men to get the hostages. After the first three lay dead in the dirt, the others decided they weren't risking their lives just yet and took cover. Hussein then made a run for the building Al Mujarab was in with Dr. Ruby but quickly had to take cover from the hail of bullets John and his men sent his way.

He then made a run for one of the vehicles and Snake made his day by shooting out the front left wheel.

"Yippee-ki-yay mother fucker," Snake chuckled to himself.

Hussein quickly got out of the vehicle before Snake could get another shot off and grabbed a gun off one of his men and finally decided he was going to fight.

Interestingly neither Al Mujarab or the other men with him made an appearance.

John was afraid they would decide to use Dr. Ruby as a shield to make a getaway and was grateful for every minute this didn't occur to them.

The next thirty minutes passed in a blur of bullets with John and his team moving positions frequently so as to confuse Al Hussein and Ali's men. He was just wondering when Al Hussein might realize there were only eight of them when Joker's voice broke in over the comms.

"Shit, we have extra guests coming to the party!" he exclaimed. "Four vehicles coming in from the north-west, approximately twenty military aged males, all armed."

John looked to his right and sure enough there were four more Toyotas making their way at speed to the village.

It was at times like these he was glad to have one of the best snipers the SEALs had ever seen on his team. He turned to Snake.

"Take 'em out. Whichever way you have to, either stop those fuckers altogether or slow 'em down."

Without a word Snake turned and pointed his rifle north-west.

John radioed command.

"Be advised, twenty military aged males approaching in four vehicles from the north-west. All armed. Possible RPGs but no visual. Recommend Alpha Two dispatch two birds for a rear-end surprise."

"Roger that," the Commander's voice crackled in reply, "Hawks one and two will be coming in from the south-west and hawks three and four will approach from the north-west. ETA hawk one is seven minutes. ETA hawk two, eight minutes."

"Roger that," John replied, "be advised target is hot."

John turned his attention back to the fight.

Snake had managed to take two of the vehicles out but the other two continued their approach.

At this rate they were going to reach the village before Assault Force Two got here.

John knew he couldn't rely on Snake alone to take them out.

He called Joker, Boots and Smurf.

"You guys are coming with me," he informed them, "we need to stop those fuckers getting to the village."

Each SEAL nodded and fell in beside John as he took off in a diagonal line in the direction of the northern tip of the village.

Three minutes later they bombarded the oncoming vehicles with grenades and were successful in destroying the lead vehicle but in doing so they had revealed their positions and came under heavy fire.

John was just wondering what to do next when he heard the choppy drone of the Seahawks approaching. He silently thanked God as he returned fire whilst calling in the enemy positions and waited for Assault Force Two to do their thing.

Minutes later the hawks demolished what was left of the approaching convoy and fired mercilessly on the enemy positions in the village. Lieutenant Mayhew and his team fast-roped in and proceeded to engage Hussein and Ali's men.

John barked over his comms for the rest of his team to make their way to the village and secure the hostages.

His heart beat furiously in his chest. Finally he was going to put an end to Maggie's ordeal and get her out of this shit-hole.

He ordered Snake and Joker to focus on Dr. Ruby and meet him, the rest of the team, and the hostages at the primary extraction point.

He and the rest of the team dodged bullets and IEDs to make it to the outbuilding where Maggie and her colleagues were being kept. The door didn't offer much resistance and before John knew it he had Maggie by the arm, dragging her to the extraction point.

At this point Lieutenant Mayhew and his team had the enemy fully engaged so getting to the extraction point was much easier than it had been to get to the outbuilding. Still their position was far from safe.

The Seahawks had retreated out of RPG range and sat waiting for them at just over a half a mile away from the village.

The hostages were in good enough shape to make that distance on foot but there was no sign of Snake, Joker and Dr. Ruby.

***

Snake and Joker approached the building Dr. Ruby was being held in. Snake thought it weird the way neither Al Mujarab or any of his men had engaged in the fighting and didn't like to think what the tattooed doc was being subjected to behind that door.

He and Joker approached it now, oblivious to the chaos around them. Their mission was to secure Dr. Ruby and get her to the extraction point.

They tried to kick the door in but it didn't budge and Snake remembered seeing a small window around the side. He ran over to it, closely followed by Joker. He quickly took a look through it to see if he could get a visual on Dr. Ruby or any of the insurgents and what he saw made his blood run cold.

A battered and bloody Dr. Ruby was on her knees on the floor, her tee-shirt and bra torn and in tatters. She was being restrained by Al Mujarab's two henchmen and Al Mujarab was standing in front of her with his dick at her mouth. One of the henchmen kicked her in the kidney and she cried out in pain. Al Mujarab sneered as he rammed his dick down her throat, grabbed onto her hair and proceeded to thrust mercilessly.

"Fuck," Snake exclaimed as he raised his rifle but as he did so Dr. Ruby bit down hard and Al Mujarab recoiled away from her, screaming in agony. The two henchmen were taken completely by surprise and she seized her opportunity. She jumped up and delivered a perfect round-house kick to the head of the one nearest to her. She was on him before he hit the floor and seconds later Snake heard a loud snap as she twisted his head and broke his neck.

Al Mujarab looked on in horror. The other henchman lunged for her but Snake's bullet stopped him in his tracks.

Al Mujarab turned and ran through a door behind him.

At this stage both Snake and Joker were through the window.

Joker went in pursuit of Al Mujarab and Snake tended to a now shaking Dr. Ruby.

Two minutes later Joker was back.

"I don't know where that slippery fucker went," he announced, "but I can't find him."

"Okay," Snake said, "let's get to the extraction point."

***

John was just about to make contact with Snake and Joker to see where they were when he saw them running towards him with a very worse for wear Dr. Ruby.

"Fuck" he exclaimed.

Maggie looked at him sharply.

"John?" she said in a shocked voice.

John shot a glance at her but then turned his attention back to Snake, Joker and Dr. Ruby. He had to stay sharp until they were all clear and out of here, then he could focus on Maggie.

Maggie continued to stare at the man who had hauled her out of the outbuilding. The man who had shielded her with his body and the man who stood in front of her now watching and protecting her and her colleagues from any further threat.

She'd thought there was something familiar about the giant of a man who had rescued her but he was wearing so much gear and his face was obscured to such an extent that she couldn't be sure. But as soon as she'd heard his voice she'd known. Tears started to fall down her face as it started to sink in that the man she loved, the man who she thought she'd never see again was standing in front of her.

John commanded the Seahawk with the three male hostages and the other four members of the team to take off. As soon as Snake, Joker and Dr. Ruby rocked up he, Maggie and Boots joined them on the other Seahawk and got the hell out of there.

For every hundred feet they lifted into the air he could feel his heart beginning to soar. They'd done it. Maggie was safe and free.

He looked over at her as she helped Snake deal with Dr. Ruby's injuries and felt a rush of relief wash over him so powerful it left him feeling light-headed.

Ruby seemed out of it and was shaking badly. Snake had wrapped her in a blanket and was holding her, telling her in a voice John had never heard him use before that everything would be okay.

Maggie was holding her friend's hand and trying to get her to talk but she was completely unresponsive.

Something had gone down in that building and it was obvious it was going to take Dr. Ruby some time to deal with it.

John reached out for Maggie.

She turned around and looked at him.

He took her hand and pulled her towards him, enfolding her in his arms.

He needed to hold her and savor the feel of her against him. He'd nearly lost her forever. The realization of that and the strain of the past seven weeks came crashing over him and the only thing that was keeping him from completely losing his shit was the feel of her in his arms.

No words passed between them and for the remainder of the flight they simply held each other tight.

Fifty minutes later they touched down at Haghedera airport in Kenya where a C-130 and a medevac team were waiting to take them to Camp Lemonnier in Djibouti.

Snake stayed with Dr. Ruby as the medevac team took charge of her and Joker and Boots took up position outside the Seahawk.

The medevac team were pissed as they were anxious to take Maggie into their care but Joker held them back, explaining that the lady needed a minute.

John grinned, only someone with a death-wish would defy Joker when he was serious.

He looked down at Maggie.

"Hey," he said.

Maggie looked into his eyes, the fathomless orbs of dark amber she had dreamed about for so many nights and smiled.

"Hey," she said, her voice a barely audible croak.

John smiled. "Listen, things are going to get crazy. There's going to be briefings and debriefings and I'll have to be a part of it all but I'll come see you when I can. Okay?"

Maggie nodded. "Okay," she whispered, not having a clue what lay ahead.

Boots stuck his head back in the bird. "We gotta go."

Maggie disentangled herself from John's arms but before she could jump out of the helicopter, John grabbed her hand. She looked back at him.

"I love you Maggie," he said, his voice breaking, "I love you."

She smiled and turned as Joker took her other hand to help her out.

John quickly followed.

The medevac team swooped on her and she was just in the process of reassuring them she was all right when she noticed blood on her hand. She knew she wasn't injured and immediately her thoughts turned to John. He walked past her and it was then she saw his back was covered in blood.

The next thing she knew she was enveloped by blackness, a blackness as dark and unforgiving as the Somali night.

THIRTY-ONE

John sat and watched the gentle rise and fall of Maggie's chest as she slowly breathed in and out. He reached over and brushed a strand of hair away from her face. Her face and hair were still dirty but he didn't care, he could sit there and look at her forever.

The doctors assured him she was okay and her collapse back at Haghedera was most probably due to exhaustion and dehydration. Whatever. Seeing her go down had finally caused him to lose it and it had taken the combined efforts of Snake, Joker and Boots to bring him under control and back to a modicum of reality. He guessed there were a few medics he owed an apology to. Still, despite what the docs said, he'd feel a lot better if she would wake up, just for a little while.

His eyes travelled down her body and he wondered about the baby. He looked at her tummy. Was it true? Was there a baby in there? His baby? It seemed to him there was a slight rounding of her tummy. He had a peculiar urge to put his hand on it but he didn't dare.

All things considered she seemed in pretty good physical shape and he wondered if she had been harmed in any way during her weeks in captivity. Just the prospect of it had him wincing. He couldn't bear the thought of any of those fuckers hurting her. What he had seen her endure at the hands of Al Hussein was bad enough.

Suddenly her body jerked and his eyes shot up to her face. She was still asleep, just dreaming.

He thought of all the things he wanted to say to her. Where did he start? He was prepared to beg her to take him back but would she? He knew she would want him as part of their baby's life, he had no doubt about that, but would she want him as part of hers?

She stirred again and he took a hold of her hand.

"Shhhh..... Maggie," he whispered, "it's okay, you're safe. No-one can hurt you now."

***

The darkness was giving way to a grey mist and somewhere, far away, she could just about hear a man's voice. The place she was in was cool. It felt good. She had no idea where she was. The mist started to disappear but there was someone there in the mist, a man. She couldn't quite see who it was but she seemed to know him and then he turned towards her and there was a blinding light and blood, so much blood and then she knew, the man was John. She reached out to him and called his name, desperate to touch him before he disappeared into the mist.

"John! John!"

But it was no good, he was gone. Panic gripped her and the light blinded her.

"John!" she screamed

"Hey, hey, it's okay, I'm here," she heard a voice soothe, as a warm rough hand gripped hers.

She looked around. She was in a hospital room. It was bright and clean and sitting in a seat beside her bed, holding her hand was John.

Sweet relief flooded through her and she went to put her other arm around him but soon discovered it was hooked up to an I.V.

He stood and took her into his arms instead.

God but it felt good to have his rock hard body against hers again. Inside his arms was her favorite place in the whole world.

She sighed. She had no idea how things stood between them but in that moment she was so happy to be in his arms and it was a moment she just wanted to savor.

She felt him smile into her hair and pull her even tighter to him. Then she remembered, the blood, his injury.

She pulled away. "You were hurt. What's the story? How long have I been out? Shouldn't you be in surgery?"

John grinned. "Relax. I got them to patch me up. I'm gonna need surgery but they're going to do it when I get back Stateside. And for your information, you've been out cold for about four hours."

Everything came back to Maggie in flashes, the gunfire, the explosions, running towards the helicopter, Ruby....

"Ruby!" she exclaimed, "where is Ruby? How is she? Is she okay?"

One of the monitors she was hooked up to started to beep and it upset and worried John to see her so agitated.

"Hey calm down, she's fine," he said in a soothing voice, "she took a bit of a beating but the docs are looking after her."

Maggie slumped into his arms.

"Thank you," she whispered, "thank you for saving us."

John held her tight and smiled into her hair. "Just doing my job."

Maggie said nothing but the irony wasn't lost on her that the very job responsible for taking him away from her was the same job that had saved her life.

John felt the change in her and wondered what was on her mind.

He would have to go soon before the Commander sent a search party looking for him. There was so much he wanted to say but he didn't know where to start. However, he could be on a transport back to the States tonight so he figured he'd better start somewhere.

He sat on the bed beside her and took her hands in his.

He looked into her eyes and was just about to speak when the door opened and a nurse came rushing in.

"Oh, you're awake," she announced as she went over to the monitor that had just stopped beeping.

"How are you feeling?" she asked Maggie.

"Not too bad," Maggie replied, "tired and a little thirsty, oh and now that I think of it, hungry."

The nurse smiled. "Well, if you're feeling hungry then I'm thinking you're doing okay. Once the doctor has checked you out we'll get some food in here for you right away. I'll just go get you a drink and let the doc know you're awake."

Maggie nodded. "Okay."

She looked back at John. "Sorry, what were you going to say?"

John looked down at her hands, they looked so small compared to his.

"Do you remember back on the helicopter, I told you I loved you?"

Maggie half-smiled and nodded. "Yes, I do."

John grinned and was just about to tell her again how much he loved her and how much he wanted her back in his life when the door opened and the nurse came in again, this time accompanied by a doctor.

John wrestled his frustration under control and let go of Maggie's hands.

"Hi Dr. O'Brien," the doctor said, "I'm Doctor Hennessy. Nurse Meehan tells me you're feeling okay. However, all things considered I just want to give you a more thorough examination and conduct an ultra-sound, if that's okay with you."

Maggie looked at John and could see from his face he didn't have a clue what the doctor was getting at but she knew he was discreetly referring to the fact she was pregnant.

"That would be nice," she agreed as a flutter of excitement shot across her tummy at the prospect of seeing her baby.

Her baby? No. Their baby.

She stole a quick glance at John.

God, she thought to herself, how will he react to the news he is going to be a father? Will it be too much for him? Will he panic? Will he bolt?

She'd just got him back into her life, albeit under incredible circumstances and he had told her in the helicopter he loved her but would he love her and a baby or would it all be too much for him?

Dr. Hennessy looked across at John. "I'm afraid I'm going to have to ask you to step outside for a few minutes sir."

John nodded. "No problem, I'll be right outside."

He smiled at Maggie and left the room.

Maggie felt a small ache in her heart as she watched him leave. She hated watching him leave.

Doctor Hennessy asked her some pregnancy related questions and then examined her tummy. "Everything seems okay," he reassured her, "but I'm sure you'd like to get a look at the little critter at this stage."

Maggie smiled. "That would be amazing."

Dr. Hennessy turned to Nurse Meehan. "Can you bring the ultrasound machine in?"

She nodded and made her way over to the door.

In that instant Maggie decided she needed to tell John about the baby and she wanted them to get their first look at their child together. It didn't seem right to exclude him. She didn't know how he would react but it was only fair she tell him as soon as possible.

Just as the nurse reached the door Maggie called after her.

"Can you ask Lieutenant Sullivan to come back in too, please?" she asked.

The doctor looked at her, obviously confused.

Maggie smiled. "He's the baby's father."

Doctor Hennessy blew out a breath in surprise.

"Well, I wasn't expecting to hear that," he exclaimed, "does he know?"

Maggie shook her head. "He's about to find out."

John came into the room.

Doctor Hennessy moved towards the door.

"I'll let you two have a few minutes," he said as he slipped out.

Maggie was immediately touched by the concern in John's eyes.

"Is everything okay?" he asked.

Maggie smiled and took his hand. "Yes, everything's fine."

She hesitated, this was it. She needed to just spit it out. There was no way to dress it up. "I'm pregnant John, with our baby."

She felt him stiffen.

"So, it's true," he blurted out.

Confusion gathered in Maggie's eyes and John felt he may have just said the wrong thing.

"You knew?" she gasped, "how on earth could you know?"

John tried to scramble his thoughts together in an effort not to say anything else wrong.

"It was part of our intel at the pre-op briefing. The whole team knows."

At the look of shock that came over her face, he was pretty sure he shouldn't have included the last part about the whole team.

"Oh," was all Maggie managed in response but her mind was going crazy.

He knew?

She couldn't fathom it. She knew rescuing her was part of his job and it was an incredible coincidence he led the team that undertook that rescue. But after the rescue had been completed there was no other reason for him to be in contact with her other than he wanted to be. She had hoped he was here in the hospital because he wanted to be with her and possibly get back together but now she wondered if he was here primarily because of the baby?

She knew a man like John would want a role in his child's life and his sense of duty and honor would mean he'd want to try and make a go of things with her.

He'd said he loved her but now she wasn't sure what that meant. He said he loved her before but it hadn't been enough to stop him from breaking up with her. What had changed? Him? Or the fact she was pregnant with his child?

Confusion and an undertow of disappointment pulled at her but before she could say anything else Doctor Hennessy and Nurse Meehan came back in with the ultrasound machine.

A few minutes later she listened in awe as the sound of her baby's heartbeat filled the room. The image on the screen was grainy but she could just make out a little beating heart.

She looked at John and the look of disbelief and indescribable joy on his face combined with the fact she was finally looking at their baby, the baby only yesterday she feared would never make it into the world, tipped her over the edge and she started to cry.

She was pregnant, something she never thought she would be, and her little baby was safe. She was so damn grateful for it all but the realization of how close things had come to turning out differently overwhelmed her and she let the tears fall.

John took her into his arms. Her tears shredded him.

"Hey," he soothed, "it's okay. You're here now and you and the little guy are safe."

Maggie smiled through her tears. Had he just said, "little guy?"

She pulled back and looked up into his face.

"Did you just say little guy?"

John smirked.

"Of course. We've got a little frog-man in there."

Maggie laughed.

"A little frog-man eh? Well what if it's a little frog-lady?"

John shook his head.

"No such thing. Ladies can't join the SEALs."

Maggie raised her chin and John smiled, God but it was good to have this obstinate woman back in his life.

"Well, if there's going to be any lady who will have a chance of changing that then it will be our daughter," she announced and crossed her arms for emphasis.

John laughed as a current of excitement shot through him. He was going to be a dad and the mother of his child was the amazing woman in front of him.

He bent down and placed a soft kiss upon her stubborn lips.

He needed to tell her everything that was in his heart. He only hoped she was open to giving him a second chance.

"I love you Maggie. I haven't stopped loving you and I was terrified I was never going to see you again."

He had to stop talking for a moment as he was overcome with emotion.

He swallowed hard.

"I'm sorry for what I did. I'm sorry for ending things between us. You were right. I reacted badly to Freezer's situation and panicked. I know it's a lot to ask and I know I broke your heart because God knows I broke my own but if you could let me back into your life, I'll show you I'm a man you can place your trust in again and I'll prove to you that you can depend on me. If you'll take me back, I promise I'll never let you go again."

Maggie looked at the wonderful man before her and was touched at the sincerity shining out from his eyes. She wanted to respond but she didn't know exactly what to say. She wished she knew for sure he didn't just want to give things another go between them because of the baby. She thought back to Christmas eve and how adamant he'd been and she remembered the weeks in New York waiting for him to call but he never had.

Fear still had a hold on her heart. He had decimated it before and she wasn't sure if she could take him back unless she knew for sure he needed her back in his life for who she was and how he felt about her and not because she was the mother of his child.

She could see him crumbling in the face of her silence. She desperately wanted to say something but she didn't know what.

"I love you John," she whispered.

It was all she could think of.

He was about to respond when a knock came on the door.

Joker popped his head into the room.

"Hi Maggie, good to see you looking better. I hate to break this little reunion up but the Lieutenant's presence is required at the post-op briefing asap."

John stood up.

"Give us a minute," he told Joker.

"Will do," Joker grinned as he waved goodbye to Maggie.

Maggie smiled, she was really fond of that goofball.

John looked down at Maggie, at his whole world. She'd told him she loved him but there was something holding her back. He told himself maybe she just needed time. He'd smashed her heart into tiny little pieces and he had to take responsibility for that. She'd also been through hell in the past few weeks and found out she was pregnant, so yeah, maybe she just needed some time. He just hoped she wouldn't need too much.

He took her hand.

"I'll try to get back to see you before they ship me back stateside. Please think about what I said. I love you Maggie. Before you came into my life I was existing, not living and I want to spend the rest of my life living it with you."

He bent and kissed her, then walked out the door.

THIRTY-TWO

John sat out on his deck in Virginia Beach, opened another beer and eased himself down into one of the Adirondack chairs. He looked out at the Atlantic Ocean and thought how spectacular the sunset was going to be. His next thought was how much more spectacular it would be if Maggie was sitting in the other chair or, even better still, on his lap.

He'd been back in the States now for four days and hadn't heard from her and it was killing him. He was kicking himself for not leaving his number with her when he'd last seen her at the hospital. He'd been ordered to board a C-17 to Landstuhl, Germany after the post-op briefing and had hardly had a chance to pack his gear much less make it over to the medical facility to see Maggie. He'd asked Joker to get over there the next day to give his contact details to Maggie but Joker hadn't been able to get past the Naval Communications personnel who had basically surrounded Maggie and her colleagues with a ring of steel. Joker had asked one of the lackeys involved in guarding Maggie to pass on John's details to her but it looked like he had thrown them in the bin. At least John hoped that was the case and not that she wasn't talking to him.

He'd arrived back in the U.S. on Tuesday and been admitted to Walter Reed that night. Once he'd recovered from his surgery and been released from the hospital on Thursday he'd made some back-door attempts to get a number for Maggie but to no avail.

He suspected there was a complete blackout on her contact details. The media were in a frenzy trying to track the hostages down for exclusive interviews and this was the best way the U.S. Navy could protect them and their rescuers from those vultures. He'd even looked for her on Facebook but it was as if she'd never even had a page. He knew her phone was long gone as terrorists weren't in the habit of leaving their hostages in possession of their phones, therefore she had no way to access his number.

The lack of contact was eating him up. Last night he'd watched the televised joint press conference all the hostages had given, an event that had been carefully co-ordinated by the Navy's Communications' Department. Maggie had looked tired and strained and all he'd wanted to do was call her and offer his support.

He wasn't supposed to drive with his injured shoulder but if he hadn't heard from her by Sunday then he decided he was going to drive to New York and see if she was in her apartment and if not then he was going to squeeze her contact details out of that crazy neighbor of hers.

He looked out at the sun as it started its descent and felt better at the thought of taking some action because he was slowly going crazy doing nothing and the need to see her was like a hunger in his soul.

He leaned back in the chair and closed his eyes, desperately trying to quell the aching need he had for the woman who had turned his world upside down.

***

He opened his eyes and was surprised to see it was dark. He'd obviously nodded off and he wondered what the strange noise was that had woken him.

Rock. He was making those crazy squeak noises he made when he was so excited he couldn't contain himself.

He looked over in the direction of the squeaks and then he smiled the biggest fucking smile he'd ever smiled in his life.

She was here.

He closed his eyes and opened them again just to make sure he wasn't dreaming and his face nearly split as he smiled some more.

Maggie was sitting opposite him in her chair, petting his crazy-ass dog and giggling like a schoolgirl.

He was so fucking happy he was afraid to speak in case all that came out of his mouth was a squeak, just like his stupid dog.

She looked over at him and her smile mirrored that of his own.

"God, I missed this dog," she laughed.

John still didn't trust himself to speak so he got up out of his chair, went over to her, took her hand, pulled her up and kissed the ever-loving-daylights out of her.

A few minutes later Maggie gasped for breath.

"Now that right there made the six hour drive worth it."

John grinned. "I've got a lot more than that planned to make your drive worth it, in fact I intend to make you not want to leave."

Maggie smiled. "Sounds good. Actually, I wasn't planning on leaving but if you feel the need for some extra persuasion to keep me here then you go right ahead."

John looked down into her smiling eyes and was thrilled to see unadulterated joy shining out from them.

"Seriously, you're staying? Does that mean I get a second chance?"

Maggie smiled some more. "I spoke to Andy."

Comprehension dawned on John.

"He told me about you turning up at my apartment and how devastated you were when I wasn't there."

John dipped his head, the memory of that night still hurt.

"Yeah," he said, his voice a mere croak, "I'd spent three weeks in hell and finally come to the realization my life was nothing without you in it. I was desperate to see you before I deployed and beg you to take me back and I couldn't believe it when you weren't there."

Maggie smiled. "Sitting around waiting for a man isn't my style, especially one who has broken my heart."

John winced. "I promise to mend it, to make it stronger than it was before and I'll never do anything to hurt it again."

Maggie placed her hands on either side of his face and pulled him in for a kiss. "Let the mending begin," she husked into his mouth as she placed her lips against his.

John pressed her against him with his good arm and moaned in pleasure at the feel of her curves along the hard length of his body.

Molten desire crackled through his veins and he didn't care if he undid all the surgeon's hard work on his shoulder, he was bringing the woman he loved inside right now and making love to her.

Then he remembered she was pregnant. Shit. He was pretty sure people still had sex during pregnancy but he wondered if it was only at certain stages. Were they at a stage where it was safe? Would he hurt the baby?

He pulled back from the kiss and looked into Maggie's eyes.

"What?" she asked, "what is it?"

"The baby," he replied, "will we...er...upset him if we... you know...make love?"

Maggie started to laugh. "Upset him? You mean like, is he going to start shouting at us and waving his little fists?"

John smirked. *Very funny* he thought. "I mean can we harm him?"

Maggie stopped laughing and caressed John's cheek with the palm of her hand, touched by his concern. "No, we won't harm him. He's about the size of a plum right now just happily floating away in there, oblivious to all the goings-on in this world and contentedly developing away."

John smiled. He liked the sound of that, then he noticed Maggie's wicked grin.

"What?" he asked

"You know," she said, drawing out the o in a teasing manner, "there's those that believe the more a mother orgasms during her pregnancy the better it is for the developing fetus, being exposed to all those love hormones."

John didn't remember going up the stairs or getting naked. He had a hazy recollection of lips and tongue, hands and fingers, moaning, sucking and licking, dipping and delving but the moment he entered Maggie was a moment he would never forget.

There was nothing between them, no thin sheet of latex, no barrier, just a perfect fusion of their two bodies, a perfect communion of two souls and as he cried out her name, he knew a part of his had finally come home.

***

Six months later.

John watched Maggie waddle towards him from the kitchen. There was no other word to describe the way she moved these days but he was never going to tell her that. She eased herself onto the couch and swung her feet up onto his lap.

"You may massage them," she informed him.

He chuckled, her initial excitement at welcoming him home from deployment was waning as the strain of being a week overdue was starting to take its toll. He was never so glad he was a man but for Maggie's sake he decided maybe he should have words with his son.

"Hey little frog-man, it was good of you to stay in there and wait till Daddy got back from Africa but I think mommy is starting to get a little fed up now and maybe it's time to think about coming on out of there."

Maggie sighed.

"Frog-child," she chided, "I thought we agreed on a gender neutral reference."

"Pffft," John retorted, "you can call him frog-child all you like, I happen to know my super-sperm made a little frog-man."

Maggie laughed. "Super-sperm?"

John looked at her, an expression of mock indignation on his face.

"How else do you account for the little guys being able to break through the latex barrier and swim to their target, baby? Super-SEAL-sperm, that's what we're dealing with here," he said as he cupped his man package between his legs.

Maggie's laughter intensified, in fact she outright snorted.

"More like it was a hole in that old condom from my purse, you super-ass," she laughed.

John's mock indignation turned to mock outrage.

"Ma-am, you do realize you are insulting the sperm of a U.S. Navy SEAL here and we don't take too kindly to that type of thing."

There was a twinkle of mischief in his eye but also a touch of disappointment, as if a small part of him had actually believed he had super-sperm.

This made Maggie laugh even more, until she had tears in her eyes and had to try to catch her breath. And then she was trying to catch her breath for another reason as a sharp pain shot across her tummy.

John was still pretending to be outraged when he noticed Maggie's expression change as she clutched her tummy.

"What? What is it Maggie?" he asked. "Are you okay?"

Maggie nodded, caught her breath and waited for the pain to subside. She looked at the man who meant everything to her.

"Your super-baby is on its way."

***

Ten hours later a slightly traumatized John watched as his son came into the world. His first thought was that he hoped the feeling would eventually return to his hand as Maggie finally loosened her grip and his second thought was he hoped the SEAL instructors never figured out a way to simulate childbirth because that would bring hell week to a whole other level of pain.

He watched as the nurses weighed and cleaned his son and then wrapped him in a blanket.

All rational thought left him as the nurse lowered his dark haired boy into his arms, his little frog-man. He looked over at Maggie and was floored by the radiant smile on her face. After everything she'd just been through, she could smile at him like that and look more beautiful than she ever had.

He smiled back. He couldn't speak. There were no words for this moment. He thought back to the note Maggie had written to him when she'd left the cabin, "you deserve someone to come back to."

He looked into her eyes, two shining emeralds of joy and he looked down at his son. The two of them weren't just someone to come back to, they were everything to come back to.

The End

Dear Reader,

thank you so much for reading Someone To Come Back To. I hope you enjoyed John and Maggie's story as much as I enjoyed writing it. If you did, I'd very much appreciate it if you could leave a quick review on amazon and / or goodreads. The importance of reviews to indie authors cannot be overstated.

I'm aiming to have book two in the series out in Spring 2017. If you'd like to be notified of the book's release then please like my author page on facebook and follow me on twitter and amazon. I also have a newsletter in which I inform readers of upcoming sales, price drops, new releases and giveaways. You can sign up for my newsletter by visiting my website – just wait for the pop-up box where you can enter your name and email address to subscribe, it only takes a few seconds. Links are as follows:

Facebook

https://www.facebook.com/roisinblackauthor

Twitter

https://twitter.com/roisinblackauth

Amazon

http://www.amazon.com/Roisin-Black/e/B00N8KIYD4/ref=sr_tc_2_0?qid=1460255772&sr=1-2-ent

Pinterest

https://au.pinterest.com/roisindoo/

Goodreads

https://www.goodreads.com/author/show/8524553.Roisin_Black

Website

https://roisinblack.com/

About The Author

Róisín Black comes from the West of Ireland, a place where storytelling is a way of life. She's a dreamer, a wanderer and a writer. In amongst extensive wandering and dreaming she has managed to carve out a successful career as a journalist, hold-down a marriage, produce two amazing children and spend her time with some pretty cool dogs. She currently lives in Queensland, Australia.

In addition to her Omega Security Series she has three novellas published.

Remember Me

Flynn Murphy is handsome, mouth-wateringly sexy and incredibly rich. He's also the new owner of Carra House, one of Ireland's finest historical houses and the primary instrument of his revenge on those who have wronged him in the past.

His wolf-like eyes hide a secret and the time has come to settle old scores and to ensure that those who barely remember him, will never be able to forget him again. But will his ruthless pursuit of vengeance for the past, cost him the chance of a future he never imagined possible.

Unfinished Business

Liberty Rose - world famous television reporter, best-selling novelist and philanthropist returns to the west of Ireland, the place where she grew up, for the wedding of her daughter. To the outside world it appears she has it all - international career, good looks, wealth, two children and a happy marriage. However, all is not as it seems and her success has come at a price. Now the emotional upheaval of her daughter's wedding throws a harsh spotlight on her own marriage and unavoidable truths must be faced. But matters are complicated by the presence of the only other man she has ever loved. A man she hasn't seen in twenty-eight years and with whom she still shares a raw chemistry. He makes it clear he wants to deal with their "unfinished business" but is getting tangled up with her past any good for her future?

Over Your Dead Body

Ryan Kennedy is the definition of tall, dark and handsome and along with his success, he seems to have it all. However, Ryan is a man haunted by the past. The time has now come for him to face all that happened before and to finally try and put the past to rest.

After eleven long years he has returned home to the wild beauty of the West of Ireland coastline, to a place that formed him in so many unimaginable ways. He must reach out to those who hurt him the most and lay his heart on the line but these were the people who destroyed him before and will seeing them again prove his salvation or his ultimate undoing.

ACKNOWLEDGEMENTS

Taking a leap into the unknown and deciding to be a writer is a difficult decision, especially in an increasingly crowded marketplace and most especially as an indie author. Following through on that decision and sticking with it is even more difficult and, for me, simply would not be possible without the support and encouragement of so many people in my life. To my dear friends, other authors in the indie community and all the amazing book bloggers who have read and shared my work I say an enormous thank you. Your kind words of encouragement and belief in me are the foundations upon which I sit down to write.

A number of people were involved in bringing all the elements of Someone To Come Back To together and deserve a special mention:

Sheryl Lee – Editor extraordinaire! You jumped in at the last minute and made Someone Come Back To better than I'd ever dreamed it could be. Thank you.

Hang Le – Cover Designer supreme! I came to you with nothing and you guided me to a stunning cover with your incredible patience and grace. Thank you.

David M Portraits – Artist and all round cool guy! You took my crazy and turned it into a beautiful work of art. Thank you.

Debra Presley at The Book Enthusiast Promotions. Always there with advice, a kind word and a cover reveal or blog tour to go! Thank you.

Lastly but by no means least, thank you to my little family. To my wonderful husband who has supported me on this journey by every means possible. To my beautiful son whose dearest wish is to sell mummy's books at the school gate! To my amazing daughter who worries every night about me not getting enough sleep. I am blessed to have you all in my life, a truly lucky woman.

Made in United States
North Haven, CT
21 March 2025

67054083R00193